To So Few

TO SO FEW

RUSSELL SULLMAN

LUME BOOKS

LUME BOOKS

Published in 2022 by Lume Books

ISBN 978-1-83901-493-2

Typeset using Atomik ePublisher from Easypress Technologies

www.lumebooks.co.uk

To my amazing Mother. I love you.

And to each and every member of the Armed Forces of the United Kingdom; past, present and future.

Thank you.

Prologue

In the cold beauty of the high-vaulted arena of clearest blue, violent death was close…

Quartering the achingly vivid sky, exactly as Granny had taught him to, an endless eternity of just a few months ago, briskly yet carefully, Harry Rose searched for the enemy.

Eyes strained, squinting against the light, throat dry and tight, and heart painfully slamming against his ribcage.

His eyes flicking from one quarter to another, not lingering for even a full second; it was not long before he caught sight of the little group of tiny dark specks, like insects in the slicing brilliance, tracking slowly across the nose of his aircraft.

He glanced quickly to the Hurricane flying faithfully alongside, piloted by his wingman, young Sergeant Morton, tucked close into his port quarter.

Rose cleared his throat. "Sparrow Red leader to Sparrow Red Two, bandits at ten o'clock, we'll give 'em a nasty nip on the arse."

God! He sounded so confident, as if he actually knew what he was doing!

"Give the tail end Charlie one quick burst, then tuck in tight, keep 'em peeled and no heroics, over," he licked dry lips.

Say it.

"If I buy it, lad, keep turning, get down low and get the hell out of it, they'll not have fuel to play with, OK? I mean it, no heroics, over."

"Sparrow Red Two to Sparrow Red Leader, received and understood, out." Calm and thoughtful, with a quiet voice.

Morton had a smooth, round eager face, bright brown eyes, and looked about ten. A good lad. But if it all went tits up, as it likely might, he might be dead within minutes.

It won't happen, at least not while I'm alive, he thought grimly. But the little voice inside whispered, *but what if you're dead?*

"Sparrow Red Leader to Baseplate, four bandits in sight, I am attacking, over."

The clipped, cool voice of the young WAAF, miles away, "Baseplate to Sparrow Red Leader, understood." And then softer, "Good luck and good hunting." What does she look like, he wondered, and what is she thinking at this moment?

Two against four, stinking rotten odds. The same bloody story all through the summer. Too few of us, too many of them. Always outnumbered, the poor bastards.

He turned gently to starboard, staying well below the height of the enemy aircraft, and taking care to keep the sun and channel behind him, to (hopefully) merge his little formation into the sunlit flickering expanse of water behind.

Any glint of light on Perspex or other smooth surfaces should be missed, with any luck, mistaken for the glittering golden light dancing and shimmering on the wave tops below and behind. There was no chance of getting above them, no matter how much he wanted the sun directly behind his pair of fighters.

The gentle turn guided the nose of his Hurricane into an approach from below and into a five o'clock position on what was now clearly visible as a loosely arranged quartet of faster sleek wasp-like Bf109s.

Oh Dear God. 109s. Was it too late to turn back?

Luckily (or not, perhaps?), the enemy fighters were flying at a leisurely pace, otherwise Rose and Morton would never have managed to close the range in time.

Only four, or were there more, waiting to spring a trap?

He was sweating, nerves crawling with tension as he waited for the enemy to react at any moment, but incredibly, there was no response to their approach, nothing hid high in the sun.

Don't muff this up, he sternly thought to himself. You'll get one chance only.

Rose had already set his guns to 'fire', and his thumb rested lightly on the button.

With young Morton keeping a keen look out all around them, Rose was able to concentrate carefully on the rapid approach, although he continued to glance in his rear-view mirror and check the clear blue around them, whilst selecting the number three aircraft in the enemy formation as his target.

He licked dry lips once more, "Sparrow Red Leader to Red Two, second pair, I'll take the number three. You take number four, but keep 'em peeled. This could be a trap."

The *Rotte* of four enemy aircraft bobbed lightly above and before them, thin, almost invisible, trails of grey exhaust streaming behind, gleaming blunt noses pointed purposefully for France, looking forward to a glass of chilled French wine and a good cigar.

Arrogant bastards.

Again, scrutinise the airspace all around, eyes hurting in the aching brightness, he swallowed painfully, trying to work up a bit of saliva, wishing for a cup of tea and still searching with those gritty eyes for lunging enemy silhouettes that would be part of the trap that spelt instant death, despite Morton's continued vigilance as his wingman.

All clear, still no signs of a trap.

In this high cerulean field of battle, the hunter and the hunted frequently switched roles.

And still the Bf109s maintained their heading. The mad buggers must be asleep, confident in their self-perceived aerial superiority.

The two sturdy Hurricanes were now behind and below the fast moving Bf109s, and their curving line of approach had brought them together perfectly, despite the higher speed of the enemy aeroplanes.

Incredibly, they hadn't been sighted during their careful approach (Thank heavens!), and now the range was close enough to fire worth a damn. The window of opportunity was a small one.

Better make it count, just going to get the one free shot.

A last glance at the pale undersides and dark dappled flanks of the bandits, quick check on deflection, press the trigger – fingers crossed!

One second…

The Hurricane juddered, the image of the enemy aircraft trembled before him, and an acrid stench of cordite filled his nostrils.

As soon as he saw the glittering casings cascading back from Rose's Hurricane, Morton opened fire on his target as well.

Rose's aim was good, and 'his' Bf109 flew straight through his burst of fire, but his only reward was a scintillating cluster of sparkling hits, a panel of metal detaching lazily from one wing and a single puff of gushing smoke.

Two seconds…

The enemy aircraft he was targeting sailed serenely through the tight spray of bullet rounds, outwardly unscathed, continuing along its line of flight. No reaction whatsoever from its pilot.

Damn it all!

4

His heart was hammering inside him so painfully that he thought he would have a heart attack. He lined it up again, brow furrowed in concentration, eyes flicking behind and above, finger mashing down savagely for another short burst.

Three seconds…

Morton, however, had had better fortune, and his bullets splashed the underside of the German fighter and chewed the tail plane of the fourth enemy machine into ruin.

As pieces of the tail were ripped away, the smoking Bf109 wobbled unsteadily and then began to skid sideways out of formation, dropping away, beginning to flat spin, cartwheeling out of control.

You jammy little bastard! Talk about beginner's luck…

Unbelievably, Morton had scored, one down confirmed, three to go.

Four seconds…

At last, with thick smoke pouring from their exhausts, less than five seconds after Rose had opened fire for the first time, the leading pair of Bf109s increased speed to climb rapidly away.

Morton gave them a hopeful, hurried burst but without result as the range swiftly widened. Thankfully, his success did not entice him into breaking formation to chase the enemy fighters. Faithfully, his Hurricane remained tucked in close to Rose.

Bollocks, thought Rose savagely, edgily lining up on the third Messerschmitt again.

Amazingly, it continued on course along the same heading (the bastard must be dozing!), and he squeezed the trigger yet again.

This time the enemy machine began to smoke and the Bf109 began to roll, to dive and turn away, but the young Leutnant from Bremen, badly injured by Rose's first, seemingly ineffectual burst, was unlucky, and he turned his aircraft with faltering hands straight into the path of Rose's guns.

Puffs of smoke and glittering flashes erupted and splattered along the length of the stricken German fighter, as Rose's bursts dashed messily across it, tearing devastation into the enemy machine as it passed before him.

The Bf109 shuddered beneath this third onslaught, first the propeller blades and then the big Daimler Benz engine ripping free of the fuselage, a big chunk of metal whirling dangerously away, the side of the sliding, turning fighter seeming to collapse beneath the onslaught.

A flickering ribbon of flame, instantly thickening, surged back from the ruined fuel tanks to engulf the ruined fuselage, now dropping straight downwards; but the enemy pilot was already dead, killed instantly in that devastating final third burst from Rose's machine-guns, dreams of glory turned to blaze and death and devastation.

A thick black plume of smoke behind marked the vertical fall of his victory, whilst Morton's, 'kill' augured into a freshly ploughed field far below.

But there was no time for looking at the tumbling, disintegrating enemy.

They had been lucky, incredibly lucky, the cards could have fallen differently, but would Lady Luck continue to remain with them?

Already Rose was desperately searching for the other pair of Bf109s – Damn it! Where the hell were they? One minute they were there, and then just so much empty sky, stained only by the pyres of their two victims.

I'm getting careless. Damn it. But at least we've evened the odds.

Unconsciously, he touched the little pink bear in his tunic pocket. They'd been lucky, he knew, incredibly lucky, but now there would be the reckoning.

"Sparrow Red Leader to Sparrow Red Two, I can't see the leading pair of Jerries, d'you see the blighters, over?" he craned his neck around to check behind.

Run or fight? Please God, let them have buggered off for France…

"Sparrow Red Two to Sparrow Red Leader, sorry, I lost sight of them, sir." Morton responded awkwardly over the R/T.

For goodness sake! Probably watching his first victory go down, Rose thought crossly to himself.

But then, it was hard to blame him after getting his first victory.

It was difficult to stay focussed after the first one, the urge to watch the vanquished fall so very strong, to marvel at the sense of success, but it was those few seconds of inattention that killed. He would have to give the boy an ear bashing once they'd got back safe and sound.

If they got back safe and sound.

He desperately continued to search the sky for any sign of the German fighters, gently rocking his fighter from side to side, his heart thumping painfully in his chest, lips like dust.

"Sparrow Red Leader to Sparrow Red Two, OK, keep looking out for those bandits, and bloody well done on your Jerry, over."

"Sparrow Red Two to Sparrow Red Leader, Received, thanks sir, bet they're not all as easy as that!"

"Sparrow Red Leader to Sparrow Red Two, dead right chum! Keep your peepers open, over."

Morton had opened the distance between them, but remained close enough to support him.

Rose was sweating copiously beneath his oxygen mask, and he desperately wanted to scratch his cheek, "Sparrow Red Leader to Base Plate, scratch two Jerries, D'you have any more trade for us, over?"

That's enough, time to return, don't push your luck…

"Well done, Sparrow Red Leader. Please stand by." Voice still calm,

7

but she sounded pleased. Had she lost someone, did the fires for vengeance burn hot in her heart as well?

Nothing to see, just empty sky, Where are the buggers?

They *must* have run for home.

Dear, sweet God, please let them be high tailing it at high speed for the French coast…

"BREAK! BREAK!" Morton's desperate scream of warning was like a sharp knife slicing through his innards and he instinctively hauled his Hurricane into a straining starboard turn, tight, tighter, muscles straining and his face set in a grimace, teeth clenched and vision greying.

Fuck-fuck-FUCK! They'd almost been killed because he'd allowed them to get bounced!

'THU-THU-THUMP!'

Three strikes, crashing close together, merging into almost one bowel-weakening sound, and he fought to control the machine momentarily as three rounds smashed through the machine guns in his Hurricane's port wing, punching through to the other side, thankfully without immediate apparent catastrophic structural damage to the wing.

At least it didn't fall off as he continued his hard turn outwards, but he could feel the bumpy drag caused by the damage.

Or was it his nerves jangling?

And then the tracer was whipping away below him as he out-turned the plummeting pair of Bf109s. The wing might break off, but if he didn't get out of the way of that enemy fire, he was done for anyway.

Morton's Hurricane had broken away to port and now he too was turning tightly, Perspex flashing, as the shark-like enemy fighters zoomed through the airspace the Hurricanes had occupied scant seconds before, battering him by the closeness of their passage.

His heart was hammering and his muscles ached, vision greying.

They didn't get us. Lucky again!

Thank God for young Morton.

Thank God.

The Bf109s had dropped away, too far, but were climbing up and away again, slick as lightning, already turning to line up into position for another slashing pass at the Hurricanes, this time from below.

Where the fuck was Morton? He searched desperately, ease back, and turn to port. Neck twisting painfully, bones creaking.

Oh. There he was. Closing rapidly from port.

The Germans would want to split them apart, but Morton was closing the distance again, was already reforming with him.

"Sparrow Red Leader to Sparrow Red Two, straight at Jerry, fire when you see the whites of their eyes. Stay close."

"Sparrow Red Two to Sparrow Red Leader," the boy was panting hard, and his voice was strained, "Yes, sir!"

The enemy were two dark dots now, racing upwards from below towards them, nose-to-nose, tracer and cannon fire already reaching out towards them, smoke trails twirling up at them.

Rose cowered behind the deceptively comforting protection of his Merlin engine as the two formations drew closer to one another.

He pressed the gun button again and his guns roared a final time, and the Hurricane shuddered around him.

A Bf109 loomed huge before him for a heart stopping instant, a dark streaking blur; was that smoke…?

And then there was a neck-wrenching blow, and suddenly the Hurricane staggered nauseatingly in mid-air, and was then flung over and was falling. The stick flopped uselessly in his gloved hands.

Time slowed, and through the top of his canopy he saw with shocked, disbelieving eyes his propeller, tips bent sideways, and turning end over end lazily, curve slowly away and disappear out of his field of vision.

It was over. The fight was over.

Time to go…

Rose reached against for the quick release lever for the canopy, fighting the forces that gripped him. With an effort he grasped the lever, and pulled hard.

It didn't shift as he urgently heaved on it.

He tried again, but no luck. His stomach lurched painfully.

No!

There was another bang and a juddering (or was it his heart hammering?) as his falling Hurricane was raked again. The instrument panel shattered, spraying him with shining fragments, and vibration in the tumbling ruin of his beloved Hurricane worsened.

He was about to bang the sides of the canopy to try and dislodge it with his elbows when something smacked his leg to one side, knee cap cracking painfully against the side of the cockpit, pain lancing upwards into his hip.

There was a dull *'whump'*, and suddenly flames, painfully bright, were licking around the edges of the cockpit. He could smell his aircraft burning, and he desperately reached again to dislodge his canopy. He was gasping now, unable to speak, eyes wide behind his goggles, muscles straining against the sides of the canopy, but still it wouldn't shift on its runners.

The world outside began to spin sickeningly as the weakened port wing bent, then broke in half, the ground and sky exchanging places with a sickening rapidity, the sun flashing on-off-on-off before his eyes.

It was becoming increasingly harder to move his arms, and detritus from the floor of the cockpit whirled around him.

GOT TO GET OUT OF HERE…!

He tried again to grab the sides of the cockpit, fighting the forces that held him in his seat, whilst around him swirling ribbons, droplets and fragments of blood, dust, dirt and glass danced and looped and spun all around him.

Shining a brilliant scarlet in the vortex, his life-blood flicking to splash against him and the inside of the cockpit, against the Perspex, and now he couldn't reach the canopy with his gloved hands.

Panic rippled through him, and he strove to control it.

Instead he reached painfully for the bump in his flying jacket that was the little teddy bear.

All that was left to him in these final, terrifying seconds.

The inside of the cockpit was like an oven now, and the rising heat was unbelievable, whilst flame continued to lick back from the ruined Merlin engine, darkening the Perspex above him.

It's finally over. I'm going to die.

It's my turn today.

He closed his eyes, holding hard onto the useless control stick, heart fluttering.

The R/T was silent now, no Morton, no calm WAAF. Nobody, and Morton was on his own now, poor lad.

He was surprised that it didn't seem to matter anymore. No regrets, he'd lived by the sword, and now he would die that way. It had been good to love the girl, and at least death would take away the pain of her loss.

The spin pushed him harder against his seat.

He could feel the darkness gathering as his consciousness slipped away. Not long to wait now.

No chance to see Molly again, no chance to tell her how much he loved her, no chance to say goodbye. To hold her gently in his arms one last time.

He'd been wrong, of course, there were regrets after all.

11

He thought of the dark-haired girl longingly, wondered if she would care when she heard of his death.

Of course she would.

Rose realised that he was crying, and opened his eyes.

Blood spattered brightly across his goggles.

Then suddenly, an eye-searing white flash.

Piercing, shocking, silent, and the world finally turned black.

Chapter 1

Rose awoke with a start, heart jangling madly in his chest and confused desperation filling his befuddled mind.

Oh no! I fell asleep after all! How long have I been asleep? Have I missed my stop? Oh God!

Dusk was encroaching outside the slowing railway carriage, but he could still see through the grimy glass that the train was wearily drawing into a small, unlit rural railway station.

The elderly woman seated facing him smiled gently at him through the gloom, "Don't worry, dear, this is Foxton station, I know it's your stop, that's why I woke you."

Trying discreetly to wipe the trail of saliva from the corner of his mouth, Rose smiled his thanks for her kindness, and turned from the grimy window against which he had been hunched, the shoulder he'd been laying against protesting and sore, neck stiff, now standing on unsteady legs, and reached up for his kitbag, re-checking for the fifth or sixth time in the gloom that the service number emblazoned on it was his. It wouldn't do at all to leave his belongings on the train.

Disturbed by the movement of his kitbag, Rose's unsecured respirator container immediately fell off the overhead shelf and onto the kindly woman's husband seated opposite him.

The cardboard box bounced off the man's shoulder, rolled down his forearm and teetered momentarily on his knee, before falling to hit the floor of the compartment.

The gas mask fell out of it to lie sullenly between the feet of the kindly woman wrapped in the faded brown coat.

The severe looking Major sitting beside her looked sharply at Rose, then disdainfully down at the mask.

In the dim blue light, the shadowed lines and hollows of his lean, angular face would have terrified a gargoyle, but instead the gas mask stared back emptily at him, unmoved by his disapproval.

Thank God the old tin-hat was securely stowed away inside the kitbag. That would have given someone a bit of a headache if it had fallen on them!

Rose stammered out an apology hoarsely, and reached down for it, scooping the respirator hurriedly back into its box, grateful to the gloom of dusk for hiding his flaming cheeks.

Outside there was the clatter of doors and the call of "Foxton! Disembark for Foxton station, please."

He had arrived.

The army officer glared at the young pilot momentarily then looked away, back out of the window, ignoring him completely.

Clumsy young oaf. You'd be useless as a soldier. You're lucky you're not in the battalion, I'd soon sort you out.

Thankfully, the elderly couple remained unconcerned, the woman smiling sympathetically at his discomfort, but Rose could hear the tittering of the little gaggle of Wrens in the corner beside the door that led into the passage.

To his dismay, he felt his blush deepening.

Embarrassment and stiff muscles made him unsteady, and he

concentrated on negotiating his way carefully between the knees of his fellow passengers to the door.

As he self-consciously wobbled his way out, clutching his respirator box and kitbag tightly, feeling like a complete idiot, he could feel the quiet, watchful stares on either side.

He was particularly aware of the girls in blue, but their upturned faces were just blurred, pale ovals in the gloom, watching his progress quietly now.

Waiting for me to fall down on to my face, damn them!

He focussed on the path to the door, balancing his kit carefully, his face feeling so hot that he half-expected a reflection of it on the glass of the compartment door, blooming a dull red in the dark.

Rose slid back the door and picked his way gingerly from the compartment through to the corridor, into the heaped jumble of humanity normally found in all trains these days, his careful steps encountering boots, and the ever-present bulging kitbags, knapsacks and other assorted boxes, bags and packs that seemed to be everywhere in wartime Britain.

The civilians, soldiers and matelots in the smoke-filled passage were tightly packed together, and it was a struggle for Rose to push through the crowded, sweating mass.

By some of the smirks and derisive glances he received, and the occasional sharp elbow, Rose felt sure that at least some of the servicemen packing the corridor were making the going harder than it should have been, delighting in the chance of making life just that little bit more uncomfortable for an officer, even one as lowly and inconsequential as a newly-appointed Pilot Officer.

But then again, the RAF was not very well thought of amongst the army at all nowadays.

There was a feeling in some quarters, unfairly, that the apparent lack of air support during the retreat through Belgium and France and the recent incredible miracle of the evacuation of the BEF at Dunkirk was due to a lack of ability, enthusiasm and professionalism on the part of the Boys In Blue.

Rose remembered the tales his father had occasionally told, of how the Tommies below would take the occasional pot-shot at his two-seater when he had flown it high over the trenches.

Bit of a love-hate relationship between the army and the airmen.

Well, hate-hate really, to be honest.

Strange, because the RAF had originally started as a part of the British Army itself.

The further he moved along the passage, making slow progress to the faraway sanctuary of the open carriage door, the more unbalanced he felt and the less well his feet seemed to respond to his wishes.

With each difficult step, Rose was becoming more and more convinced that he was about to ignominiously fall flat onto his face.

A grizzled infantry sergeant stood to one side to allow Rose to pass, and as soon as the young pilot was level with him, the NCO shrieked deafeningly, "Make way for the Orficer!"

Stunned by the blasted utterance, brain momentarily numbed, Rose briefly faltered but managed to keep his balance, feeling as if everything between his ears had been pulverised by an artillery shell.

Certain that a tumble would have delighted the troops hugely, he concentrated judiciously on each step, clasping his belongings tight.

At least the tightness of their packed bodies prevented him from falling, even on the occasions when he came close to losing his balance, but luckily, not everyone was intent on making the going difficult, and a few steadying hands helped him.

With a few mumbled apologies and thanks, he was grateful to finally stumble from the carriage out onto the platform and into the cooler night air.

Towards the end he'd felt if he'd been wading through thick treacle.

The struggle to get out of the train had sapped his strength, and he flopped down gratefully on the nearest platform bench, sucking in the cool air, and then immediately choking, for it was liberally mixed with fine soot and pungent smoke from the locomotive ahead.

But despite the fact that the air was filled with clouds of steam, soot, acrid smoke and filth from the waiting train, it was still possible to smell the sweet and earthy fragrance of the countryside in summertime.

It was wonderful, after so many hours, to escape the close, clammy atmosphere of the crowded train, to exchange the foul mixed brew of tobacco, stale sweat, bad breath, Blanco, serge and hot feet with the far nicer fragrance of the British countryside at night.

Rose took off his crumpled cap, scrubbed his face with one hand, and then undid the buttons of his greatcoat, allowing the cool air to circulate.

His neck and shoulder still ached and he lowered the kitbag gratefully on to the platform.

He'd boarded the train in a crisp uniform, but now he felt like a soiled and sweaty rag.

Someone, he recalled vaguely (had it been a doctor?), had written recently in The Telegraph that the necessity of the blackout had made train journeys far more restful for travellers, as one was no longer able to read, but obliged instead to rest the eyes; nevertheless, it was difficult to describe the experience he'd just endured as restful.

It had been more of a trial of endurance than anything else. He'd dozed, but had awoken with sore and stiff muscles, and feeling anything but rested.

Rather stressed, in fact.

The silly bugger who had written the article couldn't have known what he'd been talking about. Let him try a journey like the one Rose had just taken. He'd soon change his tune.

Hopefully, if the reports were true, they'd soon have managed to paint all train windows and light the interiors. At least then it would be possible to read, see the face of the person you were sharing the compartment with. Felt a bit peculiar silently sitting there in the dark with a lot of people you'd never met before.

It had been a long and dull trip, but, at least he was finally here.

'Here' was a sleepy rural station set in the heart of rolling English countryside, an island in the darkness, but Rose knew that the little English village of Foxton was nearby.

A little further out in the surrounding darkness would be the fighter aerodrome that was to be his first operational posting after the Operational Training Unit.

"Hallo, there! Are you destined for the aerodrome, by any chance?" Rose started in surprise at the unexpected voice.

Standing just beside him was another RAF officer, a young Pilot Officer like himself. In the midst of all the noise, and deep in thought, Rose hadn't heard his approach.

Unlike Rose, however, the young man was about six feet tall, broad chested and built like a rugger forward, quite different from Rose's meagre and lean five feet six.

However, the young officer's face was one of a mischievous schoolboy, with a big grin below bright grey eyes and a pug nose.

Probably grinning because he'd startled me, mused Rose sourly.

Or maybe even by my wretched, crumpled appearance.

The stranger was immaculately dressed in a spotless uniform, a bright red scarf around his neck (how the hell had he managed to keep so smart?), and looked fresh and strong, as if he had stepped down from a recruiting poster.

By comparison, Rose felt like the organ-grinder's monkey. An organ-grinder's monkey after a hard day on the pavement.

Careless Talk Costs Lives. "Er, actually, yes." he stood tiredly and extended a hand, "How d'you do? I'm Harry Rose."

The youngster took his hand, with a firm dry grip and pumped it enthusiastically, "How d'you do! I'm Billy Brooks. Bloody awful journey, eh? Thought it would never end. I was sitting next to a group of subalterns who were whinging and whining the whole time. Dunkirk this and Dunkirk that! By the sound of them, you'd have thought I was dropping bombs on the silly sods! I'm jolly glad to see a friendly face at last, I don't mind telling you."

Rose shook his head ruefully. "You were bloody lucky they didn't thump you, Billy. We're not too popular with the army nowadays."

Fortunately all the soldiers Rose had been sitting amongst had been from units stationed in Scotland and the North of England, and not any of the fortunate members of the ill-fated British Expeditionary Force who had been miraculously rescued under fire from the French Port.

The unfortunate ones, of course, were now prisoners of war, or worse.

First Norway, the Low Countries, and then France. The Blitzkreig had rolled up all resistance like a moth-eaten rug, with Dunkirk and Calais the definitive full-stop to the successful German campaign.

The BEF had started with the finest of allies, including the huge two million man strong French army, seemingly invincible, massive fortifications like the Maginot Line and Eben Emael, great advantages in terms of aircraft and armour, but nothing had stopped the inexorable German advance.

With a lot of Europe now under the Nazi Jackboot, Britain stood alone.

The future was looking very bleak indeed.

Like so many other RAF airmen, Rose had received more than a few uncomplimentary words for the perceived lack of aerial support for the BEF during the evacuation, and one of his friends had even been admitted to hospital after being badly beaten by some disgruntled drunken soldiers.

Behind them, doors began to clatter closed.

"By all accounts they had had a pretty rough time of it, Billy." Rose tried to be friendly, but he didn't feel it, and wished the newcomer would bugger off so that he could sit and enjoy a few minutes of the night air with its clean country scents.

He really wasn't in the mood for a cheery chat, but quelled the feeling of churlishness. "At least they didn't knock you about. Bending your ear was better than blacking an eye."

As he spoke, there was a shrill whistle, more clattering of doors, and the train began to pull out of the station, amidst a deafening cacophony of screeches and puffs, made that much louder by the natural quietness of the station.

Slowly, but gradually gaining speed, it disappeared into the darkness, leaving behind only a gradual attenuation of the clash of metal and hissing steam.

Billy, still grinning, waited until he could reply without having to shout.

"One should be grateful for small mercies I suppose. I must say they dented my brains with their moaning, though," and then, "Would you like to share a taxi, Harry?" Billy looked disconsolately around the station, "That is if they have anything like a taxi in such a place. Probably only have donkeys and village idiots out here in the wilderness."

He walked over to the entrance of the Waiting Room, and gazed wide-eyed at a faded poster glued the door. It exhorted citizens to join their local ARP (Air Raid Precautions) Units. "Look at this! You won't find me joining these silly buggers, looks a bit dangerous to me. Mummy always told me to be careful."

Another described the effects of Andrew's Salts, Billy snorted, "I don't need these, six or seven pints of beer usually help wash down my grub. No blockage in my pipes, chum."

He moved along to a little red vending machine fixed on the wall, popped a penny into it and received a little bar of Cadbury's chocolate. He waved it questioningly at Rose, who shook his head, and so Billy ripped it open and took a large bite. "I'm famished! I only had a couple of cheese sandwiches and a boiled egg at lunchtime. I could eat a horse."

At the mention of food Rose's thoughts turned longingly of a large plate stacked high with slices of steaming roast beef and yorkshire pudding, covered with rich brown onion gravy. His tummy grumbled and his mouth filled with saliva.

"Well, come on then Harry, old man," Billy mumbled wetly through a mouthful of chocolate, "shall we go and have a look outside?" He swallowed convulsively, and his Adam's apple bobbed wildly, "Mm, lovely. They may not have a taxi, here, but perhaps they'll have a donkey shackled to an idiot? Shall we go and see?"

Oh for pity's sake!

Rose grinned despite his desire for solitude after the hours amidst the packed crowd of sullen humanity of the train. He could feel the dark cloud of surliness gradually dispersing from his brow as Billy continued his inane babbling.

He sighed in resignation and reached for his kitbag.

"All right, Billy, let's go and see." The other's energy seemed to replenish him, and he could feel the excitement of joining his first squadron returning.

Billy pointed down the platform with his half-eaten bar of chocolate,

"Look, there're some more of our mob! Come on Harry, last one to catch up's a rotten egg."

A few other figures had alighted further along the platform, and now that the clouds of steam from the train had dissipated, Rose could see that a number of them were dressed in air force blue. Replacing his cap back on his head, Rose picked up his kitbag and followed after them. With a bit of luck there might be some service transport outside waiting to pick them up, and they should be able to cadge a lift.

The other RAF men turned out to be a group of NCO pilots.

Billy hailed the pilots just as they passed a pair of older men, dressed in civilian garb, but both were wearing the armbands of the new Local Defence Volunteers, and medals from the Great War, ribbons faded but hanging proudly from their breast nonetheless.

The colourful ribbons might have been faded, but their spirits weren't. They eyed the two young pilots suspiciously from beneath their broad-brimmed helmets, and, irrationally, Rose began to feel very guilty.

It was always the same for Rose. Even at school, if a window had been broken or a bottle of ink dropped, he would feel guilty for some inexplicable reason, resulting in awkwardness, and his ridiculous behaviour had often earned him punishment even though he was invariably innocent.

"Would you kindly show us your identity cards and paybooks, please," one asked heavily, peering through a pair of old-fashioned spectacles at them. "Sir," he added, almost as an afterthought.

Billy grinned disarmingly, "Of course you may, Mon ami," and he nonchalantly tossed the remnants of his chocolate into a nearby dustbin before reaching into his pocket.

Billy and Rose handed over the documentation, and the LDV man examined them minutely with a shaded torch, whilst his companion cast a suspicious eye over the pilots. He sighed. "Perhaps you could show me your travel orders, as well, sir?"

Rose started to feel a little apprehensive as their papers were examined, but while Rose broke into a sweat, Billy was relaxed beside him, casually leaning against the wall, hands in pockets and that big, relaxed oafish grin on his face. He even winked at the second of the LDV men.

Of course, everything was in order, the documents were returned, and the men of the LDV thanked them both, rendering the young RAF officers an immaculate parade-ground salute that would have made an RSM of the Guards weep with pride. Their faces were impassive but Rose could have sworn that their eyes twinkled.

We may not have the uniform or the weapons, lads, but we're here to fight too. We may be older than you, but we'll stand shoulder to shoulder with you and face the Hun when the time comes.

The two old soldiers turned smartly on their heels and marched off down the platform, arms swinging in time.

In his mind, Rose could hear, "It's a long way to Tipperary…" The only thing that diminished the effect was the civilian garb and the broom handles that rested on their shoulders, instead of rifles. Despite their age, their drill was superb.

Bloody hell, thought Rose admiringly; wish I could march half as well as those old boys. They're ancient, must be almost sixty years old…

He was well aware of his own shortcomings on the drill square, which had caused more than one apoplectic ranting session from dear old Sergeant Reynolds.

If they fight half as well as they marched…

Billy noticed his look. "If old Adolf has any sense at all, he'll not risk any of his precious storm troopers in an invasion, hm?" He murmured.

"Not half," agreed Rose, admiringly. He glanced back at the pair of old soldiers. "I don't think those two would leave anything over for us!"

He was only half-joking.

The three RAF Sergeant pilots had politely stopped to wait for Billy and Rose, and now greeted the two young officers cheerfully, and confirmed that there was, indeed, motor transport waiting outside for RAF arrivals.

Moreover, it turned out that they were from one of the two fighter squadrons that shared the airfield.

The three were Spitfire pilots, and were happy but weary after a long three-day leave of drinking, dances, girls and general debauchery in 'The Old Smoke.'

Sure enough, as Billy had predicted, a Bedford three-ton truck with RAF markings was outside the station, comfortably parked beside the single bus shelter, obviously the airfield duty transport.

So either somebody knew they were coming, had expected the NCO pilots to return, or a vehicle was always ready to meet the evening train, to collect returning personnel; most likely the latter.

Beside the Bedford stood another of the LDV men, a short, squat old man, firmly holding a gruesome looking home-made club studded with bent nails and broken glass. He was chatting with the driver; his head upturned, the weathered and lined face expressionless.

The MT driver was quite different, being a very bored looking airman, deeply engrossed in picking at an uneven set of fingernails on one, grimy, oil stained hand, deeply ingrained with a thick layer of dirt and oil, a cigarette perched on his lower lip.

Unlike the LDV man standing smartly and solidly in a position of parade rest before him, the MT driver was slouched casually against the truck's radiator grille, one heel on the fender, but when he noticed the pilots' approach, he leisurely got to his feet.

Rose had seen curmudgeonly regulars who resented the sergeant's

24

stripes awarded to NCO aircrew once they received their wings, after only a short time in the service.

Despite years of peacetime service, volunteer youngsters half their age now wore the same ranks that had taken the regulars' years, decades even, of hard work to attain, and they were often seen as upstarts and given a tough time by their regular service counterparts.

It looked for a moment as if the driver was not going to bother to salute the young sergeant pilots, or at least begrudgingly offer one.

However, once he saw the single thin blue stripe on each of Rose and Billy's sleeves, he immediately had a change of heart, straightening his side-cap hurriedly and jumping to attention. The cigarette rapidly disappeared.

For a moment, Rose toyed with the thought to give him a talk on how to smarten up, but decided against it.

Best not to cause ripples until he had found his feet. It wouldn't do to get a reputation as a martinet.

Rose was still young enough and unsure enough about his new found authority to feel some degree of embarrassment at being treated deferentially by men twice his age, with ribbons and decorations on their chests from service in wars that had taken place before he had even been born.

The two young officers returned his salute and then passed up their kitbags and cases to the willing hands of the others, before clambering up into the back of the vehicle.

Perhaps they should have got in the cab as they were officers, but, foolishly maybe, Rose felt more comfortable amongst the other pilots, and it seemed that Billy, too, felt the same.

Theirs was a kinship that overcame any differences in rank.

They would ride together with their fellow brethren of the air in the back of the Bedford, all for one, and all that.

Rose didn't know them, and they spoke amongst themselves, quietly, comfortably, yet they were just like him. The three young Sergeants wore the same silk wings on their left breast, and were dressed in the same blue uniforms, but the gap in experience between the officers and the NCOs gaped wide like an abyss.

Had they seen action, faced the enemy, and killed others like themselves from the other side? What was it like to see the enemy up close? Rose longed to ask them, to find out about what he would very soon be facing.

But he was unsure, and, if he were totally honest with himself, was also too shy to ask. They were all one and the same, yet the divide between the veterans and the new boys was too wide.

These men, Heavens preserve us, may look to my leadership in the air one day!

The thought was both exciting and terrifying. Billy seemed to share Rose's thoughts, for he sat down opposite, but appeared equally preoccupied as he too looked at their companions. His face was thoughtful, his grin now gone.

Awed into silence by these relaxed young veterans, Rose pulled up the collar of his greatcoat and settled back, his thoughts turning to what lay ahead.

And so they made their way to the airfield together, passing through the peaceful village of Foxton, on the last part of their journey.

Five young men dressed in RAF blue, jostled and bouncing around in the back of a truck on a quiet country lane, their futures uncertain and formless before them.

They could not possibly know that of them, some would not survive the grim and difficult months that lay ahead.

Chapter 2

Every little bump and imperfection in the road seemed to make the truck spring and bounce horribly, causing everybody in the back to be flung up into the air, time after time.

After a few minutes, when his throbbing bottom felt as if it had been repeatedly whacked with a sheet of corrugated iron, Rose decided to stand, but this was even worse than before. Although he held on tight to the metal frame, he continued to be thrown upwards, and Rose hit his head twice in the tarpaulin covered roof frame of the lorry, his hips, knees and ankles beginning to ache from the jarring impacts.

The wind whistled through gaps in the canvas covering, threatening to whip away his cap, and turning his sweaty shirt into an icy sheet.

Sitting down again, ignoring Billy's grin and wink, just discernible in the darkness, and surreptitiously rubbing his sore head, he cursed and wished for the umpteenth time that he had decided to sit in the cab after all. He was an officer, should bloody well act like one.

Idiot.

Rank hath its privileges and all that drivel.

Should bloody well use the privileges of my stripe, he remonstrated with himself irritably; being one of the lads was proving to be a painful decision.

After ten more minutes of driving along winding, narrow country lanes, at what seemed like breakneck speed to the unfortunate passengers, they finally came to the airfield.

All that was visible of RAF Fighter Command station Foxton in the night was a high wire fence with a simple entrance leading to the gates and gate guardhouse.

The lorry slowed and stopped beside a great coat clad sentry who came round the back of the lorry to investigate.

Hastily, Rose pulled out his identity card, papers, paybook, and movement orders from his breast pocket. After a few moments of scrutinising their documents, the Guard Corporal, a British Army soldier who had appeared beside the sentry, handed back the papers.

"If you gentlemen would stay in the lorry, sir, I'll ask the driver to take you to the Orderly Room. You're expected and your Adjutant wants to see you, he'll take care of you," finally, with a smile, "Welcome to Foxton, sirs. I'll phone ahead and just tell them you're on your way."

The Corporal exchanged in some friendly banter with the other pilots, accepted an unlit cigarette from one, a mysterious packet from another, and waved the lorry through. Luckily these soldiers seemed pretty friendly to the RAF!

Once inside the station, the truck stopped again almost immediately, to allow the Sergeants to get off. They wished Rose and Billy good luck, shook their hands, before disappearing into the darkness.

After another short journey, they finally arrived at a large brick building, which housed the administrative offices and the Orderly Room.

Waiting outside in the darkness was an officer. In the subdued headlights of the Bedford, Rose could see that he was a tall, florid, fortyish Flight-Lieutenant with a huge bristling ginger moustache.

Rose noticed that the Flight-Lieutenant, whom he assumed to be the adjutant, wore the 'Mutt, Wilf and Jeff' trio of Great War medal ribbons and the purple-and-white of a Military Cross with the single rosette of a second award below the silk winged 'O' of an observer.

So, another old warrior from an earlier war keen to do their bit in this new one.

"You pair of rascals, took your time getting here! I've had to wait here for you for the last two hours, and I've missed a game of Bridge because you young rakes have been chasing totty all around town instead of reporting here. There is a war on, you know!"

He sniffed, as if trying to detect the smell of alcohol. "Anyway, you're here now, so we'll say no more about it. Welcome to Excalibur Squadron."

He had a surprisingly soft voice and a sparkle in friendly eyes that took the edge off his sharp words, "My name is Skinner, and I'm your Adj, and once we've sorted out a few things, I'll arrange for someone to take you to your new home. Have you had anything to eat at all? You must be thirsty. Chasing totty is stiff work, I seem to vaguely remember. Mrs Skinner wasn't always watching me with her beady little eyes, y'know. I've had my share of a mis-spent youth."

He leered knowingly at them, "You should allow the little darlings to do some of the pursuing, y'know. There was a pretty little thing from Paris, couldn't speak a word of English…"

He smiled at a memory. "Well, come on, then, can't stand here all night talking about women. You're here to fight, not fornicate, y'know. We'll get some of the formalities sorted out, then perhaps we can phone ahead to sort you out a sandwich or something. OK? Follow me."

He turned and strode purposefully back into the building, not checking to see if they were following. Billy and Rose exchanged a bemused glance and followed him.

In no time at all, the formalities had been taken care of, and a Corporal was called to take them to their quarters.

It was quiet and deserted outside, the transport they had come in having long since departed, doubtless having returned to the Motor Transport Pool, duty done.

Instead, there was a dusty RAF-blue Hillman parked outside.

"All the pilots have gone into London for a show, Sir," answered the Corporal, with a vague wave into the distance, almost dropping one of the kitbags, which hung precariously from his shoulder, when Billy questioned him about their fellow pilots.

"Oh I say which show?" Billy's eyes lit up, "Was it at Queen's? I hear they do some absolutely ripping shows there." Rose was too tired to care. All he wanted was to have a wash, a bite to eat, and to lie down and close his eyes.

Corporal Fricker had sad, sleepy eyes, as if he had just stirred from his bed, "I'm sorry sir, they didn't confide in me, but they should be back soon, I shouldn't wonder." He placed their kit in the car, "You'll live outside the airfield, with the other pilots, Sir. I'll drive you there."

They drove carefully through the airfield, past the dark shapes of buildings, vehicles, and once, a pair of fighters, and back out the other side, through a different, smaller gate with an imperious wave at the lonely figure of the guard on duty. They continued once more along the main road, with the driver sniffling miserably all the while.

Rose watched the light reflected back from the newly laid cats-eyes on the road surface. Comprising spherical marbles of glass in a protective case, they were a new-fangled idea, originally invented in the mid-1930's, and they were proving extremely useful in giving a driver an idea of where he was on the road. They were a particular blessing in these times of blackout.

Rose had heard that they were invisible from the air, so hopefully there was no chance Jerry could use the roads for navigation at night time.

Thank God for these things, he thought. At least now we know which side of the road we should be on and we can stay on it, just hope everybody else does.

There had been too many road accidents after the black-out had been originally brought into force throughout the country.

At the beginning of the war, in late 1939, all street lights and headlights had to be kept off, as part of the black-out, but after a number of pedestrians were killed by cars that could not see them, and drivers killed by obstacles that came suddenly out of the darkness without warning, the situation had to be reconsidered and important changes introduced.

Like painting the kerb or some roadside objects white, or the slitted hood that was fitted to the Hillman's single uncovered headlight.

After a mile or so, and a journey that was so much more comfortable than the recent trip in the Bedford, the Corporal swung off the road into a small gap between the high hedges that lined the road like brooding giants in the dark, and onto a smaller private side-road that led gently uphill.

Rose breathed a quiet sigh of relief.

A little part of his mind had feared that in the darkness the chance of a collision with an oncoming vehicle was highly likely. He'd been hardly able to see a thing through the windshield.

Indeed, unconsciously, he'd been bracing his feet against the foot well in anticipation of an accident. Billy had also seemed a little tense. Perhaps he too was a little nervous about driving around the countryside in the darkness.

Near the top of the hill, set against the blackness of the sky, was the pale square shape of a large country house nestled amongst a darker background of trees.

The airman, Corporal Fricker, deftly pulled up into the gravel driveway in a wide curve, and parked the service car beside a collection of other vehicles.

The light from their single hooded headlight had momentarily illuminated the assorted group of vehicles, notably picking out a Lagonda Tourer, a white coach, and a rather grand looking, but strangely dented, Bentley with broken headlights.

To one side of the cars were a motley thicket of bicycles that looked hopelessly entangled.

The cars were lined up haphazardly near the main entrance of the large house. Billy whistled quietly in awe, "We'll be living in style, I reckon!"

Rose looked up at his new home, as Fricker unloaded the bags.

Crumbs. It was all a bit grand.

"Yessir, it's a home from home for the gentlemen from the squadron."

Fricker took them in, past a threadbare looking stag's head with a huge set of antlers, crudely tied to a small pillar with steel wire. It had been shot at, for there were quite a few ragged holes with stuffing poking out of it, and the pillar was badly chipped and pocked with bullet holes.

The once-treasured trophy regarded them coldly with one glassy eye. The other one had disappeared altogether, leaving behind an empty hole filled with stuffing.

They passed a rusty blue tricycle lying on its side in a trampled bed of flowers by one of the windows.

Fricker noticed them looking. "Mr Ffellowes, erm, borrowed that from the toy room, sirs. Something to do with a race between pedals and pistons. I believe Mr Ffellowes lost."

He shifted one of the kitbags on his shoulder into a more comfortable position, "I'll take you up to your rooms first, and then I'll rustle up some grub for you both, Sir. There's a lady comes and makes up grub and pots of tea, but she'll have gone back to the village by now." He led them in through a side door, along a wide corridor, peering midway along through another door into a dimly lit room.

"Nobody at home", he muttered disapprovingly, and sighed.

They glanced in as they passed. Inside was a large sitting room with overstuffed armchairs, a number of small settees, loungers and a pair of gaily-striped deckchairs. In addition was the detritus that was the usual evidence that a fighter squadron was in attendance.

Liberally scattered about were a large number of empty or partially empty beer bottles, and full ashtrays that were filled to overflowing to form little piles of dark powder and butts on the plush carpet.

Sleeping on one of the armchairs was a glossy black cat, long fur shining in the lamp-lit dimness. He looked up at the unwelcome intrusion, luminous green eyes intent, but decided the two young pilots were unlikely to come into the room to stroke him, and curled up into a neat ball again.

Beside the fireplace was a Messerschmitt nosecone supporting a tray with a cracked teapot and some teacups.

Resting against one wall was a twisted Belisha beacon, draped with a large pair of 'passion-killer' WAAF's drawers, and a female tailor's dummy clad in an Army Captain's tunic, colourful tea cosy on its head, and nothing else. One sleeve and a couple of buttons were missing, and a broad, lopsided red grin had been painted on to the featureless head.

Scrawled on the walls were a number of 'murals', most of which were air battle scenes, but a few were of women in various stages of undress.

Harry and Billy grinned at each other as they trailed after Fricker up the staircase. It seemed there might be interesting times ahead on the squadron.

On the first floor landing, Fricker pushed open the third door on the right with his foot, and stood aside to allow them in.

"This is your room, Mr Rose, Sir. I'll just place your kitbag here, an' I'll take Mr Brooks up to his room. The CO's done you proud, here. The officers of the squadron have all got your own rooms. The old boy who owns this house is an old friend of his. I believe he's a Colonel fighting that bleedin' Moo-soleeni in the desert. Most of the house staff is out there with him, 'though." He pursed his lips in distaste and looked around. It was clear what he was thinking.

Bet the owner doesn't know what these cheeky scallywags are doing to his lovely house. Fricker heartily disapproved of the cheery vandalism. Billy and Rose exchanged a look, and Billy grinned.

"Mussolini", corrected Billy.

"Yes, Sir, that's the one, ol' Benny-too", He sniffed, "Must be hot and dusty there I shouldn't wonder. Lots of flies and foreigners. Glad I'm not there, give me Blighty any day." He looked back at Rose sadly. "I prefer the rain meself, know where you are with rain. Once you're wet, can't get no wetter. If you'd just like to settle yerself in, Sir, I'll knock up a sandwich and a nice cuppa for both of you young gentlemen. Run you a nice bath as well, after. Get you settled in proper nice, like. If you'd like to follow me, Mr Brooks?"

Billy slapped him on the back, "See you in a bit, Harry."

As the door closed behind Fricker and Brooks, Rose went to the open window and closed the blackout curtains before lighting the table lamp. In the soft light, he was able to see the extent of his new home.

34

The room was rectangular, with a sloping roof and dormer window to one side. Must have been part of the servants quarters, he decided.

There was an ancient dresser and wardrobe pushed together beside the door. There were no doors on the wardrobe, and a few twisted steel hangers stared back at him, the open cavity yawing like a gap-toothed mouth.

On the dresser was an Ovaltine tin, an empty wine bottle, a chipped and cracked porcelain bowl and a matching jug.

There was about an inch of scummy water in the bottom of the bowl, a semi-dissolved scrape of soap and a large dead bluebottle, whilst the jug was bone dry.

The Ovaltine tin contained a broken lead pencil, a brass RAF button, a paperclip and a tattered piece of paper with 'Helen-Pimlico 264' written in purple ink with a rounded feminine hand. An apparently-unused French letter containing a few boiled sweets was held in place by the pencil. A book of matches from a club in Soho and another dead bluebottle completed the collection.

The drawer in the dresser yielded a pair of lacy black knickers, a bottle of ink, a severely worn toothbrush and an empty toothpaste tube.

The bed was neatly made up, and seemed strangely out of place amongst the ancient pieces of furniture. Next to the bed were a wooden chair with a cushion, and another overstuffed, dilapidated and faded purplish patterned armchair, complete with tassels, which looked as if it belonged in a Victorian Boudoir.

The table lamp sat on a bedside table on which was a stained beer glass and a few dog-eared paperback books.

Harry picked up one of the books and leafed through it. It was a racy thriller, *Scarlet Danger,* with a semi-clad blonde on the front, her mouth half covered by one hand and open in a silent scream, eyes turned back to a dark and featureless stylised male shadow outlined in a doorway behind. He tipped it into the wastepaper basket.

I don't think I'll need that, he thought.

Deadman's Gulch joined it in the bin.

Another was a copy of Remarque's classic, *All Quiet On The Western Front*, and the last (minus it's cover) was H G Wells' *War of the Worlds*. Well, these two would be joined by his treasured and well-thumbed copy of Ira Jone's excellent *King of the Air Fighters*.

The walls were quite bare except for a ripped out magazine page, which bore a large picture of a nude, nothing being left to the imagination.

Strangely, it looked like Vivien Leigh.

Rose peered closely at it in the dim light.

Bloody Hell! It was Vivien Leigh, or rather, her face was. It had been cut out of a magazine, presumably, and had been pasted on to the picture over the nude model's face, so that it appeared as if the actress was reclining comfortably in a rather risqué pose. He smiled and smoothed back a curling corner.

Good Lord! Her legs were spread wide apart, knees slightly bent and…good grief, he could see her-

There was a knock, Rose jumped guiltily as the door suddenly opened, to admit Fricker. He smiled benevolently at Rose, cocked an eyebrow.

"Ah, I see you've noticed the picture, Sir."

Rose coloured, and stepped back quickly from the wall, pretending nonchalance. He felt very like a naughty little schoolboy caught, ogling wide-eyed at one of those dirty postcards young Dabney used to bring in to school.

Fricker appeared not to notice Rose's discomfiture. He sniffed again, mournfully, eyed the picture. "She was Mr Dickers favourite actress, was our Viv. He told me once that he'd met her at a party. Great one for parties, he was. Adored her, he did. It's a shame, what happened."

Dead men's shoes, thought Rose gloomily.

He looked around the room. Dead and gone and now it's mine. Wonderful.

"What happened? Did he, er, get shot down?" Suddenly the bed did not seem so welcoming.

Fricker laughed, his braying startling Rose because of its unexpected source.

"Oh Gawd love you, no, Sir. He was a bit of a naughty boy; though it's not me place to say so, begging your pardon. He was a little handy with another pilot's lady, if you catch my drift, so he got himself posted to 13 Group. Terrible shame. Dickers by name, and dick 'ers by nature, if you pardon the expression, erm…"

He pulled out a handkerchief, and blew his nose forcefully into it. "Sorry, sir. I'm always like this, I'm not well, got bad feet , but don't you worry, I'll wash me hands before I make yer sandwich." He blew his nose again.

"I just came to say that Mr Brooks is upstairs, next floor, second on the left. The bathroom on this floor is right at the other end of this corridor." He noticed the bowl and jug.

"Oh dear, I see that the batman hasn't sorted these out," He tsk-tsked and picked them up, tucking the jug deftly under his left arm.

"I shall have to have a word with him. Nice lad, but a bit young. Used to live on a farm, bless 'im. No, it really isn't good enough," He looked around the room, sniffed again, "Dear, oh dear," then looked apologetically at Harry. Well, I'll go and sort out that grub for you. Would you like it here, or downstairs, sir?"

Rose tried not to stare at Fricker's shining nose. "Downstairs would be fine, thanks."

"Right-ho, sir, call you when it's ready. Sort you out some nice cold cuts, bit of fresh bread, and a nice bit of Picalilli." He nodded at Rose, and left.

What a strange little man, thought Rose bemusedly, but pleasant enough.

He gently unpinned the picture from the wall, peeked at it again, and slid it into the dresser drawer. The dreadful Dickers may be back one of these days for his picture. Interesting, but not really one he wanted to keep in plain sight. Particularly not on the wall.

He stole a last furtive glance.

Good Lord, it was all there, between her open thighs he really could see...um, well, her *thingummy-jig*.

Crumbs!

His mouth was dry. Could do with nice hot cup of sugary tea, he thought. Hope Corporal Fricker gets a move on. He shrugged off his greatcoat and hung it up in the doorless wardrobe, then began to unpack his kit.

Laying out his clothes on the bed, in the deathly quiet house, Rose felt suddenly all alone.

Chapter 3

The sudden knock on the door startled him awake.

He lay there for a moment, heart racing, in that momentary confusion experienced when suddenly awakened from a deep and dreamless sleep, wondering for a moment where he was. The ceiling that greeted him as he opened his eyes was strange and unfamiliar, a dark, sloping expanse above him.

There was another, louder, more persistent knock at the door, so he unglued his tongue from his palate and croaked, "Come in."

The door opened and a tall, thin officer peered in.

A smile, pale eyes beneath a peaked cap, the frame lean and spare, two stripes of a Flight-Lieutenant on his sleeve, and the diagonally-striped purple and white ribbon of the Distinguished Flying Cross.

"Pilot-Officer Rose, is it?"

"Yes, sir." But it sounded more like 'yeththir', Rose disengaged his sticky tongue from his palate again, licked dry lips, cleared his throat, "Yes, sir," he tried again, "I'm Harry Rose, Excalibur Squadron." Oh, how marvellous that sounded!

The tall stranger bounded into the room to pull back the heavy blackout curtains.

Early morning sunlight flooded in as if it could wait no longer to explore the recesses of his room, rushing in a torrent to fill the room with glare.

Rose winced and blinked at the sudden unwelcome and uncomfortable brightness. He was still half-asleep and shocked by this sudden intrusion.

But then he realised he was still in bed, in the presence of a senior officer, so he pushed back the coarse blanket, untangled his legs from the bedclothes, swung them out and stood up, wobbling little unsteadily at the sudden change in posture, swaying slightly in his striped pyjamas in front of this decorated, tough-looking officer.

Oh no! Were his bits tucked in properly? He daren't look down.

Damn! Should he stand to attention or not? He squared his shoulders manfully feeling faintly ridiculous standing at a semblance of attention.

"Yeah, I know who you are. I'm Flight-Lieutenant Jim Denis, A' Flight commander for Excalibur. You've been placed in my flight. Thought I'd come and say hello." He had a deep, gravelly voice, with an exotic and warm Australian twang. He noticed that Rose was standing at semi-attention, looking comical with his creased striped pyjamas and mussed hair.

Denis smiled to himself, and then felt a sudden wave of depression. Rose looked so young and helpless. Like so many before him. In his pyjamas he looked about twelve.

He wondered to himself, was I ever that young, so keen and fresh? He waved a hand casually at the young pilot.

"At ease." He looked around. "Relax, chum, we don't stand too much on rank most days," he smiled easily at Rose revealing even tobacco-stained teeth, "especially first thing in the morning."

Denis was in his mid-twenties, and had a pencil thin moustache above a strong jaw, lines crinkling around a pair of bright blue eyes, on a sun-browned face. It was a strong and dependable face, Rose decided.

He had brought in with him the smell of early morning mixed with tobacco smoke, a strong but reassuringly pleasant aroma.

Had he overslept? Rose turned his wrist slightly and surreptitiously looked down at his watch, and the dial read 6.34am.

Bloody Hell!

Denis noticed his glance. "I'm just back from the airfield. Had to check on my erks, God bless 'em, see that they've sorted out our kites for morning readiness. Thought I'd find you, share a spot of tucker at the Mess, and introduce you to some of the others."

Then, thoughtfully, to himself "Most of 'em will probably still be in bed, though, lazy blighters."

He looked around the sparsely decorated room again, "the Adj told me you'd arrived. I'm afraid we'd all gone to the big smoke for an Al Bowlly show. You missed a bloody good evening, y'know, shame you got in late, mate. Next time, hm?"

He noticed the bare patch on the wall. "Flaming hell, somebody's nabbed Viv! I don't suppose you saw Vivien Leigh run out of here last night without a stitch on? The little sweetie used to live in here, you know." He looked at the bed, as if he expected to see Vivien Leigh hiding under it. "You under there, Viv, love? Ah well, never mind." A smile hovered at the corners of his mouth.

Those keen eyes were now fixed shrewdly on Rose as he tried to clear a chair for Denis.

"Tell you what, Harry, why don't you get yourself dressed and sorted out? I'll wait for you downstairs. I have to pick up something from my room anyway. Your batman and our lady from the village can arrange the odd cup of tea or a snack, but we normally have our meals in the Officer's Mess back at the field." He picked up the

41

Ovaltine tin and rattled it absent-mindedly, "So, when you're ready, I'll give you a lift back to the 'drome for a spot of breakfast. There's a sweet little WAAF sheila there called Dolly who knows how to serve up a smashing kipper. Hand's and eyes off, though, she's mine!"

He put down the tin, and chuckled, "Oh, and I heard about your AFC, you did bloody well. Well deserved." His eyes crinkled again, "Frank Ruddock and I trained together. Good man. I'll see you downstairs in ten minutes, OK?" He winked at Rose, and closed the door behind him.

Rose stretched, stifled a yawn, then sauntered barefoot to the window, opening it and inhaling the fresh sweet fragrance of flowers, hedgerows and recently cut grass.

His room looked out over an expanse of beautifully cared for gardens, rich with bright colourful blooms, neat rectangles and squares of green grass glistening with a heavy dew. Icy droplets had pooled on the sill, and Rose doodled a meaningless pattern in it, enjoying the iciness on his fingertips, the sweet freshness in his nostrils.

The birds were twittering their daily morning chorus, and he stood there at the window for a moment savouring the peace, closing his eyes and tilting back his head, enjoying the warm sunlight playing on his face, even though there was still a chill in the air.

Below him, he could hear the boots of the army sentry crunching against the gravel as he marched around the building.

Hm, didn't see him last night. Lot of bloody good he is. We weren't challenged when we got in. The house could have been filled with Jerry paratroopers and we'd not have known it.

So much for security. The bugger was probably having a crafty fag around the corner. Hope the Wehrmacht doesn't try invading this part of the world any time soon.

How sweet the air, so peaceful here…

However, Denis would be waiting downstairs for him, and sighing regretfully, he carefully closed the window.

Whilst Rose and Billy had been tucking into the cold cuts of chicken, thick-sliced corned beef and piccalilli sandwiches, with large mugs of hot sweet tea the previous evening, Fricker, bless him, had thoughtfully replaced the bowl and jug with a clean basin, fresh water, a thick cake of soap, and a small hand-held mirror.

Now, staring at his reflection in the mirror, Rose worked up a thin lather, and began to scrape tentatively at the sparse growth that had begun to bristle on his chin.

The clear sky had cheered him up.

With a bit of luck, there might be a spot of flying today. He began to whistle.

The Officer's Mess was a long low brick building, situated close to the group of structures that made up the station headquarters and admin block.

There were already a number of pilots sitting down to breakfast at one of the long tables in the dining room when Rose and Denis arrived.

Billy was already sitting in front of a half-eaten kipper, listening earnestly to another pilot, cup of tea poised.

"So, there I was with the sauciest little redhead in London, a proper piece of popsie, more bosom and bum than a man can handle, all giggly and terribly keen on accommodating one of her aerial heroes, namely yours truly, very accommodating, if you know what I mean?" He smirked suggestively, "And so I thought, polite gentleman that I am, where more romantic on a warm summer night than Hyde Park? How lovely to gaze at the stars with a lady, hm? Of course, it happens to be handy that there're the trenches there, thought it would be quite cosy. She could lie on her back to

43

ogle the stars, with me on top, to protect her from the Hun bombs, of course."

The others laughed. Trenches had been dug in Hyde Park after the outbreak of war, to accommodate local residents in the event of a bombing raid. Luckily there had been no need for them. Except that is, by courting couples who found the privacy useful for their amorous activities.

"So, because I'm well brought up, not like you ugly mutts, I thought I'd help her down first. Problem is, those flaming sandbags were a bit past it, and we lost our balance. Arse over tit, headfirst, if you'll pardon the pun. Nice tits and arse they were, as well."

He looked around pathetically, held up his hands, and, "How was I to know there would be so much mud in there! Apparently nobody bothered to dry them out! Deirdre was quite put out, and it stopped her from putting out, if you get my drift."

He gazed mournfully around. The others, delighted at the tale, and the disconsolate look on his face, began to laugh again.

The teller of tales wiped away imaginary tears, "And then, to cap it all, the local ack-ack wallahs decided that a pigeon passing by was a Heinkel in disguise, and started having a pop. Bang, bang, bloody bang. I s'pose you can't blame it for unloading its load. I just wish it hadn't been all over Dierdre. So, y'see that was the only banging going on that night…"

They roared, Billy included. Rose smiled.

Then they noticed Rose and Denis standing behind them, and turned to look curiously at the newcomer.

Billy pointed at Rose with his fork, "This is Harry Rose, boys, we came down on the train together last night. 'Morning, Harry, come and take a pew! Are you in B'Flight as well?"

Denis snorted, "No chance, this lad's been spared the shame of joining your pitiful shower, Billy. He's been chosen for A' Flight, cream of the cream."

"Bollocks, Dingo!" called one of the pilots, a Flying Officer, rudely. Like Denis, he too wore the ribbon of a DFC.

Rose looked with discomfort at the WAAF's in the room, but they had not, or at least appeared not to have heard anything.

Probably hear a lot worse every day.

"Here, plant your posterior here with us, Harry. You may not be in B'Flight, but we'll let you have breakfast with us, you too, Dingo."

"Oh quieten down, for Pete's sake, Dicky! My blasted head feels like it's about to blow up." Another of the pilots muttered viciously.

The Flying Officer, Dicky, smirked at his other companion as he spread jam onto a piece of bread, "That'll teach you to over-imbibe, you naughty boy. You should learn to control the amount of beer you sup. When one has had the benefit of a chorister's upbringing, as have I, one knows that one pint is always more than enough." He nodded piously.

Denis shook his head, "Take a seat with these reprobates, Harry. I'm just going to check on our kippers, and then I'll be back, don't let 'em ruin your morals."

Dicky leered again, "You're the danger to the poor chap, old man. Check on our kippers, my arse. Going to check on your little Dolly, more like, you old devil."

"In order to truly appreciate a dish, one must first understand and appreciate the cook, in every sense," Denis said pompously, and walked away towards the kitchens amid catcalls.

"Is this Dolly a bit of a dish, then?" asked Billy quietly, with interest.

Their other companion, a gaunt looking youth of no more than twenty, nodded. "I'll say, old boy." His voice was low, "The girl is lovely. Not often you see such a veritable beauty." He sighed, "Wish she was mine."

45

"Not half! I dunno what she sees in an old colonial like Dingo."

Harry, hearing what sounded like a terrible slight of his likable new flight commander, his first operational flight commander, felt the pricking of new found loyalties. "He seems nice to me. I'm sure Flight-Lieutenant Denis has many endearing traits that, er, Dolly can appreciate," he said rather stiffly, regretting the words as soon as they came out, knowing how priggish he sounded.

Damn! He looked around, anxious not to fall out with his newfound colleagues.

They looked at him curiously, sensing his imprudence. Rose reddened, "What I meant to say-"

"Well, I'm bloody glad that one of those endearing traits you're blathering about is being effective at killing Huns," This from another pilot who walked over and sat down. He too, was a Pilot Officer, tired old eyes in a round, young face, "though I'd be willing to bet the outrageous size of his wedding tackle may play a part." He smiled wistfully, "Dolly must be a hell of a woman."

The wistful expression vanished. Now he stared belligerently at Rose, "Who the hell are you, anyway?" Are you one of ours or do you belong with those Spit bastards? If you do, why don't you just piss off back to them?" He said referring to the Spitfire squadron sharing the airfield. A couple of heads turned for a moment, and then looked away again.

"Oh my Gawd! You're not a blasted sprog are you?"

Then he noticed the shiny new ribbon of the Air Force Cross on Rose's chest and looked more searchingly at Rose. "Not a sprog, then?"

"Whoa, Wally!" cried Dicky, "Bloody Hell! Calm down! You really must learn to relax a little! This is Harry Rose. He's in A' Flight, poor fellow. It's not his fault. You mustn't hold it against him, though, you know. Harry, poor chap, thinks that Dingo is a choir boy and that little Dolly's a girl guide. He'll learn, the dear wee thing. Say hello nicely to Harry."

Dicky winked at Rose, "Don't mind this moaning old misery-guts, Harry, this is Wally Wilson, used to be a lawyer, hence his sunny disposition and cheeky smile." He waved to a passing WAAF waitress, as Wilson raised a hand, wiggled his fingers and curtly nodded at Rose. "Hello nicely, Harry."

There didn't appear to be any neat white-coated waitresses here, just the three overworked young WAAFs with rolled up shirtsleeves, stained shirts and harassed faces.

"Holly, my love, some tea for our brave young new boy, here." With a smile the WAAF retired to fetch Rose's tea. "You mustn't take any notice of old Wally, here. He's always been a miserable bastard. Born like it, poor sod. They all are where he comes from, in the benighted North, comes from living in the rain, clouds and smoke," he whispered the last in a conspiratorial whisper, as if confiding a great secret.

"Anyone with an AFC," he continued in a normal voice, nodding at the red and white diagonally striped ribbon on Rose's chest, "Particularly a nice new boy like you deserves to be pleasured by the delights of Dolly's gorgeous kippers. They positively seduce the tongue, and copulate vigorously with your senses. However, I'm afraid our supply of butter has disappeared this morning, though. Those Spit bastards have nicked it all, I suspect, so we shall have to use some of that dreadful oily margarine stuff." He made a face.

"Dicky, you are such a silly sod, and you talk such a load of old cock, as I'm sure poor Harry's noticed. I'm from the north, Lancashire. It's lovely." Wilson glowered at them. "We're happy, decent folk, y'know. We haven't all been born with a silver spoon up our arses. Just because everything north of Cambridge is foreign to you."

47

Ffellowes ignored him, instead sipping delicately from his teacup.

"You'll understand our desperate jealousy when you gaze upon the scrumptious Dolly, chum," said the haggard youth, holding out a hand, "I'm Johnnie Farrell and this smooth-talking rogue is Dicky Ffellowes."

"With an 'e', young Rosie, with an 'e'." Added Ffellowes languidly, "Don't forget the 'e!' We Ffellowes earned it at Agincourt, you see. Proud of our heritage, doncha know?" He smiled calmly.

"I daresay you fellows are," retorted Rose, tongue in cheek. Billy grinned and slurped his tea.

Ffellowes smiled too. "Very good, old boy. Heard it all many times before, of course. You know Billy, of course, and the alluring but obdurate Wally. He doesn't like the Spitfire bods very much, because one shot him down over Dunkirk."

Wally Wilson had a broken nose and a shock of curly black hair. He nodded, morosely. "Had to go for a blasted swim, and then the fucking brown jobs almost shot me before they pulled me out." He picked up a fork and studied it closely, "When they found out I was RAF, they had a go too. That's how I got my broken nose. Pongo bastards."

"Doesn't like the Army much, either, I'm afraid, in fact, I don't think he likes anyone, but it's only to be expected with someone as ugly as he is." murmured Ffellowes sadly, "But overall, he isn't such a bad fellow for a northerner."

"Or for a lawyer. Just piss and wind really, but very dependable and stolid, bit like a cow, just not as pretty or as useful." agreed Farrell.

"Fuck me. You're such a pair of bastards," scowled Wilson, chin thrust forward and hands flat on the table. "If you'd appeared before one of my judges, I'd have got the pair of you sent down for a few years of hard labour."

"The kippers are on their way," announced a voice, and Denis collapsed onto the chair beside Rose. It creaked alarmingly, and for a moment Rose thought his new flight commander was going to make an ignominious second landing, via his bottom, on the floor.

"I managed to cadge some butter from Dolly for us. Apparently she'd kept a little back. Imagine that." His eyes twinkled as he picked up a thick-cut slice of bread.

Dicky smirked salaciously at Rose, and Wilson shook his head and blew out his cheeks.

"So what's the chance of a flight?" Rose asked.

"Oh, I imagine Dingo will take care of that for you." Ffellowes murmured nonchalantly, not looking at him.

"Any chance of some aerobatics or maybe gunnery instruction, do you think?" Rose knew that if he could fly his fighter as well as possible, he had a far better chance of surviving the combat that was to come. He still felt very inexperienced, and the thought of a confrontation with a gaggle of Messerschmitts filled him with more than a little trepidation.

"Oh we don't talk shop over breakfast, old man." Replied Ffellowes airily. "It's bad form." He picked up his tea cup and looked into it "Dear, oh dear. Cold."

It'll be worse form if I get shot down and gutted by cannon shells because nobody could be bothered to give me a spot of advice when I needed it, thought Rose, annoyed and exasperated, but he remained silent.

Billy caught his eye and winked.

Another of the WAAFs brought them a fresh tray of plates piled with sliced bread.

Denis crammed a slice of bread into his mouth, then patted Rose's sleeve, reassuringly.

49

"Don't worry, Harry, old man, it's all in hand." He mumbled around the mouthful of bread. "All in good time, mate. I've made arrangements for all that."

He swallowed the bread convulsively and looked up as the waitresses reappeared. "Hm? Ah!"

This last as plates of kippers and preserves appeared, and Rose's nose twitched at the delicious pungency.

There was a scrape of butter decorating the side of each plate, except for one, burdened with a pair of kippers, a fried egg, and a very much larger knob of butter, which in comparison to that on the other plates, looked like the Rock of Gibraltar.

This latter plate was carefully set before Denis, like a tribute being placed before a king. He leered at their envious faces, and reached out for another slice of bread.

They tucked in with great enthusiasm, and no-one talked for a while as they ate. Wally Wilson smiled beatifically as he chewed. His face changing completely with that smile.

Rose picked carefully at the yellow flakes of fish, savouring the flavour.

Denis was right; the kippers were really delicious, beautifully done.

"You don't deserve her, Dingo," muttered Farrell jealously through a mouthful of fish, a smear of butter on his lips. He was eyeing Denis' plate.

Denis cracked a smile, eyes twinkling. "I know, mate." He generously buttered the slice of bread, and his smile widened, "Terrible, ain't it?"

Chapter 4

Flight-Lieutenant Skinner, the squadron adjutant, was waiting at the Flight offices, perched on the edge of a desk 'manned' by a pretty little WAAF, when Billy and Harry arrived to check about their position on the flying roster.

"Good morning, gentlemen. Had a good breakfast? Fantastic kippers, eh? Well, I'll have to arrange a time for you both to see the Stationmaster today as well, of course."

He noticed Rose's perplexed look, "Oh, that's just what we call the Station Commander, but that'll be for later. For now, the CO would like to see you both. Just a few words of introduction, explain a few things. Say hello and welcome to you both. He's already had a word with me about sorting out some flying for you both today. I'll go through the form afterwards, once the old man's seen you. Fair enough?"

He looked down at the little WAAF. "Look out for these two, my dear, they're die hard skirt-chasers, real reprobates, don't give 'em the time of day, OK?"

The little WAAF smiled prettily at Rose and Billy, "OK, sir."

"That's my girl. Good, good, well come on then, chaps, follow me."

He led them to another office. The door was partly ajar, and Skinner knocked, once, before pushing it fully open.

"The two new boys are here, sir. Would you like to see them?"

"OK. Please bring them in, Uncle, and thanks." The voice was mild, almost gentle. It didn't sound like that of a demanding fighter squadron commander, more like that of a mild mannered classroom master.

Skinner beckoned them in, and, automatically, they both checked their collar buttons, belts and ties (or scarf in Billy's case), even though they'd already checked them each at least once.

Rose nervously pushed the door closed behind them before following Billy to stand at attention before the desk.

A blotter, a couple of pens, some scattered forms, a picture frame facing away from them.

The Commanding Officer of Excalibur Squadron was standing at the window, back to them, looking out at an AA machine gun nest.

"Welcome to Excalibur Squadron, gentlemen. My name is Donald." He turned to face the two. Skinner stood impassively beside the desk, staring at them.

Edward Donald was a slight young man, no taller than Rose, of twenty-five. He had calm grey eyes, a prominent nose and a firm mouth. At first glance he looked no older than they were, but a second, closer, look revealed grey already beginning to sprout at his temples, and a network of fine lines at the corner of his eyes and mouth, lines engraved by a bright sky whilst endlessly searching in that wide arena, the indelible marks of strain.

A thin white scar began halfway up his forehead, and disappeared into his hairline. On his breast, below his wings, he also wore the ribbon of the DFC.

Another veteran, than. France or Norway maybe? Even though the war was less than a year old, there had already been so much fighting and so much loss.

"At ease, gentlemen." He stuck out his hand. It was rock-steady, a hard grip. "Unfortunately I was off the field when you arrived yesterday, so I couldn't receive you. Settled in OK, then, met the boys?"

He cast an eye over them. Both young men smartly turned out, young, expectant faces.

One of them serious, slight and dark, the other smiling, taller, and fair. Shy eyes and a red and white diagonally-striped AFC ribbon on the chest of one, the top button confidently undone and a colourful scarf on the other.

Fine.

A new boy then (but one with a calm head and courage in the face of adversity, if the act that had earned him the immediate award of an Air Force Cross whilst still in training, meant anything), Rose; and a Fighter Pilot with some experience, or at least one who fancied himself to be so, good reports, Brooks.

Billy Brooks, Gladiator biplane fighters. Has he been taught the old, flawed and outmoded ways, or has someone managed to instil modern tactics and ideas in him?

"Yes, sir, thank you," they chorused together. They looked like a couple of schoolboys (but then, hadn't they all?), and for a fleeting moment, he felt a wave of unhappiness wash over him.

Would they learn and survive, or...would they just become more faces and names to remember in those quiet, pensive moments when he was alone?

He smiled, a warm smile, and for a second the carefree young man he had once been returned, but only for a second. "You've both been allocated flights, so I shall leave the details to your flight commanders. Rose will be in A' Flight and Brooks will be in B'. There'll be a couple more lads joining you in a few days. You'll get to meet the other pilots during the day or this evening at dinner. They're a fine bunch."

Donald had a soft Scottish accent. "I've organised some flying for you both today with experienced section commanders from your flights. Uncle here," He glanced at Skinner, "Will give you the details."

Skinner nodded firmly, "I'll give the little blighters the gen when you've finished, Sir."

"Good." He turned once more to look out of the window. "'A' Flight from this squadron fought in Belgium and France just before the end, and we provided air cover for the BEF's withdrawal at Dunkirk."

The Miracle, as it had been called in the popular press, the retreat of an army from a smoke-stained, blasted and burning seaside town, only made possible by the courage of a rag tag navy made up regular and irregular sailors. The Navy helped immeasurably by civilians, old men and boys.

He crinkled his nose and frowned at the memory, shook his head ruefully.

"We learned some important lessons fighting Jerry. Lost a lot of men learning them, ground crews and pilots, including the Old Man, Squadron-Leader Bolton."

The old man, dead at twenty-six years of age. What a loss. He reached out and gripped the ancient radiator beside him. They had been his men. The CO had been a great man, a man who had died to save those men and others.

"I assume you've both got at least a few hours solo on the Hurricane? We had a lad turn up yesterday who'd only ever flown a Battle, so back he went. No damned good here."

"Twelve, sir." Said Rose. A pleasant faced boy, clear brown eyes and dark hair. Achingly keen, eyes eager but anxious. Very serious. A schoolboy in air force blue, but already proven under stress, not found wanting when really needed. Well thought of by his instructors.

And the saviour of one of them.

"Ten, sir," Billy.

Ten and twelve. Dear God.

"But plenty of hours on biplanes, too, sir." Billy hurriedly interjected, "My flying assessments were good."

Jerry will sober you up, son, should you live that long. Another young man, but God-willing, at least one with some experience of operational flying. Thank goodness for that.

Somewhere outside, a Merlin engine coughed, spluttered and crackled, then burst into noisy, throaty life.

Spitfire or Hurricane?

"Yes, of course. Brooks, hm." Donald raised his voice to be heard above the sound of the Merlin. "Gladiators, yes, fixed undercarriage." He scowled, "I've seen some good Hurricanes written off by some careless pilots, and not just the ones who've only flown biplanes. I don't want to lose any of mine, OK? Make sure about the position of your undercarriage when you're coming in, then, check again. Keep checking your wheels are down. I don't want any of my Hurricanes bent, understood?"

Or any of my fine young men, words he couldn't say.

Nearby, at one of the air defence machine gun posts, an Army Sergeant raucously shouted vile oaths at his men.

Skinner smiled inwardly at his CO's words. You wait until I tell them about the shiny new Hurricane you wrote-off last year when you were grandstanding, Eddie, my boy.

"Understood, Sir. I'm familiar with retracting undercarriage." Billy sounded hurt.

Donald had to raise his voice above the sound of the taxiing Hurricane, his eyes like flint. "Yes. Well, we'll see, shan't we?"

The CO transferred his unyielding gaze to Rose. "Oh, yes, sir, yes indeed." He hurriedly replied.

The growl of the Merlin outside gradually receded as the aircraft taxied away.

Donald's voice softened. "I don't want to lose any men or any kites through stupidity or cockiness. I'll not stand for grandstanding or showing off. There'll be no aerobatics or beat-ups on my squadron. Bloody behave yourselves." He looked back at Billy, "You might think you know everything there is to know, and I'm assuming that you're both well versed in squadron operations, formation flying, tactics and fighter area attacks, and all the rest?"

They nodded.

Donald smiled grimly. "Well, you're both going to have to forget everything of what you've learnt about fighting in the air. Those were the old ways. We've learnt to do things differently now. So will you. As I mentioned, we've learned a few painful lessons, courtesy of Jerry." And we've suffered in the learning.

Unbidden, the memory of Bolton's Hurricane falling, falling, just broken, burning pieces, that loud braying laugh silenced forever, and endless, endless waves of deadly enemy fighters.

His eyes had turned heavy and dark, and the two youngsters shifted uneasily beneath his scrutiny.

He realised he was staring moodily at them. "The old ways are outmoded, useless. Your section commanders will be taking you up for some instruction, including mock air fighting. I want you both to have some airborne gunnery practice at RAF Sutton as soon as possible, too. God willing we can show you what you'll need to know."

Thank God! Rose thought, relieved. The Training Unit had not given any practical instruction whatsoever in air shooting. He wasn't sure if he could hit a barn door at fifty paces, and the thought of taking on an enemy machine flown by an ace of the blitzkrieg had given him more than one nightmare, and plenty of unsettled nights.

Donald picked up a picture that had been perched on the sill. A young woman with a fair bob and dressed in a simple white dress smiled up uncertainly at him, the flush of recent laughter still caught in her eyes.

He stared intently at the smiling girl, as if burning each detail onto his mind, even though each line and angle was permanently marked in his mind. *I still miss you, love.*

He noticed the two young men looking at him quizzically.

Wondering about him, about the scar and the DFC, perhaps? Well, let them. They'll find out themselves what it was all about, soon enough, poor little sods.

His voice hardened. "I want you both to have a lot more hours in these kites before I allow you to become operational." He saw their expressions, and held up a hand before they could protest. "You have to be a useful part of the squadron, so you'll have to learn how we do things, and how we work. Think of it as an additional course of instruction. A little bit more training, hm?"

His gaze was intense now, the voice harder. "At the end of the week I'll ask your flight commanders on how you've each progressed, and, depending on that, I shall decide on your individual readiness for operational status. I'll not send you against Jerry unless you're ready."

He glanced out of the window, then back at them. "One last word of warning. If you're not up to it, I'll send you back. No duffers on this squadron."

If only I could really afford to send back the ones who weren't ready.

They looked suitably cowed. Good. Better not to be over confident. There was more to being a fighter pilot than a pair of silk wings, a cocky smile and a fancy scarf.

He carefully set down the picture frame, as if it were a fragile and priceless, which to him it was (I love you, my sweet!), and leaned forward on his desk, "We work together, and are stronger for it. All for one and all that sort of thing."

God! How do I keep saying this? How easily the words slip out, but in reality I'm just a man like either of you. You think I have all the answers, but I have none. Just false assurances for an uncertain future.

On the runway, the unknown pilot blipped the throttle on his aircraft saucily, and then began his take-off run. The taped windows vibrated.

"We are currently under-strength, so I can't afford to keep you away from the war for too long, but I want you better prepared than you might be right now. Learn as much as you can, as soon as you can, because what you'll learn will likely help keep you alive, and, hopefully, help you remain in one piece. We lost quite a few of the squadron over Dunkirk, so we're still awaiting more replacements, but they should be joining us over the next few days or so, as I mentioned before."

There was a gentle smile on his lips now, "I'll expect you both to pass on to them what you're about to learn. Learn well, because one day it might be you doing the teaching." The smile disappeared, "That is, if you can prove to me that we should keep you."

And if you survive, of course.

Don't look at me with those trusting eyes, those eager, shining faces. If I have to, I will send you to your deaths, and you'll not be the first, God help me. Because it's what I may have to do. Will I have to write to your parents one day, too? I hope you're able to learn what our hard-earned experience has taught us. If you can learn, maybe you'll live. If you don't, there's no hope at all.

For you, or for any of us.

If I could give you more time, I would, but, God help me, I need you now. The enemy is coming.

There is no more time.

He shook their hands again, and smiled at them, but his heart mourned the many dead of this war, and the many more of those yet to die.

Skinner gazed at Donald with compassion, as the two chastened young pilots left the room.

You poor boy, you've already been through the mill. Belgium, France, Dunkirk, what next? You've grown old before your time, seen things that no man should, and now you have to go on sending more boys out to fight, and if needs be, die. If I could take your place, bear your responsibilities, I would.

His thoughts drifted back to another war, another place. Seems so long ago now.

I, too, have known the hell you are in now. May you live to look back on this time in your old age, so that it is only a bitter faded memory.

My memories are still crystal clear, even after twenty-odd years, but at least they're only memories now. We have more hard times yet to come.

New memories yet to make.

Donald turned to him with a smile, slowly rubbing his hands. As if wiping away the terrifying enthusiasm of the two boys.

"Well, Uncle, they seem a promising pair of lads. Brooks has a reasonable number of flying hours, and he's used to flying fighters, so he knows the score, and although Rose may still be wet behind the ears, that AFC means there's hope for him. I just hope they're good students. Fingers crossed, eh?"

"Don't worry, sir. Granny and Dicky will set them straight, teach them a thing or three. I have a lot of faith in those two. God help Rose and Brooks!"

"Quite right, Uncle." Here was the boy again, "All this jawing's made me thirsty, how about a nice cup of tea?" He pulled out his pipe, clamped it firmly between even teeth.

Skinner's gaze softened. "Certainly, Sir, I'll give Jenny the nod, tell her to put the kettle on, on my way out. I better go and tell those boys who they've got to fly with." He, too, looked at the photo.

Skinner put a fatherly hand on Donald's shoulder, squeezed gently. "Come to think of it, I could do with a cuppa, too."

Though I'd prefer something a bit stronger, he thought, and a cigarette or two.

God help us, but it never gets easier.

Chapter 5

Rose had been told by Skinner to meet with a Pilot Officer Daniel Smith, who was, apparently, the section commander for A'Flight's Yellow section.

Billy had found his section commander straight after the interview with the CO, as Dicky came out of the Mess. Ffellowes was to be his (Brook's) section commander.

The same could not be said for Rose, however, and after a series of fruitless trips to the main store, the latrines, one of the blister hangers, and then the cookhouse, he was finally redirected to some of the fighter pens at the far end of the field, situated near a large copse of trees.

Beyond them, smoke curled peacefully from the chimney-stack of a farmhouse outside the airfield perimeter.

Nearby, a Fordson 15 cwt truck loaded with a khaki clutch of soldiers slowly trundled its way back to the guardhouse. It was one of two vehicles that were part of the airfield defence detachment immediate response section.

The other was a Morris truck with a pair of dustbin-like turrets, mounting machine guns. Wouldn't like to be on the receiving end of that, he mused, cautiously eyeing the grim faces beneath the helmets.

The fabric at the bottom of his trouser legs were damp with the still-present morning dew, whilst his once beautifully polished shoes were now wet and covered with bits of earth and grass.

There were three Hurricanes lined up in adjacent blast pens, sturdy and exciting, and one of the three had its engine cowling pulled back with an airman on a ladder hunched before the big Rolls-Royce Merlin II engine, his hands disappearing inside the workings of the engine.

Another airman stood beside the wing root of the fighter, standing ready with some tools.

A third 'erk' was perched precariously on the tip of the fighter's black nose cone, which had been removed from the aircraft and placed on the ground before it. He was polishing a small nondescript metallic object industriously. An overpowering stink of dope, grease, oil and glycol clung to the air about them.

The metallic clatter and cheerful voices floated on the morning air to him as he walked towards them.

They did not see him approach, and he listened with interest as the lanky, dark-haired mechanic working on the engine told a dirty joke whilst still tinkering with the complex innards of the engine.

The internal workings of the modern monoplane fighter engine were a confusing near-mystery to Rose, and, despite attempts during training to teach him the basics by well-meaning and kindly teachers, he remained the worst of students, and would most likely permanently ruin any aero-engine he was allowed to tamper with. The most generous of engineering officers were usually reduced to raving incoherence by his difficulty with even the most fundamental points.

He still found it hard to believe that he'd satisfied the requirements of his tutors. They must be desperate.

Thus, with this woeful lack of understanding, he marvelled as the mechanic worked skilfully, never seeming to falter as he tightened something one moment, then adjusted another next.

For some moments he stood and watched in mystified fascination.

The airmen finally noticed him, and they sprang to attention. Except, that is, for the dark-haired and lean mechanic on the ladder, who casually glanced at him momentarily, then returned to the business at hand, without any sign of acknowledgement.

Bewildered and annoyed by the rudeness of the discourteous mechanic, Rose waved the other two to rest, and asked, "I say, could you tell me if P/O Smith is around, at all?"

"Who wants to know?" The unhelpful answer seemed to emanate from the bowels of the Merlin, as the man continued to labour industriously, refusing to look at Rose.

"Quite why that involves you, airman, I don't know," answered Rose firmly, "However the fact is that the CO has asked me to report to him. I'm to fly with him today."

Firm, be firm, you're an officer! They're supposed to be respectful towards you!

"Perhaps if you'd just direct me to him, airman?" He irritably wiggled his cold toes in the wet socks.

The mechanic finally turned around and looked at him, hard.

"Ah. You'll be Rose, then."

Really, the bloody man had little respect for rank! Rose could feel his little authority slowly sliding away from him. He hadn't experienced such blatant disrespect before.

"Yes, Pilot Officer Rose to you, *airman*." He emphasised the rank. "Do you have any idea where the hell I can find Smith?"

The mechanic eyed him with distaste. "Oh, you'll find him in hell one day, I shouldn't wonder," he said, coolly. "But not today, I daresay you'll find him a sight nearer than that right now." He hawked and ferociously spat a glistening blob on the grass to the side.

Good Lord! Rose's feet were uncomfortable, he was tired, and he wanted to sit down. He'd chased all over the airfield to try and find Smith, and now to top it all off, some half-witted moron was being extremely insufferable and unhelpful. He was beginning to feel very prickly, and why the hell were the other two grinning like idiots?

"Look here, I don't like your tone. So if you can't…" His voice tailed off as a terrible suspicion began to dawn.

Awful comprehension.

Rose's face reddened.

"Oh, I say. Are you…I mean to say, you're not P/O Smith, are you?" he blurted out incredulously.

The mechanic threw his tools into the nearby toolbox, with a discordant clang that made Rose's teeth ache, and jumped down from the ladder.

"Yes. I'm P/O Smith. I was told by Uncle you'd be looking for me. Well, you've found me. Took your own sweet time about it, though. I've been waiting bloody ages." He turned to the groundcrew. "Could you finish off here, please, lads?"

He reached up for a battledress tunic carelessly draped over the wing behind him, and shrugged it on. Like his shirt, it too, bore the stains of his labours. Rose caught sight of an angry red scar on Smith's forearm before it was covered up with an oil-stained sleeve.

In addition to the stains, the tunic was also decorated with RAF wings and the tightly striped ribbon and rosette of the Distinguished Flying Medal and Bar, as well as another ribbon, somehow strangely familiar, and the General Service Medal ribbon.

Rose was awestruck. The man had been decorated twice already, and commissioned recently as well! He must have absolutely bucket-loads of experience, had to be an ace, yet he looked little older than Rose himself!

Pilot Officer Daniel Smith, Distinguished Flying Medal and Bar, Croix de Guerre avec palme, RAF, known as 'Granny' to one and all, was twenty-four years of age, had been part of Air Marshal Barratt's AAF (The air component of the British Expeditionary Force) during the phoney war, had then fought in the disastrous French campaign as the German Army rolled over the low countries, being shot down twice, and ending the disastrous campaign in the smoke-stained skies over Dunkirk.

He held his hand out to Rose. It was patterned grey-black with grease, black beneath each oily fingernail.

Without hesitation, and still slightly taken aback, Rose grasped it firmly, and they shook hands.

The master had received his apprentice, and now he looked him over critically.

Smith looked at Rose's AFC ribbon, then back into his eyes. "The CO has asked me to show you the ropes, including some flying training, Rose. Show you the form, so to speak."

"Please, call me Harry," answered Rose automatically. He was still in awe of Smith. The war was less than a year old yet, this man had already earned a DFM and bar!

Bloody hell!

Rose blushed, wincing inwardly at the thought of how he'd spoken to Smith just a few moments ago.

The dark, brooding eyes bored into his, as if searching for weakness, the pitiless eyes of an eagle, of a hunter. There was no softness there, and the thin, tight face was equally without softness. The fires of war had forged hard steel from this one, turned him into a killer and a warrior.

"You're to be in my section, Rose, and you'll fly as my number two for the moment, so in the air you'll always be Yellow Two. The third member of the section has not been allocated yet, but we'll probably get someone who's going to arrive sometime tomorrow. This morning I'm going to go over the basic rules we have here on Excalibur squadron, about flying, etc., then we'll see what you're like in the air. I've read your assessments. The CO has placed you in my charge so that I can make a fighting man of you. And a fighting man you'll be, if I have to kill you to do it, because if I have to fly with you, you're going to help me stay alive."

He wiped ineffectually at his sleeve. The grease stain remained stubbornly resistant to his half-hearted efforts, instead seeming, if anything, to spread further. Rose had never seen such a poorly turned out officer, and he tried not to stare.

"If I don't find you to acceptable standards, though, I'll have you off the squadron. I'm not flying into combat with some rubbish pilot, gong or no gong." It sounded like a challenge.

He stared at Rose once more with those cold, killer eyes. "It's not an idle threat; you know," he said quietly, "The CO will get rid of anyone who doesn't look like they can handle the job. He's already posted three pilots away this week that were useless. So if you can't keep up, either you go back to the Training Unit, or to another Group where there's no danger you might hurt someone. Understand?" Smith's voice was ice-cold, uncompromising.

Trying not to be overwhelmed, but also feeling a burgeoning spark of irritation and resentment, Rose nodded.

He didn't speak, for he was sure his voice would quaver, and this was the man who could answer all his unanswered questions, the one who would teach him how to fight and fly, and hopefully, help him to survive whilst in harm's way.

Was the dreadful Dickers one of those pilots who'd been sent away? He wondered. He'd left his picture of Vivien behind, so he must have gone in some sort of a hurry.

Apparently satisfied with Rose's cowed silence, Smith grunted, and indicated the Officer's Mess with a nod of his head.

"Well, now that you know where you stand, and what I expect of you, let's make a start. Why don't we talk about some of the basics of flying and fighting in the Hurri over a nice cup of tea?" He sniffed, "How many hours?"

"I beg your pardon?"

"Bloody hell! Are you deaf as well as rude? Hours on Hurricanes, man! You have flown a Hurricane before, haven't you?"

"Sorry. Twelve, sir." Rose was ashamed. He had meant to speak with a firm, confident voice, but it had come out as a chastened murmur.

"Twelve! God help us. The Old Man must think I'm a ruddy magician. I'm not a miracle worker." Smith looked grimly at his grubby hands.

"We're going to have to improve on that, because there're some very nasty flyboys not far from here who are praying for the chance to come up against a new boy like you, and I've no desire to see you peppered into pushing up daisies. If you're rubbish, better you spend the war sharpening pencils or making sandwiches, or something more useful."

Nasties. The same word as used by Churchill, the new belligerent Prime Minister, a mispronunciation to denigrate the Nazi's.

Smith saw the growing resentment in Rose's eyes, and smiled inwardly. Good, might be of some use after all, this one. Had a bit of fire in his belly.

He pulled a grey, stained handkerchief from his pocket, looked at it for a moment, and then wiped his hands on it.

There was no effect whatsoever upon the ingrained grime on his palms, and he frowned.

"I'll arrange for us to go up this afternoon for an hour or so, because we don't have long before Adolf has a go at us, and there's a lot you need to know, I suspect. We're going to do a lot of flying over the next few days, OK? None of the training shit they've filled your little head with, though. I'm going to show you how to fly and fight in a Hurricane properly. Forget about gongs and glory, though, I'm teaching you to keep me alive, and if you stay alive too, well, that's a bonus."

They started walking back towards the Mess.

"Yes, sir. Thank you, sir." Great! Some flying! This was exactly what Rose had been hoping for.

Smith scowled. "Don't call me, sir, for heaven's sake. I may be your section leader, but we're the same rank. You might even have seniority. Anyway, I'm called Granny by all and sundry around here, Lord knows why, so you'd best call me that. Just take my advice, and do what I tell you to, and do it when I say you should. Let's try and keep me and you alive. I intend to die when I'm grey and very old, preferably clutching at least one pretty young lady at the time."

He looked at his hands, and scowled again. If anything, his hands looked even dirtier than before. He bunched the handkerchief up and pushed it back into his pocket.

There was a drone, which suddenly turned to an onrushing roar as an aircraft shot across the airfield at very low level directly towards them and over their heads. The sound was deafening and he could feel the passage of air wash over and buffet him.

Startled, scared witless, Rose instinctively threw himself face first down onto the glistening grass, only to look up and see Smith gazing up into the sky, hands thrust into his pockets, a frown still on his face.

In the distance the Spitfire that had so rudely 'buzzed' them arced gracefully up into a smooth, steep climb, whilst also executing a cheeky barrel roll. His cap had been blown off his head by the low flying aeroplane.

"Those silly buggers from the Spit Squadron just love to show off. One of these days the pongoes in the machine gun posts are going to bring one of them down. The Army isn't renowned for its aircraft recognition." He looked down, eyes dark, "They showed that well enough in France and during the retreat."

Red-faced and trembling, Rose stood up and brushed his uniform. The dew had left some rather damp patches. He looked around for his cap.

He was mortified. "I'm s-sorry about that."

"Don't be. You did the right thing. If that had been Jerry, I'd have been Swiss cheese. The only way any of us have any chance of surviving this war will be to carry out our job, but not to take any unnecessary or stupid risks. Live to fight. Live to kill. Better to have a wet uniform than a peppered arse. I've had both, believe me, and I wouldn't recommend the latter."

He clapped Rose on the shoulder, leaving a faint greasy stain on his sleeve. "Something tells me that you'll do alright." He almost smiled at Rose. Almost.

"Come on then, Harry, let's go and get that tea, and I can make a start on your re-education."

He waved to where his cap had been blown by the Spitfire's propeller wash. "I'll get my hat, and then we can talk. Tell me about the flying formations that they taught you..."

Rose was assigned to fly T for Tommy for the first of the training exercises, a tired looking Hawker Hurricane, which incidentally, had been one of the trio of fighters lined up in the pens where he'd first met Smith.

Apparently she had seen service in France, and proudly bore four black swastikas on her fading paintwork to show the combats she had triumphed in, and survived.

Unlike poor Rose, T was no virgin. She'd lost her innocence in France, and had accounted for four of the enemy in that time.

Smith and he had discussed flying and fighting in the Hurricane for over two hours, their cups of tea cooling between them, after which they had adjourned for a light lunch, following which, Rose had met the Station Commander, an ancient (Forty seven years of age!) Wing Commander, who had flown Bristol Fighters during the Great War, amassing a tidy score of victories and a vehement desire for peace.

The station CO had been a provincial Bank Manager until 1939, when he had decided to offer his services to his country once more, despite his abhorrence of war.

His country over his ideals.

He was aware that there was no longer any chance of his being able to fly the modern monoplane fighters that were now the mainstay of Fighter Command, but he would serve where he could.

The Top Brass had decided, in their infinite wisdom, that his authority and experience were best suited to a desk job, so he had gracefully accepted this assignment to station command, and did his best to make his little station a happy but efficient part of 11 Group.

Rose had found him welcoming and kind, and watched with interest as the young WAAF secretary fussed fondly over him. It seemed he was very popular amongst his personnel.

A 'very nice old bloke' was how Smith had described him. The 'Stationmaster' had talked with interest to Rose and Billy, a round and kindly figure with a gentle manner and a voice that was indulgent.

Rose had to listen carefully to catch every word. It was impossible to visualise him ever giving a 'rocket' to anyone.

There was a superbly carved foot-long mahogany model of a Brisfit (as the Bristol fighter used to be known to its aircrews) on the battered desk, amongst the piles of paperwork, with an inscription, *'Presented to Captain Edmund Albert Heart DSO, MC, CdeG, RFC, by the Officers and Men of 317 'Hawk' Squadron RFC, Rouvres, October 1917.'*

It had been in every office in which he worked, and now it was back once more on an operational fighter airfield.

A mass of photographs on the wall, a cavalry sword, a decrepit looking elephant gun, and assorted trophies told of a well-travelled and sharp shooting ex-army officer and ex-RAF aviator.

There was also a sepia photograph of a pleasant looking woman of about forty framed with black velvet. They had met in France, she driving ambulances, and their love had lasted, even though he had outlived her. He knew she waited for him on the Other Side, yet he also knew his duty lay with the men and women of his command on this.

The Service and his station were the only things that the Wing Commander had left now, and he guarded them, and loved them jealously.

There had been an incident of disorder at the local public house two months earlier, involving broken glass and furniture, following a difference of opinion between some soldiers and a number of his airmen. He had paid for the damage, and spoken out for everyone involved, including the soldiers, after giving them a stiff talking-to, which coming from so gentle a man, came as sufficient shock to make even the most hard-bitten of the soldiers to tremble.

There had been no further incidents since.

After all, he had been a soldier in the British Army first, well before he became an airman. And even though he may rescue them all from gaol, he had to maintain discipline. After all, adherence to discipline and authority are vital to any service at all times.

And he was still an aviator, for Rose had seen the wistful look in his eyes whenever an aircraft took off or landed behind them.

He did, of course, have his own personal Gloster Gladiator (assigned as a headquarters staff machine), but running a station ensured he had little time to fly, although he made efforts to find time and on the occasional Sunday the airfield was lucky enough to see him putter sedately around the local area, like an old gent out for a Sunday jaunt in his motor car. It was also proving to be handy transport to have available whenever he attended meetings at Group or at the Air Ministry.

His two young squadron commanders made sure that there was always a fighter in the air nearby whenever and wherever he flew, should a hostile aircraft choose to make an unwelcome appearance. They loved him too much to leave him in the air without protection, despite the fact he had more combat experience than the both of them put together.

The old boy had been a crack fighter pilot once, but a lot of water had passed under the bridge since, and they were not convinced he could fling an aircraft around as he must once have done when he battled with the Kaiser's finest.

It was now the turn of the young men, the brave new eagles of the Royal Air Force, and although he may have envied them, and wished himself with them above the fields of the land that he loved so dearly, he knew that he had to allow them the foremost place of danger.

His role was to keep them free of concern when it came to being on terra firma.

He loved them, as a parent will love their children. They were the ones who would take the lion's share of the fight, who would give their all and then some more, perhaps all that they had, so it was his dearest, most fervent desire to make their precious lives as easy as possible.

Their interests were his own.

And so it was, with a warm handshake and a beaming smile, like an authoritative yet favourite close relative, he welcomed Rose and Brooks to the Station that was now his home and theirs, and into the service that was his family.

On the ground, at least, he would do his utmost to protect them.

They were his kin.

73

Chapter 6

The smell of 100 Octane fuel, glycol, dope and wet grass made for a heady, electrifying mixture, and it made Rose feel slightly light-headed, although it may also have been because he was standing alongside the solid and powerful shape of T-Tommy.

It was early afternoon, and Smith had arranged for some formation flying and simple combat practice in the bright sun, to assess Rose's abilities as a combat pilot. Furthermore, the trip aloft would also give Rose an idea of the local geography whilst visibility was good, show him where everything was relative to the airfield.

After all, he would likely have to make his way back home alone one day, perhaps even today, and it was important he had some idea of where to find it when he needed to. Smith would first show him some of the local landmarks like main roads, railway lines, water-courses and other features that were the visual aids which usually helped guide home lost pilots.

But it was also of paramount importance that Rose familiarised himself with his newly-allocated aeroplane, before he began any risky, complex manoeuvring in it. It was essential to be aware of the safe flight parameters before trying to exceed them.

T-Tommy had been produced at the Hawker factory in Brookland two years previously, and after the ending of the 'Sitzkrieg' and the beginning of the now famous 'Blitzkrieg', or 'Lightning War', it had been sent across to France as one of the replacements to try to make good the terrible drain on fighter resources that the BEF Air Component and the AASF had been suffering once the Nazis had finally got going.

T-Tommy had returned safely to Britain three weeks later, after confused and heavy fighting, with battle-damage and a wounded pilot who had been instructed to evacuate himself and his valuable aircraft to safety.

Many other aircraft, now sorely needed for Britain's own defence, had been destroyed in France by their ground crews because they could not be flown out, due to damage or lack of pilots or essential spare parts.

Oh, how desperately they were needed now in these dark hours!

But this one was his! His first aeroplane!

Mine! He thought, *all mine!* (or at least for the next hour or so… after which he'd have to return it to Chiefy and the ground crew).

Even now he could feel the senior ground crew NCO gazing balefully at him from the side of the pen.

Rose thought of cheerily shouting out that he'd look after her, but he was concerned that he might appear careless and flippant, so he walked slowly around the machine, eying the surfaces carefully, trying to ignore the NCO instead.

T-Tommy was an early Mark I Hawker Hurricane, a fabric-winged aircraft with a Watts two-bladed wooden fixed pitch propeller, kidney shaped exhausts and eight .303 Browning machine guns mounted in the wings, in two bunched clusters of four per wing.

Wing-mounted guns were a recent, innovative step in fighter weapon mounting. Up until the last few years most fighters, like the Gladiator or the Hart, had still carried fuselage mounted machine-guns.

He reached out and touched Tommy. She felt alive beneath his fingertips, and he could feel the tingle of electricity thrill through him. She was as exciting to him as any woman could be (not that he had any personal experience of such delightful creatures, unfortunately!).

T-Tommy wore the dark green and brown European theatre camouflage pattern, patched in places, paint chipped on the fuselage and the wings, streaked and stained with exhaust and fraying at its edges.

She was no sleek debutante, but in his eyes, she was truly gorgeous.

External checks and walk-around complete, engine started, Rose climbed up onto the port wing of the aircraft, and then, with the assistance of an airman, clambered into the cockpit, trying to make sure he avoided any contact with hot metal.

Even though he had a slight frame, the cockpit still seemed tight and enclosed once he sat down on the bucket seat, but nonetheless, it felt right, perfect.

He wiggled himself into a comfortable sitting position, and then adjusted the straps of his Sutton harness, but not too tight, as Smith had emphasised, leaving them a little slack purposefully, so he could change position should he have to fight the loss of consciousness that comes with manoeuvring ("But tighten 'em up if you have to take a brolly-hop, unless you want to feel you've been strung up by your balls when your 'chute opens!").

The airman crouched on the wing handed him his flying helmet and gloves, and Rose nodded his thanks as he pulled them on.

He ensured he was properly connected to the oxygen tank, checking that there were no blockages and that there was an acceptable flow of the precious gas, and then he connected the other cord to his R/T, and tested it to ensure the set was functioning correctly.

He then ran through his checklist, T.P.F.F. (Trimming Tabs, Prop control, Fuel, Flaps).

Good, everything seemed correct.

Rose gave the thumbs up to the airman, who now crawled out along the wing, out of the backwash from the spinning propeller, to lie down beside the large blue and red roundel on the port wing, hanging on tight and facing forwards.

Another pulled away the chocks from the undercarriage and waved to Rose who nodded, excitement and anticipation building within him.

Having ensured all was as it should be with his aeroplane, Rose turned to look at the other Hurricane that was now taxiing out of its pen alongside. Smith was going to lead him to the main runway, so Rose revved his engine, testing the running, and the growl remained smooth.

Satisfied, he eased off the brakes and T-Tommy slowly began to trundle forward, out of her bomb-proof pen, following on after Smith.

Once clear, he relied on hand-signals from the airman on the wing to guide him. The long nose of his aircraft, angled upwards due to the arrangement of the undercarriage, effectively blocking the view directly forward of the aircraft. As a result, the presence of the airman, whose view from the wing was unobstructed, was necessary for any taxiing around whilst on the ground. It really wouldn't do to drive the kite into the station-commanders office.

Lovely man, but he wouldn't like it.

Once at the runway, the airman, with a last wave and a thumbs up, jumped off the wing, and ran back the way they had come.

Rose tucked himself into position beside Smith, checking the distance between them, and then with a curt nod from Smith, and a last look around and with clearance received, they began their take-off runs.

Rolling forward, slowly at first, then faster as each of the Merlin II engines drove their respective airframes along with 1,030hp unleashed.

Faster, and faster still, pushed back hard in the seat, one eye on Smith, stay in position, the other on the instruments…

One moment they were speeding along the runway, everything to either side a blur, and the next they were airborne, like horses leaping a fence, they seemed to jump, float, and were slicing quickly and effortlessly through the air, airscrews spinning.

They retracted their undercarriage, the ground dropping steadily below them, the airfield disappearing behind, and the wide open rich and lush land stretched before them, a stunningly diverse range of natural colours, the horizon sinking away below.

The R/T crackled, "Yellow Leader to Yellow Two, take a good look around. We'll nip up to 5,000 feet, then stooge around for a few minutes or so. Keep your eyes and ears open, and I'll just show you what and where everything is. OK?"

"Yellow Two to Yellow Leader, received and understood." Rose looked around, trying to imprint as much as possible into his mind. As he stared out a sudden flash of light caught his eye, and he looked up to see a pair of racing silvery dots in the distance. His heart suddenly began to beat faster, and his mouth felt dry.

Bloody hell…

"Yellow Two to Yellow Leader, bogies at four o'clock high, descending, over." He forced his voice to remain calm. 'Bogies' was the term for unidentified aircraft, whereas 'Bandits' were enemy aircraft. He found himself hoping that the dots were friendly.

"Yellow Leader to Yellow Two, well spotted. Don't worry, it's a couple of Spits," Rose looked carefully, but they still looked like a pair of distant unrecognisable blobs. Smith must have very sharp eyesight, he decided.

"Probably back from a patrol over the Channel, might think we're Jerry, or they may just want to show us who's the top dog here. The silly buggers'll try and bounce us, I fancy. We'll go to a head on interception, OK? If they see us like that they'll break off. They'll see they can't catch us napping. They'll not want a fight after their patrol. They're just after a quick bounce. No harm in being a bit careful, though. Wouldn't be the first time Spits have attacked Hurris."

Sure enough, as they turned towards them, the blobs rapidly turned into a pair of Spitfires, and as Smith had predicted, they curved away as soon as they saw the two Hurricanes turn towards them. The Spitfire leader waggled his wings as they flew back to the airfield, and Smith waggled his own in reply.

"Yellow Leader to Two, let's finish off our geography lesson, then climb to Angels Twenty for a little re-familiarization with the controls, a bit of formation flying, then for a spot of interceptions and dogfighting. OK?"

"Yellow Two to Leader, Wilco."

For a few minutes more the two Hurricanes circled the area of Foxton in a wide, graceful arc, as Smith pointed out all the salient features that Rose would have to learn.

"Remember where the sun is whenever you take off…"

All the while his eyes automatically flicked from land to sky, quartering the sky, searching for an enemy that may suddenly appear.

Given time, and a little luck, Rose would come to know the surrounding area as well as the palm of his hand. But time was a commodity they had precious little of, for at any moment the Germans could begin their final push.

Britain was next on the tyrant's list.

Then, one lesson over, Smith led Rose in a powerful, steep power climb to 20,000 feet, to begin the next, more important, one.

Chapter 7

It was a sober and exhausted Harry Rose who dressed for dinner that evening.

What a day!

He had learned a lot in the short period of flying above the fields of southern England today, about how to hunt, and how it felt when it had been his turn to be the one hunted. He had also been able to see that Smith's Hurricane, with its variable-pitch propeller was an improvement in performance over the fixed-pitch prop kite he had had to fly.

Luckily though, additional variable-pitch replacement aircraft for the squadron were to be delivered to them over the next couple of days.

His arms and legs still felt bruised and sore from the extreme manoeuvring in the arena high above, the tiredness from turning, diving, climbing, and the horrible sensation when grey out began, and consciousness began to fade.

Luckily, he hadn't blacked out, but his body complained now, and he ached as if he had swum ten miles.

But he welcomed the pain, for it was little enough to pay in comparison to what he had learned already in that first session, and he felt the first creeping shoots of confidence inside now.

Even Smith had seemed pleased with his performance, "But you must try and look in your mirror more often, every couple of seconds at least, if not less! Keep a good lookout all around! Mirror! Mirror! Mirror!"

He had grabbed Rose's arm to emphasise the point, "And when I say look, I mean you must *really* look. Not just a quick glance, but a proper check of the sky behind you. Jerry can appear out of what seems to be a clear, empty sky in just a few seconds. One second the mirror's empty, and then, before you can say 'bugger me with a broomstick,' he's there, and he's trying to pump lead right up your arse. Not the best cure for constipation, believe me."

Granny had wiped the sweat from his nose, "in between checking the mirror, keep sweeping your eyes all around the sky, 'cause the bastards may try and fillet your backside from the side…and when you're not checking all around or looking into your mirror, then you can try taking the odd pot-shot back at them. Nothing to it, really…"

Rose realised there was so very much to learn, but fortunately, Excalibur squadron had been taken off operations for a week as it absorbed the new intake of pilots that were to make up for the losses suffered by the squadron over Belgium and France and finally at Dunkirk.

There had even been a couple of Fleet Air Arm pilots and an Army co-operation pilot. All of whom had thus far only been flying low-performance aircraft by comparison to the high performance Hurricane fighter.

As usual, there had been the usual share of duffers and rejects that no-one else wanted, so the CO, Donald, swiftly sent them back whence they came.

Rose applauded the possibility to continue his training with Smith for as long as possible, the whole week if at all possible, although

Donald would ask Smith of his opinion after another five days. He could see now how much there was yet to learn, and a week seemed too little time to squeeze in all that learning.

A young Pilot-Officer who was also to be in Yellow section, as Yellow Three, had turned up whilst they had been flying that afternoon, so now Rose would have to share Smith's time.

Less time with Smith for me, he'd thought morosely, looking at his reflection in the mirror. He fancied that his eyes looked a bit more practised than before.

He set a suitably heroic pose, and admired himself for a moment.

The newcomer was called Barsby, and was a tall, thin, youth with straw-coloured hair and quiet, almost reserved disposition.

Rose had thought him sullen, conceited, and hadn't liked him at all.

Barsby already had twenty-five hours on Hurricanes, and like Billy, had recently converted from Gladiators. He seemed to see the training schedule for new pilots as a total waste of time. "I think I know how to fly a Hurryback, old man." He had drawled to Rose, waving a fragrant Turkish cigarette for effect, "I've had quite a few hours flying one already. Talk to me later, I'll give you some hints and tips."

Smith would love him…

Rose had also met his new rigger and fitter, Aircraftsman Baker and LAC Joyce. They were both from the East End of London, Baker from Whitechapel, and Joyce from the Isle of Dogs. Although they came from the same part of the world, they were completely unalike.

Baker was short, sturdily built and dark haired, with a penchant for crunching boiled sweets (which likely accounted for his gap-toothed yellow smile).

Joyce, on the other hand, was tall, painfully thin, and had a thatch of fair, almost white hair on his head. He whined endlessly about everything. Despite this, Rose had found them both friendly and pleasant. He resolved to spend time getting to know them, and more about the jobs they did. They were the ones who made sure his Hurricane worked the way she should.

Without them he could not fly.

It would be Barsby's turn to fly T-Tommy first in the morning, and he could show Smith just how well he could fight, but first there would be another ground-based tutorial, for two this time, on tactics at 8 am sharp.

Smith was slouched in his favourite battered armchair, nursing a half-empty glass, brooding. The other pilots could see he was preoccupied, so they left him alone.

He had determined that he was going to make the two young men who had been entrusted to him, Rose and Barsby, as ready for combat as much as was humanly possible before the squadron became operational again, and the inevitable fighting that they would soon experience, for it was coming, and quickly.

The lull in fighting that they were currently experiencing was permeated with a heavy pervasive dread.

Smith almost wished the fighting would start. This waiting was very wearing on the nerves, but at least Rose looked promising, he was competent, and he learned quickly. He'd done well today. God-willing he would be a good, reliable, wingman.

As for Barsby…well, time would tell. The lad was capable, but he knew it too and more than once Smith had wanted to deliver a hefty kick up that smug little beggar's backside.

Time would tell.

Smith sighed, and rubbed his tired eyes wearily.

Just give us a few more days, he prayed silently.

All of them could sense the heavy atmosphere of dread and expectancy that hung over the country. It was the expectant moment before the storm, but the calm was a falsehood, for the storm was coming, and it was going to break soon, very soon.

Rose, too, was experiencing the strange feeling of strange expectancy, like one of being under siege, and he was also desperately keen to enter the fray, if only to know that he would be able to deliver that what was required when the time came, and to take part in what could well be one of the last battles of the war, if the speed at which the Germans had bulldozed their way through the Low Countries was anything to go by.

The yoke of fascist oppression may well be upon them all even before the onset of autumn.

In the last war they had boasted it would all be over by Christmas.

Time had proved them tragically wrong.

It looked as if it could easily be over for Christmas 1940, but this time, unlike as in 1918, might it be possible that Germany and her allies were the unbeaten ones?

God forbid.

Rose shuddered at the thought, as he fastened the tie, automatically folding the Windsor knot. He ran a finger around the collar, his neck still sore and chafing where it he had rubbed it raw against his collar by the continuous swivelling of his head in flight during the mock fights with Smith.

He made a mental note to purchase a silk scarf at the first possible option.

Preferably a nice bright one resplendent with polka-dots (white and red perhaps?), yes, dashing, like the one which Smith wore. Or stripey? Only to protect his neck of course, nothing whatsoever to do with cutting a dash with the ladies.

Good Heavens, no.

Never.

He was greatly in awe of his trainer, wished to be like him, yet Rose could not imagine himself ever to be like Smith, so coldly calculating and yet so thoughtful, throwing the Hurricane around so casually without apparent consideration for safety parameters, but with such cold fluidity and precision, so quick to teach, firm yet fair.

The man was both an extraordinary, skilful pilot and a patient teacher who did not tire at the simplest mistakes of his pupil, although Rose suspected that a slow student might soon arouse Smith's ire. He determined to be a fast learner.

If he had been born a German, would one of those Teutonic heroes of the Luftwaffe be as forgiving and patient an instructor as Smith was with him?

Unlikely.

It must be so grim living in Hitler's Germany.

A number of Rose's classmates at school had visited Germany in 1936 for the Berlin Olympics, and had spoken of the feeling of national pride, the resurgent vibrant economy, innovation and development, the Nazi rallies and the swaggering bands of uniformed young men and women of the so-called 'Aryan Master Race.'

It had been impressive to see such a proud country rise triumphant from the ashes of defeat of 1918, its subsequent dismemberment, and the cruelty and suffering of the depression, to see so many radical ideas working in a modern society and the foresight of some, yet somehow the achievements were cast into shadow and belittled by the dreadful philosophies and dubious policies of the country's arrogant leadership, and the apparent attitudes of a once more proud and strong people.

Rose found it impossible to see Britain like that, any different from the relaxed land that he knew. Of course there were the British

Fascists, the Blackshirts, but Sir Oswald Mosley and his repugnant kind had been interned since the beginning of the war.

It was impossible to imagine Britain as a Fascist state. Yet if Hitler were to conquer Britain, he would conspire to create a Fascist Britain, a mere province of the empire of Greater Germany. With twisted ideals and a cold inhumanity, it would no longer be the gentle and tolerant land of his birth.

Hitler had spoken recently of peace, yet he spoke as the Commander in Chief of the German Armed Forces, and the carrot he held out was overshadowed by the size of the stick he held in his other hand. What kind of a peace offer was it when the alternative was to be bombed to submission?

Hitler did not want peace, rather, he wanted Britain to roll over and surrender itself to him.

No, he thought. I'll not see it happen, for I'd rather die a hundred times than see my land stolen and turned into a organised reformatory for its people. How could one not sacrifice oneself to resist such a cruel and oppressive occupation, the theft of what was theirs?

He looked at himself in the mirror, at the steady, serious brown eyes. I will fight to the last for Britain, he thought. I'll not see us prisoners or slaves in our own land. Winston Churchill had given his famous speech in the House of Commons less than two weeks previously, stirringly ending, *"... We shall never surrender."*

The rousing words created such passionate emotions in Rose that he had sworn to himself that he would give his life to ensure the continued liberty of his country.

Things may look bleak now, but we've halted and beaten tyrants and oppressors in the past.

The Virgin Queen had trounced the Armada, and then Britain had stopped Napoleon when his Empire had stretched across Europe.

And when Germany had started beating the drums, Britain had stood against it, and given the Kaiser a drubbing.

And now we'll do it again to bloody old Adolf.

He grinned as he saw the serious expression of his reflection, and it smiled back at him.

Listen to him! Here he was thinking like some great philosopher, but he was only a lowly pilot-officer, and nobody cared for his opinions.

He tried to push back his thatch of thick dark hair, but it just fell forward again, into an untidy fringe, as it had been since he was a little boy.

He sighed. It wasn't easy looking like a hero. And at the moment, it wasn't a hero who stared back at him from the mirror.

But the boy was now grown into the man. A man who was more than a little scared, certainly, but his fear of the danger to come was far outweighed by another fear.

The cloying fear, a constant undercurrent in his thoughts of every waking hour. It was the fear that when the time came he might be found lacking in the qualities he needed as a warrior.

The fear of cowardice.

He knew how to fight, but when the time came, would he, *could* he?

He was terrified that he would be unable to be the fighting man that Britain so desperately needed when the darkness that threatened to envelop them all finally came. He didn't want to fail them all.

He looked critically at himself. At the pleasant face, the way the dim light of his room threw shadows onto his face. He quite liked the shadows, for they made him appear older than his twenty years, more of a man.

Was this to be the face of a proud warrior or a snivelling coward?

The nose was straight, a snub nose, and he felt, in personal moments of anxiety and self-doubt, that it may make him seem soft, not what you'd expect of a Nelson or Leonidas.

Wellington's grand old beak was legendary.

His lips were soft, and he pursed them in dislike. Why can't they be thinner, with a confident sardonic curl like the soldiers in the films? Like Denis or Granny?

"Some girl will see those lips, one day, and she'll be unable to resist you." His mother had once teased.

He was not reassured.

In his mind, he felt he would not measure up to his heroes of 1914-18, like Mannock, Ball, Barker and the rest of them.

His father had not shrunk from danger, had served in that same, terrible war with those heroes, a war where the casualty figures had been so great as to become incomprehensible in their enormity.

He, too, had been a hero, and the row of medals in the drawer, the uniform in the cupboard, the memories of the man she had loved that Mother kept so proudly was a sign that when his testing time had come, he had not been found wanting.

All that Rose could remember of his father was a kindly, tired man made prematurely old, with a hacking cough that could be heard faintly throughout the house at night, and a tremor that made it hard for him to eat or smoke his pipe when on occasion he had one of his 'turns'. He would sit in his armchair, alone in the drawing room, arms clasped around him, eyes closed, shuddering and silent, face pale and drawn.

Father had finally died in the winter of 1928, when Rose had been eight years of age, yet another of the countless victims of the 'War To End All Wars.'

Smart and solemn and cold to the touch, father had been a

waxy stranger, lying in a casket in the living room, all the laughter drained from Rose's home, with a mourning mother who rarely smiled thereafter.

Rose sighed and pulled on his tunic, buttoned it up, the bright splash of his AFC beneath his wings making him seem much more than he really was, demanding from him that which he desperately feared he lacked.

He undid the top button, did it up again immediately. He hadn't earned the right to be a fighter pilot yet, so much yet to learn.

Despite her husband's loss, and her fears, mother had sent her son unflinchingly to fight in this new war, for although she loved him and dreaded the likely consequences, she recognised that it was something that he had to do, and it was something that their country needed. Proud, brave and terrified, her heart hollowed by fear, but buoyed by pride, she accepted what she might need to sacrifice.

Will I fear death, or will I be able to handle the danger with a careless smile like the boys in the Mess? They seem so cool, indifferent to the dangers. I want to be like this.

Will my first time in a fight panic me, or will I be able to keep a cool head and an objective mind?

He played with his top button again.

His wonderful, beloved sister was a Second Officer WRNS, based at the Naval Dockyard of Portsmouth, and she'd already experienced how it was to be under fire.

She had the resolute heart of a lion, the spirit of a warrior. He smiled fondly; the little girl she had once been had always been a fighter, having a fearsome reputation in the village, following the scrapes with local bullies.

Once, when a boy had said something derogatory about Rose

within her earshot, she had sent him home with a black eye and two less teeth than he had had minutes earlier.

She'd not hear a thing said against her own.

I hope I have half your courage.

Although he still felt apprehensive that he may fail at the vital moment, he tried to control the fear.

He felt the same as he had that night less than a year ago.

The night in question had been the one before his first flight at the Elementary Flying Training School; and then he had felt the same, cloying fear again when the time came later in the course for the instructor to pass control of the Tiger-Moth over to him for his first solo. The flights before had been fine, but his fears had resurfaced once more.

Like a cold murmur, the thoughts coalesced in his mind, telling him that he could not do it, and the treacherous whispering fears of his mind that had almost immobilised him.

Whilst his friends had slept undisturbed by such thoughts on either side of him, he had thrown back the rough grey blanket, got up from his iron cot with its' hard 'biscuit' mattress, dressed, and gone out. Unable to sleep, he had walked for a while, savouring the iciness of the air on his skin.

The first time he had driven a motorcar had been an experience of confusion and downright terror. Which way should the wheel be turned, what gears engaged? His limbs had frozen in terror and his mind had become blank, much to his chagrin.

Had there not been an instructor in the car, he would have fetched up in hospital, or worse.

Would he be the same in flight? Would he freeze at the vital moment, and shatter the dream?

After walking for what seemed like hours, he had returned, and sat watching the stars on the step of the hut which he shared with three other cadets.

Occasionally the distant barking of one of the perimeter guard dogs or the calling of an owl would float across the night air, to remind him that there were others awake this night, but most of the time it was quiet, almost silent. There was only a faint rustling, which he fancifully thought was the grass growing, and the low, rhythmic snoring from Cyril Newton, an ex-office boy from Darlington, who was now with a squadron flying a new type of two-seat fighter made by Boulton-Paul, the innovative single-engine Defiant.

In the mirror, his forehead ridged as he tried to remember the number of the squadron. Was it 141? He couldn't recall. Perhaps they would meet in the air.

He had stayed there on the step, huddled in his greatcoat, with his smart new cap with its white band jammed onto his head, into the small wee hours of the morning.

At one point he had taken out the big red apple his mother had given him on his last day at home on his last visit.

He had taken great bites out of the fruit, unmindful of the juice that dripped onto the step, watching the leisurely passage of the moon across the dark blue heavens, and the dancing moths illuminated in the moonlight as they pirouetted gracefully, chasing one another in an unceasing dance.

He had wondered what the next day would be like, wondering about that dreaded first solo flight. It had been one of the coldest winters on record, and his breath had come out as billowing white clouds of steam, that were caught on the wind and whipped away, dissipating into the icy night air, like dreams evaporating from promise into nothingness. It would be even colder up there in the sky.

It was this same fear that had now returned. He had thought himself ready for the great test, but Smith had shown him that things might never be what they seemed. There was much for him to learn, and he was eager to prove himself, confident in his abilities, after all hadn't he flown well? But the treacherous apprehension would come again, and make him wonder, was it enough?

He wanted to prove himself a worthy wingman to Smith. He could not bear to be sent back to the O.T.U., or worse still to a Group where all he would have to protect would be empty fields, a few sheep and little else.

Rose was desperately keen to fly operationally in 11 Group, the group at what would be the frontline. It was similar to the hungry desire he'd felt to wear the silken wings with the RAF emblem embroidered on.

The immediate award of the AFC he'd received so very recently was still like a dream to him, still unreal, but it was the wings that meant so much.

He'd later dreaded the solo flight as well, and had he known the experience that was to occur with his instructor in the preparatory flight before the solo, he might never have stepped into the aeroplane, might never have received either the coveted wings or the medal.

Instead there had been the shocking emergency, he had taken over, the worries and fears evaporating as he struggled to return and land his damaged aeroplane, the injured and unconscious instructor helpless.

The nerves had gone and he'd done well, he knew. And when he landed, the visiting Air Marshal had been standing there with the ambulance and fire tender, wearing a smile and the news that he would be rewarded for his bravery and skill in the air.

Of course, the wings and the AFC were both a huge source of pride to Mum, but he felt a fake, the panicky minutes of 'heroism' just blurred and confused images in his mind.

And now, the next step in his life, operational flying and the terrors of war. Once more he questioned his abilities.

Again he was on the verge of new understanding, of combat, and the thought of it simultaneously terrified him and thrilled him. He wanted so desperately to be able to face the experience with fortitude, yet the apprehension of failure in the face of the unknown was like a heavy knot in his stomach, almost uncomfortably heavy so that his spirit felt weighted down, and it was this apprehension that made him appear so reticent, so aloof.

There were footsteps outside, then a crashing knock on the door, which made Rose jump. Fine warrior you'll be, he thought. The bang had been so loud he thought the door would come off its hinges, or at the very least, thump open. He looked around, to see if it was chipped or dented.

"Are you ready yet, Harry? Are you dressed yet?" Billy squawked from outside. "Christ! I swear you take longer to get yourself dolled up than any Popsie I've ever known! We're only going for dinner, you know, not for an audience with the King, y'know! There won't be any crumpet on offer downstairs, so don't dandy up too much, for Heaven's sake!"

He sounds like a schoolboy banging on the loo door, desperate for a pee, thought Rose with amusement, and chuckled, all the maudlin thoughts and fears of before dispelled.

His mind made up, he finally undid his top button. He would face all that came his way, and do battle with all his heart, as best he could. His fate lay ahead, and possibly his death, but he would do all that he could to fight *and* to survive.

To the death, then, if needs be. It may sound dramatic, but it was how he felt.

For he was an RAF Fighter Pilot, and all that he had, he'd give gladly for those he was sworn to defend.

There was another bang on the door. "For goodness sake, Harry, have you got a girl in there?"

Rose smiled. He would be in good company, whatever happened.

Chapter 8

Rose sat back in the armchair shyly.

Around him the conversation was muted. Billy sat across from him, deep in conversation with Flying Officer Tim 'Fatty' Barrow. Like Billy, he too came from a biplane squadron. But, instead of Gladiators, he had flown Gloster Gauntlets with 13 Group. He was a tall, wan young man with prematurely grey hair and a stoop, presumably from trying to hide from the cold gusts in the open cockpits. Despite his appearance, he was a very amicable young man with a wicked sense of humour.

Rose was seated with the other officer pilots in the Mess as they waited for dinner to be served.

Excalibur squadron still consisted of only eleven officer pilots and three NCO pilots. The normal complement should normally have been twenty pilots altogether.

Apparently, they were to receive more pilots over the next few days. Granny had even mentioned that a pair of Fleet Air Arm pilots would be arriving the next day.

He had sounded horrified.

Sailors in his beloved air force?

Whatever next? Nuns?

Donald stood at the fireplace with his two flight commanders (there were not enough pilots to form a C'Flight yet), Uncle the adjutant, and the other three pilots that had taken part in the May fighting in France, Wilson, Ffellowes and Farrell.

Sitting separately in the armchairs around them, listening quietly, were the new boys.

Apart from Rose himself, there were two other pilots straight out of O.T.U. They were both pilot Officers.

One was an ex-bank clerk from Hilltown in Dundee. He was a friendly boy with a wispy fair moustache that only served to make him look younger.

The other pilot was from the Midlands. He was a fashionable and worldly wise man of twenty-four named Renfrew, apparently an ex-used car salesman. He had already, in only two days on the squadron, been seen walking out with two separate WAAFs.

No problem with confidence there, and he had a good line in patter, which explained his success with the women, and senior officers.

The remaining pilot officer, a young bewildered looking specimen named Cavell, was also a regular transferred from a biplane equipped squadron. Like Barrow, he too had flown Gloster Gauntlets. Thank Heavens I don't have to fly one of those things, thought Rose with a shudder.

Hurricanes are a far nicer aeroplane to go to war in.

Dinner was another delight to the tastebuds, and a far more carefully prepared meal in comparison to his first on the squadron. To be fair, though, Fricker's sandwiches of the previous evening had tasted pretty wonderful, too.

At the head of the table, Donald sat, still chatting quietly with his two flight commanders, seated either side of him. B'Flight was commanded by a humourless Flight Lieutenant named Sinclair. Like a small number of the pilots who made up the core of the squadron, he too was a newly-promoted veteran of France with the DFC.

On either side of Rose sat the other members of A-flight.

Granny sat to his right, clearly enjoying the last of his Spotted Dick, whilst on his left was seated the French Air Force officer, Capitaine Phillipe Desoux.

Desoux was a very dapper young man with slicked back hair and a pencil moustache, and hailed originally from just outside of Paris. He had arrived in Britain with the remnants of the Hurricane squadron with which he had been liaising. He had been flying Morane 406 fighters up to one month before the end had come in France. Barsby sat beside Desoux, idly picking at his teeth with a silver toothpick.

And of course there was Flying Officer 'Wally' Wilson, Rose's round-faced companion at breakfast, looking far more relaxed than he had earlier.

For the next few days of early July, 1940, there were some attacks by small formations of Luftwaffe fighters and bombers on coasters and other small vessels in the English Channel. The Junkers 87 Stuka particularly showing the effectiveness of dive-bombing against shipping, whilst also showing how exposed and unprotected the coastal convoys that hugged the coastline of Southern England were to airborne assault.

At the same time there were some low and medium-level intrusions by German fighters over Kent and Sussex, with the intention of luring RAF fighters into combat, and reducing the defending fighter force piecemeal.

These fighter skirmishes usually ended with losses.

On the 4th of July, a Spitfire from 97 Squadron was bounced and shot down by a Rotte of Bf109's, the pilot being killed as his aircraft blew up. The mood fell at Foxton as his loss was reported.

Other squadrons also lost pilots, an example of which was the loss of three Spitfires of 65 Squadron and their pilots when they too were bounced. However, the losses of early July were not all due to the enemy.

No. 79 Squadron lost their CO, Squadron-Leader Joslin, when he was shot down into the Channel by Spitfires who misidentified his Hurricane as a Messerschmit 109.

It was not an uncommon mistake. It was an incident similar to those of earlier in the war that once more illustrated how easy it was to misidentify an aircraft in the heat of the moment, or when one was eager for a quick 'kill'. Despite the tragedy of the 'Battle for Barking Creek', loss due to friendly fire was still a dangerous reality.

The ground crews did not escape the enemy's attention. Manston was bombed by enemy raiders, but was not put out of action.

The losses were on both sides, but Lord Haw-Haw, the traitor ensconced comfortably in a Berlin studio, crowed gleefully as he made claims of inflated victories over the ether.

For the people of Britain, his broadcasts were as widely listened to as other, friendlier programmes, such as ITMA, or the 'Radio Doctor', broadcast by the BBC.

None of this really affected Rose very much as he was trained hard with Barsby under Smith's tutelage, spending many hours first in the cockpit of T-Tommy, then in the new Hurricanes that were being daily delivered to the squadron.

The recently formed civilian Air Transport Auxiliary now ferried the new aircraft to Foxton, although Rose was allowed to pick up his personally from the Hawker airfield at Brooklands.

His new Hurricane was a pleasure to fly, and it was completely different from flying the 'clapped-out old hurri-bag' that Barsby had contemptuously termed poor T-Tommy. Rose had been quite fond of the veteran machine, despite the reduced performance in comparison to the variable-pitch Hurricanes that were now being flown by the squadron.

They had spent many hours sweating profusely as he strained in intensive high speed and low speed aerobatic combat exercises, at high altitude and at low level, whilst on the ground they would endlessly discuss tactics, some of the cardinal rules of air combat learned through harsh experience by the early combat pilots of the RFC, and sometimes, rarely, they would go over some of Smith's own experiences in action.

Practising, practising.

As the days passed, and his hours on Hurricanes gradually increased, they rehearsed again and again, going over the same ground again and again, learning the art of aerial war. Rose began to gain in confidence, as he realised that he was able to thrust and parry attacks with more and more proficiency, to be able to actually counter attacks with success. The first time he 'shot down' Smith in a mock dogfight, he shrieked with excitement, much to Smith's quiet amusement.

Rose became a regular visitor to the hangars and hardstandings of Foxton. He came to know many of the groundcrews, as Smith had advised. As Smith had said, "'Groundcrew, aircrew, and aircraft are all vital components of the same machine. Without one part, the rest are useless. Never forget how important the ground crews are for us.'"

He had also become much more aware of the WAAFs on the station.

However, being young, and painfully shy, he was unable to muster the courage to actually engage one in conversation. So the tentative approaches by some of the young women interested in this quiet, shy and sincere young man remained unexploited. Even their dark-haired officer had noticed him, and wondered about the bashful young pilot.

Despite his reticence, and because of the natural thoughtfulness of his character, he was becoming very well thought of throughout the station.

Rose, being Rose, remained blissfully unaware of his acceptance and burgeoning regard, but instead concentrated on becoming better at the things that mattered to him.

Smith, meanwhile, was pleased at Rose's progress, but continued to push hard, giving little praise and generous with his criticism, because he saw that Rose was not disheartened when he made mistakes, but instead the youngster was eager to correct them on the next occasion. Criticism only made him stronger.

He was a talented pilot with a natural flair, but even excellent pilots can make mistakes, can get shot down, can get killed; so Smith drilled his charges again and again. Rose became ever familiar with flying and fighting in the Hurricane, and this further helped to boost his confidence and abilities. He even began to recognize more than the rudiments of the Merlin engine.

Barsby, however, though a good, confident pilot, was resistant to change with regards to some of the new ideas that Smith was trying to instil in him.

He learnt what he was taught, flew well, but he did not appear as buoyant and enthusiastic as was Rose in the air. Nevertheless, he would make an appropriate addition to Excalibur Squadron. And truth be told, there was little choice in the matter. They needed pilots too urgently. Excalibur could no longer afford to be selective. Spaces needed to be filled, regardless.

Smith was aware that the increasing activity over the Channel and the coast were likely just the beginnings of a more intense campaign that could escalate any day.

Hitler's so called offers of peace were not going to bear fruit, and the time for more fighting was drawing closer, and so he trained his students with a greater will. And although the efforts he put into the training drained him, desperation gave him greater strength.

It would not be long now before the storm broke. Soon his young apprentices would be thrust into the ferocity of the storm.

Thank God they weren't a pair of fools who would throw themselves away at the first opportunity. These boys flew with thought and consideration, and they would be a worthy opponent for the victors of the Blitzkrieg. They just needed a chance.

Please, God, give them that chance.

Please save them.

One evening later that week, long after dinner, when most of the other pilots had adjourned for a 'beano' at the local Inn, the Horse and Groom, followed by a trip to the Palais, Rose went back to his room to relax, and go over the day's training in his mind.

The pilots of Excalibur had welcomed him warmly, and they liked the quiet, shy young man with the AFC, but he was not a drinker, and he did not feel he could truly be a member of the Squadron until Donald had told him that he had passed his period of training.

He would not join them until he felt he was worthy of their company.

This reticence, however, had not been shared by the other pilots of Excalibur squadron, and Rose had been forced to escape more than once from the ribaldry that all groups of young men, the world over, engage in, when they embrace one into their group.

But as they were fighter pilots, they misbehaved even more so.

More often than not, he had not been able to avoid his pursuers, and had been debagged once, thrown in the river once, and forced to listen to an execrable rendition of 'If I only had you' once, sung by a tipsy and haughty Ffellowes, bumpily riding his 'borrowed' tricycle.

The last was, without doubt, the worst experience of the three he had suffered.

He had been able to escape the wild mess games, though. One of the other new pilots had not been so lucky, and now lay in hospital with a broken ankle and wrist. He'd not be trying any of his patter on the WAAFs of Foxton for some time.

The CO, Donald, had been mightily annoyed with them, and there had been a (slight) reduction in high jinks since.

But these gave him no cause for concern.

Initially, he had been more fearful of the threat of being sent back to the O.T.U., but now he felt quietly confident in his abilities, and was sure that he had satisfied Smith. After all the training he had received to date, he was infinitely more sure of himself, and he knew himself that he could now fly (and hopefully fight) a Hurricane far better than he had been able to a mere week earlier.

The tomcat that lived with the Squadron pilots was a large jet-black creature named Hermann, in honour of the Luftwaffe Field Marshal that he resembled so much in shape. He was as well known amongst the local female cat population as were some of the pilots of Excalibur Squadron amongst the showgirls of London.

For some incomprehensible reason, Hermann had taken to Rose, and demonstrated his affection by taking up permanent residence in Rose's room.

Every evening before bed, Rose would sit in his battered, threadbare armchair (since made even more threadbare by the not-so gentle ministrations of Hermann's long claws), with Hermann sleeping contentedly in his lap, and occasionally suck his unlit virginal pipe, for an hour or so.

He had tried a cigarette once, but the effects had put him off, so he avoided actually putting any tobacco into the pipe and lighting it.

The illumination in his room was poor, so he would usually sit in the dark, resting his body and mind (If he could stop thinking about the day's lesson), with his window open and uncovered. The liquid lustre of moonlight would spill in, and the fragrances of the gardens would flood in with it.

It was also a good time in which to formulate a letter home, and tell his mother he was well and enjoying himself. He wanted to able to write more, but the official Station Censor would take a dim view of his writing all his experiences to her.

Every word nowadays had to be watched, for spies could glean much from a few, careless words. Of course, there was always the telephone, but Rose had an aversion to speaking on it, and his telephone conversations were always stilted and cold, no matter how much he tried to sound animated. He felt he could be more himself on a piece of paper.

So, almost one week after arriving at Foxton, he sat with his eyes closed in his usual place in the corner beside the bed, Hermann sleeping on his lap, one hand on the warm, coarse fur, the other holding his pipe.

All was quiet. Not even the crunch of army size nine boots on the gravel outside. The sentry had been banished back to the airfield, as the pilots had complained that his crunching around and nocturnal whistling prevented them from getting a decent night's sleep.

His secretive rendezvous' with a local girl had not helped, particularly now she was in the family way.

Only Fricker seemed to be sorry to see him go. He didn't mind that the sentry had fired a warning round at a drunken Wilson. This had been because Wally had taken a pot-shot at his tin hat, with his service revolver, instead shooting out the stag heads' remaining eye. "I wanted to see if the helmet's bullet-proof."

Oh well.

On his bed were the crumpled, precious sheets of his most recent letter from home. Mum wrote of the mundane goings-on of the local branch of the WVS, how she had carefully packed away her precious Pye television console in the basement, and also of her worries about her decision to keep Tinkles, her little cat. With rationing in place, hundreds of pet cats and dogs were being put down all around the country, but she wouldn't, couldn't, follow suit, despite her feeling that she were being unpatriotic.

But Rose was glad, because it would have been too much like murdering a close relative.

She had managed to avoid giving voice to her worries for her son, although reading between the lines, he could feel her anxiety for the dangers she knew he must face.

It was good to hear from home, and know that life went on as normal, or at least as normal as was possible in these times.

He felt tired but also relaxed, for the day had been a pleasant one.

He had spent an exciting time with Smith and Barsby that afternoon, on yet another training flight, pursuing and trying to shoot down a rogue barrage balloon they had been vectored onto by sector control. It had torn loose of its moorings and was leisurely drifting along the Thames Estuary and out to sea, like a jolly old gent out for an afternoon stroll on the pier.

They had made repeated interceptions and attack runs on it as Smith used it for an impromptu training session. They had also been given more practice in deflection shooting as they had finally sent the great flabby silver monster flaming into the water below.

Doubtless the ten or twelve men and women responsible for raising and lowering the balloon would get a rocket for allowing it to break free. On the flight back Granny had made a detour to show them the mysterious masts of an RDF station, although he had seemed more interested in waving at the tiny figures of a pair of WAAFs on bicycles below. Back on the ground, he had said enigmatically, "Those masts will win the war for us, you know."

Barsby and Rose had looked at one another and wondered.

It was all very hush-hush.

Yes, it had been a good day.

The others must have driven to London by now, to a dance at the Hammersmith Palais. Billy had tried to bundle him into the car, but Rose had managed to escape his clutches.

Although the entrance fee at the Palais was far more than a ticket to the pictures, Farrell of B'Flight was (currently) seeing one of the girls who worked at the Palais, and she managed to get all the pilots in for nothing.

Apparently, Geraldo and his Orchestra (whoever they were) were going to be playing there, and the house was quiet.

There was a light knock at the door.

Surprised, Rose opened his eyes. Who on earth could that be?

"Come in!" he called out.

The door opened to reveal Smith. He came into the room, blinked a few times to try and adjust his eyes to the darkness.

"Hullo, Granny, what can I do for you? I thought everyone had gone to the Palais." Rose indicated Hermann, "I'm afraid I can't get up, but you're welcome to take a seat." The cat stared unblinking at Smith, stretched, adjusted its position, and then curled up again, purrs rumbling loudly.

"Hello, Harry. No, I thought I'd let the other boys have a crack at the crumpet for a change, poor sods. Thought I'd turn in early for a change, must be getting old." He smiled to show he wasn't being serious.

"I'm sorry to disturb you, but I thought I'd nip in and have a quick word with you before I pop to bed." He sat down gingerly on the wooden chair, brushed it.

Rose noticed that the seat of Smith's trousers was stained with engine oil (at least he hoped it was engine oil).

Pilot Officer Granny Smith DFM and Bar, RAF.

His leader, his friend, his hero. Great leader, formidable fighter pilot, and absolutely rubbish at keeping himself smart. Rose smiled affectionately.

But why was he here?

Smith noticed the curiosity in Rose's eyes.

"I just wanted to tell you about what I shall be saying to the Old Man tomorrow." Smith spoke formally, but smiled again; a sight that Rose was seeing more and more often in the last few days. It converted the cold, skilful killer into a pleasant faced young man.

"I'm sure you know that I think you've done satisfactorily," Rose grinned, elated, but not surprised, "and I shall be advising Squadron-Leader Donald that I consider you an adequate pilot," Granny returned his smile.

Adequate! Cheeky bugger!

"And I believe you are now ready to fly operationally in combat. I'm sure he'll also be pleased that you've managed to increase your flying hours considerably. You've managed to become sufficiently familiar with your Hurricane, and I think you've got a pretty good idea now what its strengths and faults are."

He leaned forward, held out his hand. "Well done, Harry. I shall be very pleased to have you in my section. I reckon you're ready."

A thrill of fear and anticipation ran through him, yet Rose grinned and shook hands with Smith.

"Thanks a lot, Granny. I can't begin to thank you for all the time you've spent teaching me." Rose was embarrassed. "I want you to know that I will be very proud to fly with you. I will do my very best. Dingo seemed happy yesterday when we went up together. I'm really grateful." The words came out sounding hackneyed, and he cringed at how they sounded, but Smith only smiled.

"Harry, I want to take you and Barsby to the Armoury tomorrow, because you should have one of these," He reached into his tunic pocket, and pulled out a revolver. It glistened silver-blue in the moonlight as he passed it over to Rose.

"This is an old friend of mine. I take care of it, and once or twice, it's taken care of me."

Rose hefted the gun gingerly. He was fascinated by the feel of the weapon, by the faint aroma of oil and metal that came from it. It felt heavy, solid. As he turned it, he noticed the scratches and dents on the surface of the weapon.

Like its owner, it was obviously a veteran. Although he had had a basic course in weapons instruction whilst a cadet, he was more used to the idea of using the guns on his aeroplane. The revolver felt strange and warm, but exciting to hold, like holding a girl's hand in the stalls at the cinema in the dark, during a film. Warm and smooth and ever so slightly slippery in feel.

"Every pilot should carry one of these. Old Winnie said we need to drill with rifles, but I prefer carrying one of these. We usually fight with our kites, so we tend to neglect our skills with side-arms, but, it's something we need to be capable of. You're not bad with a rifle; I'd like to see how you are with one of these."

He took back the gun, "I found it very handy when it comes to learning deflection shooting, and shooting at moving targets. You can practise for hours. I'll show you and Barsby, and it's actually a lot of fun, too." He looked at it reflectively, and then put it back in his pocket.

Smith had flown with Rose and Barsby on to RAF Sutton Bridge in their new Hurricanes for some gunnery practice, and he had spent considerable time explaining how a pilot should correct his aim according to the speed, angle and direction of flight of the target aircraft. The mysteries of deflection shooting could take some learning.

They would have to learn to shoot at the spot where the enemy aircraft was likely to be when the ordnance reached it, not where it had been.

Enemy aeroplanes only went down if bullets actually hit it.

The busy training station at Sutton Bridge had been a miserable, muddy place, but the experience invaluable. A Czech pilot had crashed into the marshland and rescuing him had been a tense, drawn-out affair.

Rose had initially come closer to shooting down the drogue-towing aeroplane, a Hawker Henley, than hitting the target being towed, but he had quickly managed to grasp the principles behind leading with his shooting, and his gunnery had improved drastically. Barsby, to his very vocal chagrin, had not been much better.

But thankfully, they had both learned so much, and had become capable shots. Not quite the dead-shots of the movie westerns, but good enough. At least that was how Rose felt now.

He had shown it this afternoon in the attacks on the barrage balloon.

"The three of us will be going tomorrow after breakfast to sign out a revolver for each of you." He stood up. "In the afternoon we'll go for a little flight, and then when we get back, we can do a little shooting practice with some tennis balls, OK? Well, I'm off now." He paused. I'm going to ask the CO to make Barsby operational tomorrow as well, Harry. I'll tell him at breakfast, if he wakes up in time for it. We should be available as Yellow section when the squadron is back on operations. I'm just glad the new Hurricanes arrived when they did. You two needed to get used to flying the variable pitch model. Definitely an improvement on poor old T-Tommy."

He turned to go again, "Well, good night then, Harry. Sleep well. Enjoy it, because there's no reason for you to miss a beano again. The boys will be glad. Tomorrow is a new day for us all. Cheerio, chum."

He nodded amiably at Rose and closed the door quietly.

Operational! Even though he had expected it, and had worked so hard for it, Rose glowed with a warm, self-congratulatory feeling of achievement. Smith thought him ready, and he felt it.

Bring on the Messerschmitts, he thought, bravely.

I'm ready for you now, Adolf.

I'm ready.

Chapter 9

The morning of the 10th of July, 1940 dawned with rain and cloud driving in from the south-west. It was a dirty, grey start to another lovely summer's day.

It looked as if there would be no flying with conditions such as these, but nonetheless, B' Flight of Excalibur Squadron was slated for dawn readiness. Billy had woken bleary eyed to a cold and wet darkness, as if the world had disappeared into an empty windswept void, leaving only the Station in the midst of lonely grey countryside, so that he felt as if he were lost in the midst of a desolate wasteland.

Whilst Rose slept peacefully in his bed, Hermann a silent companion curled comfortably beside him, the service car slowly crunched its way up the gravel path that led to the Manor House, to take the yawning pilots to an early breakfast of a steaming cup of sweet tea and a toasted crumpet scrimped with butter, before the inevitable journey to readiness.

"Bloody Harry Clampers, again," moaned Flying Officer Warburton, eyeing the morose clouds. "I hate bloody cloud, especially low bloody cloud, that bastard. Can't see bugger all." He flung the last of his crumpet at a crow that was eyeing him and his breakfast. "Here, have it then, you sod!" It landed on the grass, and the crow ran to it eagerly.

Billy collapsed tiredly onto a wooden park bench that bore the legend 'Shoreham Parish Council.' It was dark with moisture from the early morning air, and it creaked disturbingly.

Billy didn't care. Despite the wetness seeping through the seat of his trousers, he could feel his eyes closing with tiredness. He put down his mug and closed his eyes, sat back. Warburton moaning again! Why, if it wasn't the weather, it was the brass, or the kites, or the food or it would be something else.

"Oh Lord, Burt, put a sock in it." Warburton made a face, threw the dregs of his mug of tea onto the grass, and walked off towards Flight-Lieutenant Spink, the new C'Flight commander, who was chatting with the airman manning the telephone.

Early morning was no time for jokes, and Billy was in no mood for making any. All he wanted was to close his eyes and sleep, but at any moment he may have to get into his aircraft and chase one of the Hun recce planes that flew over the channel or Southern England every day, gleaning intelligence. With the amount of cloud up there, they would be lucky to make an interception successfully.

Although two days had passed since the squadron had been made operational again, there had not been any contact with the Luftwaffe, Billy and his squadron-mates had only been involved in convoy patrols and fruitless interceptions, which had ended with the Hurricanes usually being vectored onto an enemy aeroplane that had dived for home well before they were able to get anywhere near.

Billy had yet to see an enemy aircraft, and the excitement of being on active service again had now dulled somewhat. The thought of a warm bed seeming far more attractive at this time of the morning.

He yawned hugely, and tried to make himself comfortable on the bench. He tipped his cap forwards and closed his eyes.

With a bit of luck, maybe he'd get the chance of a quick forty winks.

Half an hour later, still bleary eyed, he and his section were taking off on an interception near the Thames estuary.

The third scramble of the day saw A'Flight take-off in mid-afternoon to the request for assistance by the standing patrol of the small coastal convoy 'Teacake.'

Rose was Yellow Two in the second section element of the six aeroplane flight. Flight-Lieutenant Denis led his flight as Blue one.

Climbing quickly, they flew to the coast. There was no radio chatter as they flew. The enemy raid was a large one, and already some coasters had been hard hit.

Other fighters had also been scrambled and the first of these smashed into the Luftwaffe attackers, to the relief of the hard-pressed defenders.

As they neared the coast, they could see the thin dark trails, in the distance, stark against the pale sky, marking where ships and men fought and bled and died.

Dry-mouthed and heart beating rapidly, Rose was transfixed by the distant sight of battle, and the first warning of trouble was when Granny Smith suddenly shouted desperately over the intercom, "Break! Bandits above! Break, break!"

Seeing the burning ships before them, they had not noticed the high level bandits, the raider's escort.

Cursing, Rose instinctively kicked right rudder, pulled the stick back hard into the pit of his stomach, as far back as he could. Like someone wet behind the ears, he had allowed the sight of burning ships make him forget to keep checking his tail. Thank God for Smith!

Pulling into the sudden, vicious manoeuvre, Rose blacked out momentarily. The Hurricanes of A'Flight shot apart in all directions, like a flock of startled birds as the Staffel of Me110 twin-engine fighters fell on them from above. However, thanks to Smith's desperate cry, miraculously, not one Hurricane was downed in that first pass.

But the formation was broken, whilst nearby sailors raged and bled and called desperately for assistance.

As Rose turned sharply, sight blurring, sweat sprang out on his brow, and his heart thundered like a kettle-drum. He could feel abject fear engulfing him, an inexorable tide that threatened to overwhelm and engulf him.

He had felt this way once before, when he had been scrumping with Fred Hinds. The farmer had set his dogs on them, and they had fled in terror. Rose had wet himself in his fear.

Thank goodness that at least he hadn't done that again now.

Suddenly, as he looked up, a black shape hurtled past him, huge and dark. The Hurricane wallowed in the shock-wave of disturbed air, and he instinctively ducked his head.

What in the hell was that?

Whatever it was, it was sufficient to snap Rose out of the frozen moment of stark terror that many fighting men experience as they go into combat for the first time in their lives.

Look around you; check those danger areas below and behind.

Calm down.

Calm.

Calm. Pretend it's just another practice combat.

Breathe slowly.

He craned his neck around, glanced quickly up, down, to the sides, just as he had been taught to do by Smith

The blood was roaring in his ears, heart fluttering violently. He willed himself to slow down his rapid breathing.

Dear God. Was this what it was like?

114

Most of his companions had already disappeared. Surely they were not shot down?

No, of course not. He could hear them calling out to each other.

Far below, he saw a Hurricane chasing a pair of Me110's three thousand feet below. He could not tell if it was Granny or Barsby, or one of the others.

Another Me110 was going downwards, seemingly out of control and at full throttle in a steep dive, almost vertical, away from him. Apart from the distant solitary Hurricane, there was no sign of the other members of A'Flight.

Where could they all go, so suddenly?

Then his heart lurched painfully again in his chest, for just below, perhaps a couple of thousand feet was another Me110, and it had just pulled out of its own dive, and was turning to gently climb to port, its wings waggling uncertainly.

That must be the aircraft that had just passed so close to him, almost hitting him in his turn. The speed of its dive had prevented it from levelling out and chasing him at his own height. It had probably prevented the German pilot from drawing an accurate bead on him.

Lady Luck had smiled on him, saving him from the mid-air collision.

Already the panic was lessening, as Granny's teachings took control.

Time was of the essence, a quick glance in the mirror.

Satisfied that there were no more enemy aircraft behind him for the present, he quickly half-rolled so that he was inverted, and pulled the Hurricane into a dive to follow the Messerschmitt.

The carburettor of his Merlin, not being fuel-injected, would have become starved of fuel and would have cut out, so he had to roll inverted before he could dive. A few small lumps of earth from the floor of the cockpit swirled past his face. He had to act quickly, because with its advantage of speed over the British fighter, the 110 could escape if not tackled immediately.

Below Rose, in the Me110, Leutnant Carl-Gustav Schnee was having an extremely anxious time. Up until a few minutes ago, he had been revelling in the fact that he was a member of the invincible Luftwaffe's elite Bf110 Zerstorer force. It had felt so good to be flying wing to wing with the finest pilots in their powerful heavy fighters.

He had caressed his firing button lovingly, anticipating the moment that he would pour fire from his nose mounted cannon and machine guns into some hapless Tommy fighter. The tales he had heard from his squadron mates had fuelled his hunger for combat.

The enemy fighters had been there one moment, but as he fired at them, there was just empty space ahead as the British *schwein* scattered.

But now, he had lost the Staffel, the formation broken as he tried to follow a Tommy with his sights, but the enemy fighter had disappeared and, worse, he had lost sight of his leader. He was alone, his crewmen offering little comfort.

It suddenly felt very lonely and vulnerable in this small patch of sky, and the enemy coast so nearby.

He suddenly wished desperately for the sights of his home town of Dortmund instead.

Suddenly Rudi, his gunner, screamed urgently, "Spitfire! High and behind! Hard turn!"

Directly before Rose, the Me110 suddenly tightened into a turn as the enemy pilot became aware of the danger from above.

The enemy gunner opened fire at him, but the stream of tracer, a line of fiery blobs, curved uselessly away below and to one side harmlessly as the gunner tried to track Rose's Hurricane, whilst his pilot began to manoeuvre desperately.

The enemy aircraft banked sharply to starboard, then to port again, jinking poorly, and then the nose of the 110 went down as the other pilot tried to pull away from the diving Hurricane, whilst also trying to give a better field of fire to his rear-gunner.

As the German plane disappeared momentarily from view, Rose rolled to right his fighter, and the enemy popped back into view.

Quick, quick!

As the distance closed he saw that the twin-engine machine before him was not painted all-black as he had originally thought but wore patterns of black and dark-green, and had large crosses on the wings and white spinners on its propellers. Each detail, from the glinting of the long, narrow glasshouse-like canopy to the ineffectual short bursts of fire from the rear-facing machine gun burned into his mind as the enemy plane began to dive again, as if realising the danger suddenly, and trying to escape, rather than fight.

He realised also that he was well within range now, and gauging the degree of deflection, he sighted and pressed the firing button.

The eight Browning machine guns spat fire at the German fighter, and the Hurricane bucked with the recoil, so that the image of the Me110 seemed to tremble and jump before him. The enemy gunner's aim seemed to be improving as well, though.

Tracer ripped up towards him, as if it was reaching for him, but then at the last moment shooting past, seemingly only a few feet above his canopy, like a blazing trail of comets. His breath came in gasps from the effort, and the rush of adrenaline coursing hot through him. He could smell the cordite, acrid and choking.

His own aim was not much better than the enemy gunner's, the tracer from his guns passing just below the enemy's tailplane, so he pulled back the stick a little, adjusted his aim, led as he had been taught, and fired another two-second burst. This time the trails of smoke converged just ahead and then onto the enemy aeroplane, and he was rewarded with the sparkle of glittering hits on the 110's starboard wing just inboard of the engine, and along the starboard ailerons.

A detached part of Rose watched as some of the rounds from his guns left unusual, corkscrewing trails of smoke behind them. The German fighter was still turning, but the Me110 could not out turn Rose's Hurricane, and his aim was good.

There appeared to be no immediate physical effect on the enemy machine, but there was more of an effect on the enemy pilot, startled by the shocking clatter of the hits so close to him and by the sight of the torn fragments of metal that began to peel away from his starboard wing.

Schnee suddenly pulled up, twitching the Me110 as if stung, so that his machine suddenly leapt back upwards into a desperate climb, upsetting the gunner's aim completely, and tracer sprayed out below, impotently into the void.

This tactic to gain precious height was a terrible mistake on his part, presenting more of his plane as a target, whilst also allowing Rose to catch him.

Following him from above and behind, Rose fired again, reflexively, without sighting properly, and his bullets also curved away uselessly, beneath the other plane. He muttered to himself reproachfully. The excitement of the situation had got the better of him.

The stink and smoke of cordite from his guns filled the cockpit as he pulled back, back, then back again, as he strove to keep the twin-tailed fighter in his sights as it jinked, firing short bursts. Most of the bursts connected and he was rewarded with further twinkling hits on the wing-root and fuselage, and a streamer of smoke began to trail thinly behind the starboard engine.

What was it that Granny used to say?

"Get as close as you can, as close as you dare. Then, get closer still."

Still flying at full throttle, he cut across the wide arc that the climbing Me110 made, closing the distance between the two aircraft rapidly, heart hammering. He began to reduce the throttle as the German aircraft seemed to swell in his GM2 reflector gun sight and pressed the gun-button again, convulsively.

Someone was shouting hysterically, and at first he wondered who it was cursing over the R/T.

With a shock, he realised that the voice was his own. He lapsed into a tense embarrassed silence. His eyes were smarting and his arms felt stiff as he held on to the stick tightly, as if it were his lifeline, as if to let go were to let go of life.

A blazing cluster of hits sparkled brightly once more on the 110, but this time a number of larger warped pieces flew off, and a great gout of black smoke erupted from the starboard engine. The shining arc of the propeller broke up as it began to windmill, and the engine cowling was ripped completely away.

The glass of the long canopy exploded, shattering into a million glittering fragments, and for a split second created a strange, eerie, shimmering and hazy halo around the German plane before being whipped away in the howling slipstream.

The Messerschmitt wallowed and slowed as it lost the power of one engine, pulled to one side, and just as it seemed that they must surely collide, Rose realised the danger and heaved back the control column hard, deep into the pit of his stomach again, spasmodically pulled the flap lever, and the Hurricane clawed upwards.

He tried to curl into a foetal ball, and instinctively closed his eyes tightly in terror, threw up his arm over his face, as the black shape loomed, filling his windscreen, and the cockpit radio aerial stood out before him from the long glasshouse canopy that had been devastated by his Brownings.

In his terrified mind it seemed like a lance, as if to impale him.

Even though his eyes were closed he could still see, fixed in his mind's eye, the pale ovals that were the faces of the German crew, incredibly not killed, as they stared back at him, transfixed with shock, or fear.

A tableau frozen in time, imprinted on his eyeballs.

Dear God! He wasn't going to make it!

He waited for the crash of impact, eyes closed tight, and teeth clenched, but it did not come. He could hear the sound of the rear-gunner's 7.9mm machine gun as he passed over the Me110. It sounded like a strange, dim and distant popping, like the backfiring of a motorcycle on a summer's day, a spatter of pebbles against the underside of the aircraft. Then there was a faraway thunderclap of sound, *'Boom!'*

He cringed at the thought of hot metal that could punch through the floor of the cockpit at any moment. There was a second, louder, thunderclap of sound, *'BOOM!'* Not the high pitched, rending crash of metal on metal that he had been expecting, but a deep, visceral sound, that he felt in his bones.

After a few, long, seconds, Rose opened his eyes.

Incredibly, unbelievably, he had not crashed into the heavy German fighter, although it must have been pretty close.

The Hurricane was still climbing steeply, screaming upwards, with bullets still spraying from the guns. He released the button, and the guns fell silent, and gulped in great whoops of air.

He realised that he must have been holding his breath.

Rose relaxed his gloved hands on the stick, palms greasy.

There was nothing but emptiness in front of him.

120

Where the enemy aircraft had once filled his windscreen, just seconds ago, there was now only a beautiful empty, deep blue sky.

He was still alive!

He suddenly realised with a shock that he hadn't once checked behind him during the attack, glanced into his rear-view mirror, then twisted around to see behind him.

The enemy fighter that he half-expected to be sitting behind him, dark and threatening, spitting deadly fire, was not there.

In fact, there was nothing behind him at all, not even the Me110 he had just attacked. It was as if it had disappeared into thin air. He undid his mask and wiped his face with the back of his gloved hand. The combat and near collision had left him feeling fiercely excited, and he was exultant that he had survived his baptism of fire.

He had passed The Test without flinching (well, sort of).

But, more importantly, he was Still Alive.

He laughed, the terror of a few seconds ago forgotten.

"I'm alive!" he shouted, joyously.

There was the taste of blood in his mouth, where he had bitten his lip.

"I'm alive!"

But then he sobered.

Idiot! After all that Granny has taught you, you overshot! You just went at it like a bull at a gate. All that training and you make a balls-up of that attack. Missed half the time! Lucky to be alive.

But I'm still here. That was just the beginning. There would be more fighting to do yet. The convoy was still under attack.

You've got another chance of doing it better. Don't make such a mess of it next time.

He looked into the curved rear-view mirror like the one Granny had.

Far below there was a splash in the sea, a white, expanding scar, which boiled for a few seconds, before the water settled, and it disappeared, leaving behind an expanding circle of disturbance, but he could not tell what had made it.

Was that 'his' Messerschmitt? Or was it one of his countrymen? He felt quite sure that the enemy fighter could not be able to get back to its aerodrome with only one motor.

He pulled the Hurricane around and headed back towards the burning convoy. The ships were still under attack, and it was his duty to go and protect them, even though he was now on his own.

This time, he kept a careful look-out all around him. He had been extremely lucky not to have been shot down, but this time he would not trust to luck, but would maintain a good lookout as he had been taught to by Smith.

Amazingly, there were no other aircraft visible in the air around him. How many Me110s had bounced A'Flight? Where had they gone?

He was Still Alive!

God be praised!

As he drew closer he could make out the bursts of anti-aircraft fire peppering the sky above the convoy. There was something falling slowly, burning. Above it silvery shapes wheeled and dived. The aircraft were flying away from him now, and were too distant for him to catch up with. The R/T was filled with the sound of men fighting, swearing…dying?

But there was something, a shadow, just skimming the sea, not quite as far away. At first he thought it was a boat, but, as he got closer, he could see that it was another Me110. A thin, almost invisible, trail of smoke limned from one engine.

It was heading east towards sanctuary, away from the pitifully small collection of coasters that were the battered convoy 'Teacake.'

The 110 was flying low, so low that the slipstream from the propellers was creating furrows in the surface of the sea. Hazy plumes of spray swirled away lazily behind it. It was as if the enemy aeroplane was a speeding motor boat, leaving its wake behind.

He wondered if it was one of the planes that had bounced A'Flight.

The rear-gunner had also seen him, and a line of tracer sped from the gun as the enemy tested the range. This one was a better shot, but the range was still too great, and the fire curved away from him uselessly.

Thank God for bullet-proof windshields, thought Rose again, as he swept down at full throttle. As the range closed, he fired a one-second sighting burst.

This time he had calculated the deflection better, and the Me110 seemed to fly through the glowing lines of tracer.

Lines of splashes shot up from the surface of the sea, like an avenue of surreal trees, with the German flying through them. His propellers carved the water into spiralling vortices that whipped backwards towards the pursuing Hurricane. Already water was speckling Rose's windscreen unevenly, unevenly smearing the shape of the 110.

He fired again, a longer, three second burst this time, hunched forward, willing the bullets onto their target.

The enemy gunner had already begun to fire back, and Rose felt something hit the Hurricane, once, twice, three times, as if someone were hammering at the airframe, and then he was out of the deadly hose.

But the shock of the impacts had scared him enough that he brought the throttle back and dropped further behind. He kept care to keep the 110's tail-plane between them, hiding the Hurricane in the gunner's blind spot, whilst the gap widened safely again. His Hurricane bounced the disturbed air caused by the enemy's slipstream and from ground-effect.

Water vapour from the disturbed sea and spray streamed over the canopy, as if he were flying through rain. It was difficult to see ahead, and it was difficult to aim. With the recoil of the guns and the low speed his aircraft teetered on a stall.

A small piece of metal, ripped from the enemy aircraft, appeared and disappeared in an instant. A stream of tracer whipped close but not close enough to do damage.

He felt rather than heard a handful of impacts on his kite, but they were not bullets but pieces of the 110. He fired again.

And then the return fire suddenly ceased, and although the Messerschmitt continued to fly, the rear-facing MG15 machine-gun drooped impotently downwards; the gunner slouched behind it, head lolling.

A lucky shot had hit and disabled, perhaps even killed, the gunner.

Lucky for Rose. Not so for his opponent.

Don't forget your mirror. Keep checking the mirror…

Thank you again, Lady Luck. He pulled up slightly, dropped back a little.

Despite the enemy hits, the Merlin engine still roared healthily. The gauges read normal, and the aircraft responded normally to his commands, so he pushed the throttle forward again, but the Me110 had managed to pull away again as it tried to escape. He fired another burst hopefully, more tracer this time, the strikes showing hits, but without any appreciable result. A black blob, the size of a marble, hit the windscreen, spreading out unevenly, partially obscuring his vision for a moment before being spread thin into invisibility.

Oil! The Messerschmitt was leaking oil! He had added to the damage further.

He waited for the oil to thin on his windscreen, before he pressed the gun-button again, but this time the roar of gunfire was replaced by the pneumatic hissing that came from empty chambers. He tried again, with the same result. He banged the side of his cockpit in frustration.

Damn it! He was out of ammunition. Now what?

He trailed the Messerschmitt for a few miles as he pondered. Perhaps he should try and scare the enemy into ditching?

Rose was about to make a dummy attack when he noticed another aircraft coming down from above and behind him. Oh Hell. The situation was going progressively from bad to worse. Who was this?

Friend or foe?

He pulled back into a climbing turn, keeping a wary eye on the approaching single-engine fighter. He needed to get into a favourable position. At low-level and without ammunition, he was very vulnerable.

Please don't let it be a Me109, he prayed silently. I can't outrun it and I can't outfight it.

The R/T crackled, "Blue Three to Yellow Two, nice shooting, Sir, how about letting me have a go?"

The other plane was a Hurricane. It was another aircraft from Excalibur Squadron, an experienced NCO who had survived France with two victories, Flight-Sergeant Jimmy Carpenter. Rose breathed a sigh of relief. He keyed his microphone.

"Have a go, Jimmy. I'm out of ammo. Good thing you turned up. He's all yours." To his ears, he sounded high pitched and trembling.

"Understood, Yellow Two."

Oops. Callsigns were there for using.

The canopy hood was pushed back, and Rose saw Carpenter wave when the other Hurricane shot past, as the Flight-Sergeant took over pursuit. He tucked himself into the wingman's position for protection, although it was as much for himself as for Carpenter.

With Rose watching for enemy fighters, Carpenter concentrated on the fleeing German aircraft.

They caught up with him as they passed close by the tail of the convoy. Luckily there was no ack-ack from the ships.

With the rear-gunner out of the game and a disabled engine, with two RAF fighters on his tail, the odds were against the Me110 pilot, and as the first long burst from Carpenter's guns chewed up his starboard engine and tore off shreds of wing, he decided to ditch his heavy, ailing fighter.

A plume of spray shot up behind the bandit as it touched down on the sea, and then it disappeared for a moment in a bigger cloud of spray, emerged to shoot up for a moment, shedding debris, then fell back on the sea, propeller blades bent back by the initial impact. A tail fin spun away from the Me110.

"'Strewth. He didn't try very hard, Sir. I think you'd already knocked him about quite a bit." Carpenter sounded disappointed.

"Yes." Rose watched as the Luftwaffe pilot struggled from his cockpit. The wings of the Me110 were already awash, and the tail was slowly lifting up, as the heavier nose and engines began to sink below the waves. He glanced back inside, saw that there was no-one left to help in the torn cockpit, and that he was the only survivor. He scrambled down the wing, and cast himself away from the sinking plane in a little inflatable dinghy.

Already a yellowish-green stain was spreading out from the dinghy's marker chemicals to make rescue easier.

The remnants of the Me110 settled lower, like a dark monster sliding back into the grey and silent depths of the Channel. Within seconds, it had slid beneath the surface, and there was only the dinghy with its surrounding stain to mark the 110's watery grave.

One of the convoy escorts had lowered a boat, and it was making its way to the sinking aeroplane.

"We'd best head for home soon, sir." Carpenter said respectfully.

"Yes, you're right. Of course." He said shakily. "Just a minute while that boat gets here, then we'll go. Would you take the lead, please, Blue Three?"

"Yes, sir." Rose tucked himself gratefully behind Carpenter's wing again.

Together they orbited, Carpenter in the lead, over the solitary German until he was picked up by the excited sailors.

Not once did he acknowledge that he was aware of the two Hurricanes circling overhead. Instead he sat with his head dejectedly bowed, the picture of misery. No longer a powerful and capable conqueror, but a sad and lonely man, his colleagues dead and gone. Rose searched for feelings of guilt in his heart, but there were none.

His body ached all over, his hands were trembling and he was drenched in sweat, but he was filled with a new found vigour, and could not remember a time when he had felt so very alive and conscious of his surroundings.

But there was relief, too. The dice could have fallen another way. That German below, struggling in his dinghy, could so easily have been him if the enemy gunners had had a better aim, or had been more fortunate with their shooting.

Skill and ability were important, but Luck played as great a part of this game, he understood now, and today, it had been with him. He realised with a shock that the fear that had lain in him, coiled up in his stomach like a slumbering serpent, was gone. All that was left was the exhilaration.

He looked across and waved at Carpenter.

God be praised, he was Still Alive!

127

Chapter 10

They were the first ones back, and Carpenter landed first.

Rose was excited, but drained. Mindful of Granny's warnings, he did not make the victory roll that he had promised himself in flight training, although to be honest, he really didn't feel like doing one anyway.

He wasn't quite sure that he was even entitled to a victory roll.

Right now, he just wanted to get down safely, and close his eyes.

Safely back on the ground, he wearily pulled off his oxygen mask, and as Baker pulled back the canopy, his nostrils were assailed by the pungent smell of fumes, hot metal and machine oil.

Baker helped him loosen his harness, and Rose caught a whiff of liquorice, sweat and grease from the fitter, banishing the dryness slowly from his airways.

Rose closed his eyes for a moment as cool air played on his face.

Like an old man he fumbled his goggles off and unplugged his leads. The tension suddenly seemed to drain from him, like water from a colander.

Carpenter patiently waited for Rose to climb down stiffly from the cockpit before he made his way over to join him. Rose's legs felt like jelly, his body shaking from reaction, and he discreetly leaned against the Hurricane's rudder.

He was fearful for a moment then that he might pass out.

His rigger, Joyce ran up to the Hurricane, his face shining hopefully, like a schoolboy about to be given a pound of sweets.

Like Baker, he had noticed the torn and stained fabric over the gun ports, the black trails from the leading edge, and the scattered bullet holes, and had heard the tell-tale whistle from those open ports as Rose had come in to land.

They knew that he had seen action, and had fired his guns.

"Any luck, Sir?" Joyce looked expectantly at the young man with the marks of his oxygen mask and goggles on his strained face. As usual, Baker joined them, his jaws working agitatedly as he chewed the tough fragment of liquorice.

Rose blew a strand of hair out of his eyes, and tried to appear nonchalant, although he felt he was about to fall over at any moment. He felt slightly sick and was not sure he could speak without his voice trembling. He spoke slowly, carefully, but with a wide grin that felt painful and contrived, stretching skin that felt as tight and hard as dried leather. Surely they must see how shaky he felt? The voice sounded like someone else's, he thought with some detachment.

"Wizard show! Had a crack at a couple of Me110's. As I was feeling generous, I let 'em have all my ammo. Certainly gave 'em a bit of a headache."

Mm. That sounded suitably fighter-pilotish. His stomach ached. "Definitely two damaged, or one damaged and one shared, although they gave me a bit of a squirt, too, as you can see."

Would they see through the façade?

They grinned excitedly back at him and, almost shyly, he thought, shook his hand in turn and congratulated him, before clambering up onto the fighter. Despite the paleness of his face, they glanced quickly at each other, marvelling at his calm, unhurried manner.

"He's a cool 'un," whispered Joyce. "If it wuz me, I'd've shit myself."

"Aye," agreed Baker, "He'll do me." He stroked the Hurricane, "Two damaged! Good girl!"

Joyce grunted in agreement as his practised eyes took in the bullet damage to his beloved Hurricane. "Yeah. Told you all along, din't I?" He stared at the battle-damage with a professional eye. "No major damage. Have this right as rain in a tick."

"Told me, my arse..." replied Baker.

Rose closed his eyes and leaned his head back.

Now, if he could just lie down...

Carpenter reached him and pumped his hand, then whistled at the shredded tailplane surfaces. "Whee-oo! Jerry certainly took a swipe at you! Well done, sir!"

They looked up when another Hurricane appeared in the distance, and watched in silence as it approached and came in to land. They could hear the strange, resonating organ-like tones that came from the wind passing through the open gun ports in its wings.

It was Smith, and he, too, had fired his guns.

He taxied to dispersal, blipped the engine twice, impertinently, and then switched off. They walked, Rose rather shakily on still unsteady legs, to him as he jumped down.

"Wotcher, Granny!" Carpenter greeted Smith warmly. "We had a little party. How about you, any luck?"

Smith's hair was dishevelled, face stained and his eyes tired, whilst his uniform was even more rumpled than normal.

He removed his gloves and ran a hand through his tousled hair, but it just stood up all the more. Carpenter lit a cigarette and passed it over to Smith.

Rose felt like giggling hysterically. Granny's hair was standing up like a sheaf of corn.

Smith took a long drag on the cigarette. "Got one of the bastards. Dornier 17 over the convoy. Blew him to buggery into a thousand flaming pieces."

He exhaled a long plume of smoke. "Still had his bombs on board. Stopped his shenanigans good and proper. Had a hell of a time getting away from the 110's, though." He spoke in a staccato, the words coming out like machine-gun bullets. He looked Rose over, his face oily and unreadable, and his eyes were cold.

"I'm glad you managed to get back. How was it, Harry?" He looked carefully at Rose, taking the strained, drained expression and the too-bright eyes. The feelings of excitement and the exhilaration of combat were still powerful in him.

"Wizard, Granny! I'm sorry I lost you. I tried to look for you, but there was a 110. I hit him quite hard, I think, but then I lost him. I didn't see him go down or anything, but he was damaged, I'm sure of that. Then I had a go at another one, but ran out of ammo. Jimmy, here, finished it off."

Smith shook his head tiredly.

"Actually, Harry, I'm just glad you managed to come out of that OK. It was a bit of a shambles." He wiped his forehead, dropping ash from his cigarette onto his Mae West, "The Huns could have had us. We were bloody lucky to escape that bounce. It just so happens, though, that I was below you when you were attacking that first one. I had one of the bastards turning after me, and I'd lost too much height, so I couldn't help. Sorry."

He grinned then, tightly, the lines on either side of his mouth pronounced, "You did really well. I saw your attack on the 110, and I also saw it blow up just after you made your firing pass. I even thought you were going to ram him, actually."

Carpenter coughed and looked away.

131

Granny smiled wisely, "A definite kill, and I'll confirm it, but you cut it a bit fine. Would have been a bit of a waste of my fine training if you'd left it a bit too late, eh?"

He cocked an eyebrow quizzically, and Rose blushed in chagrin, despite the unexpected revelation of his success.

Bloody Hell! He had shot down the first Messerschmitt 110 after all! A confirmed kill!

It was hardly believable. He was amazed at how elated he suddenly felt. It was if his tired body was electrified.

He'd shot down a Hun!

More, he'd done it on his first operational combat flight!

But, warned the little voice, he'd almost rammed the 110, as Granny had chided. His self-discipline and flying should have been better. He'd achieved his first 'kill', but more by luck than ability.

He mentally resolved to take greater care, to try and control the excitement of battle.

"Are you sure, Granny?" He asked.

Smith, nodded, spoke quietly. "As eggs are eggs. You got one confirmed, there, definite. No doubt about that one. I was watching." He smacked Rose on the back, almost knocking him down, and he tottered shakily, "You did well. But most of all, you managed to survive. That's the most important thing. That's something you can't learn."

He smiled slightly, and shoved the cigarette back into his mouth, "Better still, you'll learn from the experience. Bloody well done!" He drew on it, then passed the cigarette back to Carpenter, pulled out his pipe, and clamped it, unlit, between his teeth. "My first was a 110, too."

Rose found it difficult to believe it. The Me110 had exploded. That must have been the strange thunderclap of sound just after he had almost collided. He hadn't even felt the shock-wave of the explosion; although he was so close it could have torn the Hurri to pieces, or thrown him out of control and into the sea. The thought made him go cold.

"Are you sure, Granny?" He asked again, and shook his head dazedly, "I didn't see him go down."

"I did. He went straight in. Out of control. No parachutes."

Carpenter laughed, "Well, sir, you can add one half-shared to that, because you certainly gave the other 110 a pasting before I had a go. He would have probably gone into the drink anyway, without any help from me. Anyway, we got the sod!"

I must tell Joyce and Baker, thought Rose. They'll be really pleased.

Carpenter gripped Rose's arm. "Come on, I'll stand you a cup of that flippin' awful NAAFI tea." He indicated the NAAFI van that was making its way to dispersal. "Maybe we can get a piece of cake or a roll to celebrate. I'm starving!"

Donald had driven up in his shooting brake. He had Skinner, Toby, his Labrador, and Farrell of B' Flight with him. They had heard the tail-end of the conversation, and now they too offered their congratulations. Farrell looked at the dazed Rose with surprise and not a little envy, who was almost knocked off his feet by the ever-affectionate Toby.

"You damned lucky hound! One confirmed and one shared! You've only been with us five minutes and you've already given half the blinking Luftwaffe the chop. This isn't on, you know. All the totty's going to go after you, now. No chance for a poor old sod like me!" He said, half-seriously. Farrell's score card was still blank, even though he'd been in France at the end, and flown over Dunkirk. He heard shouting, and saw that other members of the squadron were on their way.

Smith shook his head again. "With one and a half kills, I think you should be getting the tea in, Harry, old son."

He looked up into the sky, "No sign of the others yet."

Then Rose realised that the spaces at dispersals for Denis' and Barsby's Hurricanes were empty.

Donald shook his head. "I heard that they're on their way back. I believe Dingo got one, too. Renfrew got a few hits in his motor, so he took to his umbrella."

Poor Renfrew, so eager for a victory, but having to bale out instead.

He noticed that Donald's attention was elsewhere, and his eyes followed those of Donald's to where a petite, fair-haired WAAF was standing forlornly some distance away, one hand shading her eyes, searching the distance.

Dolly was waiting too.

"Oh dear, poor Dolly. I'd best go and tell her not to worry." With that he bustled off, leaving Rose, Granny and Carpenter to be carried off in triumph by the gaggle of newly-arrived, excited pilots. Skinner smiled benevolently at them.

It certainly brought back a few memories of another field, another war, another time.

The sun was low in the sky when Rose managed to slip quietly away from the celebrations in the Mess. Excalibur squadron had not been called upon for any more sorties after A' Flight's action over the channel.

Although there had been further raids, other squadrons had been tasked with interception. Unlike earlier days, there had been a noticeable increase in enemy activity.

Behind him, in the Mess, Farrell was trying to dance the can-can on the bar. He had already lost his trousers, and he was waving his shirt-tails seductively, amidst the catcalls and jeers of his fellows.

The occasional glimpse of his underpants and his suggestive leers at the catering officer were enough to make her scowl, whilst pretending not to see the leers.

In addition to the two Me110's that had been shot down, Smith and Denis had each accounted for a Dornier 17, Barsby had been chased by Me110's, but had managed to escape, shaken but unhurt, whilst Pilot officer Renfrew, Blue Two, had been shot down, but was safe. His Hurricane had been the only casualty of 'A' Flight.

Donald had flown down and picked him up in the station's Miles Magister.

On his return, he had drunk heavily, 'To wash the taste of seawater from my mouth,' and was now lying snoring and insensible in a quiet corner of the mess, minus trousers, shoes and tie.

Needing to be alone for a little while, Rose walked slowly along the road leading back to the squadron's adopted home, enjoying the coolness of approaching night and inhaling the sweet fragrance of the countryside in summer.

Joyce and Baker had already painted one and a half German crosses (Rose's score having been officially confirmed) onto the side of P-Peter, his machine. They seemed even prouder of his victories than he did himself.

What a day! Everything had changed.

Smith had taught him that they were all members of the same team, each as important as the other. 'A machine cannot function unless it has all its' parts,' he had once said.

Rose had thanked Joyce and Baker quietly for the vital part they had played, and had promised to buy them each a pint or two.

Joyce had spoken for them both when he had said, "Just take care of dear ol' Peter and keep on shooting them Huns down, Sir. That's the best thanks you could give us." He had patted the fuselage fondly, "Give 'em hell!" Rose wasn't sure if the last comment had been addressed to him or to the fighter.

The bullet holes were greater in number than he had imagined. He had thought that only a handful of bullets had smacked into the Hurricane, but there were twenty strikes in total. Some rounds had even passed vertically through the wings, probably from the first Me110's machine-gun. He had been extremely lucky not to have received a disabling hit, particularly, as Smith would have put it, indelicately, in the 'Crown Jewels.' He could not even remember the impacts as he had passed over the Me110. He must have been a wonderful target for a split-second of time.

The gunner had not been such a bad shot, after all. Rose had been luckier than he had realised.

On impulse, he decided to walk through the field that ran alongside the leafy road. This was after all, what he was defending. Even if it were private land, he had the right to walk through it at least. He was going to do his best to prevent some jack-booted Nazi infantryman from making it into some battleground.

Unbidden, a picture from a history book came to mind. It had been a photograph of the ravaged French countryside at Ypres following a prolonged artillery barrage during the Great War. It had been a sterile and lumpy panorama, a dark land of water-filled shell craters and torn tree trunks.

He stopped for a moment and looked around him, trying to imprint the peaceful image into his mind.

Taking out his unsmoked pipe, he thrust it into his mouth, clamping it firmly between his teeth. It made him feel heroic and pugnacious.

Rose thought of the clumsy attempt he had made to thank Granny for the training. Had it not been for that, it was more than likely he would be represented as a little roundel painted onto the side of an enemy kite right now. The words had stumbled out, and Granny had smiled briefly.

"You were alone in the cockpit today. If you were a duffer, nothing I said could have helped. Those Jerries were yours alone. But, if you feel you owe me, well, you can buy me a beer." Then he had slapped Rose on the back and turned to speak with Skinner.

With his hands deep in his pockets, Rose began to walk again. It was hard to think that the beautiful countryside around him could be changed into a nightmare of mud and death, but that was exactly what could happen if he and the others of the RAF failed to stop the continuing advance of the German war machine.

Dad had often spoken of how the French fields had been turned into a barren and destroyed landscape with very little effort on the part of the fighting armies.

He leaned against a large tree. The wood of the thick trunk felt dry and knobbly beneath his fingers, and he sat down against it, sucking noisily on the pipe.

Smith favoured cigarettes over his pipe, and had smoked innumerable numbers of them during his talks with Rose and Barsby. Rose just kept his stock of issued cigarettes in his wardrobe, for Granny, Baker and Joyce. He was content to suck his empty pipe, although he found the smell of tobacco vaguely pleasant.

He closed his eyes and turned his face up to the sky. He could still see the image of the Me110 frozen in his mind.

The halo of glass shimmering silver and gold where the canopy had shattered explosively, the smoke, the faces seen dimly in the dark shape of the fighter.

Smith had said that there had been no parachutes, which meant that he had killed at least two men today. Three, if the gunner of the second Messerschmitt were also included. Although some reports said that three men flew in a 110.

At the time, he had felt as if he were fighting an evil machine, an inanimate collection of metallic parts. It had seemed like a great monstrous insect, buzzing death. And he had felt pleasure at swiping it.

But after the action, and on seeing the lonely German survivor in his dinghy, the realisation had set in. The duel had been between men.

This morning, as he had got out of bed, three, perhaps four young and maybe as many as five men just like him had also stirred in France, and prepared themselves for the coming day. They had had breakfast, joked with each other, and not realised that in a few short hours they would be dead with their remains lying in their smashed aeroplanes in the cold waters of the channel.

Before they had met their ends, had they been thinking of their futures? Had they intended to meet with a girlfriend, see a film? Or might they have intended to write home to a household in Germany?

It was a sobering thought.

Had he stolen a father from small children, or a doting son from elderly parents? He realised that the consequences of his actions over a period of only a few minutes had ended the lives of at least three men, but perhaps more importantly, he had changed the lives of those left behind completely. He had gained so much, but others had lost everything. Today he had been responsible for their deaths.

He remembered his father. If he had not returned as he had, would Rose have been a better man?

He shook his head. Those unknown men would not now be dead if they had stayed in Germany. They were flying from one conquered land on a mission to help conquer another. If he hadn't killed them, more British sailors would have died this day.

They were servicemen who knew the dangers, and the likely consequences of flying in combat, as did he.

He felt suddenly angry, the morose mood evaporating.

What the bloody hell was he feeling sorry for them, anyway? What did they think they were doing? Why couldn't the bastards have stayed on their side of the puddle? They had come over, bombed the convoy, just because they coveted what was not theirs to have in the first place.

If they had left loved ones, well sod them! The sailors on the coasters had families too. Families who today had had the full effects of the war brought brutally home to them. What had they ever done to deserve the unwanted attention of the Luftwaffe?

The pipe stem was slippery with saliva, so he wiped it on his sleeve, then placed the pipe on the ground beside him, and picked a stalk of grass. He chewed on it absentmindedly, and rubbed his sore neck wearily.

He had not started the war, he was just one of millions who had been forced to come from their homes, and from a life of peace, and been thrown into the maelstrom because of the crazed machinations of a madman in Berlin.

The guilt that skulked in the deep recesses of his mind had no place in his life. It was a luxury that could not be afforded in wartime.

He gazed at the orange sun that seemed to shimmer just above the trees at the far end.

Had the positions been reversed, would the Germans have mourned him? He thought not.

Had the bounce been successful, they would have celebrated his death with Schnapps and a sing-song, as they must have already celebrated the victories of the last few months or so. There was no place for guilt in the life he now led.

139

It would only serve to make him weak. Weakened steel breaks so easily, he thought, I must ensure that I do not break. Britain needs me and those like me.

Britain may yet have to fight for its very survival, and the last thing it needed now was a warrior with a guilty conscience. He wondered for a moment how the others came to terms with the killing.

Did they have these thoughts? He must ask Smith. Perhaps this was why Father drank so heavily.

But what it came down to in the end was that he, with so many other men and women, both military and civilian, was fighting for the way of life that he had always known, and one which he wanted to continue. Those young men he had killed had been the soldiers of the tyranny that now threatened them all, and he had to fight them. He was fighting for his flag and his country, but more importantly, for his people.

The People of Britain and of the free world.

A warm feeling of pride, in his country, his service and for himself, permeated his being.

He banished the guilt back into the dark recesses of his mind. There was no place for it in the world he found himself.

The sun had disappeared behind the trees, and the darkening sky had turned a glorious blend of various deepening shades of gold, red, purple and blue. The weather had been wonderful, after the miserable, wet start, and sunset brought a kaleidoscopic collage of magnificent colour.

The sun had gone. And with it, the guilt.

What came in the future could not be changed. He would meet his destiny with fortitude.

Fate had granted him the precious sight of this day's sunset.

He got to his feet, stretched, and yawned. He felt shattered.

In his tiredness he could not appreciate the beautiful lilac half-light, or where the sun's last dying rays caught the undersides of the clouds with red-violet fire.

The boys can play, he mused, but I need my sleep. What a day!

It was a day in which Rose had finally seen action, had overcome his fears, had killed the enemy, and his life would never be quite the same again.

Chapter 11

The next day dawned wet and miserable, too.

A fitful light rain spattered the windows of the dispersals hut, whilst a low bank of thin fog eddied around aircraft and buildings.

"I don't fancy a take-off in this muck," complained Barsby, but Rose only snored gently in reply, untroubled in sleep.

He managed to sleep almost until the end of readiness, although his sleep was disturbed twice, once by a call to advise them that tea was on the way, and the second time when the tea arrived. He waved it away, preferring to doze, then changed his mind and struggled up to claim a cup.

His mouth was sour tasting and sticky, and a nice cup of the hot sweet NAAFI tea was just the thing to wash it out.

They flew twice that day, both times a convoy patrol in the Dover Straits.

There was no sign of the Luftwaffe on the first patrol, and they returned to Foxton for a late lunch. Later in the afternoon they rushed back with the squadron when the same convoy was attacked by a small raid, but when they finally got there, they were too late.

The Heinkels had already bombed and left the scene of the crime, leaving behind their escort, but the Staffel of Me109's were low on fuel and not interested in a fight. Seeing the British fighters, they turned away and flew towards the approaching dusk at full throttle.

Donald, leading Excalibur, boosted his throttle and tried to close the distance, but the Messerschmitts, with their speed advantage, and probably low on fuel and ammo after battling the convoy standing patrol, disappeared into the late-afternoon murk. They had already downed a Spitfire and damaged two others, all without loss, and were well satisfied with their day.

As the formation lost some of its cohesion, Rose was one of the tail-enders of the formation, and maintaining a careful watch behind, almost crashed into Barsby who was also watching behind. The near-collision scared them both badly, but neither pilot was anxious to be bounced again by high-flying bandits.

Fortunately, there was no further enemy activity, and the squadron returned to Foxton with a frustrated Donald, and a greatly relieved Rose.

Fighter Command lost four aircraft, but the balance for the day was worse for the Luftwaffe, suffering twenty losses.

That evening, after dinner, following the usual rough and tumble, the pilots of Excalibur squadron elected to spend their evening at the local watering hole in Foxton.

The Horse and Groom had a long association with the aerodrome, and the Inn, once a favourite of the famous highwayman Red Tom, was now proud of Tom's flying successors.

The old landlord, an ex-RN sailor named 'Jack' Ayres, always welcomed the men and women of RAF Foxton with open arms.

His old pub was decorated with memorabilia from Ayres's time in the Navy, a few mementoes of the time when Red Tom had frequented the locale, and more recently with photographs of RFC and RAF fighters and squadron members, past and present. The propeller of an

Avro 504 was nailed above the great fireplace. The place had a long association with the men and women of the air force.

Feeling comfortably full with meat pie and vegetables, the bruised and battered pilots piled into two cars. Rose wavered a little at seeing the way the cars were overloaded, but a wink from Smith made him forget his worries, and he pushed himself aboard with a shout, placing an elbow accidentally into Billy's side. Billy yelled in turn.

They were in Fellowes' dented Bentley, a vehicle that came with a questionable past, "Won it in a poker game, old boy. Don't worry; I let him keep his shirt." A thoughtful look, "Had his trousers, though."

As the cars strained their way haphazardly down the winding lanes, they sang a number of bawdy songs, as well as a few recent hits. It had been a day with no action, but plenty of tension, and the pilots were full of energy.

Just as they were beginning the final chorus final line of 'Lords of the air,' they pulled into the courtyard of the Horse and Groom.

Amongst the irreverent it was otherwise known as the 'Nag and Bone,' mainly because the picture of the groom on the sign depicted a rather strange looking cadaverous creature standing beside the horse.

Old Jack affected not to hear the name given to his establishment whenever within earshot.

Other parked vehicles included an RAF station car and a three-ton lorry. The RAF presence was already there in force.

Catcalls and hisses greeted their entrance, as some of the Spitfire boys of 97 welcomed them in.

Some of them shifted to allow the newcomers in. Rose noticed that there was a fair smattering of young WAAFs present too. His face reddened as one caught his eye and held it daringly.

He continued on behind Smith and the others as they pushed their way through to the bar.

Behind the bar, Jack stood solid, built like the Rock of Gibraltar. Pink-cheeked, stout and with a broad smile on his round face he was the very epitome of a senior lower-deck Royal Navy rating.

He was talking affably with one of the two Sub-Lieutenants loaned to Excalibur Squadron by the Fleet Air Arm. Rose had spoken with one of them earlier, a young man of twenty called Grayson. He had told of flying the Skua in the Norwegian campaign.

Rose shuddered at the thought of having to fly such an obsolescent aircraft. He was now speaking earnestly with Jack.

"Lord knows what his real name is," muttered Billy under his breath, "everybody calls him Jack, but that's only because he used to be a Jack Tar."

On the wall behind the bar were a number of photographs showing destroyers dashing through the sea under thick black clouds of smoke. There were also some carved wooden models of sailing ships. Skeins of pipe and cigarette smoke hung heavy in the air, thick and torpid.

Standing apart from the others, Rose marvelled at the intricacy of the modelling. Each of the ships was fully rigged with cannon run out of tiny open gunports.

"These're what used to be called Frigates. The one you're looking at is a model of the old *HMS Arrow*. The old wooden walls of Nelson's time."

Jack had come across, and was watching him. He had seen Rose's interest in the models. His voice was placid and low, and Rose thought he could detect a Cornish accent. He reached up and brought down the model for Rose to hold.

"Here, take a look at that." His hand was huge and rough, but he handled the little ship tenderly. "She was a 32-gun ship. Her descendants of today are destroyers. Like the ones that captured that Jerry supply ship, *Altmark*, in Norway a little while back."

145

He regarded Rose with curiosity. "You boys don't usually take such an interest in the Navy."

"Oh, my maternal grandfather was a Captain in the Navy. He died a few years ago."

Grandpa Arthur, who treated his grandchildren with the same discipline and firmness as his matelots. A scowl or a sharp word from him turned the blood cold. Rose handed the model back to him carefully.

"But a life in the air force was the life for you, eh?"

Rose grinned, "Well, the thing is, I read all the W E Johns novels," he had read every Biggles novel he could find, "But, I also get seasick." He grinned again.

"Well I hear you've already given the old Hun a bit of a bloody nose. So the next drink is on me." Jack replaced the model back on its plinth, and then pointed at a black and white photograph.

"This was one of the ships I served on during the war. The last lot, that is," He smiled fondly, "She was the HMS Lizard, when we were in the First Destroyer Flotilla at Jutland."

Rose peered up at the smudged picture. The ship was just a grey shape in the dimly-lit inn, but to this proud old man she had been a home. As his eyes focussed, he picked out the long lean shape at anchor. Her upperworks were mainly a bridge superstructure, three funnels, and deck gun, whilst flags waved gaily from the mast.

Men were waiting for drinks and the barmaid was rushing from one to the next, but Jack did not seem to care.

"That was a terrible day, that was," Jack seemed faraway. "There were great ships wherever you looked. Blowing the living hell out of each other. Ships just blew into tiny little pieces, took all their crews with them. The smoke was so thick at times you couldn't see a thing, just the flame from the muzzles, and that awful ripping sound as the shells would pass over us. One fell short, near us. Fair shook us up, that did." He cackled. "That could have been it for us, but I'm still here. A lot of good lads weren't so lucky."

Rose's glass was empty. "I'll get you that other drink. Mr Rose is it?"

"Please, Jack, call me Harry." The other beamed and turned to his bottles. "I'm busy boys; Mabel will take care of you." He called to the pilots lining the bar. They groaned out aloud. Mabel's lips turned down, and she shook her head. Denis shouted, "Come on, Jack, I'm one of your heroes. Give me a pint, mate!"

Jack just waved at him as he poured another drink for Rose.

Rose leaned against the bar and looked around. He noticed the WAAF still staring at him over the rim of her glass. Her eyes glinted across the packed room, and he looked away again hurriedly. She was really pretty, but she was not alone. Luckily (for Rose, at least), her companion, a pale flying officer, had not noticed him looking.

She had shoulder length wavy fair hair, bright eyes and very red lips. Had she been on her own, and shown him the same interest, Rose may very well have gathered up his courage and made his way over to her.

But he had no intention of competing for her interest whilst she had a burly beau in tow, besides he did not want to create a feud between 97 and Excalibur. Or, rather, be on the receiving end of a thumping. They all had to share the same aerodrome, after all.

But he was quite tempted.

She was really, really pretty.

"Here you are, lad. Have a sip of that." Jack placed the cold glass down before him.

Billy was being held upside down by a couple of boys from A' Flight, Carpenter and Renfrew, as he tried to 'walk' across the low ceiling, tracing the path of a trail of ink marks that looked strangely like feet on them. His foot caught one of the beams, and he 'tripped,' losing what precarious balance he had managed to achieve.

The three of them collapsed in a jumble of arms and legs, to catcalls and howls of the onlookers. Rose leaned forward anxiously, but the three got to their feet, Billy nursing his head, but raucously demanding a pint and medical attention.

"That Billy, he'll do himself a mischief one of these days," sighed Jack affectionately. "Here, Harry, you ain't the sort who does all that sort of stuff, are you?"

"No, Jack, that's not me, really. Sometimes I think I must be in the wrong place. The boys are quite crazy sometimes, and I think I'm a bit too boring."

Jack placed his hand on Rose's forearm, "No, son, you may be quiet, but we all go crazy sometimes. When you feel it, you be crazy, but when you don't, you stay as you are. I've seen all sorts of crazy, so I know boring ain't bad at all. You're alright, you are." He squeezed gently.

"Cripes, Jack, you telling poor old Harry all your war stories again?" Smith placed his pint glass on the bar next to Rose's drink, peered myopically at the drink in Rose's hand. "Oh, dear. I see you're drinking some of that weak piss again. Jack, be a dear and get our Harry a pint of something manly. You need something a bit stronger to last through our Jack's tales of Jutland."

Jack shook his head mournfully. "Ah, Granny, I dunno what we're going to do with you, lad."

"Just keep pulling the pints, Jack, and you'll not go far wrong." Smith winked at Rose, "You could let Harry tell you one of his own war stories, too."

Another sing-song had started; Smith patted his shoulder kindly, and winded his way back through the crowd, singing at the top of his lungs in a wicked high falsetto.

Rose smiled fondly. It was amazing how Smith had become so much more approachable since the end of his 'training' period.

The heady mixture of alcohol, cigar, pipe and cigarette smoke and the warmth of the pub were making his eyes smart, so he raised his glass to Jack, and made his way to the side door. "I'll be just a moment, Jack."

His host cackled and made a shooing motion with one hand. "I'll tell you about my time on the China station when you get back, lad!"

Outside, it was cool and fresh. The sky was partially cloudy, but a patch was lit up by the moon, brilliant white in the darkness. He gazed at it. How clean and pure it looked, just as it had looked on that frosty night when he had been unable to sleep at the O.T.U.

Across the channel there would be Germans who must surely be enjoying that very same sight at this very instant.

Did they wonder about what must come tomorrow, as he did?

He stood for a moment, comfortable in the darkness, enjoying the muffled sounds of the men and women inside, tunelessly murdering a song in the inn.

The voices lingered hideously over a particular note. Rose fancied he could hear Smith screeching above the rest, and laughed quietly to himself.

"It is pretty awful, isn't it?"

Startled, Rose dropped his glass. It hit the edge of the wall with a sharp *crack!* Like the retort of a pistol shot, making him jump a second time. Then the pieces smashed into the ground, shattering and flinging shards of glass everywhere, and lemonade splashed against his feet and legs. It was so loud he imagined the sound in the inn checked for an instant, before continuing unabated.

For a second, unexpectedly, the image of his first Messerschmitt 110 surrounded by the golden, coruscating cloud of splintered glass appeared in his minds-eye. He shook his head to dispel it.

"Oh, I'm sorry; I didn't mean to startle you." The girl standing nearby spoke calmly. "It's just that I've been standing out here for five minutes, to escape that awful hullabaloo inside." A low throaty laugh, she paused, then, with concern, "I say, are you quite alright?"

The unexpected sound of her voice struck him dumb, and for a moment he could only stare mutely towards her.

In the darkness, his unaccustomed eyes could just make out a dark shape leaning against the darker wall, just beside the door. He must have just brushed past her as he had stepped out.

He had not even noticed her.

A thought struck him. It couldn't be the girl who had been staring at him so openly earlier, could it?

Oh My God. What do I do?

At last, he found his voice.

"Oh, uh, I didn't realise anyone else was out here." His voice sounded high-pitched. He made an effort to deepen it. "It was a little stuffy in there, so I thought I'd nip out. I was just enjoying the night air."

It couldn't be that little WAAF. He was certain she had still been sitting amongst the crowd of pilots when he had come out.

The singing inside suddenly stopped. The sudden quiet was deafening.

"I know. Me too. It's awfully poky in there when all the boys decide they need a bit of watering, and pile in together." She breathed in deeply, "And it's dreadfully smoky too."

The shape moved as the girl came closer, "So its evens as to whether or not you're going to get crushed first, or pass out from the noxious atmosphere."

He could sense her smile, "Perhaps I should have brought my respirator, but it's just so tiresome carrying that blessed box everywhere."

150

Despite the moonlight, she was still in shadow, and he could just make out her trim figure, a pale oval that was her face. Not wishing to seem to stare, he averted his eyes.

It was quiet behind them, and then the singing began again, interspersed with the tinkle of glasses and the occasional shout or laugh.

They stood in companionable silence for a while. They were so close that Rose could smell her perfume, and he found it far more enjoyable to the sweet fragrance of the honeysuckle in the air.

Mixed with the alcohol of her drink, it was a heady mixture, and he felt positively light-headed.

And tongue-tied.

Curse it! I need to say something witty and clever before she decides I'm a dense troglodyte and goes back inside.

Think, think!

What was that certain something about ladies that turned him into an awkward, speechless, red-faced idiot? When he most wanted to seem humorous and interesting, he could only behave like a brainless dollop of a schoolboy.

As he was searching frantically through his mind for something special to say, she broke the silence for him.

"I saw that you were looking at the sky. The moon looks lovely tonight, doesn't it?"

Ah! "Oh yes. I love the way the moon illuminates the clouds up there. When it's bright and cold, like tonight, the clouds look like frosted patterns on a clean, clear sheet of glass." The words rushed out, like an unstoppable flood, "Like a painting really, thin, milky skeins stretched taut across a dark canvas."

Oh God. He cringed inwardly at his words. Say something, something else, for goodness sake, before she falls asleep listening to you. "It's strange."

151

"What is?" She asked.

"Oh, I just think it's funny that the light makes everything look so different. Different and quite strange sometimes. I wonder sometimes what it would be like to look at the earth from the moon. What a sight that must be!" His voice took on wistful tone, "Perhaps there is someone up there looking at us?"

Oh no! *No!* This conversation was going rapidly downhill! He sounded grave and dull, *boring*, not like a proper fighter-pilot at all. He should be standing there shooting a line to her. He winced silently.

"Oh, I see that you must read some of those stories about life out there in space."

She sounded amused and he felt like a bit of a chump.

"Well, I like to keep an open mind. There're so many stars up there. I've always wondered what the world must look like from a distance. It must be a grand sight." He said it defensively.

"I've never met a pilot who was a dreamer before. You seem very philosophical."

"Just a few careless thoughts," He turned to look at her, "Sorry. You did ask."

"Indeed." she agreed, solemnly. They lapsed into silence again. It seemed that his usual ineptitude was in the ascendant. He sighed sadly.

Behind them the door creaked open. They turned. Outlined in the light was the slight figure of a girl, the light making her hair a golden-red halo. He could not see her face, but he knew at once that it was the little WAAF. She stood there for a moment, looking at the two of them, said "Oh" in a surprised sort of way, then turned on her heel and walked back inside, the door partially closing behind her.

"Oh dear. I think poor Janet may have wanted to speak to you. I rather seem to have queered her pitch. What a shame." There was no regret, and there was still that note of underlying amusement in her soft voice. He reddened again.

So he'd managed to bore this one and alienate the other. Well done, Harry, lost two girls in just a few minutes. Must be some kind of a bloody record. You can shoot down Jerry, but you're a dead loss with the fairer sex.

Useless.

He cleared his throat to cover his embarrassment. The door was still a little ajar, and the light from it fell on them.

He looked at her, seeing her properly for the first time.

Wow!

She was the same height as he, and large brown eyes gazed warmly back at him from beneath arched eyebrows and a fringe of dark hair. She had high cheekbones and full red lips that appeared almost black in the faint light.

Very welcoming, smiling sensuous lips, a long shapely neck. He felt his heart flutter ridiculously in his ribcage. Like Janet, the girl before him was a WAAF as well, and she was lovely.

Really, really lovely.

The corners of those lips turned up even more than before in amusement.

"Don't you think you should close it?"

Was he standing there with his mouth open like some thick dolt? Dear God!

"I beg your pardon?" he managed to stammer.

"The door," she pointed, "Don't you think you should close it? I'm sure Jack wouldn't like it if some German bomber decided to bomb him. The Inn isn't really an important military target, although I think the pilots in there may disagree. Nonetheless, I would prefer not to have a bomb fall on me tonight, I must say."

At last he understood what she meant. The blackout! He rushed to close the door. The stream of light was extinguished. He was going to say that he could not hear any aero-engines, so there was probably little danger, but thought better of it.

She sighed. "Much better."

The light had shown that she had rings on her sleeves, and that she was an officer, although he couldn't remember seeing her at the aerodrome. He realised he hadn't introduced himself. "I'm Rose, by the way." Should he offer her his hand? He decided not to.

"Yes, I know. Pilot Officer Harry Rose, isn't it? You're from Excalibur squadron, aren't you? A'Flight?"

"Why, yes." He was surprised that she knew of him.

"I've heard a lot about you from some of your friends. They think very highly of you, you know, although they're always grousing about how you never come here for a drink with them. They say you never get drunk, and they're always joking that they can't understand how you passed out as a fighter pilot."

How could he explain his aversion to drink? She had never seen his father late at night, drunken, to dull the pain and the memories. He could never drink so.

She spoke into his uncomfortable silence, "I heard you were successful a couple of days ago." She had heard of him! Good Lord!

"May I congratulate you on your victories?"

"Thank you." He hesitated, then, "Actually, I feel a bit of a fraud. I was lucky to get the first one. I got a bit excited, peppered him, and then lost sight of him. I didn't realise he had gone down until I got back, and the second one went in only when Sergeant Carpenter shot him down. Everything happened so quickly."

"Not quite what I heard, but, whatever happened, you must have kept your head, acted the way that you needed to at the right time.

The attacks you made were successful, and, in the end, that's what counts, isn't it?" her head tilted questioningly.

He blushed at her words, nodded in response.

"In the end, it doesn't matter how you did it, the important thing is what you achieved." She sighed again. "We watch you and all the others go up every day, and we know that you're all up there to defend us, and I can think of no nobler duty than the defence of this green and pleasant land and its people. I wish I were up there with you all, too."

She took a sip, and her glass glinted, the drink inside like quick-silver in the moonlight. It was delightful even just to watch her take a sip.

"Of course, we're all are doing our own bit, but you are the tip of the spear, so to speak." She laughed, "I'm sorry to sound so awfully serious, but you aren't full of bravado, like some, quite the opposite, in fact, so I feel I can speak quite candidly to you. I hope you don't mind my speaking so?"

"Erm, no." He mumbled. I'm just happy you're talking to me, he thought, gratefully. You could be giving me a meteorological report or reading out your shopping list. I'd still listen raptly to your lovely voice.

They sat there quietly for a moment. He was embarrassed by her words, and she seemed a little embarrassed by them as well now, but she had spoken sincerely, and had obviously meant every word.

He also felt pleased, and flattered. He had to say something, but what? He cleared his throat.

"Can I get you another drink, Miss, um...?"

"I'm sorry, how terribly rude of me. I'm Flight Officer Digby to my girls, but my friends call me Molly." She turned to face him, as he shifted uncomfortably. Flight Officer!

That was the same as Flight-lieutenant, if his hazy recollection of WAAF officer ranks was correct.

She was his senior officer.

"Oh dear, maybe I should have saluted you, or something?"

"We'll overlook the serious lapse in regulations this time, seeing as you shot down those German's yesterday," she said lightly.

"And, now that we've met, I think we can safely say you're a friend, so you'd better call me Molly. But what should I call you? Harry, or would you prefer Pilot Officer Rose?"

Molly!

What a lovely name.

He wished that there was more light, to see her better again.

"I'd be very pleased if you'd use my first name. The boys have a number of names for me, most of which I'd never dream of repeating to you, but most of 'em call me by my first name."

"So Harry it is, then. And, in response to your question, yes, I'd like another drink, a small gin, please." She laughed again. It was lovely, a light thing of dancing beauty, "You had better get yourself another drink, too."

"Yes, you took me rather by surprise, then. I thought everybody was inside," he said ruefully, as he gingerly took her glass, revelling in the momentary contact of their fingers. His heart was still racing.

"I better tell Jack about the pieces of glass out here." He pushed the pieces near him carefully to one side with his shoe. "Would you like to come back inside, or shall I bring it back out here?"

He looked back at the building, "It seems to have got a little bit quieter in there, now." Whilst they had been talking, the din inside had lessened. The sounds within the inn were now somewhat muted in comparison.

As if to make the lie of his words, there was a loud crash inside, followed closely by the tinkle of a glass or two shattering, amidst laughter and shouts.

"I'd prefer it out here, please, Harry. It's pleasant to chat in the night air. I'm not really one for parties, and the boys are getting a little carried away in there. Sounds more than a little wild, to me. Besides, you can tell me more about the Messerschmitts you shot down? I'd love to hear about them."

They smiled conspiratorially at each other in the darkness.

Inside, the party was in full swing. A gaggle of pilots were wrestling weakly on the floor, drenched with beer, whilst Billy was still nursing his head over a pint. Amongst the crowd he picked out Granny, who was sitting amongst a bunch of giggling WAAFs. He seemed to have lost his trousers. It was hard to associate this pilot with the vacuous grin, and his shirt tails hanging ridiculously around his skinny pale legs, with the hard-eyed man whom he had greeted just over a week ago. Granny waved to Rose.

"Harry! Get your worthless carcass over here." He slobbered cheerfully, "I've saved a girl for you, her name's Sue and she loves fliers, even old dull stick-in-the-muds like you! Get yourself a decent bloke's drink, then plant your bottom down here!" Sue simpered and waved at him.

Rose waved back, continued to make his way to the bar for their drinks. The little fair WAAF, Janet, pointedly looked the other way as he passed.

Jack was grinning at Granny. "'Strewth! For Gawd's sake, Granny, put them flippin' knobbly knees away, 'else I get 'old of old Bill to cart you orf for lewd conduct!"

Rose held out Molly's glass, "Jack, may I have another Lemonade, and a small gin too, please."

Jack took it and grinned at him. "A lady already, eh, George? My, you're a fast worker. You sure you're not a sailor?" He winked salaciously, then leaned closer and lowered his voice conspiratorially, "Looks like I'll have to save my China station stories for another time. She's a very nice girl, is Molly, my lad. Just right for a fine lad like yourself."

Rose flushed in embarrassment, "Just a friendly drink, Jack." He cleared his throat, "I'm afraid I broke one of your glasses outside, though. I'm terribly sorry. Perhaps I could brush it up for you? Could you give me a dustpan and brush?" on the far end of the bar three tiddly Spitfire pilots (one wearing a WAAF's cap back to front) were slapping the bar counter, "Come on Jack. We need more beer!" they started to sing, "Come over here, we need the beer, we need your beer, without our beer we're feeling quite queer, so come on Jack, come over here…"

Jack ignored them, instead favouring Rose with another wink, "Don't you worry, son. I'll brush it up in the morning. It's been a quiet night. The lads are behaving themselves at the moment. You should see how this place looks after the boys have had a good party!" he shook his head, rolled his eyes, "Heaven help us!"

Chapter 12

Rose felt as if a ton of sand had been poured onto his eyes. They felt itchy and gritty. His mouth was dry, and his muscles ached abominably. He longed to put back his head and close his eyes.

The sun was shining bright here, high above the fleecy white clouds that stretched out cleanly before them. He was callsign Slipper Two of a flight of two, on an interception of an unidentified trace.

It had been four days now, since the fight with the Bf110's.

The squadron had taken part on more patrols, although the weather had not always been on their side, and more than once they had been stood down.

He had not seen any action since, although there had been more than one opportunity.

Which was just as well, as he could not keep the girl with the dancing brown eyes and lovely smile out of his thoughts. He had spent an hour chatting with her that night, magically becoming more at ease as they had talked, revelling in sound of her voice, the delightful sound of her light but throaty laugh. He had been too shy to ask her out when a cheery Granny had come for him, grinning foolishly, but she had given him a beautiful smile, and touched his hand in parting. Murmuring "Au revoir, Harry..."

Until next time. He smiled wistfully at the memory.

Today, Smith, with Rose as wingman, had been vectored onto what they would find to be a lone, low-altitude reconnaissance Heinkel that had first been reported by a motor launch, and then spotted by the Observer Corps.

They flew tensely, each of them hunting vainly for the first sight of the bomber, but the cloud cover was thick, and could have hidden a squadron of bombers.

He tried not to think of the lovely WAAF officer he had shared such a short part of that evening with, tried to concentrate on the task in hand instead.

But it was hard, and she continued to return unbidden to his thoughts.

Molly was lovely, and like it or not, he was smitten. He wanted to get to know her even better, despite his feelings that such a relationship was not a good idea for a single man in wartime, when death was always so near.

He wanted her. Even though she was senior to him.

Anyway, there was so little free time available to get to know her in.

He must stop thinking about her. What could she ever see in him, anyway? It was just a pipe dream.

Granny always emphasised the importance of single-minded concentration. The slightest lapse could mean death.

He sighed and cast his eyes around for the umpteenth time.

Nothing, and clear behind, above and all around (Thank God).

The sector controller directed them in cool, measured tones, like one of the commentators on the BBC.

He was very efficient, and continued to guide them as they searched. He did not seem impatient as they struggled to see the invisible enemy.

They had gone up to fifteen thousand feet, down to nine, and then back up, to eleven. The controller had continued guiding them.

But, like so many times before, the bandit was evading them. Was it to be another frustrating and fruitless interception? They had had two like this yesterday, once while on escort duty.

Smith was about to turn for home when his eye caught a flashing glint of light. Sure enough, it was the Heinkel, flitting from cloud to cloud like a little fat beetle scurrying from stone to stone, two miles from them, at the same height and heading south-west.

Granny had seen it too. With a terse, "Enemy at two o'clock, Tally-Ho!" Smith opened his throttles, so that smoke trailed thickly from his exhausts. His Hurricane shot forward and Rose worked to remain close.

They closed quickly, but the bomber entered another dense bank of cloud and disappeared again.

Smith cursed over the R/T. "I'm going to follow him in, Harry. Climb and watch out for him from above and maintain the current heading." The other Hurricane entered the cloud about the same place as the Heinkel and disappeared as well.

Rather him than me, thought Rose, don't fancy flying around in thick cloud, playing hide and seek with a bloody fat Heinkel.

Rose flew on for a few minutes, straining to catch a glimpse of either of the two aeroplanes playing hide and seek in the clouds, whilst also anxiously watching for enemy fighters. The sun was perky today and made the clouds a brilliant white sheet. The glare was making his sore eyes hurt all the more.

Then, "Enemy in sight! Slipper Leader to Two, Harry come on down! The Heinkel's broken out of cloud and going down, heading one-twenty."

Why had he not stayed safely hidden in cloud? Must be bloody mad.

Half-roll, dive. Switch guns from safe to 'fire,' reflector sight on. Aiming dot and circle appear as if by magic before him. Open throttle, increase oxygen flow, all done automatically. Descend at an angle to the enemy's heading, join up when everybody's in clean visibility.

Heart racing, try to slow it.

Vision greys as the forces strain against him. Cloud rushing up to meet him, closer, closer, then diving through it, so that the sun and bright blue sky disappears and the world becomes a limbo of milky emptiness. He felt so alone there, as if there was nothing else outside, just beyond his canopy.

Merlin engine running smoothly, propeller slicing through swathes of cloud, finger caressing the gun button gently, and then out of cloud again, out of the whiteness, into a duller, greyer world.

Cloud below and the sea above him now, grey and fitful. Roll right way up, check behind, all clear, now, where's Granny? Keep a look out for him...

Turn, turn.

Rapid check all around, no sign of him, nor of the Heinkel.

Bollocks! Where on earth were they? Had he kept to the correct heading? Yes, the instrument still read one-twenty degrees. So where were they? He muttered fretfully. Calm, calm, look again. Careful check, look, look.

Yes! A dark grey shape sliding down, another, smaller one above, turning. Quick! Catch up, full throttle. Enemy not trying to evade, just diving at full speed. Trying to get away. Granny turning for another attack.

No enemy fighters, yet. Range closing rapidly, standby.

"Slipper Two attacking," he called. He had built up his speed in the dive, closing in behind quickly, pull up a little, stay behind and below, keep the tailplane between himself and the dorsal gunner. Stay out of his line of fire. A wide shape, two propellers spinning, wings sweeping back.

Damn! A line of tracer. Bloody ventral gun! Hunch down, grimace behind goggles and facemask. Concentrate on the shaking image of bandit in the GM2 gun sight. The forces of the dive pressed him back into the seat.

The enemy fire curved away uselessly to one side.

In range, get closer, closer.

There! Seeming to fill his windscreen, enemy bomber swollen and dark, evil and insectile. Enemy gun flashing but no hits.

Press the 'tit' and the eight Colt-Brownings roar out their song of anger. The Heinkel blurring before him.

Careful. Correct for deflection.

Acrid cordite smoke penetrates the facemask, dry throat hurts all the more, and eyes smart despite the goggles.

Kite vibrating wickedly from the recoil, but his aim was true, there, the sparkle of hits, clustering around the starboard engine, wingroot and fuselage of the Heinkel.

Leaden hatred hammering into the enemy.

There! A trace of smoke, streamer of fire from the Daimler-Benz DB 601A-1 engine as the starboard undercarriage falls out and hangs uselessly, tyre spinning listlessly. Pieces of German aeroplane spinning past.

Eyes suddenly watering and still smarting.

No enemy fighters, clear sky around and behind clouds too far for safety.

He was engulfed by the sudden black cloud that billowed out of the engine, recoiled with shock as it leapt back at him, like a hungry beast. He could smell the hot, choking, bitterness of it.

For a stunned second he could see nothing, trapped in the darkness that was to be the bomber's shroud, and then he had burst through back into the light.

Pull up, up! Fire again, hits on the enemy fuselage, sparkling on the dorsal gun position. Almost strike the tailplane? No, loads of room, could drive a bus through that!

The enemy bomber flashed past beneath him, a streak of dark grey and green, tracer from the dorsal gunner's MG15 reaching out, far behind, it's alright, no danger. Three thin yellow bands painted on the starboard wing.

Strange markings, wonder what they mean? Section leader perhaps?

Eyes still smarting, filling with tears. Blink rapidly to clear them.

Heinkel disappears in an instant behind him. The enemy gunner doesn't manage to connect with Rose, thank God!

Clear in front. Where's Granny?

Turn hard, keep out of field of fire of the front MG gunner. Careful, careful.

"Good shooting, Slipper Two!" Granny calling.

Where is he, watch out for him.

Rear-view mirror.

No enemy fighters? Good. Must keep looking.

Keep turning. Line up for another attack.

Twist around.

Movement? No. Just shadows at the periphery of his vision. There would be no enemy fighters today to save the Heinkel.

It was far behind now, turning too, climbing now, desperately seeking sanctuary in cloud, thick smoke flowing darkly from one engine. Granny tucked in close behind, throttled back, raking the bomber mercilessly, burst after burst.

More smoke, and pieces of burning aircraft. The other engine begins to smoke. Fire streaming a searing yellow-white from both engines now. Undercarriage flops down, is he surrendering?

No. He's still heading for cloud cover. Have to attack again.

No enemy fighters.

Curving into the attack again. Cloud getting nearer, he's going to get away, hit him hard!

Jerry turning from Granny who curves smoothly away, desperate to escape, plan view of aircraft looming before Rose, press the trigger!

Another long four second burst, no return fire from dorsal gunner. Strikes on fuselage and tailplane. An aileron flaps, tears off and rolls away. Pieces whirl off into the slipstream. Bandit carries on flying, cloud very near now. He'll disappear into it in just a few seconds.

Wait. He's not climbing anymore. Starting to lose height now, turning slightly, fuselage and wings well alight, broad trail of dirty smoke marking his falling.

Granny, breathless, "Break off, Slipper Two, he's done for."

Turn away; get out of range of his MG15 machine guns.

No enemy fighters, sky all clear.

Throttle back, take deep breaths. Wet with sweat and tense.

Relax.

The Heinkel was falling now, uncontrollable and now unable ever to reach the cloud, both engines wrecked, the machine could take no more. The smoke was a long thick black trail now. A parachute blossomed, then another. White silk umbrellas drifting down.

They waited, but there was no sign of a further parachute.

Just two survivors from a crew of five.

A coffin for the dead members of its crew, the Heinkel dived a further thousand feet before the fire burnt through the main spar. The wings folded, and the remnants of the bomber fell vertically down. A molten pyre dripping fiery blobs, spiralling into the sea.

Above it, the two survivors hung disconsolately beneath their canopies.

But they had survived. They were the lucky ones.

"I'm alive." He had spoken out loud. "I'm alive," He said it so that he could hear it again, know that he was still there.

"Still alive." He was sopping wet.

"Well done, Harry, that's another one in the bag for us. There's a bit of gen that fat old Herman won't get his greasy paws on." Granny, laughing and still breathless. "That's another half for you, my old son. That one makes your score two. One confirmed, two shared. You'll be a hero soon, like me, though not as pretty!"

Another laugh, that sounded strangely like a sob, "I thought you were the bloody escort when you came down shooting out of that flipping cloud like God only knows what. You scared the hell out of me! I was about to clear off! Christ!"

A half share. Add that to one and a half, makes two. Two kills! Or is that one and two shared destroyed? All in just a single week of operations.

Who'd have thought it just a few weeks ago?

He almost felt like a veteran. And this time he had not felt the guilt, even as the Heinkel had fallen flaming straight down, the survivors to an uncertain and cold fate.

More dead by his hand. More empty chairs across the channel.

Just that fierce exultation again. The fire burning liquid through his veins. But there was a dark shadow of something still cast by it.

There was a pleasure coursing through him, he had defeated a deadly enemy, victorious in this duel to the death. He knew that the killing was necessary but it was undesirable.

There was no guilt, but still it did not please him to send men to their deaths. But it was necessary. It was his duty, an honour even.

He formed up on Smith's wing as the other broadcast news of the victory and giving a 'fix' of the location of the survivors for RAF

Search and Rescue. With a bit of luck the survivors would be picked up shortly.

They were still very close to the coastline; it was just visible as a dark line on the horizon, so they should be able to rescue the Germans before dusk. That's if the cold, hungry sea did not claim them first.

"Alright, Slipper Two, time to head for home. Jerry may have called for fighters, so I think we'd best make ourselves scarce." Granny paused, "I think he gave me a light peppering too. Doesn't look like he hit you at all, though, you lucky dog! Anyway, I've called for help and a launch for those poor devils should be here within twenty minutes, well before one of their own rescue planes. With a bit of luck, they're in the bag."

"Understood, Leader." Calm, professional. I'm alive, thought Rose, as he searched the sky endlessly with sore, slitted eyes.

Still alive. Thank you, God.

Chapter 13

A Bristol Blenheim IF fighter was in the circuit when the two of them returned from shooting down the He111 bomber.

There was a thin tenuous trail of smoke coming from one of its two Mercury VIII engines, and the dorsal turret was a ruin.

They waited as it made a perfect approach and just a slightly bumpy landing, before it taxied off the runway, followed by a fire tender and one of the station's ambulances, the huge red cross inside a white circle standing out on its' side.

Once the remaining propeller had stopped turning, two men stepped down from the aircraft, one leaning against the other, whilst the figures of the firemen, bulky in their asbestos suits, ran forward to douse the engine.

Rose was unaware of the slight, raven-haired figure watching him from a balcony on the HQ building, skirt whipping in the wind, as he came in to land.

She brushed the loose strands of hair from her eyes, and the wind promptly blew them back. For about the twentieth time that afternoon, she wished she had tied up her hair as she usually did whilst on duty, or at least worn her cap.

As if it could read her mind, the wind snatched off the cap of

Flight-Lieutenant Skinner, Excalibur's adjutant, who was standing below watching the aircraft, and with a mumbled curse, he scrambled to retrieve it.

She often stood here, when she had a few minutes, so that she could watch the fighters come in or take off. Whenever she could, she wanted to see the men and their planes returning after their missions. And now she watched the two Hurricanes as they lined up for their approach, now that the Blenheim was safely out of the way.

Bartle, the engineering officer called up pleasantly to her as he walked past, and she waved a friendly greeting. He was a pleasant man, always had a smile on his face, nice to everyone.

It was important to see them all, to see the individuality of the squadron. Most of the time when they were in the air, they were just represented by little red and black coloured numbers on wooden markers on the great table below. But they were men of flesh and blood.

For the umpteenth time she wished that she had an administrative duties job in the Ops control room, instead of the duties of code and cipher officer.

Her girls pushed them around like the counters of a children's game, but they represented real young men. Even now, most of Excalibur squadron was deployed on the table, called to intercept a convoy attack just when it had already broken up. There was no chance that Excalibur's pilots would get there in time, so they were returning empty-handed.

Conversely, Slipper flight had managed a successful intercept, and she was please for Rose's (and Granny's) success.

Another of the enemy that would not threaten Britain again. Once more, Rose had faced the enemy, and quite probably had killed again. How many had died this time at the hands of the quiet boy with the shy eyes that she found so fascinating?

For some reason that she chose not to examine too closely, it troubled her that he had been involved in the fight. More than when she heard the other pilots in an air fight. She was pleased for his success and his strength, but felt a strange disquiet that he'd faced danger.

She watched the second Hurricane side-slip as it passed over the boundary fence on its way in to land, undercarriage and flaps extended. The young pilot had pushed back his hood, and the bright silk of his scarf fluttered gaily, a cream and scarlet speck of cheer against the drably painted Hurricane. The prefix letter on the side read 'P.'

It was P-Peter, Harry's aircraft. It settled gently on the runway, and despite the distance, she thought she saw the tension in his posture ease, as if the very act of landing had released him, and he was finally able to relax.

But then, perhaps she had imagined it.

Her gaze followed him as he taxied to his pen, the breeze forgotten. On the far side the Blenheim boys watched his progress indifferently as they awaited transport.

Harry was quite different from so many of the others. She respected Granny for his honesty and decency, and could see that he too liked the young man. Something indefinable about him set him apart from the others.

It had been two days since they had shared that quiet drink outside the Horse and Groom, and she smiled at the memories, his bashfulness and at his obvious pleasure in her company.

He was so very shy, yet painfully eager to talk, those dark eyes so wistful.

In the little while that they had spent together, something had happened to her. It was impossible to explain, for he was much the same as those other young men, but somehow she could feel herself being strangely drawn to him.

She could not explain to herself the strange attraction, for he was no charmer, no silver tongued devil.

Just a boy, really, and so young! He must be at least five years her junior! Dear Lord!

What on earth had created this attraction (and it *was* attraction she felt, she knew) for this young man who, until quite recently, had been just a schoolboy? What had come over her?

During random moments of the day, whatever she was doing, wherever she was, thoughts of him would come unbidden to her mind. She would wonder about him. Just a mysterious young man, so serious and self-critical, sweet and shy, brought to this place from some unknown corner of the land to fight.

Her girls had noticed the occasional distraction of their Flight Officer at odd moments of the day, her momentary smiles at nothing at all, and already some were talking of Rose as 'her young man.'

She held tightly to the railing that ran around the balcony, idly picking at the flaking green paint.

The crew of the Blenheim were joined by some groundcrew, as they surveyed the damaged heavy fighter. Pilots of single-engine types of fighter did not envy them against the lighter, more manoeuvrable Luftwaffe fighters. The Blenheim was seriously unsuitable and hopelessly outmatched in daylight air combat.

Try as she might, she could not get Rose out of her mind. A wartime romance was not something she wanted, yet here she was.

She wanted to stay apart from the young men. It would not do to become involved with one of these boys, better to remain apart, remote. That way you could never be hurt if, or when…

But, there was that strangely compelling something about the gentle, thoughtful man she had met in the inn courtyard. Some

171

quality that made him so very different from the brash, loud young men with whom he belonged.

It was easier to be the distant, cool senior WAAF officer, feared by her girls, and respected by both the aircrews and groundcrews.

He had almost fallen over his own feet in his eagerness to get her that drink, and she had seen his face whenever he gazed at her momentarily. She had seen that gaze before, but the men in whose eyes she had seen it were usually bolder and confident. They usually had dead, cold eyes, or hot dangerous ones.

Harry's were neither. Instead, they had seemed softer, his gaze calmer. Less penetrating, less intrusive. He was just a boy, like all the others, yet not like the others at all.

Yes, there was something indefinably different about him.

Not a boy, though, but a man, she reminded herself sternly, he had already come face to face with death in the air. He had come to terms with his own mortality, risking death himself, and being responsible for the death of others.

And it was apparent from what she had just heard over the R/T, that he had just fought, killed and survived again.

But although he had done such things that made him a man, she knew that inside, the man and the boy were one and the same inside, and that this man/boy must face the daily trials and terrors of aerial combat, and also the awful yet necessary responsibility of fighting and killing.

She was so aware that she was older than he, goodness, so much older! But she felt like enclosing him in her arms and holding him tight against her. Dear God, It was ridiculous to have these silly, secret thoughts! This longing to take him into her arms should stay only as that, to run her fingers idly through his hair, a silly, secret daydream.

She pulled her hand away and cursed quietly. Her girls would have been amazed that she knew such naughty words. Though they'd not be shocked, they were a pretty worldly bunch and knew far worse ones, she thought affectionately.

A flake of paint had lodged under a fingernail and now dug deeply into the nailbed beneath. She pulled it out and sucked her finger, grimacing inwardly at the mixed metallic taste of the railings and of her blood.

She thought of his strong hands. When she had shaken his hand the dry firmness of his grasp, and the warmth in his eyes, had awakened feelings she did not think she had.

The passing contact had made her heart beat faster, like a silly schoolgirl's, and she had felt mildly irritated and surprised that she would feel like this when she prided herself on her usual calm reserve and self-control.

The hands that had once flipped through history texts or logarithm books now directed his fighter plane. She felt he was like a modern knight on his trusty warhorse, eight .303's his lance, fighting an honourable fight.

And now she wanted those hands on her.

She smiled for a moment at herself, and at her foolish thoughts. If the girls only knew their feared officer was such a romantic fool! It would not do for them to know she could feel like this.

She thought of how Dolly Atkins had stood waiting on the tarmac for Denis after that fight with the German fighters over the channel, and she had thought to herself, I'll never allow myself to become like that. Never allow myself to die a little bit at a time every time that special, treasured one is late.

Except now it seemed that it was not so easy to behave and think so.

Dear God, what was happening, *had* happened to her?

She could remember the look on Janet's face when she had made her way out that night.

Disappointment and surprise.

Janet was a good girl and a reliable one, but she was too kind, and her kindness extended to the pilots in more ways than it reasonably ought. She was far too fond of the boys. And from what she had overheard, Janet was excessively fond of more than one of them.

I must have a serious chat with her, she made a mental note. The poor girl would get a reputation if she wasn't careful (if she hadn't already).

Yet here I am, swooning over this young boy I've just met – what madness!

Harry had cut his engine and now jumped down from his Hurricane. She saw Granny Smith walk over and throw an arm around the young pilot, laughing.

Dear Granny, like an older brother, so protective, but he had spoken warmly of Harry when she'd asked about him during the enforced training all the new pilots had undertaken. Harry had been so absorbed in his flying he'd not really considered anything else, so he'd not really *seen* her when their paths had crossed a few times.

He really was shy.

Harry was grinning, and talking animatedly with his ground crew. The smiles on their faces were wide enough to see from here.

She had almost laughed out loud at his shocked expression when his glass had fallen and shattered on the worn flagstones outside the inn.

Looking for a brief moment as he did in the moonlight like a startled schoolboy caught stealing biscuits from the tuck shop, eyes wide and mouth open.

She laughed at the memory. He had been so disconcerted by her appearance that he had not noticed her own startled reaction when the glass had broken.

She had almost dropped her own drink at that moment, but the darkness had hidden her own momentary fright, and it had also allowed her to quickly regain her usual composure. Poor Harry, however, had been completely at sixes and sevens, totally off-balance.

How was it that a man could fly and fight with such boldness, wore the ribbon of the Air Force Cross on his chest, yet, when she stood talking with him, why did he become so shy and uncertain?

Which was the real Harry? Most of them were so full of life, raucous and high-spirited; both in the air and on the ground, although there was so much pressure on them to appear unaffected and urbane by the terrible experiences that they had to face each and every day.

She decided at that moment, as she watched his groundcrew pick him up, to get to know him, to find out what he really was like. There, it was decided, and bugger the bloody war. What mattered was now, not the future.

Somehow, he was special. And she'd bag him first.

Molly smiled at her foolishness, still watching Granny and Rose, at their horseplay and relief.

Just as she had watched his progress across to the bar that night, the quiet smiles in response to the banter, and seen how he had spoken so earnestly with Jack.

Jack had said afterwards to her that, "that Mr Rose was a proper gent, and anyway, 'is Gran-da' was in the Andrew, so he must be a good 'un."

The Andrew. That strange name that the lowerdeck matelots used when they talked of the Royal Navy. Jack would always be a sailor, to his very last breath, even when he was so far from the sea.

Skinner had pulled up in his car, cap firmly pushed down on his head, to take Harry and Granny for a debriefing of their combat with the 'spy,' and to file a report. They threw their caps gaily into the car, and clambered in, still laughing.

She had better get back down into the operations room, before the controller sent out a search party. Anyway, the girls seemed more efficient when they felt her frosty gimlet eye on them.

She wished that she could speak with Rose again, for they had not met again since that night outside the inn.

As they drove past, Rose looked up at the HQ building and noticed her. He gave her the thumbs up, and smiled hesitantly. His face was drawn and pale beneath the smoke stains, but his eyes were bright.

Her mind knew it must be because he had just been in combat, but her heart preferred to think it was because he was looking at her. She smiled warmly back, half raising her hand in greeting.

Harry turned his head so that he could continue to gaze at the girl.

The sight of the slim, raven-haired girl on the balcony above was a wonderful sight. Molly's shirt sleeves were rolled up above slender forearms, and her tie loosened, showing her smooth neck. The wind flicked lightly at her skirt to show her smooth knees and calves tantalisingly. His eyes lingered with pleasure.

The wind was in her hair, and had blown it awry, but even being windswept, she was truly lovely, and the beguiling smile on her face made her lovelier still. He found that he was staring, and dragged his eyes away from her, embarrassed that she must have caught his gaze on her body.

She could not have smiled that lovely smile for him alone, surely? He looked surreptitiously at Skinner and Smith. Perhaps she had been smiling at one of them?

What could such a special girl (and a senior WAAF to boot!) like that see in such a junior pilot officer like him?

His companions, however, did not seem to have noticed. Skinner was telling Granny about the alert that had called away the rest of the squadron.

He felt like singing with happiness, the recent combat with the Heinkel forgotten in favour of that beautiful vision of the girl.

She found herself still smiling back warmly. He really was very nice.

I *will* get to know him better.

Damn it, I will!

But nothing serious, of course. They could offer each other an escape from the harshness of their lives, and she really wanted to know him better.

After all, he could not be more than twenty, if that, whereas she was twenty-five last birthday. She felt old when she looked at him. He should have someone younger, more his own age. Like Janet.

She shook her head, smiled to herself.

No. Not like Janet.

Granny turned his head and saw her smile, and he smiled himself.

Hm. Harry was a saucy little devil. He's been keeping that close to his chest. Must be true what they say about still waters running deep. When Rose looked at him, he winked. Harry smiled uncertainly back, shifted in his seat, and then looked away, but a red flush crawled up above his bright scarf.

Smith pretended not to notice.

Little devil. Good luck to him. Molly really was a lovely girl, and he was such a sincere, decent lad, they were right for each other.

The Blenheim gunner sat on the grass, trying to smoke a cigarette and watching his pilot talking to the ground crew who had rolled up. He had a fresh bandage neatly tied around his left hand, but already it was soiled, a bright red smear of blood where the bullet from the

Bf109's machine guns had grazed him. The ambulance crew were seeing to the navigator. Poor old Duffin had got one in the leg, and it looked like it had shattered the bone.

The wound had made him retch, and now the acid in his emptied stomach churned.

When they had been in the air, he had lost all hope.

He had become convinced that they were going to surely die, that they had no chance. The two 109's had been playing with them, but the pilot, Mike, with judicious use of cloud, and some sharp moves, had managed to escape, and the enemy had been robbed of their prey. Mike had saved them from certain death.

He was trembling in shock, as he thought of the fight, of the minutes of terror as the enemy fighters had attacked again and again. Those few minutes had seemed like hours.

I'll never get into one of those things again, he thought. He pulled out his wallet and opened it so that he could look at the photo he had taken of his wife and child, in Clacton. His hand was shaking so much that he had to put it down onto the grass, so that he could see them clearly.

I'll fucking go to jail first.

A tear trickled unnoticed from his eye.

The pilot turned from surveying his once lovely aeroplane, to look at his dazed gunner.

Poor old Briggsy. He'd been a great gunner, but now he'd come to the end of the line. The bandit had not been able to badly hurt him, although his turret had been wrecked, but the experience that he'd just been through had finished him as a member of aircrew. He had lost his nerve completely, but he would make sure that no-one outside of the crew knew of the gunner's breakdown. He'd get him remustered without comebacks.

178

Yet who could blame Briggsy? He had escaped death only by a miracle. He did not want to tempt fate a second time, it would be crazy to.

When they got back to base later, he would do his best to get Briggsy transferred to ground duties. He would make sure that his friend kept his mind, and that his godson kept his father.

He looked enviously at the two Hurricanes parked nearby.

What I'd give for a chance to fly one of those gorgeous crates against the Hun. You had more of a fighting chance when flying against the 109's in one of those.

Perhaps he ought to try for a transfer onto one of the fighter squadrons based here?

Yes, he decided, time to apply again for a transfer to single-engine jobs. Fighters weren't designed to fight with two engines.

Duffin was not going to be able to fly for a long time now (if ever), and Briggsy was hopefully never going to have to fly again in operations.

So he was without a crew. It would help him to wangle a transfer to a single-seater squadron.

Anything had to be better than trying to take on the Luftwaffe in a fighter like the Blenheim IF. It was unlikely that she could fly far anymore anyway.

His A for Annie was a lovely aeroplane, but she was no fighter, and the six .303 machine guns she carried did not make her one.

It was madness to expect her to take on the roles expected of a fighter.

He made arrangements for the handling of his aircraft with the ground crew sergeant, whilst behind him the other members of his crew were carefully loaded onto the ambulance.

Make that application first thing in the morning, he decided.

There was no future in flying Blenheim fighters.

Chapter 14

Sergeant Kenneth Howes picked absent-mindedly at a shred of meat that was caught between his upper central incisors, scanning the sky around the Defiant carefully. As before, it stubbornly remained stuck between his teeth, continuing to resist all efforts to dislodge it.

Babs made a great meat and pickle sandwich, but he wished that she wouldn't use such a lot of cheap, tough cuts. They were playing merry hell with his dentition. He'd already had one of his molar teeth extracted after it had fractured on the tiny bone that had been in one of her Cornish pasties.

Barbara Howes (nee Garrett and curvy blonde Essex beauty pageant winner) and he had been married for all of a year, but what a year it had been! It had been the best year of his life.

The early afternoon sun shone down upon him in his machine-gun turret, and the intercom was quiet save for the occasional comment or direction from the formation leader or the ground controller.

On either side of his two-seat fighter, a further eight Boulton-Paul Defiants formed the formation on convoy patrol duty, south of Folkestone. With their impressive endurance and powerful turret armament of .303 Browning Machine guns, they had already achieved amazing successes against unsuspecting enemy fighters and bombers.

They shared many of the same characteristics of the other single-engined fighters in the RAF. Except, of course that there were no forward firing machine guns in the wings, and it carried over a ton of extra weight with the turret and gunner.

German fighters, expecting an easy kill when bouncing the Defiants (thinking them to be Hurricanes or Spitfires), ended up getting a nasty surprise when the rear-facing Browning's blew them out of the air.

Howes had already shared in the destruction of a Bf109 and a Dornier 17, and claimed a Heinkel 111 all of his own, and was looking forward to the next encounter. Having the triggers for four Brownings in his hands made him feel indestructible, and the palms of his hands were itching, hungry for action. Although Babs always said itchy palms meant he had money coming, "rub yer arse to make it fast," was another. He tried to reach back to rub his backside.

Carefully placed in the mechanism of the turret, the photo of Babs smiled sweetly up at him, wearing that ridiculous wide-brimmed hat that she loved so much.

Still twiddling at the piece of meat between his teeth, his eyes on Barbara's sweet smile, Howes didn't see the slim shapes as they came down out of the light.

The German fighters fell hungrily onto the Defiants, out of the glaring sun, like a pack of wolves.

One by one, they began to be shot out of the sky.

This time things were different, as the Bf109's were flown by pilots who were aware of the British fighters design, and keen to exact revenge for their many countrymen who had been lost to the Defiant.

They were careful to approach from the beam or head on as much as opportunity allowed, with high speed, slashing attacks. With no forward facing guns, the Defiant was particularly vulnerable to this type of attack.

And although the turrets swivelled desperately from one side to the next and back again, the gunners were unable to draw more than a momentary bead on the attacking bandits.

One Defiant whirled away from the formation, a blazing torch carrying two young men of Fighter Command into the darkness of death, whilst another was blotted out by a shattering explosion that left a few twisted pieces of metal, to drop away to the sea below.

In return, a single German fighter broke off the action and limped home, trailing smoke and a semi-conscious injured pilot.

Howes gripped his handles with tight claw-like hands and depressed the triggers as a Bf109 swept past. The turret vibrated with the recoil, and an enemy fighter flipped sharply over onto its back, and fell away with a white smoke trail streaming thinly behind. Perhaps the damage had been fatal, he thought and hoped.

"Two more coming from ahead and above, Kenny." The voice of his pilot, Pilot-Officer Newton was terse and strained.

Howes swung his turret, but the enemy pair split apart and dived away beneath the formation of Defiants, well before they entered the deadly envelope of the turret's arc of fire.

Fuck!

Another Defiant fell away, its wings shredded by bullets and cannon shells. Fire licked from it, curling back to swallow the rear half of the British aircraft.

Howes caught a glimpse of his friend, Ernie Dent fighting to get out of the rear turret before fire obscured him from sight.

He felt like retching and weeping as he turned to find a target.

What the fuck had happened? He couldn't draw a bead on any of the enemy fighters for longer than a couple of seconds before they were gone from his sights.

As it fell lower, a pair of Bf109s raked Ernie's Defiant again, setting off a series of small explosions. The black smoke became thicker and thicker, but a small figure fell away. Howes did not stop to watch the survivor, for already more German fighters snapped around them, and he and his squadron were fighting a losing battle, their numbers dwindling rapidly.

But even as the Defiants fought and died in the one-sided battle, reinforcements were on their way.

Hurricanes from nearby patrols were being desperately vectored on to the area.

Newton threw the Defiant away from the now seriously depleted formation.

They had to try and escape. Perhaps if they went further down, they would be able to protect their vulnerable underbelly. There was no chance that they could dogfight with the nimble little Bf109's.

There was no security now in the formation, anyway, there were too few of them, and the damaged aircraft straggled unprotected behind, easy pickings for the Jerry fighters.

Newton's Defiant spiralled downwards sickeningly, desperately seeking safety.

Howes was pressed forwards and sideways by the strong forces of the dive, head against the side of his turret, and he groaned involuntarily at the pressure. The world spun violently, faded, and his full stomach protested painfully. With the aircraft spinning like this, there was no chance that he could track the enemy kites with his guns. Every time he fired, he was just uselessly throwing away ammunition.

The delicious sandwich that Barbara had so lovingly prepared for him threatened to re-surface.

Bitter acid filled his mouth, and he spat out, the gobbet falling into the well of the turret, and onto his left flying boot.

He cursed foully, before his mouth flooded again.

Pilot Officer Michael Newton strained to look back over his shoulder, fighting against the g-forces. Behind them, yet another Defiant fell burning from the sky.

Already, some Bf109's had broken away from the main battle to pursue him. He could hear Howe retching over the R/T, behind him.

The airframe was vibrating, and the engine was screaming, yet he still continued to strive to lose more height. The sea was rushing upwards to meet them, but the only chance of survival lay in slipping away from Jerry at low altitude.

When he reached 500 feet, he levelled out, arms straining against the force of the dive, heart pumping fit to burst.

He breathed a sigh of relief once he had managed to get the aircraft back into level flight, but then he felt and heard the roar of the four browning machine guns behind him as Howe fired at the Jerry aeroplanes that came down towards them.

Desperately, Newton pulled the complaining Defiant into a series of turns to port and starboard, cutting as sharply as possible.

One Bf109, miscalculating it's closing speed, overshot and screamed past their wing, turning hard away. Newton instinctively swung around to follow, but then remembered that he had no forward-firing guns, and swore bitterly.

Ahead of them was the convoy they were supposed to be escorting. A pitifully small collection of coasters and trawlers that hardly seemed to justify the name.

But, at their head was a destroyer. And that meant anti-aircraft guns.

Newton pointed the nose of his aeroplane at the grey shapes ahead, pressed hard on the throttle lever again. Already the hope of salvation was germinating in his head. If he could use the protection of the destroyer's ack-ack, there may be a greater chance of getting away.

It was more than likely that the naval gunners were liable to fire upon the Defiant, but it was a risk worth taking if it scared off the Messerschmitts snapping away at his heels.

And in truth, there was no other realistic choice. Without some help there was little chance for survival.

So far, Newton had managed to evade the Jerry barrage, but with a Bf109 on either side and behind, the enemy had him boxed in. He continued turning and swerving, but they were closing his space for manoeuvre. It was just a matter of time before they nailed him.

High above, Hurricanes had arrived on the scene, and the Bf109's attacking the main Defiant formation were breaking off the action, well satisfied with the results.

Five Defiants had been ripped out of the formation, another was smoking and it looked as if it would be unable to make it back home.

Three, widely separated and rather battered looking aircraft were all that were left of the original nine-strong Defiant formation.

Donald, at the head of his squadron, gritting his teeth in frustration and fury as he led them in a fruitless pursuit of the departing German fighters, when Granny called out to him.

"Yellow One to Red Leader, looks like there's some trouble below." Donald looked downwards, and a flash of light from a turning aircraft below showed him where more aircraft were yet battling.

"Okay, Yellow One, I see 'em. Take your section down and see what's happening. Looks like these bloody Huns are going to get away, anyway. They've had enough already, those-er hum…' Then, mindful of the WAAFs listening, he fell silent.

"Understood, Red Leader, Yellow section, let's go."

Granny dipped a wing and dived down, closely followed by Rose and another new Sergeant-Pilot, Burton.

The Defiant was less than a couple of hundred yards off the port quarter of the destroyer *HMS Shilton* when a burst from the pursuing German fighters tore at the rudder, and smashed its way along the fuselage of the two-seat British fighter plane.

Howe was firing desperately, without sighting, and also looking fearfully at the oxygen bottle between his legs. If the bottle catches one...

The cannon shells and bullets burst along the aircraft and into his small turret. A bullet ripped through his sights and smashed its way between his upper central incisors, dislodging and pulverising the shred of meat that had bothered him so greatly scant minutes before. A second followed closely behind it.

The photograph of Babs fell to the floor of the turret, but Howe was past caring.

There was no pain, just the fleeting sensation of a sharp blow to his mouth before the sudden oblivion as the bullets exploded through the back of his head, heaving him backwards into death.

Newton did not see his young gunner fall back from his guns, but as they fell silent, his canopy was holed, and his instrument panel blown to scrap. The impact of bullets into his back threw him forward, painting the windscreen bright red with his blood.

He hung forward, pain and confusion blotting his thoughts, sucking in air painfully, his hands still tight on the control-stick, wondering why he could no longer see out of the cockpit, why the world had gone so red. Where was Ken? Nothing made any sense.

The mainspar broke, and the wings folded back, so that the faltering Defiant fell at full power in to the sea, blowing up as it hit. One second a well flown and lovely flying machine, the next a collection of shattered scrap metal.

Newton did not feel it, though, because he was already dead.

The men on the side of the little warship were soaked by the water thrown up by the explosion. Fragments of the wings and the still turning airscrew scythed in an arc over the forecastle, dangerously close, forcing the onlookers to duck.

The destroyer vibrated like a tin can as the shock-wave from the explosion slammed into it, threatening to cave in hull-plates.

Appalled, the gunners on the Destroyer, up until this moment shooting enthusiastically at both the RAF plane and the Luftwaffe fighters, stopped shooting as one.

All except for a light-calibre machine gun firing from the bridge.

Disdainfully ignoring the popgun firing defiance, the two Bf109's that had shot down Newton, swept low on either side of the *Shilton*, before curving up and away as they headed for France, their victim leaving only a subsiding and expanding circle of disturbed water. In seconds the wind had blown away the thin skein of smoke.

Behind and above in the diving Hurricanes, the pilots of Yellow section saw the Defiant go down, and raged ineffectually.

"The Navy shot down our kite," breathed young Burton over the R/T, horrified. And indeed, it did appear as if the ack-ack bursts peppering the sky around the British plane had plucked it from the air. Rose was silent with shock and sorrow.

"Yellow Leader to Yellow Three, shut up and stay in formation," Grated Granny coldly.

They shot past the convoy, and this time, the appalled naval gunners remained silent.

The speed of their dive allowed them to close with the fleeing

Bf109s, and Granny tried a testing burst at long range with his machine guns. Trails of smoke tore back from his guns.

They were just too far, although a piece of metal flicked from the hindmost 109, pirouetting and catching the light, but the enemy aircraft continued to fly as the pair put down their noses to take advantage of their higher speed in a dive.

Rose was keeping an eye for German fighters behind, when he became aware of a strange rattling against his Hurricane, like a sudden flurry of hailstones against a window pane. The thumping was against his wings, and he could see where a number of dents appeared on the wings.

Thinking they were under attack, he glanced again into his rear-view mirror, before realising the truth.

Spent cartridges and ammo links from Granny's machine-guns were streaming back from his wings, and into his path, so that Rose flew his Hurricane through a shower of small metal casings.

He grinned humourlessly under his oxygen mask at his foolishness.

"Break, Yellow!" The scream seared through Rose's ears, and he pulled back hard on the stick instinctively, kicking the rudder pedal.

Damn it! Bounced again! He hadn't even seen anything! Bloody useless wingman he was! They were being bounced by a second group of enemy fighters. Why hadn't Excalibur squadron called a warning?

The three Hurricanes broke away hard, splitting sharply from each other, Granny split-essing to face the new threat.

The sky immediately behind them was empty. They circled warily, but the feared Messerschmitts were not there.

"Who called out that warning?" Granny demanded. He was almost incoherent with rage.

The Bf109s, their pursuers checked, disappeared gratefully into the distance, until they were quickly swallowed up by the haze.

"Yellow Three to Yellow One, I did, sir. I was being hit, so I called out the warning." Burton sounded confused. His Hurricane turned slowly. Good lad, at least you've owned up.

"Did you see anything at all? Harry?"

Rose shook his head, "No, Yellow One, nothing."

"Where the fuck are they, then?"

"Yellow Three to Yellow One, no, sir. I just felt some hits on my Hurricane. I thought, I was sure, we were under attack." Poor Burton sounded close to tears.

"Those flipping Huns have cleared off as well, now, blast it!" Granny waggled his wings. "OK, can't be helped, form up Yellow Section, we'll re-join the squadron. Probably have to stay as escort until the relief for those poor sods in the Defiants turns up."

Then, ominously, "I'll speak to you later, Yellow Three, back at the 'drome."

Burton, you poor chap, thought Rose pityingly, I'll bet any odds the hits you felt were the same ones I did. Except we weren't under fire as I thought; it was only the spent cartridges from Granny's guns. I'll have a quiet word with you when we get back. If I say anything now, the boys will never let you forget it.

And Granny, red hot and denied vengeance, will string you up by your balls.

I'll bet those blokes in the convoy will be wondering what the hell was wrong with us, what the sudden aerobatics were all about, why we let the Jerries get away from us when we had a slim chance of getting even.

He scowled beneath his mask in frustration.

But then he remembered his own startled reaction when the phenomenon had occurred, the way his heart had beaten painfully by the sudden hail of shell cases, and he felt ashamed.

He, too, had almost called out that they were under attack. The tension of the past few minutes drained out of him, and he suddenly felt very tired, and horribly dejected.

Men in the same uniform as his had just died, he'd witnessed the deaths, and the killers had escaped scot-free from the wrath of the avenging Hurricanes. We let them escape.

Oh God. I'm sorry, chaps. We failed you.

Forgive us.

Forgive me.

Chapter 15

The next day brought a number of enemy raids against convoys and coastal targets, with the resulting give and take of successes and losses to both sides.

The squadron saw no combat, the flights of Excalibur Squadron taking part in just two uneventful patrols.

Rose, however took part in neither patrol, although his day was more eventful.

His faithful Hurricane P for Peter was in for maintenance, so he had to take up a newly delivered fighter, G for Gertrude.

Immediately following takeoff for the first patrol, the cockpit began to fill with petrol fumes, making him gag and his eyes water, despite his mask and goggles. He was about to call up the control tower, when a thin line of vile-smelling liquid suddenly began to spray out.

A thin stream hit him in the face, and he thanked his lucky stars that he was wearing his goggles over his eyes. Ever since the near-crash during training that frosty February, he always chose to take off and land with his mask and goggles firmly in place.

Just in case.

The fluid was squirting everywhere, soaking into everything, fumes filling the cockpit. He began to feel a little light-headed as he advised the control tower of his problems, and requested permission to land immediately, slowly and carefully pushing back his hood, and leaning forward into the slipstream.

He was eager to land, as he had heard all the horror stories of unexplained accidents and fighters suddenly blowing up in mid-air. The flame coming from the stub exhausts was terrifyingly close, and hurriedly Rose slid the hood closed again.

On landing once more (a very bumpy landing not up to his usual standard, but due more, in equal parts, to his eagerness to get back down and the sprinting of his heart), he immediately switched off his engine, rapidly made his way out of the aeroplane.

In close attendance were a fire tender and one of the station ambulances.

Rather than offering him reassurance, their presence only made him more nervous. When he gave them a thumbs-up, the ambulance crew seemed disappointed.

It transpired that the fitter for Gertrude had failed to correctly place the cap on the Hurricane's reserve tank, and that it had worked its way loose during the takeoff.

The station Medical Officer, Squadron-Leader Lamb, checked him over carefully, bathed his eyes (despite protestations from Rose) liberally with sterile water, made him swallow a dubious looking milky-white colloidal suspension ('Just to rid you of the sickness, laddie') that actually made him feel more ill than he had before, and confined him to bed in the Medical quarters for a few hours for observation.

Lamb was a large man, well-built with a ruddy complexion and a ready smile. He looked the very model of a typical rural practitioner.

More of a bull than a lamb thought Rose in irritation as he tried not to heave up the chalky slimy liquid that churned in his stomach.

* * *

Under the ministrations of a hard-faced male sick quarters attendant named Griffen, Rose found himself lying between stiffly-starched crisp white sheets, wearing only his socks and a gown tied up at the back, within an hour of landing Gertrude.

He itched to be allowed back into the air with a reserve machine, but they had been flying quite a few patrols over the last few days, and his body welcomed the chance of a rest, even though his heart ached to be with his squadron mates.

Forty-five minutes later there was a light tap at the door.

Rose opened his eyes, and there, at the door, was Flight-Officer Molly Digby. She was leaning comfortably against the door jamb, a slight smile on her lips, alluring and exciting and, oh, so very desirable.

His heart jangled inside him.

"Oh! Molly! How very lovely to see you."

Dear God, the beautiful girl was here, and all he wore was this monstrous diaphanous gown and his socks!

He cringed beneath the starched sheet, drawing it up to his chin protectively.

"Hello, Harry, I had a little free time, so I thought I would come and visit the wounded hero." She tilted her head quizzically.

He grinned foolishly at her. "Well, not really wounded, and hardly a hero, to be honest," he managed to mumble at her, his throat uncomfortably tight.

"Well, as you're not in uniform, we'll forget about the salutes." He realised he was almost naked, and he tried to pull the sheets even higher around him unobtrusively.

Dear God.

She smiled, as if she could read his mind. "I haven't had a salute from you yet. Honestly, standards are really slipping! I think I shall have to speak with your CO!"

She pulled off her cap, releasing her lustrous, shoulder-length black hair to swing delightfully into the light.

With one finger she tucked a swathe of hair unconsciously behind a small and delicate ear, exposing her slim, smooth neck.

Cor!

Just by looking at her, his senses felt sharper, heightened. The smell of steel and polish and ether seemed sharper, the brightness of the clean walls and surfaces even more so, the steel taps glinted sharply.

But he had only eyes for her. She was the glorious centre of the universe.

She sat down on the bed next to his, and her voice was serious.

"Honestly, though, I heard that you'd pranged, so I thought I ought to come and see you." She looked with concern at his reddened, sore eyes and pale, streaked face. "Are you alright, Harry? I must say that you look a bit, erm, peaky."

"Oh no," He said, "I hadn't pranged the kite. It just sprung a leak, so I had to pancake. The reserve tank on my Hurribag decided to empty itself into the office."

There. That sounded suitably *savoir faire*. He tried looking heroic, but it was difficult whilst sitting up in bed under a clean white sheet dressed in a gown that felt as if it were a frock (and not even a pretty frock).

"To be honest, Molly, the MO made me drink some appallingly obnoxious concoction, and I think it might be that making me look a bit peaky."

"I heard that you had been hurt. I thought I should visit."

"Oh no," he said again, "Not really. The MO thinks I may have had a whiff or two of petrol or glycol or something else like that. He thought I should lie down for a little while."

"Oh, perhaps I should leave you to rest for a little while?" there it was again, the concern in those beautiful brown eyes.

"Please don't, Molly, you really are a sight for sore eyes," he smiled self-consciously, "Quite literally!"

It was so difficult to reason with her being so near. The way her hair fell around her face was divine. A tiny pulse throbbed in her neck, and his heart seemed to beat in rhythm. In his peripheral vision he sensed rather than saw the firm lines of her slim figure, the curve of her hips, and his heart beat even faster. Easy, Harry, he thought, or else you really will need the doctor's care.

"You're staring, Pilot-Officer," she scolded, reprovingly.

Rose blushed again, looked down, rested his eyes on the delightful curve of her breasts, realised what he was doing and hastily looked back up again.

"Ah. Um, sorry, but the fumes made my eye water a bit. I have to focus on you, otherwise my attention wanders. Something to do with the fumes apparently."

"Hmm. I see." Her face was stern but her eyes sparkled. She reached behind her for the small wax paper wrapped package she had brought with her. He took the opportunity to run his eyes admiringly over her body.

I'm in love, he thought dreamily.

"Sorry, did you say something?"

Oh, Lord God! For one horrifying instant he thought he may have vocalised his thoughts.

"Perhaps this will help your poor eyes," She leaned forward, and held out…a carrot!

She wrapped up the package again, but not before he saw the sandwich that was the rest of her lunch. He reached out and grasped it, and for a second (oh, so short a second!), their fingertips touched.

He looked up, and saw that strange something sparkle in her luminous eyes too. Then she withdrew her hand self-consciously, leaving him clutching her carrot. He did not feel the dry, mottled surface of the carrot; instead he could only feel the warmth of her skin where she had touched him.

They were silent for a while, smiling shyly at each other. He racked his mind for inspiration.

He cleared his throat noisily. "Harrumph! Well, seeing as you've treated me to your lunch," He waved the carrot triumphantly, "Perhaps you'd allow me to take you out for a meal or a drink?" desperately, he pushed on, "Perhaps the pictures if you'd prefer?"

Damn my treacherous flaming cheeks! They must be glowing like a blessed beacon again.

Sitting up in bed, with his hair rumpled, streaked cheeks and his swollen eyes pleading, it was all that she could do to resist from wiping the thin smear of oil still on his forehead and hugging him.

She thought of the other young pilot, the one who meant so very much to her.

The young man who flew Hampden bombers at night to take the war to the enemy in his stronghold. She feared for Edward so much, and now she was allowing herself to make another young man important to her.

He saw the indecision in her eyes and mistook it for doubt, "Please will you come out with me Molly?"

Why did good young men such as these have to risk everything when their lives should be only filled with less dangerous pursuits?

Alright, I shall be your less dangerous pursuit, Harry.

So, despite her misgivings, she laughed and said, "Yes, that would be lovely. I'd love to go to the pictures with you. 'Wuthering Heights' sounds super, but I'm quite busy in ops at the moment, so maybe we can settle for lunch one day."

196

He smiled with such touching gratitude that she felt like smiling and weeping, she just wasn't sure which. He was just such a sweet boy, really, just like Edward.

She stood again, trim and smart, patted her skirt carefully. "I must be off. Otherwise they'll be calling for me over the Tannoy. I'm glad you weren't hurt, Harry. I think you're nice. When the MO releases you from this purgatory, come and see me. We'll have a cup of tea and see about having lunch together then, alright?" The sudden rush of words over, she turned to go, seemed to hesitate as if coming to a decision, and then reached into her tunic pocket.

"Here, Harry, I'd like for you to take care of this for me," amazingly, her cheeks coloured slightly, "A keepsake from me, a good luck charm, of sorts, to help you when you're up there." She pulled out a little teddy bear, smaller than her hand, and gave it to him.

"Her name's Genevieve. I've had her a long time, since I was small, and she's always brought me good luck. Hopefully she'll do the same for you." She smiled, "Please take care of her for me, and she'll take good care of you." she paused, "For me."

Rose held the little bear in his hand. It was a lovely little thing, only three inches high, and wearing a pink ribbon around her neck in a bow. It regarded him gravely with soft brown wooden eyes.

Still warm from having been in her pocket, a keepsake and lucky mascot that she had entrusted to him.

"But, she's wonderful, Molly, I don't know what to say...shouldn't you keep her with you? Are you sure-?"

But she had gone, leaving only the indentation of her bottom in the next bed, the memory of her warm brown eyes, and the faintest trace of the subtle fragrance that she wore.

He hadn't even asked her to stop for a cup of tea.

He hopped out of bed, one eye open for the orderly, and placed both hands, palms down, onto the faintly warm indentation left by her buttocks.

For a moment he allowed himself to imagine what it would feel like to cup those delightful buttocks in his palms (Gosh!), and then he sighed wistfully, and got back into bed.

He carefully placed the carrot and teddy bear under his pillow, then lay back and closed his eyes again. He tried to envisage Molly's lovely face in his mind. He would try and get some paper and a pencil later, try and draw her from memory.

Perhaps she'd let him have one of her photos?

"Are you alright, sir?" Griffen was regarding him suspiciously from the doorway. "Can I get you anything at all?"

"Yes, thank you Griffen. I'd be grateful if you'd get me a cup of tea please."

"Of course, sir, how are the eyes?"

"Feeling much better, thanks. Oh, and Griffen…?"

"Sir?"

"Could you get me some paper and a pencil, please."

"Certainly, sir." Griffen nodded sagely. "Remember what the MO said, though. You mustn't over-exert yourself."

Rose smiled beatifically at the ceiling. He felt like jumping out of bed and dancing around the little ward, but of course if the MO saw him, he'd probably keep him under observation for even longer!

He hadn't been able to fly with the squadron, and it looked like there would be no flying for him today, but nevertheless, it had been an incredible day! Molly had been to see him, and she was worried about him!

And she had said she thought he was very nice! I ought to go and shake Gertrude's fitter's hand! By not tightening that cap on the reserve tank, he'd done Rose the greatest favour in the world.

This is the happiest day I've had for a long time.

Thank you, too, Gertrude. I'd kiss you if I could. Your fitter as well!

When Granny and a crowd of pilots arrived to see him some time later, they found him still smiling, with the rough sketch of a smiling dark-haired girl on the bed beside him.

They gathered around him, laughing and teasing him, but they wondered. He was a dark horse, and no mistake. The Flight Officer had been to see him! Lucky sod!

Granny just lit a cigarette (in spite of a disapproving frown from Griffen), and smiled secretly to himself.

Good lad.

Chapter 16

Rose missed the first patrol the following day, as the MO had insisted upon another cursory examination before allowing Rose to be rated as being passed fit to fly. He stood near the Headquarters building, moodily watching his flight takeoff, but also secretly hoping for a glimpse of Molly.

Granny was flying with Burton and Barsby today. The former had returned from a private talk with Granny a very sober young man. He would not mistake casings with enemy gunfire ever again.

The Hurricanes of A'Flight arrived at their patrol area to almost immediately plunge into a turning inconclusive tussle between a section of Spitfires and a number of Bf109s.

Soon after the Hurricanes had arrived, the German pilots decided that the odds were no longer in their favour and dived out of the fight at full boost, seeking the sanctuary of the French coast.

After the initial manoeuvres, the members of A'Flight only managed to get in a few long-range bursts at the enemy planes.

When all the combat reports were collated, they were only able to claim one damaged. The Spits had lost one, though.

Granny had stumped off in a grand old rage after landing, so Rose had had a word with a flushed, excited and still-shaking Burton.

Despite an initial scare, Burton had had an exhilarating time pursuing the German fighters with the rest of the flight, taking regular pot-shots all the while (despite a lack of personal success on his part) until he had used up all his ammunition. He proudly showed Rose the line of four ragged bullet-holes in his rudder, the result of a snap-shot by an escaping Bf109.

"I thought my time had come," he croaked ruefully. "After that, I was so excited, I went after one that was a good half mile in front and gaining ground. I tried some high-angle shooting to bring him down, but I think it all fell short, because he took no notice of us."

Rose had not yet met any Bf109s in combat, had only seen them from a distance on the single occasion with the Defiants, and he stared at the holes silently. The thought of taking on one or more of the feared single engine cannon-armed German fighters filled him with a great sense of unease. Even though Granny had simulated a Bf109 during the aerial training, and Rose had some idea what it was like to fly and fight against the nimble Luftwaffe fighter.

Meanwhile, whilst the squadron had been skirmishing, Rose had received a clean bill of health, and Donald was pleased to see the young pilot operational again. Granny said nothing but his wink said it all.

At Rose's request, he was allowed to take part in the second patrol of the day, a coastal convoy escort patrol by B' Flight at Angels Fifteen between Dungeness and Beachy Head.

The scene was a peaceful one. The sun shone brilliantly down onto the six Hurricanes of B'Flight droning serenely through the clear air, gently bobbing up and down in the unsettled mid-afternoon warmth.

Down below the RAF fighters, a small convoy of ten little ships ploughed stolidly through the flat plain of a glittering sea, a single destroyer plodding along beside them on a southerly beam, a thin grey shape alongside a line of darker, fatter shapes. The trailing white wakes made by the ships were striking and bright against the deep blue.

Control had warned of possible activity, bogies nearby, but there had been no word for the last two minutes. Despite the serenity of the scene, none of the six pilots were relaxed, six pairs of eyes scanning the surrounding environs carefully and anxiously.

Sinclair was looking forward, maintaining position over the convoy. This left the others to keep station on him, whilst watching for enemy fighters. As one, the other five pilots searched tensely in their cold cockpits, heads craned every which way, eyes straining against the blazing sky, watching their positions in the formation and the skies around them.

Rose was flying as Red Three, and he quartered the sky as Granny had taught him, a quick but careful gaze, searching for movement in his peripheral vision, before moving on to the next area.

Mustn't spend too long gazing at a particular area, behind, up, right, down and left, then behind again.

Quick look at the instrument panel, then back out again. His eyes felt sore, and the goggles and facemask stuck uncomfortably to his face.

Sinclair's voice crackled over the R/T, "Honey Flight Leader to Jamjar," 'Jamjar' was the callsign for sector control, "Still no sign of bandits. Please advise." He sounded irritable.

Rose pulled up his goggles and quickly rubbed his eyes. The gauntlets felt rough, chafing the skin on his forehead. He sighed, but did not relax his tense muscles.

"Hello, Honey Leader, Jamjar calling, twenty plus bogies at Angels Ten. Vector to 160, repeat vector 160."

The voice of the controller was calm and unruffled.

"Received and understood, Jamjar. Honey Flight turn to vector 160."

The pilots of B'Flight followed Sinclair onto the new heading. The Hurricanes turned as one onto a south-south-east heading, carefully maintaining their position as well as continuing to maintain a careful lookout.

Not an easy task at all. All the while trying to look all around and watch expectantly for an as yet unseen enemy.

Rose gazed eagerly forward, but there was only empty sky, no tell-tale glints, still no sign, and he returned to watching the space behind.

Forcing himself not to look for the bogies ahead. Sinclair and the Red section leader, Farrell, would watch for the bandits.

After what seemed like an age, but in truth must have been less than a minute, the R/T crackled again. It was the controller again, "Hello, Honey Leader, Jamjar calling, twenty plus bandits at your two o'clock, closing."

Rose turned on the reflector sight. His heart was thumping.

Farrell called out excitedly, "Red Leader to Honey Flight, bogies in sight, two o'clock low," Rose stole a glance forwards, ahead of the six Hurricanes a growing group of black dots suddenly became visible against the shimmering water. They quickly sprouted wings and resolved into, black (no, not black after all but a dark green, why did they always look black?), gull-winged shapes, with fixed, spatted undercarriage and long, lustrous canopies. Five waves of aeroplanes stepped up, flying eight abreast, forty dive-bombers neat and orderly as if on parade.

Then, Sinclair again, "Whizz-o! They're Stuka's! And no bloody escort! Follow me down, two vics. Line abreast. We'll split 'em up, then every man for himself! Tally-Ho!"

Rose's heart leapt with excitement.

Stukas! Granny was always wittering on about how Stukas were a 'piece of cake' to shoot down, and about the losses they had suffered already during the blitzkrieg and at Dunkirk. It was his turn to find out the truth.

But where were the escort? There were no enemy fighters at all, had they missed the boat?

Sinclair's Hurricane nosed down, and B'Flight followed him into the dive head on with the enemy. Rose looked nervously around. Still no sign of enemy fighters. Where on earth were they?

The Stukas rapidly grew in Rose's reflector sight, and whilst just out of range, with one last, quick glance behind, he aimed carefully ahead of the Stuka he had picked out for himself on the port side of the formation, and squeezed the trigger on his control-column for a two second burst.

Immediately his Hurricane juddered from the recoil, spraying out a stream of bullets in front of the oncoming target, the strange corkscrewing grey trails converging on the ugly gull-winged shapes, now distorted by the vibration of his Hurricane's airframe.

He had misjudged the closing speed, and his fire missed the first two waves altogether. However, the third Stuka in line was not as fortunate.

It flew through the concerted storm of bullets, hits flashing along its cowling and fuselage, a brilliant burst of fire, debris torn from it, spinning away like a leaves in an autumnal gust.

Then it had disappeared beneath him.

All in less than a second.

To his side, other trails of grey smoke and cartridge casings streamed back from the wings of his companions as they, too, opened fire on the serried ranks before them. In an instance they were through the enemy formation, and he pulled back, tilting into a curving attack from astern. He couldn't tell which of the enemy planes he had targeted and hit, for the sky seemed to be full of the frantically twisting black gull-winged dive-bombers, the formation hopelessly broken up. Two of them were falling, trailing thick smoke.

Tracer curved dangerously close then fell away.

They were everywhere, a cloud of dark enemy machines, some desperately racing for sanctuary amongst the few clouds or diving down, whilst others continued doggedly on course towards the convoy.

B'Flight had broken up the formation with their attack from above, and already another of the Stukas was spiralling down in flames, whilst below there were waterspouts where the bombs jettisoned by some of the startled Luftwaffe pilots had landed.

He felt a stab of gladness and pride. That was some explosive that wouldn't take any British lives.

A single Hurricane was turning tightly after a group of four bombers that had maintained their heading. Another was racing after a Stuka, firing long bursts into the stricken aeroplane as it fell away, already burning and out of control.

Of the others in B' Flight there was no sign, although he could still hear them shouting and swearing over the R/T.

Rose ignored the chaotic communications and looked around, searching for escorts, and more importantly, for more targets. There certainly were enough of them.

No dark shapes from the sun. Where the hell were the fighter escort?

A Junkers 87 flashed past, and was gone, tracer reaching out, falling away.

Chase him? No. He had no bomb, and was heading for home. Some bombers were still heading for the convoy.

Those were his priority. He had to stop them. He looked around again.

Another turned lazily above him, wobbling uncertainly, turning onto a heading for the ships.

God! They were so slow!

Any fighters above or behind? No. Thank God.

Pull up, tighten the turn, pull hard inside the German's turn, watch that gunner, aim slightly ahead, and gently squeeze the firing button. The eight machine guns thundered out again, firm on the stick, strain to keep the deflection correct. No return fire. The poor fool didn't even know he was there! Flashes on the stained pale blue underside of the other aircraft, a white plume of glycol whipped back thinly.

Eyes flick quickly around, then back at the Stuka.

Flame gouts out of the enemy plane's Junkers Jumo 211 engine, and there go the bombs, a big one and four little ones, falling and turning, end over end, jettisoned by a pilot who knows he can no longer deliver them onto their intended targets. A flash of smoke and one spatted wheel flies off, spinning ridiculously.

The Ju87 tightened its turn, extended its speed-brakes, looming dangerously before him. Rose desperately threw the Hurricane the other way, his heart thumping painfully in his chest, and half-felt, half-heard a splatter of bullets pierce the fuselage somewhere behind him once, twice and three times.

Sounds like a cricket bat smacking into a wet sandbag. No time to worry about them.

He passed through the gout of thick, oily black smoke that billowed out of the Ju87 suddenly, staining his windscreen.

The world went dark momentarily, and, despite the facemask being strapped tightly to his face, he choked on the pungent stench of the smoke and from the cordite.

Another Hurricane shot past him, close enough to touch, steadied to fire a burst into the stricken dive-bomber, and was gone again.

Bloody Hell! Where on earth did he come from?

Keep a proper look-out! Didn't see him at all! Could get shot down by the next one!

The Junkers was burning like a torch now, it tipped over, and fell away, burning pieces detaching from the main body of the aircraft. It seemed to collapse like wet paper. On the way down, a single parachute opened.

Swinging like a pendulum.

Got one!

Eyeballs straining for escorts.

One survivor. An escapee from the torch that was the now tumbling Stuka.

Another for me! Or is that a half? That other Hurricane may claim it, he thought.

Cheeky bastard.

A fierce exhilaration gripped him tightly.

Another glance behind.

Still no fighters. Thank you, God.

All around was a confused picture of aircraft fleeing everywhere.

Ah. Two more of the Junkers 87's were close ahead, far below, tucked closely together, diving gently. Towards the convoy. They had a clear run in, no other Hurricanes apparent nearby.

Up to me to stop them, then.

Turning again, he closed quickly from above and astern. He was beginning to feel a little light-headed from the forces placed on him by the sharp turns, and the raw excitement pounding inside him.

The range closed rapidly and mentally he berated himself; reduce the throttles, Harry, or else you'll overshoot. These kites are slow, dead slow. If you overshoot and end up in front of them they may take a quick pot-shot with their wing-mounted machine guns at you, too.

What a terrible thought. Being shot down by a bloody Ju87 Stuka!

He was not aware that he was muttering meaninglessly under his mask, encouraging himself with directions and meaningless remarks. His thumb stroked the gun-button. Not yet, he reminded himself, get in close, really close.

He thought they might separate from one another, but doggedly they held formation, relying on the security of combined fire from their rear facing guns.

The rear-gunners were firing back at him, and their fire drew close so that he was certain that it would hit him, but he side-slipped again and again and the blazing balls of fire would sear past.

So close, he felt he could reach out to them. Can't you do any better, you Jerry bastards? His anger burnt away the creeping fear.

His testicles felt as if they had been turned to ice. Despite the armoured glass of the windscreen, and the comforting bulk of the engine block in front of him, he could not help but hunch down in the face of the return fire. Side-slip, jink.

Four hundred yards, then three hundred. Reduce the throttle.

Glittering webs of tracer reaching out. Something *spanged!* off the side of his cockpit, startling him, but he held to his course grimly. The engine still growled smoothly, and she continued to fly.

At a range of less than two hundred yards, with the worn and dirty-looking Stukas looming large in his gunsight, he placed the dot onto the leading aircraft, and pressed down the firing-button convulsively. The machine guns clattered, a harsh reek of cordite filling the cockpit again. At exactly the same instant, he finally felt more bullet-strikes on his fighter.

Ahead of him, the shuddering vision of the lead Stuka shook under the onslaught, as Rose kicked the rudder pedals alternately and nudged the control column to spray a spreading cone of gunfire over the pair of Stukas.

The dive-bomber's wing man pulled up and broke away, out of the lethal hail of lead. The flaming blobs of tracer swirled around the port aircraft, and it sparkled from multiple hits on its fuselage, wings and tailplane, small pieces of metal and thick grey-black smoke escaping in a couple of billowing puffs. Fire flared briefly, went out, flared again. Yellow-white tinged with red, lancing back like the flame from a blow-torch.

Shreds of metal, tailwheel and then one tail-strut were ripped off. Unsupported, the port aileron shook then folded back. The wingtips wobbled as the pilot fought desperately for control of the aeroplane.

Something smacked against his starboard wing tip but he retained control, heart pounding.

Meanwhile, the Stuka wingman was frantically diving away in an attempt to escape the hail of lead.

And then Rose's bullets set off the bomb slung low under the Ju87.

One second the enemy aeroplane was in front of him, burning, pieces falling from it, the next Rose was flying inverted, six thousand feet above the sea, hanging downwards in his straps, mind muddled and disorientated.

He realised after a few confused seconds that the glittering sea was now above, the sky beneath.

All he could remember was the sudden bright white flash as the bomb exploded. It had been a dazzling whiteness interspersed with black spots, and a pointed wing had twirled dizzily past, close enough to touch, the black and white cross on it just a blur, and then nothing.

He must have been unconscious for at least a few seconds. Nothing was audible on the R/T. It was completely dead. And his ears were ringing strangely. Was he deaf? No. He could still hear the roar of the engine.

Best roll right way up, come out of this dive.

Dazedly, he righted the Hurricane, shook his head like a punch-drunk boxer, and pulled back into level flight. The light-headedness persisted, and he could taste acid at the back of his mouth. He swallowed painfully.

At least his kite was still airborne, seemed responsive, and the engine sounded healthy enough.

He closed his eyes tightly, counted to three, opened them again. Blinked.

And almost threw his Hurricane into a hard turn of evasion to port.

Flying close off his starboard wing was a Spitfire with unfamiliar squadron markings. The other pilot had pushed back his canopy, and was staring at him beneath thick black eyebrows, white silk scarf flapping in the slipstream. He held up a hand.

Rose waved weakly at the other, aware that his earphones were completely dead. No static, nothing. The only sound was the roar of his engine and the whistling of the slipstream through the holes in the fuselage.

He keyed his microphone. "Jamjar from Honey Red Three...do you read me....please respond." No response. His R/T was useless. Must have been damaged by the explosion.

He looked across to the other pilot, tapped his ear, shook his head, pointed to himself, and gave thumbs up gesture.

The Spitfire pilot nodded his understanding, waggled his wings, drew his gauntlet dramatically across his forehead, in a gesture that cried out 'Phew!', winked and gave Rose a thumbs-up in return, then opened his throttles wide open and curved away.

Presumably after the remaining Stukas. He looked around, but there was no sign of the second Stuka or any other Stukas. Had it been hit by the bomb blast too? Had the surviving enemy plane gone down? Had the Spitfire pilot shot it down?

210

Or was it, even now, limping back home, with a crew, thankful to be alive, just as dazed as he?

Thank Heavens that it had been an RAF kite that had been sitting on his wing. It could just as easily have been a Jerry fighter.

Thanks a lot, chum, he thought warmly of the other, I'll stand you a drink or three if I get the chance to meet up with you. I owe you a lot more than that.

My guardian angel. You kept me safe in those seconds or minutes whilst I was out of it.

Quick glance around and into the rear-view mirror. Nothing.

There were Jerry kites still in the area, and he was still in the battle area, so Luftwaffe fighters could still jump him. He pushed back the hood, then, gingerly, he tested the controls. She seemed to be OK in level flight.

Should I get back into the fight?

No, perhaps not. He was still feeling peculiarly light-headed, and he'd definitely accounted for one (all by myself!), shared one, and maybe had a probable with the other Stuka? That was enough for today.

Two confirmed, two shared, and a probable, at least. The score was mounting, and he still lived!

There was probably only a couple of second's worth of ammunition left in his ammo trays, his aircraft had suffered hits, and the fighter escort, notable in its absence, could arrive at any moment. Flying along, on his own in that wide open sky, he felt very, very, lonely. He'd had enough.

Best get home. I'll remember the squadron letters of that Spitfire, try and find out who it was who thought to protect me. He must have been itching to get into the fight, but instead he was looking after me. He certainly shifted fast enough when he was sure I was alright. Hope you're lucky, too, my friend.

211

Lady Luck again, giving me a guardian when I most needed it. I would have made easy pickings whilst I was out. Why, even one of those Stukas could have downed me, with its single forward facing popgun!

He shuddered at the thought, and then, remembering, patted his breast pocket. Yes, Genevieve was still there. He could feel the little bear with the slightly faded pink ribbon beneath his gauntleted fingers.

Thank you, Genevieve, and Thank you, Molly. I think she works for me as well. You and the unknown Spitfire pilot looked after me today.

He shuddered, suddenly feeling very cold. A few yards closer, and the explosion would have shredded his aircraft like tissue paper. The sight of the flaming wreckage of the first Stuka he had helped shoot down was still fresh in his memory.

I could have died, he thought shakily, and not even known it. A telegram would have arrived on the doorstep at home, perhaps even a letter from the Palace.

A letter of Royal sympathy. *'The Queen and I offer you our heartfelt sympathy in your great sorrow...'*

His legs began to tremble from reaction.

Well, no damned telegrams or letters today! Mother would not be shattered by loss today.

For some reason that he could not fathom, tears were spilling from his eyes, slowly dribbling out of his goggles, along his cheeks where the slipstream caught them.

In the distance, thin trails of smoke threaded the sky. A faraway flash, flaring bright briefly.

Mute testimony of the deadly struggle still raging.

Was he imagining it, or did the engine sound a bit rough?

His fight was over for today, he felt exhausted, and he desperately wanted to see Molly, to hear her voice, inhale the sweet scent of her fragrance. He craved her cleanness, the warmth of her nearness, and he had had more than enough of the stink and sight of war for one day.

He felt Granny's absence, and was uncomfortable high over the channel, all alone.

He turned carefully for home and safety, keeping a wary eye out for enemy fighters.

Still alive, he thought, fatigue mixed with gladness.

But, for how much longer?

Chapter 17

The sun was warm on his face, and slowly, he allowed his muscles to relax. The sound of bees and birdsong, and the rich fragrance of earth and wild flowers, lulled him peacefully like a soporific.

Rose lay on his back in the field where he had lost his first pipe, and felt at peace. Dry blades of grass scratched gently against his neck.

It was hard to believe that only yesterday he had been almost killed by the sudden, violent, explosion of the Stuka.

Altogether, B-Flight had claimed ten Stukas definitely destroyed, six probable, and many more damaged.

At least he now knew first-hand what a 'Stuka party' was.

Rose himself had been credited with two confirmed (It had been Farrell who had been stepping on his toes, but he would not claim a share in Rose's kill, saying that the Stuka had already been on its way down when he'd fired his passing burst, and anyway he'd got two of his own), and two damaged.

One of the damaged claims was the second Stuka of the pair Rose had attacked. It had been damaged when its companion had blown up under Rose's fire. It had last been seen rapidly descending, with smoke issuing from the engine, but it had not been seen to crash. So he had only been allowed a 'damaged' claim.

Granny had been so pleased with his success that Rose had feared Smith would kiss him, whilst simultaneously being furious and envious with having missed a 'Stuka party'.

Molly, too, had been pleased, but sadly, unlike Granny, she had not come near to kissing him.

The celebrations, however, had been tempered with sadness.

The squadron had suffered two aircraft losses, and the death of a pilot.

Pilot-Officer Renfrew, an addition to the squadron who had arrived the day before Rose, had collided with one of the Stukas, and had been killed.

Unlike the combat on the 10th of July, this time he hadn't managed to get out.

Sinclair, to his great chagrin, had been shot down, but had been rescued.

The loss of Renfrew had been the first fatal loss that the squadron had suffered after becoming operational again. It had cast a gloomy light upon the success, and Donald had walked around with a melancholic face for the rest of the day.

A-Flight was not rostered for operations today, and the pilots had the day off. Granny had disappeared in his ancient Austin Seven, in the direction of London, on one of his forays to what he termed the 'Gin and Popsie Palaces.'

Donald did not approve of Granny's tomcat-like behaviour, but as Skinner had soothed, "'Don't worry. When Granny's willy drops off, he'll have nothing left to play with, and then he'll be able to concentrate even better on his flying and fighting." He'd smiled gently, "'His girls will likely be grateful for the rest.'"

Rose stayed at Foxton, despite the invitation from Granny to further his non-RAF training (or what Granny termed his 'social education'). He planned to air test his Hurricane later, but his lunch would be a picnic alone with Molly. They would have a sandwich together in the short time available to her.

In the distance they could hear the muted sounds of the busy fighter aerodrome. But even the faraway sound of engines and machinery, or the crackling of the Tannoy, were unable to dispel the peacefulness of his surroundings.

He sighed dreamily, glad for the peace, for the rest after tense days of being on stand-by or in the air.

"It's so peaceful here; I wish it could always be like this." Molly's voice was hushed, as if she were afraid to disturb him.

His eyes were closed, the sun warming his face, "Isn't it wonderful? That first day, after talking and flying with Granny, I needed some time on my own, try and get everything straight in my head. So I decided to go for a walk, and I found this place quite by chance, and since then, this has been my favourite place to come to whenever I have some free time. It's easy to forget about everything for a little while, here." He sighed contentedly, "I could just sit here for ages, listen to the birds and smell the sweetness of the air. It's nice to just lie here quietly, forget about the war, and enjoy the blissful peace."

"Oh! I do hope I'm not intruding on your blissful silence?"

This time, he did open his eyes, turning to look at her anxiously. "Oh my goodness! Of course not!"

He was relieved by her mischievous smile, "No, Molly, what I was trying to say was that I thought it was idyllic before here, but you weren't here with me then, and I didn't know any better." He smiled back at her bashfully.

"Now that you are here with me, I know what true bliss is. You being here makes it truly perfect."

Molly stuck out her tongue at him, and he gazed at it with great interest. What a lovely little red thing. It was the sort of tongue that he had always imagined she would have, small, delicate, and very desirable. Every part of her was beautiful to him.

"I suppose every apple has to have a worm."

"You're certainly no worm, sweet Molly." He marvelled that he found it so easy to talk to her now, that he was no longer as tongue-tied as he had been before. Even then, despite this new-found familiarity, he could still sometimes look at her, and feel speechless and shy.

"How do you know I'm not speaking about you, you dreadful child?"

He sat up. "I know that you could never call a fine, brave warrior like myself a worm, you sweet girl. And I can't understand how you can call me a child. We're about the same age."

Rose sat there before her, a young man in rumpled air force blues. Unruly brown hair that had never seen Brylcreem curled gently, two or three wisps of grass sticking out of it. His scarf loosened, and the scarlet and white of his striped ribbon bright in the light.

"Hmm. About the same age, eh? You forget the simple matter of five years or so as if they were nothing." She examined her fingernails. "I am twenty-five, you know." She made a face, "Oh dear, you see what you've made me do now? No woman should have to admit to their age, even an ancient fossil like me."

He reached into his pocket and waved his briar pipe at her. "Twenty-five? Is that all? But that's nothing!" He stared at her beguilingly. "I think you're very young and so very lovely."

Molly wrinkled her nose at him. "I wish you'd get rid of that smelly nasty thing, Harry." She was pleased by his words, but ignored them. What was it she always said? 'Flattery will get you nowhere!'

He raised his eyebrows, questioningly, "What do you mean?"

"That horrible thing you're waving around, it's disgusting!"

"But this pipe is a part of me!" He stuck it belligerently into his mouth, sucked on it. "It helps me to think."

"You've never even lit it, you shameless fraud. I doubt it's ever seen a shred of tobacco in its life! You just sit there and slobber on it like some dirty old man. I think it's disgusting. Get rid of the rotten thing."

"Get rid of it? This is a part of a fighting man's armoury."

"Yes, I shouldn't be surprised. The thing's so whiffy, it's dangerous. If you chucked it into the Reichstag, they'd probably surrender before passing out. It's such a horrid, stinking thing; I wish I'd brought my respirator." She conveniently forgot that it was beside her; instead she waved a hand theatrically under her nose, and rolled her eyes. "In fact, I feel rather faint. I think I may pass out." She coughed delicately.

Rose's eyes brightened, "Perhaps I could minister tenderly to you?"

"Ha! Try it, and I'll do something dreadful to you, fighting man or no." She held out her hand. "Come on. Give it to me."

He stared at her. "What? You're not really serious are you, dearest Molly?""

She tried not to laugh at his shocked expression. "Come on," she scowled, "Give me that infernal thing."

"Why? What are you going to do with it?" he clutched it against himself, "Don't tell me you want to smoke it? Get your own one. This one is mine!"

"I'm going to get rid of it. Horrible thing. Smells bloody awful."

"Oh, no, Molly! I love this pipe! Please?" He gazed imploringly at her.

"If you don't give it to me, I'm leaving. You and your horrid pipe can enjoy the flowers here together."

She stared stonily at him, her hand outstretched, palm upwards.

"Come on, Harry, me or the pipe, you choose."

"Must I?"

She threw his cap at him and made as if to stand.

Sighing, with eyes downcast, he grudgingly handed it to her. She gingerly took it from him with two fingers, as if she were handling a dead rat, took out her handkerchief and wrapped it up.

"Yuck! Don't worry, Harry. I'll see the nasty thing is disposed of decently." Her eyes twinkled mischievously, "I have a friend whose brother works in bomb disposal!"

He pouted at her, and pretended to wipe away a tear.

Two Hurricanes roared past above, canopies flashing in the sun, brave and glorious, and together they looked upwards to watch them. She turned to look at him, at the dark circles beneath his eyes, at his narrowed serious eyes as they followed the aeroplanes.

"Is it grim, Harry?" Her voice was soft.

"Pardon me?" He turned to her, confused by the sudden change of her tone, firm one moment, now gentle.

"Up there. You know. What's it like? Is it hard for you, for all the boys? Please tell me. I'd like to know, to share it with you." She tilted her head, waves of hair cascading to one side, and her eyes glistened. "You risk everything for us. I want to know everything about it."

He thought for a moment.

"We-ell." He ran a hand absently through his unruly hair. How could he tell her of the exhilaration and the gut-wrenching fear as enemy bullets sped to greet him? The buttock-clenching terror as bullets smacked into the armour plate behind his seat. The dry mouth and iciness in his heart as men fell away in shattered planes, be they friend or foe. How could he explain, how could he make her understand?

219

He affected a light tone, "It's the best thing a boy could ever wish for. Lot of aerobatics, pop off a few bullets, then home for tea."

"All sounds like real Boy's Own stuff!" She smiled gravely. "I'm sure there's more to it than that, however. Why don't you tell me about it? I'd really like to share it."

Molly picked a buttercup and held it delicately beneath her nose.

Rose sat up and brushed some grass from his tunic. "I always used to wonder, as well, you see, before that first time. My father was in France in the Great War, first in the PBI, wounded at Ypres, then into the RFC." He looked back up at the sky, but not really seeing it. "He hardly ever talked about the war, but he used to think about it a lot. He would be digging in the garden, or writing in the study, when he'd suddenly stop. Just stop. As if he was somewhere else. And the look in his eyes…"

Rose rubbed the back of his neck vigorously. "I wanted to know what he'd had to endure, so I read as much as I could about the war, about Ball and Bishop and Mannock. About the Red Baron's Flying Circus, the slaughter, the mud and the Trenches. I wanted to know about my father. What he had done, where he had gone, what he'd seen. He wouldn't talk about it."

The sound of machine guns came faintly in the distance, like ripping fabric, and he momentarily cocked his head towards the sound. Was Jerry visiting?

But they were only Brownings. It was some test-firing and adjustments being done down in the firing butts.

"I saw all the films, you know, Hell's Angels, All Quiet On The Western Front, that sort of thing, but that's not reality, really. I read everything that I could find, but it only told me the facts, some of the feeling, only not really the true realities about what it was like to be there. They are so impersonal. The books can only tell someone about battles and campaigns, not real first hand experiences. At least not the ones I read." He stopped, then, "I'm not very good with words, and it's hard to explain, Molly, but…"

His mouth was parched, and he was feeling more than a little awkward under her searching eyes.

Two sparrows pirouetted close overhead, diving down to skim just over the grass before shooting back up into the air, their chirps sharp and excited, but he was not even aware of them, caught up in the web of his memories. Instead, he moistened his lips and pushed on, "Even the accounts I read by the aces weren't enough. I don't think they gave the full story. It's one of those things you can only know by experiencing it, So, when Hitler started this madness, I knew I had to do what Father had done, as he would have done it again if he had to, I would do my duty." He shrugged, "And so now, I'm here."

She smiled that heart-achingly warm and beautiful smile at him again. "Good thing, too, if you ask me. I would never have met you, otherwise."

He was thrilled by that, and she was surprised how her words brought him so much simple happiness.

O.T.U., Granny, operational experience and combat had taught Rose to be a competent fighter pilot, but underneath it all, underneath the trappings; he was still the quiet boy.

Her voice was still soft, "Tell me about your father…" she hesitated, "is he…?"

"Yes. He's dead." He held up a hand at the stricken look on her face. "No, it's alright; I don't mind talking about it with you, besides," He looked away, unable to meet her eyes, lest his gaze reveal too much of what he felt for her, "You're special. I want to tell you everything. I want you to really know me."

And to love me, he thought to himself.

She half-smiled again, but her eyes were still troubled.

"Anyway, he had a disease of the liver. He used to drink, quite heavily, sometimes. He was hurt quite badly in the war, so he had to take a lot of medicines. I don't think he should have drunk, but he did. I loved him very much, but the drink could make him... unhappy. That's why I don't often drink. Almost never. I can't bear the stuff, because of what it did to him. In the end, it killed him."

He lay down again, cradling his head in his hands, his face brooding, "I thought I could find out about it, understand what it was like for a young man at that time. I wanted to know why he had become the man he was, what had made him into that. He once said that he had seen thousands of men dying needlessly beneath him, and the sight would be with him always."

She shivered, at the image of grey death reaping the fields of young humanity, leaving shattered landscapes and endless carpets of the ruined dead.

He paused, immersed in reflection, eyes faraway, and it was as if he had forgotten she was there.

She held her breath, and then he spoke again, "apparently he was completely different before he went to war. The man I knew was quiet, and patient, and often kind, but then, he would suddenly get angry for no reason at all, shouting like a madman. Screaming suddenly in the night. In the end he was like that even if he hadn't had a drop. Mummy said he was the gentlest man she'd ever known, and that he had captured her with softness. I wish I'd known him when he was like that. I used to think it was so unfair." His voice was flat, colourless, as he relived the sorrow. "I suppose it was like that for a lot of people."

The pain was dulled by time, but not the sadness, the sense of loss.

What must she think, he wondered, and, Dear God, how maudlin he sounded!

But, in his mind he could still see his father, raving senselessly, weeping. Memories of a lost generation, of friends eternally young, and never forgotten.

And those who would die young, years later, after the armistice, just like Dad.

And the terrible, horrific, handful of times his father had hit him. The shock fresh and awful each time. It had worsened over the years.

Rose's face felt tight, his ears and eyes hot. He was scared that his voice might quiver, but he wanted to share it with her.

"So I decided to learn to fly. Air Force kites like Dad. See what it was like for him. To try and understand it all. To try and understand him a little more. He didn't shirk, though it cost him so much. I want to be like him. Protect others as he had protected all of us."

She tossed her hair back, and his heart ached to see the way in which the sun caught the glistening strands with gold. How wonderful it would be to touch her hair! He almost reached out to her, but his courage failed, and instead, he pulled out a blade of grass, uncomfortably twisted it between his fingers.

"Mother didn't say anything, but she didn't really want me to go. Thing is, she'd always taught us that we had to do what we thought was right. So she didn't try and stop me, either."

Suddenly he peered at her, "Gosh! Listen to me babbling! I'm sorry, Molly. Your ears must be feeling a bit sore! You should have told me to be quiet!" He looked at her apologetically.

Molly shook her head, her hair shimmering, and her face thoughtful, "I like to hear you talk, Harry, and I told you, I want to know about you, and the people who are or have been important in your life. I like to think that you and the other boys are fighting for all of us, and that we're all family." She spoke quietly, but with feeling, "Please carry on, if it isn't hard on you, because I really want to know all about you and your people."

Her gaze was intense, but her voice was soft. "You see, I think you're very special, too. Very special for all of us, of course, but also very much for me." She reached out and took his hand lightly, her grip gentle, soft and warm. "But I'm too old, Harry. It can't go on, you know."

Rose could feel his neck suffusing, and he coughed to cover his mingled pleasure and ridiculous feelings of embarrassment. "You aren't old at all. Stop talking such nonsense. I don't want to hear it again." He could feel his heart banging hard against his ribcage. Surely she must hear it? It sounded like an artillery barrage! *Boom-boom-boom!*

"Phew, it's hot." He fanned his face with his cap. "It's too lovely here to talk about gloomy things. Let's just enjoy the sunlight?"

She had said he was special! To her! Bloody hell!

She smiled softly, "I'd like that, but," she looked at her watch. "Unfortunately, I'm back on in fifteen minutes. You're not off the hook, yet you know. I want to know more. Thank you for trusting me, and telling me about your Dad." her hand gripped his tighter, "Would you walk me back to the airfield?" She gathered the crumpled paper bags with her free hand and placed them carefully in her respirator box.

He smiled back, squeezed her hand (God what a pleasure it was to touch her again!). "Nothing would please me more."

"Good." Then, she smirked, "Don't forget your sauce-pan."

Rose looked down at the black and yellow-brown stained steel pot near his feet, then back at her, and rolled his eyes.

When they had been walking down the lane earlier on the way here, a little boy had shot out of a nearby cottage, holding it out to them. Eight or nine years old, with grimy knees and a snotty nose.

"Hey, Commander, 'ave this for yer Spitfires." The little boy's face was flushed, and Rose did not have the heart to decline. He had tucked it under his arm, saluted the boy solemnly, and thanked him. The warmth of the boy's smile had been palpable, Molly's even more so.

"You are nice, Harry." Then, "But don't bring that pan anywhere near me. I don't think it's ever been washed. Now we had better run, because his Mum may not know he's given it to us, and I don't want to be accused of theft!" she'd laughed as he'd looked at it. "You are nice." She'd repeated.

And better still, she had held his hand for the rest of the journey here.

He could smell her, clean and fragrant. Unbidden, the popular slogan *'Elizabeth Arden soap really washes away the day'* flashed into his mind.

She got to her feet in a single fluid movement, like a ballerina gracefully rising, patted her skirt and tunic. She offered him her hand again. He took it and stood, making a great show of using her assistance.

"Thank you, Ma'am."

She looked at him silently for a moment, and then she made up her mind. God help her, she would give it to him after all, even though she had resolved not to, the moment she had bought it. She opened her respirator box, and drew out the red and white striped silk scarf. It shone brightly in the sunlight.

"I want you to have this, Harry. You belong to Excalibur squadron, and I've heard the groundcrew call you all Donald's 'Knights of the Air.' I think his people have painted 'Arthur' on the side of his aeroplane."

He stared at the square of shining silk, wondering where Molly was going with this, "Well, every knight has a warhorse, and yours is that Hurricane you're so attached to. A knight usually has a lady too, whose colours he wears, and whose honour he upholds." She looked away, blushing in embarrassment, "I'd like it if you thought of me as your Lady."

Rose grinned, and croaked, "I'd be honoured, m'lady!" He bowed deeply, almost losing his balance, and tugged his forelock theatrically.

"Well, I thought I should have some colours, and I've chosen these as mine. I thought you could wear this as my banner into battle?"

He took the scarf from her, discarded his own, and wrapped hers around his neck in its place.

She was looking at him, her eyes suddenly glistening with unspilled tears.

"I suppose you think I'm being terribly silly?"

He smiled. "No, no, not at all. I think it's a wonderful thought, and I'm glad you picked me to wear your colours. I'd be honoured to take your standard into battle with me." His throat felt tight, and for some inexplicable reason, his hands were shaking. "I can't tell you how much it means to me. Thank you, Molly."

She sniffed, "You're very formal, all of a sudden, Pilot-Officer."

Greatly daring, he took her hand between his, and brought it to his lips. He held it there for a long moment. He waited for her to pull it away, but she just stood motionless, a slight, strange smile on her lips, her cheeks colouring a delicate coral pink, and her liquid eyes on his.

Her palm was dry and fragrant. He closed his eyes, shutting out everything but the scent and the touch of this lovely woman.

Elizabeth Arden soap washes away the day.

The scent of her, the sound of her voice, washed away all his tension, all his worries.

"I've nothing to give you in return, except…would you like my old scarf, Molly?"

"Yes please, I'd like that very much."

She took the scarf from him, folded it carefully, and placed it carefully into her respirator box.

Then she placed one finger on his chest, just below his wings. "Perhaps you could tell me about the medal, as we walk back? It's the Air Force Cross, isn't it?"

Eyes still closed, he said, "The tale of my heroism will take many hours in the telling, for it has many embellishments and praises of my character and nobility." How easy it suddenly became to talk like this with her! "It will need to be told at some later point, when we have more time. Perhaps over dinner one evening? I always tend to go on about myself. Next time, you must tell me about yourself. And we still have to go and watch 'Wuthering Heights.' Come on, you know I'm irresistible! How can you refuse me?"

He could sense her acceptance, feel her smile. He felt her other hand come up to caress his cheek gently.

He opened his eyes, and saw such a look of tenderness on her face that instinctively he took her into his arms and hugged her tightly, as if it were their last embrace, and not their first. She was warm in his embrace, and he felt as if he were as light as air, and might float away at any instant.

He had imagined the first time he held a girl that he would be all fingers and thumbs, but instead it felt the most natural thing in the world.

Standing there, cheek-to-cheek, she felt so right, so natural, curving against him, as she hugged him back. They fit so perfectly together.

He felt at peace, his heart filled with joy, yet her very nearness initiated excitement and treacherous desire stirred in his young loins.

He was embracing her! He could hardly believe it! Already, he could feel the beginnings of an erection, and shifted awkwardly so it would not press against her, but he did not let go of her.

She placed her hands on his face, one on either cheek, and gazed deep into his eyes. Then she kissed him lightly on his lips, soft and moist, just for a second, and he thought that he would pass out from the surprise and the burgeoning delight that thundered through his veins.

She tasted of freshness, cool, sweet, and so very soft.

First kiss.

Such a gentle, chaste kiss, not at all like the frenzied, lustful, hungry kisses he had watched with envy at the train station, filled with fire and passion, but the tender kiss of two people who care deeply for one another, still too shy to show their mutual longing. The caress of her lips was like eiderdown, so light.

It was his first proper kiss ever, and he felt ten feet tall with the experience.

"Will you come for dinner?" He squeaked.

"Alright," she answered, simply.

As they walked slowly back, not saying another word, hand in hand, Rose felt that should he live a hundred years, he could never experience such joy as this ever again.

She had kissed him, and he had held her in his arms.

And she had given him her colours.

Molly was his Lady.

Chapter 18

The following day, Yellow section, flying as 'Slipper section', were scrambled to intercept a plot approaching from the south east. They were expertly vectored to the bogie by another efficient controller.

Unlike the previous day, the weather was a grim, with low, heavy grey cloud hanging like a miserable curtain before them. It had rained heavily earlier, but had come to a fitful stop, but the cloud was pregnant with the promise of further rain. Visibility was bad in the grey light, and the three pilots strained as they looked through the murk for the unseen aircraft. Rose thought of the fire in the Mess, and he clenched cold gauntleted fingers.

Come *on*; let's go home, he mentally urged Granny.

He thought back to breakfast.

Ffellowes had cocked a questioning eyebrow at him, as he bit into a piece of toast. "You're looking decidedly chipper, old man?"

Granny had sniffed from behind his usual copy of the Daily Mirror, rustled it, "It'll be a woman, mark my words. Don't believe in 'em myself. No bloody good to man nor beast. Give me a Pint of Best any day."

"Oh, I wouldn't go so far as to say that, chum." Denis waved a fork at the hidden Granny. "And I happen to know that you're incapable of resisting Popsie."

Granny sniffed disdainfully again but said nothing.

"I take it that the rather glamorous Flight Officer Digby is responsible for that rather silly grin on our young friends face." Ffellowes smiled benevolently, and crunched another mouthful of thickly buttered toast.

"Poor, innocent sweet boy." Granny sighed sadly, and continued to leer at the lewd cartoon pictures that chronicled the antics of Jane, as she shed items of clothing in her latest adventure.

They were a good bunch. Rose had merely smiled and remained silent.

His thoughts slowly drifted to Molly, and tendrils of warmth crept over him from within, but they were quickly dispelled as the voice of the controller came over the ether again.

More instructions, but no sight of the enemy in this brooding grey half-light.

Naughty boy, he chided, you're leaving all the work for poor old Granny and Speedy.

Down below, an equally grey and cold sea chopped fretfully, the crests making Rose imagine hungry, biting pointy teeth. He shivered in his cockpit.

Earlier they had passed a convoy, cutting ponderously through the hard sea, a few small barrage balloons straining above some of the small vessels, like banners being carried by knights into battle. Funnel smoke trailed darkly behind before being whipped away, making the grey day even gloomier.

Unlike his mood, or the banner Molly had given to him. Unconsciously he brought up his hand to touch the silk at his neck. He had seen Granny's eyes flick with interest to his new scarf, but his friend had not said anything, despite the curiosity in those eyes.

The ships looked as grey as the sea, their red ensigns the only speck of colour in the miserable scene, and it made him feel cold just to look at them. I don't envy you, he thought, tossing around in the freezing wind, soaked to the skin on an open deck or bridge.

If they had to abandon ship, they wouldn't last long in that freezing, hungry sea.

Nervously, he hummed 'I'll never smile again', the popular tune that Ffellowes had been playing endlessly on the gramophone in the mess.

Even the ship's barrage balloons looked wet. Thank God father never chose the Navy. I might have been down there now if he had!

He stole a glance at W-Wally, flying to one side and slightly behind him.

W-Wally was being flown by a pilot who would most probably feel right at home, bouncing around down there. Sub-Lieutenant Harold 'Speedy' Sampson RNVR was one of the two pilots on loan to Excalibur squadron from the Fleet Air Arm. The other young naval pilot, Grayson, was seconded to Sinclair's B-flight.

Fighter Command's ranks had been swelled by over fifty naval aircrew from the Royal Navy's Fleet Air Arm.

Rose had found Sampson a friendly but quiet young man, unlike the devil-may-care Grayson, who had only flown 'Stringbags', Swordfish torpedo bombers, up until this point. He had confided his fears of inadequacy as a fighter pilot quietly to Rose one evening, yet nonetheless, he climbed into his aeroplane and flew every day two or three times on patrol.

And more importantly, he continued to survive.

Sampson would sit quietly by the fire, resplendent in dark blue, with a single wavy gold stripe on his sleeve, occasionally murmuring a sentence or comment. Each word was carefully enunciated, spoken with concentration. He was a man who spoke seldom, but, when he did, it was to say something of value.

Hence his nickname.

Rose found him congenial, as did Granny, who managed to get Sampson to fly with his section whenever possible. He too, had recognised the worries afflicting Sampson, and wanted to keep an eye on the young sailor.

The naval pilot was not always so quiet, though, for now he squawked loudly on the intercom, "Slipper Three to Leader. Bandit at ten o'clock high!"

Two other pairs of eyes wrenched around to see a dark shape disappear into the grey clouds above. It had gone quickly, but not before Rose had recognised the twin radial-engine bomber, on a heading for the convoy they had left behind.

But before he could say anything, Granny cut in, "Slipper Leader to section, I see it. It's a bloody Junkers 88, and it's heading straight for the convoy. It's up to us."

They turned sharply on an intercept course, but stayed below the cloud. Formation flying in cloud was an extremely unwise and unhealthy pursuit.

Twice, the enemy aircraft appeared before them, wraith-like before fading away again. The second time, it was so close that Granny tried a short burst, but without result. Then, they lost it.

Granny took them back down, cursing the cloud impressively. Rose thought of the WAAFs listening in the operations room, and blushed.

"We aren't going to find the bastard in this muck, boys. We'll circle the convoy. If he finds them, we'll be able to give him a smack on the chops."

At full throttle, it was not long before the convoy materialised again out of the murk, off to one side.

They circled it, but carefully kept out of range of the naval gunners.

As the crew of HMS *Shilton* had shown, naval gunners were not always terribly good at aircraft recognition, and were definitely not shy of 'having a go' when in doubt.

Grayson and Sampson, to their endless chagrin, had been teased mercilessly about it.

Within a minute of reaching the convoy again, Rose saw the black twin-engined bomber burst through the swathe of cloud about a mile distant. It noticed the ships, and turned towards them.

"Slipper section attacking! Tally-Ho!"

Within an instant they were closing on the Junkers. Just when Rose began to think they might catch the enemy aircraft by surprise, it turned to starboard sharply, and tracer stabbed at them, bright and deadly in the gloom, before zipping past to port.

"Break formation, and attack in line astern," ordered Granny, turning with the bomber.

Rose nudged rudder and skidded out of formation. As he did so, he glanced at the raider ahead. There was something strangely familiar... He looked again.

Gazed with disbelief at the red and blue roundels.

"Christ! Break off the attack, Granny! It's a Blenheim!" But already Granny had seen the markings and was turning away.

Rose hauled back on the stick, noticing how close they had got to the convoy, but there was no anti-aircraft fire from the ships below. They must be wondering what the hell we're doing, he thought with consternation and more than a little mortification.

With one last quick burst from the Blenheim's gunner, it fled back into the sanctuary of the cloud, heading for the English coast. There're three lucky young men, thought Rose. They came within a hair's breadth of the end.

Doubtless there'll be a few shaky hands downing pints tonight.

And a pointed telephone call to Fighter Command from their CO.

"Slipper section to Footlocker, be advised bogie is a Blenheim." Complained Granny. "He's pushed off. We'll stooge around for a little while, just to make sure that there isn't really a Junkers in the area. Why don't you tell those bods to tell us they're flying around out here."

"Received and understood, Slipper Leader," acknowledged the controller. "Please advise when you end patrol." Then, surprisingly, "Well done."

"Understood, Footlocker, and thanks." Then, to Sampson and Rose, "What a party! Form up, Slipper section."

They were about to re-form when another black shape detached from the cloud, on the far side, and dived at full speed for the convoy.

Surprised, they banked around again.

"Bugger me with a boot brush!" shouted Granny over the intercom, almost bursting Rose's eardrums, "It's a bloody Jerry for real this time!"

Once more, Granny led them in a straggly line after the other aircraft. It looked as if they may catch it as they bored in at full throttle. It saw them coming at it almost head on, and levelled out of its dive, and turned away.

The enemy bomber dumped a stick of bombs against a small steamer on the flank of the convoy at the same time as it turned.

Lightened of its bomb load, it seemed to bound upwards.

Waterspouts shot up all around the little ship, but when they had subsided, it reappeared, wet and shining, seemingly undamaged, with an almost jaunty air, like a cheerful tramp doffing his cap.

It looked untouched. But appearances can be deceptive and even now there could be men down there coughing up the last of their blood.

Small puffs of smoke appeared in front as the convoy began to fire upon the Junkers with a wide variety of calibre of weapon.

Disconcerted by the anti-aircraft fire, the enemy pilot almost flew into one of the barrage balloons, just clearing it by a small margin.

As the Hurricanes took up the pursuit, the gunners targeted them. All around, a fire storm erupted. Dirty grey-black puffs of smoke blossomed suddenly, and tracer lanced upwards for them.

Rather than fly through the naval gunfire, which resembled a lethal fireworks display, Granny and Rose broke upwards and away, but disregarding the vicious explosions, Sampson weaved his Hurricane through it and out the other side, buffeted and stained, but miraculously undamaged.

He seemed determined to close with the German aeroplane, knowing that the enemy could easily escape into the murkiness. Trails of grey smoke streamed behind the Junkers as the German pilot slammed on full power and tried to climb back into the nearby cloud.

But he hadn't reckoned on Sampson's tenacity.

Granny and Rose watched disbelieving as the Hurricane shot through the devil's brew of tracer and explosions, the unscathed emergence.

He closed rapidly with the 88.

Grey-white trails streamed back from the wings, hammering from in close, and the enemy began to smoke almost immediately from the starboard Jumo engine. Pieces of aircraft broke off, and then Sampson was over and curving around for another attack.

Rose remained circling over the plodding convoy (from a safe distance), in case of further attack, whilst Granny pursued the two fighting aeroplanes as they dwindled into the distant muck. Thankfully the naval gunners had ceased firing, but he kept his distance, nonetheless.

Sampson attacked again, and more smoke issued from the engine. This time it was denser, marking the path of flight of the escaping bomber. It was difficult to see the two aircraft as they melted into the cloud, but the lines of tracer fire lit it up from within, so Sampson still had him.

Then there was a flash, as if from an explosion. Rose watched anxiously. Had Sampson strayed too close? Or had the Junkers paid for his courageous foray over the channel?

After a few seconds, an aircraft reappeared. First, all Rose could see was a splash of flame, trailing back a long line of fire, a bright flare, carving a parabola in the poor light. It was impossible to see who it was, but then, "Got him!"

No screams of delight, just two words, filled with satisfaction for a job completed.

Sampson's Hurricane reappeared, close behind the burning Junkers.

The Junkers 88 had checked in its upward dash, flipped over, and dived down towards the waiting sea. Before it hit the surface of the water, there were two further flashes of light, close together, as something (Distress flares? Ammunition?) on the bomber exploded.

The second explosion tore the raider into pieces, the separate fragments slowly fluttering down to burn momentarily on the sea before they were extinguished. There were no parachutes.

Joining with Granny, Sampson returned victorious. It was his first victory.

"Slipper Leader to Slipper Three. Well done, But I think we ought to have a word with each other when we get back." Granny was obviously not amused at Speedy's risky flight through the ack-ack, even though he had managed to down the enemy bomber in doing so.

Rose watched the two as they returned together to the convoy. Below them, he could see tiny figures lining the decks of some of the vessels, perhaps cheering?

How did it feel to kill them, Speedy? Are you experiencing the same mixture of exhilaration, fear and horror?

Or are you just glad that you're still alive? Whatever else you are feeling, at least you will be glad that you've struck a blow against the foe, and proven to yourself that you are a fighter pilot. Sometimes, it's hardest to convince oneself of that.

It was fast approaching dusk when they emerged from the debriefing hut where they had seen Skinner, and the airfield's intelligence officer, the Spy. He had been particularly fastidious today about submitting the action report.

Rose had drunk a glass of water, and despite talk of a jolly drink at the Horse and Groom, what he really craved was a hot, sweet cup of tea.

Then he noticed the lovely girl outside.

Molly was waiting for him, and Granny turned, tipped Rose a wink. Molly watched them as they walked towards her, a trio of fine young men, one of whom was that extra bit special to her.

His once-white, immaculate flying overalls were now stained and worn-looking, and he seemed to have mislaid one of the rank badges from his left shoulder strap. His eyes were tired, but his obvious pleasure at seeing her was both pleasing and touching.

Granny slapped Speedy on the back.

"Come on, Speedy. I think we ought to have a little talk about your endangering HM equipment. If the Navy had managed to shoot you down, you'd have to spend a year filling in forms and attending courts of enquiry. At least you got that Jerry, so it ain't all that bad. I think I should stand you a pint, and the boys will be in there. I daresay they'll be waiting for you!"

Sampson turned to Rose, "Come on Harry, and, er, you too, Flight-Officer."

"We'll just be along shortly, Speedy."

Granny and Sampson walked away, and he stood there looking at her. He was conscious that he did not look his best, and he desperately wanted to wash the grime and tiredness from his face. But she didn't seem to care.

She reached out her hand shyly, and he took it in his.

They were quiet for a moment, just looking at each other, enjoying what each saw, the slight, weary young pilot, and the lovely girl in the powder blue uniform.

"I can't tell you how good you look, Molly, but you do."

The skin at the corners of her lips creased as she smiled faintly, and she looked away. He loved the gentle way she smiled, the way she would look away when embarrassed. She always did that.

"You're a very silly boy, you know. I feel positively ancient when I look at you. I can't imagine why you're so interested in me?" She reached out with her other hand, and gripped his sleeve playfully. "Anyway, you are in the Royal Air Force, you know, even if you are a dreadful child, and you still don't have any idea about dress regulations. So, come on, where's my blessed salute?"

Rose flipped up a casual salute, tried to click his heels. As he was wearing his flying boots, there was only a dull clump and Molly laughed a single peal of laughter that brought joy to his heart and another smile to his face.

He placed his hand over hers where she held him. He could smell her scent, and was conscious of the fact that he reeked of battle.

"Are you free now, then? Will you come and have a drink with me? If you can, of course."

"Yes, please. Of course I will, Harry. Always." He flushed with pleasure as she put her other hand in his, and he held on to her hands tightly, to his lifeline.

Chapter 19

The following day was one with very much improved weather.

The Navy had been hoping to take a large convoy of ships, CW8, through the Straits of Dover unnoticed by German observers, but the improvement in conditions dashed their hopes. The light haze was not enough to prevent attacks or to even make them difficult.

All three of the German armed services took part in the assault on CW8 that day.

The Wehrmacht gratefully made use of their coastal battery big guns based around Cap Gris Nez to shell the motley and unwieldy collection of vessels.

The Kreigsmarine sortied forth their light coastal forces, the powerful E-boats rolling out of the wretched waters of occupied France to attack repeatedly with torpedoes and cannon, like hyenas snapping incessantly and painfully at the heels of a bulky and outraged bull elephant.

Up above, with the improvement in visibility, came the air attack. Massed ranks of Junkers 87 dive-bombers wheeled and dived above the ships, and left the convoy trailing smoke and burning wreckage.

For the crewmen of those besieged vessels it must have seemed like an unending hell, as bombs and shells rained down from the heavens, and torpedoes cleaved the waters, all around them, to split hulls and extinguish lives.

Existence became a weary, umending story of waterspouts and explosions, the whine of ricochets and the clatter of gunfire.

This time the Stukas had come with a substantial fighter escort, and the defending 11 Group squadrons fought hard to cut their way through to the gull-winged dive bombers, but cut through they did.

A' Flight arrived on the scene of carnage to be bounced immediately by a force of Messerschmitt 109's. Once again, the Luftwaffe had supplied their bombers with a strong escort, yet once again, the sharp eyes of Granny Smith warned them of the impending doom just before the trap could be completely sprung.

Unable to reach the Stukas, the flight broke up into individual aircraft fighting lonely and desperate fights that mirrored the dogfights that were going on all around the area.

Rose had glanced once into his rear-view mirror, the desperate warning still ringing in his ears, as he hauled the control column back, back into the pit of his stomach.

His Hurricane twisted around violently to starboard, and he opened the throttle with a jerk. The hairs on the back of his neck stood up as he saw the swarm of monoplane fighters just a few hundred yards above and behind. His chest knotted with tension and dread, the tension making it feel as if an ice-cold stone had been placed inside his chest cavity.

As the Hurricane formation exploded apart, so too did that of the enemy.

The Germans split up into pairs, each choosing a different Hurricane to pursue.

"Keep turning, Yellow section." Granny gasped over the R/T as he too hauled his aircraft into a violent turn.

The same bloody thing, every bloody time. Why do we keep on getting bounced?

As he began to climb away, he watched some of the enemy fighters begin to turn after him, the control surfaces catching the sun as they, too, manoeuvred hard.

Despite the fact that he was turning, and the 109's streaked past below, the image of one of those fighters was burned into his mind. Even as he tightened his turn, grunting and cursing to himself, the darkening of vision encroaching, Rose was able to admire the deadly beauty of the trim little fighter, with its neat, sleek design and grey and blue paint work.

His very instincts screamed at him to reverse his turn and chase after some of the other 109s, but he knew that if he followed his instincts, he would be lost. The greatest safety lay in trying to out-turn the enemy. He could be out-performed in the vertical, but he held the edge in the horizontal turning fight.

As Granny had said before, "If a 109 tries to turn with you, it'll stall and fall out of the fight. Then he's at your mercy. If you're ever unfortunate enough to have one up your arse, for Christ's sake keep turning. It'll get you out of trouble. Scout's honour."

In his rear-view mirror he could see the pair that were slipping in behind him.

Oh God! He could feel his insides turning to jelly. He braced himself, his testicles shrivelling to ice.

No! I'm not going to die, not today, he railed himself defiantly.

The enemy leader opened fire, and his nose and wings twinkled prettily, belying the true lethalness of the lights.

The fire from his cannon and machine guns zipped past the Hurricane, close, but far enough away to show Rose that the Bf109 could not turn with him. He was safe from them, at least for the moment, anyway.

Thank goodness.

Keep an eye out, though, for others slashing through the fight.

Those cannon shells were explosive, and just one could do a lot of damage to P-Peter.

Rose kept the stick pulled hard back, right into his stomach. Arms and legs moved without conscious thought, just as Granny had taught. Two weeks of operational flying had given the polish to what he had learned, and what now came automatically. Even as the cold sweat came, he kept calm, and kept his head.

Automatic responses that helped to extinguish the heat of his fear. Turn. Keep turning. Slight adjustments. Oh, God, keep me safe! Steady pressure on the rudder. Keep the nose pointing at the horizon. That's it. Just keep on turning. Just like Granny showed you.

Keep looking around.

Jerry can't keep it up.

But can I?

Eyes stinging, mouth open and gasping. Keep the nose pointing at the horizon.

With its higher wing-loading, the Messerschmitt was unable to match the Hurricane. It could not match him in this turning fight.

Watch out for others…

More shots streaked past ahead, fiery flecks, closely followed by another Messerschmitt, which had tried to hit him in a slashing pass, but the shot was a difficult one, and unsuccessful.

It was difficult to line Rose's Hurricane up for a shot whilst he was turning so hard, and the attempt almost proved more dangerous for the attacker than the attacked. As the enemy fighter shot past, tantalisingly close, Rose spasmodically pressed his gun-button, knowing that there was little chance of a hit, for the German had already shot past.

His guns remained silent, and he realised that he had not slipped the safety catch off in all the excitement.

He cursed and berated himself foully, although he knew there would have been little chance of a hit. He was breathing hard, resisting the effects of the turning on his body.

As Rose turned high above, one of the destroyers escorting the convoy received a direct hit from a Stuka; it curved out of position, and immediately began to settle in the water.

Fully engrossed in personal survival, Rose did not even notice the death-knell flash amongst the distant grey huddle of ships to show the successes of the Stukas.

One of the two 109s behind had disappeared (where's it gone?), but the other was still following him.

However, with his tighter turning advantage, Rose now found himself creeping up behind the other plane and slowly closing the circle. The pursuer had imperceptibly turned into the pursued.

Pressed back into his seat, he gazed up at the 109, once again admiring its shape. It was an attractive aircraft, in a waspish, dangerous kind of way.

Keep turning. He was banging his knee with his fist as he urged his faithful Hurricane to close with the German kite. His heart was thundering monstrously, and his face was fixed in a grimace as the terrible forces pressed him back into his bucket seat.

Automatically he continued to check all around, continuously swivelling his head, to ensure that another enemy plane was not positioning itself to make an attack from the side or from behind.

So far, so good.

The Luftwaffe pilot in front, not unmindful of the danger, but scared to break out of the turn, continued to turn with him. Amazingly he had not yet stalled.

Keep turning. Almost there! Granny was right!

Tighten the turn further. Is it safe? Yes.

Reflector sight? Yes. On.

Guns? On.

Good.

Tighter! Keep turning.

The Merlin was roaring powerfully. Don't fail me, please.

The 109 crept ever closer into the crosshairs.

Help me, God, please!

After what seemed like minutes, but in truth could not have been more than scant seconds, Rose had pulled around and was finally able to sight on his one-time pursuer. He wanted slightly more lead, but fearful that the German may finally awaken to the danger, he pressed the gun-button once more.

This time he had slipped the safety catch off, and his machine-guns spat fire out at the 109 before him.

Hits registered as his bullets clipped the port wingtip, close to the huge black cross outlined in white. There was a sudden puff of smoke from his bullet strikes.

Another one second burst ripped into the fuselage, and started the Daimler-Benz DB601 inverted V12 engine smoking.

Startled by the sudden impacts, the German pilot finally realised the folly and danger of continuing the turn and dived out of the fight, disappearing with thick dark smoke and debris streaming back from his exhaust stubs and wing.

The 109 could out-dive him, and he let it go, his eyes already searching for another target. He tried to moisten dry lips with an equally dry tongue, grateful and slightly surprised at having success-fully out-fought one of the dreaded Bf109s that he had secretly feared for so long.

Did Dad feel like this when he'd flown against the German Jastas?

Another aircraft screamed past, climbing steeply, buffeting Rose, and he instinctively tried for a deflection shot, but his burst failed to connect, which was just as well, as the other aircraft turned out to be another Hurricane. A pale, terrified face looked back at him as it swept upwards.

"Cripes, watch out!" Rose cried involuntarily, although it had been his shooting, his bullets clawing out at a friend, and his heart was thumping painfully, erratically.

He'd almost shot down Cutts!

Almost immediately, a second aircraft streaked past. This one was a Messerschmitt, and it too was firing at Cutts' Hurricane. On the R/T he could hear Denis shouting for Cutts to turn.

Rose was about to follow, when a thought suddenly struck him. Granny always warned that where there was one, there was likely to be two (at least).

Was Cutts being chased by a pair of Huns? And if he were, where the hell was the other one?

Damn it! He was about to throw the Hurricane into a violent manoeuvre, half-expecting to feel the crash of projectiles into his aircraft, when a second Messerschmitt skidded past, already manoeuvring, rocking the Hurricane.

The second German pilot, the wingman, obviously climbing at full throttle, had noticed him too late, and had been unable to draw a bead on him.

Thank God they had not seen him earlier.

Now the German was curving around, contrails streaming from wingtips, ailerons working as he tried to turn, but in his eagerness to fight his reactions were poorly thought out. Instead of adequately protecting his leader, he merely became an easy target for Rose's guns.

Rose was amazed as the slightly foreshortened plan view of the Bf109 appeared in the lower half of the ring of his reflector sight. Like the first, it too was painted a silvery grey and blue.

It was a sitting target! Was it a trap?

No, nothing behind.

Too far in front. Fuck it! Fire anyway.

Turning after it, he fired a long burst that tracked forwards as he followed the curve more tightly.

The Messerschmitt floundered as Rose's bullets smashed into it. Hits sparkled like short-lived harbingers of doom along the rear fuselage and starboard wing root. A cloud of what looked like dust or powdery debris (flakes of paint?) plumed back from the enemy aircraft. One strut parted from the tail plane to whirl away in the slipstream.

Mirror. Keep watching your tail.

One eye fixed on the one in front, the other feverishly scanning the immediate surrounding area for more enemy fighters. Or so it seemed.

Too many 109's around. I'll be cross-eyed after this.

His target rolled to port, and Rose hammered another endlessly long four second burst into it. Wing panels and ailerons flew off, and the airscrew had begun to slow down and windmill, a searing streamer of flame, bright yellow shot through with vivid orange, jetting back from the wing-root.

Behind the goggles he squinted at the sudden glare, allowed the range between the aircraft to increase. The distance had closed to almost nothing, and he fancied he could feel the heat from the flames.

Out of control, the 109 rolled further to port, when the tail unit, already weakened, snapped off to whip past Rose's Hurricane. It was more than fifty feet away as it whirled past, but it gave him a good scare. It seemed to him that he could have reached out and touched it as it gyrated wildly past.

If it had hit him, he too would have gone down too. In its death throes, the Messerschmitt may still have been able to wreak its revenge on its killer.

Deprived of the stabilising forces provided by its tail unit, the 109's nose dipped suddenly, but forward momentum carried it along its path of flight, and it flipped forward end over end, into a series of somersaults, pieces breaking away.

All control of the aircraft was lost, and it began to spin wildly, falling away. Pinned to his cockpit by the tremendous forces, there was no way that the German pilot, if he still lived, would be able to escape from his aircraft.

Subject to these unbearable forces, the wings suddenly bent back and then sheared completely off.

Rose watched as the wreckage of the rapidly spinning, burning remnants of the Me109 disappeared below. It was hard to believe that such a beautiful and potent aircraft could be converted to flaming debris so quickly.

Cutts and the other Messerschmitt had disappeared, but there would be other aircraft still around. A quick glance behind showed a Hurricane turning towards him about five hundred yards distant.

"Bloody good shooting, Yellow Two. There's no doubt about that one." It was Denis in his D-Dolly. He formed up with Rose, his Hurricane smoke and oil streaked. Some of the fabric on the fuselage had been ripped back, exposing the wooden dorsal section formers within.

"Thanks, Leader. Any luck?" Rose looked at the now far distant convoy, faint and ghost-like in the haze. Palls of heavy grey black smoke hung ominously over the just visible, muted, silvery dots that were the barrage balloons above the clump of ships on the horizon. The underside of the low hanging dark smoke cloud glowed red from the fires that burned below it.

The fight of the last few minutes had taken him far from the naval battle below, which, at least for the time being, had finished. *How on earth did I get so far away from it in such a short time?*

"Yeah, got one, mate."

The German bombers had escaped whilst Rose and the others had been facing the 109s. At least he and Denis had managed to score.

Another quick all-around check revealed a seemingly empty sky. The rest of the 109's appeared to have beaten a retreat as well.

Denis' voice sounded weary, even over the VHF. "I got a Stuka for certain, and damaged a 109. I was going after the two Huns that were chasing Cutts. I'm out of ammo, though. At least you got one of 'em. Did you see where they went?"

"Dunno, Red Leader," he gasped. Suddenly he felt like a wrung out sponge, dried out and empty of feeling. "I lost them when I went after that wingman." He marvelled at the steadiness of his voice. *I should have pulled Cutts' nuts out of the fire. But if I'd followed the 109 leader, the wing man would have nailed me.*

Denis seemed not to have heard. "They got the new boy, curse them. Flamer straight down, no 'chute."

Without thinking, Rose brought up his hand to check on Genevieve. Yes, she was still there, tucked away safely in his tunic pocket. *She was definitely gaining a lot of combat experience (and keeping me safe at the same time! Thank you, Molly).* He realised that he could not even remember the new pilot's name. He had been a Sergeant-pilot who had arrived only the day before. There was just the vague memory of a round faced young man, cropped blond hair and rosy cheeks, a ready grin, asking what time dinner was.

Had he died instantly, or...? His mind shied away from the thoughts of the painful and horrible death that the boy may have suffered at the end.

Damn it.

His mind returned to the events of the previous day. Sinclair and his flight had cornered a He 59 Luftwaffe red-cross rescue plane, twelve miles east of Boulogne.

They shot it down into the sea, despite the fact that there were many German fighters in the area.

Then, they had fled, leaving the enemy fighters circling empty-handed over the burning pieces of metal.

Originally Rose had thought it an unfair victory, but Granny had explained how the big floatplanes were more often than not flying with a heavy escort, and always seemed to be in areas of military significance, spying. Churchill himself had declared the big flying-boats to be hostile aircraft, despite the large red crosses.

Besides, a rescued pilot was a pilot that could shoot you down tomorrow. That was why Churchill had declared them to be legitimate enemy targets.

Rose had understood the importance to the enemy of the spy planes, and now, with another loss, it did not seem wrong at all.

When you fight, Granny had said, you fight to win. Total victory or nothing. "It ain't a game, Harry. And being dead ain't much fun. Don't ever forget that."

Winning was the only thing that mattered. Otherwise, there's no point.

His heart was still hammering painfully. The edges of three bullet holes showed on his starboard wing. He could not even remember being hit.

Copeland. Ah, yes, that was his name. Sergeant-Pilot Copeland, the new boy on the squadron.

Just a young boy, killed on his first mission. Rose had hardly spoken to him. How many more would there be before it was all over? Would he himself be one?

RIP, Copeland. God bless.

And RIP the poor chaps in the convoys. Why on earth are they still sending them out? What are they thinking? It's not worth the lives lost or ruined.

But whatever the machinations of those hidden away in safe, secure offices, I'm still here, surviving once more.

Thank God.

Scrapped with Bf109's, definitely got one, damaged another, but better still, I managed to avoid getting shot down myself by some stroke of good fortune, and I'm still alive to tell the tale!

Still alive. Thank God.

But, like Granny had said, the best fighter pilots are not just good, but also lucky.

Still alive, and still lucky.

For today, at least.

Chapter 20

"Balloons," said Molly dreamily.

"Hmm?" responded Rose languorously, voice muffled, from beneath his cap.

Molly leaned over him and grasping the peak of the cap, tipped it up. He squinted in the bright sunlight, his lips stained green by the stem of grass that he had been squeezing between his lips.

"I said, Balloons." She repeated in a low, deliberately throaty voice.

One eyelid raised slightly, and he frowned. What was she talking about?

"Balloons? What about them? Do you want one? Shall I get you one, Molly? What colour? Tell me?"

"Not that kind of balloon, simpleton," she scolded. "I meant barrage balloons."

This time he opened both eyes, shading them with an upraised hand and stared at her in bafflement. "You want me to get you a barrage balloon, sweetie? I would, truly, but aren't there regulations or something that stipulate that any old Tom, Dick or Harry can't take them as a present for their sweethearts? I don't think I could fly one of those things. I mean, I could get in awful trouble, and you'd not want that, would you?"

251

He was all wide eyes and innocence, "Say you wouldn't, do."

"You're so silly," she sighed, "Heaven's preserve us." Molly rolled her eyes in mock exasperation.

She was sitting beside him on the thick grass, her long legs folded neatly beneath her.

She placed his cap on her head, and looked across the adjoining fields.

On the far side, the farmer was early collecting his grain sheaves.

The tall stalks had been scythed down, and then gathered into loose piles at regular intervals around the field. The farmer had then harnessed his horse; he would tie a rope around each pile, and then use his horse to pull it to a hay stack. It was back-breaking work on this hot day, but the farmer and his work hands had not stopped even once for the last hour.

Rose raised himself onto his elbows. "Honestly, it's easier to steal the station commander's Gladiator then it is to nab a barrage balloon, my dear."

"Oh, Harry," she sighed. "You can be so dim, sometimes. I wanted to call your attention to the balloon they were putting up over there." She pointed with a slim, well-manicured finger.

Rose sat up. The two of them were lounging on the side of the low hill that bordered the road that led to the airfield.

In the distance a barrage balloon shone silver as it slowly emerged from behind a line of trees, obscuring the windmill behind.

The balloon swayed gently in the light breeze, and they could hear the peculiar whistling notes where the wind caught its cables. As with many of its fellow brethren, it seemed to sprout two cauliflower-like ears, one above, one below; the stabilising fins.

"Oh. It looks like a nice one. Very shiny…urm…and, uh, bulbous." He looked at her. "But not as nice and shiny as you, my lovely Molly."

She tilted her head, and a swathe of lustrous hair escaped from beneath his cap to swing delightfully, catching the light.

"Flattery will get you nowhere," she repeated tartly.

"Oh, no. No flattery intended, believe me. I'm only speaking the truth. You are very lovely. Very lovely indeed." His voice caught as he looked at her. It was true. When he looked at her, it was so very difficult to look away again. At her full, soft, red lips, her high cheekbones and dark, almond shaped eyes. Her teeth gleamed momentarily and he thought longingly of licking them.

"Flattery will get you nowhere," she said again, lightly, "You are such a silly boy." She leant forwards and kissed him gently on his lips.

Mmm. Lovely.

"But at least you're a moderately nice silly boy." She took his right hand between hers and squeezed. Gently, he squeezed back.

"Someone will catch a packet if they keep the thing there," she said thoughtfully, eyeing the balloon professionally, "If they put it too close, they'll damage the windmill."

Wonder why Jerry would target a windmill, Rose wondered.

Seeing the question in his eyes, she explained. "When I first joined the WAAF, those were the things that were my bread and butter every day."

Rose looked at her with interest, "Really? Tell me?"

"Well, there were fifty or so of us girls in the company. We were one of the first balloon companies."

"Balloon companies?" Rose was all agog. His eyes looked huge, the dark shadows beneath them making them appear even more so.

She looked at him, to see if he was being facetious, and seeing that he wasn't, she continued.

"Yes. Number 20 RAF (County of London) Company of the ATS, to be precise. Just before the WAAF was formed in June, last year. It was decided that we would be affiliated and sent to one of the balloon centres. That involved making balloons, or patching up those that had been damaged by the elements. Weather really can be quite cruel to the poor old balloon, and electricity in the air sometimes sets off the hydrogen they contain. How would you like floating around in all sorts of weather?"

She adjusted Rose's cap, peak lower over her eyes, "Of course, we didn't get the ones that were shot down. All the effort of patching them up and getting them in the air, and then, after all that work, someone comes along and shoots it down."

She glowered pointedly at Rose, who blushed, remembering the wretched runaway balloon he had helped to shoot down whilst training with Granny in his first week on the squadron. Hell's teeth! Did she know everything there was to know about him?

"A couple of the girls went into the Skyrockets," she continued, referring to one of the new force's dance bands.

"Our first uniforms were berets and overall, and it was damn hard to be a credit to the Air Force in those. Not very fashionable, either."

Rose smiled wickedly. "I'm sure that you looked lovely, but I can definitely say that you look absolutely terrific in your blues."

And he made a show of examining her trim uniform and gleaming buttons. She looked like a fashion catwalk model even in her air force outfit. A little voice murmured something in his mind that she'd look even better without them but he quashed the thought immediately.

He was quite sure that if she stood naked before him he would pass out or that his heart would shudder to a stop in wonder.

But the thought of her naked was most delightful, and was not a vision easily dispelled. It lingered pleasantly.

Molly sniffed haughtily, "Yes, well. What did I say about flattery?" She stared down her nose at him, but the effect was ruined by Rose's cap tipped over her eyes. She looked ridiculous.

Achingly beautiful, but absolutely ridiculous. Beautifully ridiculous.

"Anyway, we did all sorts of admin type jobs before they sent some of us to a balloon centre in Essex. Now that was fun, and the girls there were a jolly bunch. Sometimes we spent a few days with balloon squadrons in London's docks or on barges on the Thames."

She looked at him severely, "Did you know one of those things," she waved vaguely at the distant balloon, "Needs over a thousand yards of fabric?"

Bewildered, Rose mumbled, "Crumbs!"

"Oh yes! Over six hundred pieces of fabric in each of the things!"

Rose tried to look suitably impressed.

She released his hand and looked at her palms, "My hands were like pincushions. I abhor needlework at the best of times, you know, and we had to use herringbone pattern with a single thread or one of those big oily sewing machines for the bigger tears in the material."

He widened his eyes and raised his eyebrows in an attempt at awed wonder.

"Hell on the dungarees, you know." Rose had visions of truckloads of girls in dungarees speeding madly through the countryside, towing colossal sewing machines behind them, the way army tractors were used to tow artillery pieces.

He tried not to laugh at the mental picture.

Not knowing a single thing about needlework, he asked, "Um, wouldn't the needle make the thing leak?"

"You poor, sweet boy, you don't know anything, do you?" She patted his cheek kindly. "Never mind, Molly will take care of you."

He perked up at that. "Oh, jolly good!"

She waggled a finger at him in admonishment, attempting to scowl, "Don't get any ideas, buster."

Rose pouted, but to be honest, he was so comfortable in the easy relationship that had formed between them that the implications of a physical relationship terrified him.

He was still a virgin, and although he was desperately keen to change that, Rose wanted so desperately to please her, and the thought of performing poorly when the time came made him go hot and cold in consternation.

"So why aren't you still driving a balloon around, or running around with a needle and thread, or, um, something?"

"You'd rather I still was, do you?"

"Oh no, sweet Molly. Just wondering."

"I decided I had had enough after a particular incident, and asked to be transferred."

"Oh?"

"We used to be sent inside each completed balloon…"

"A sweet Jonah into the silvery whale…"

"Hm. Quite. Erm…oh, bother. You've made me forget now. Ummm, where was I?"

"Sorry. You were about to venture forth into a balloon." He stared dreamily at her. Even if she wore a barrage balloon she'd look divine.

"Ah yes. We-ell, once we had made a balloon, or patched one up, we had to paint the whole thing with dope on the inside. Just to make sure it was airtight."

"Sounds very sensible."

"Well it was my turn, so in I went with a couple of tins of dope and a paintbrush. While I was in there, the girls forgot about me and they all trooped off for their usual eleven o'clock glass of milk."

"Milk? D'you mean elevenses? A cuppa?"

"No, milk. Supposed to counteract any effects the dope may have, apparently. Then, while they were there, the CO decided to have a practice air raid, so off they all trot to the shelters. Meantime, good old Molly is still going great guns with her brush inside her balloon. I didn't even notice the passage of time. Next thing I can remember is waking up with the girls dragging me out by my feet from the innards of the damned balloon. Had a stinker of a headache for days afterwards. After that, I decided that my association with the dear old silver beastie was at an end. Time to seek new climes, and all that."

"Thank heavens they rescued you," exclaimed Rose, fervently. "I'd not have met you otherwise."

"And would that have been so terrible?"

"Oh, Molly, lovely Molly, of course it would have been. I cannot imagine life without you. I know I don't say so, but, er, you mean very much to me." With one finger he traced the line of her cheek down to her chin. "You mean everything to me. I think you are wonderful."

Pleased, she said, "Do you really mean that?" even though she could see his sincerity.

"Molly, I've never said a truer word. When I'm with you I feel so comfortable. I feel truly at peace when I'm with you. You are like my sanctuary from the world."

He sat up," I know that you really care about me. And the thing is, I really care for you. When I'm not with you I don't feel whole. You are so lovely, so perfect, and I feel so free with you. I don't feel as if I have to shoot lines or be anybody but myself. You are the tranquillity and beauty in my life." Goodness! Where did that come from? He was surprised at his outburst.

She looked away, her eyes bright. "Oh, Harry. You are such a lovely boy."

But, of course, he wasn't. He was a man, a sweet, wonderful, gentle, quiet and strong man. So different from all the men who had tried to impress her in the past, so full of themselves, both in the RAF, and before, when she had worked as a fashion model.

She looked back at him, eyes swimming, "Of course I feel the same. Of course I do. I think you're such a special and dear person, and I can't begin to explain my feelings. But the thing is, I care very much for you."

Molly shook her head sadly, "But we can't. I'm too old for you."

"You must never say that, lovely Molly." He said fiercely, "Promise me you'll never say that again?"

Instead of answering, she pulled his hand to her, and placed it beneath her left breast. "Can you feel my heart beating? Every time that I'm with you, or when I see you, it thumps so. Aren't I silly?"

He was struck dumb. Beneath the material of her tunic he could feel the soft curve of her body, the tightness of it, where the underside of her breast pressed against it. He looked at her as she leaned back; her eyes closed, with her hand holding his against her, and thought he had never felt anything so exciting, even in combat. He could feel the blood roaring in his ears, and he thought he would swoon.

Her breath was rapid, whilst conversely he, caught in this stunned moment, held his breath without realising he was doing so. He was frozen (in fear? Or was it stunned wonderment?)

His every instinct screamed at him to slide his hand upwards, to cup the fullness of that lovely breast, to feel her sweet womanhood in his palm, but he was afraid it might insult her to do so, and did (could) not.

He had never been with a woman, never even kissed one (not counting *that* kiss cousin Barbara had given him last Christmas, but *that* had been more of a slobber) before he had met Molly, and now he was here with this beautiful girl, whom he loved, her body warm and compliant beneath his fingers.

258

Yes, loved. Why skirt around the truth?

There was no reason to fear the truth, was there?

He loved Molly. So it must be alright to touch her.

Mustn't it?

She had taken his hand and placed it on her, after all.

But he was fearful of her reaction. She might be outraged. Mother always warned him of the girls that picked up men. Of course he knew Molly was not like that, but she mustn't think that he thought she was that kind of girl.

She was so gentle and lovely he wanted everything to be right. She was the only thing that brought him peace. She was everything. Nothing else mattered when she was near.

God, I want to be with you for the rest of my life, Molly.

Oh, come now. Come on, a little voice whispered, chidingly, you're just scared she'll find out you've never been with a girl.

It's your first time, and you want her, but you're too scared. You don't deserve to touch a girl like her. Admit it. You've never been so scared. More perhaps than when you faced your first solo flight, or your first combat patrol.

No. He wouldn't touch the things that he really wanted to. The things that made his mouth dry, his head spin and his heart race.

It was important that he did everything just right. He could remember the whispered stories of frenzied and confused coupling that his friends had boasted of during the summer holidays, during OTU, but it held no attraction for him. He had listened with envy, but he did not want a girl like that.

When he finally lay with a woman, it would be with the one that he cared for, and one who felt the same, for surely love added the special something to the experience, surely the experience was intensified by love? The experience should be special. It would be with Molly.

Everything had to be just right, to be perfect. He would go slowly, savour each sensation, and wonder at each experience. He wanted to appreciate the sight of her, the fragrance of her, the feel and taste of her.

But she was lithe and firm beneath his hand, and how lovely it would be to enfold that firm, rounded breast, to feel it as he squeezed it gently, grip it against his palm.

How easy it would be to touch her, as she lay there before him.

But he would not. It did not seem right, even though he ached to do so. It seemed almost sacrilegious. She was glorious, and he didn't want to spoil it in any way.

He was a gentleman, not some desperate youth, and he would not paw her. Not his perfect Molly.

Oh, he would touch her and caress her when there were no distractions, when there was just the two of them, alone. Naked and welcoming on a soft bed, clean white sheets, with all the time in the world to enjoy her completely.

Oh, Molly. I love you. I wish that you could love me the way I love you. I would give everything to be loved by you. You're marvellous. And I want you.

In every way.

After a moment (seconds, minutes?) she brought his hand up to her lips and kissed his fingertips tenderly. Such soft lips.

"Oh, Molly, I think I'm in love you."

Oh God, NO! He was appalled. Had he just said that?

What will she think?

Oh. My. God.

The words had come out before he could stop them. She'll think you say such things without meaning or sincerity.

That you're only saying them so that you can have your way with her...

Oh you stupid fool!

Bleating out your most intimate thoughts like some silly little schoolboy! He cringed inwardly.

But it was how he truly felt. So why hide it? Damn it! In for a penny, in for a pound! Fortune favours the brave, and all that nonsense! "I mean it. I love you. I do, honestly."

She did not let go of his hand, but just gazed back at him with that wonderful soft smile.

"I know that you do, Harry. I've always known how you felt, and I want you to know that I feel the same." She kissed his hand again, "I shouldn't, but God help me, I do."

He stared at her, disbelieving. Could it be true?

She paused, gazing into his eyes searchingly, and then repeated, "I love you. I shouldn't; but I do." She laughed at his expression. "I love you very, very much, my darling, with each little part of me."

Astonished and joyful, he felt as if a firework had suddenly gone off brilliantly inside him. Electricity tingled and thrilled from his toes to the top of his head. It was a joy even more intense than that when they had shared that first kiss.

She loves me!

Dear God, she loves me!

Oh, thank you! Who could want more?

She put his hand against her cheek. Despite his growing happiness, he heaved a mental sigh.

His hand had been very comfortable where she had placed it before, beneath her breast, thank you very much, and he could still feel the warmth of her body on his skin. Please put it back there. I'd rather like it if you did. Wish I had the courage to touch you there myself. But what you think, how you feel, means so very much to me.

So I daren't. I want you only to think well of me.

I'll never do anything to hurt you. I promise it.

"I love you, Harry, for your honesty, your kindness, your decency, for your modesty. You are everything I've ever wanted, and everything I knew you would be. You are a very, very special, man, Harry. I can't fight the way I feel about you anymore. I really want to be yours."

"Oh, Molly, will you really be mine? I want nothing more in life than that you should be mine." His voice, sounding stilted to his ears, stumbling with embarrassment.

So much for keeping your feelings to yourself, you daft twerp. What happened to your ideas about remaining single for the duration of the war, twit?

But they were his thoughts before he had met her. How was it possible to continue to still think so after meeting anyone as lovely as she is?

"I will," a pause, "for as long as you want me."

"Forever. I want you as mine always." He gulped.

"Then you shall have me, always." Words spoken quietly, but with great intensity. Powerful words. "I love you, my dearest Harry."

"I love you, my lovely Molly," he said it again, wonderingly, and hugged her as if he would never let go, burying his face into her sweet, luxuriant hair.

It was like a dream.

I've been on the squadron for just less than a month, he thought, and I've brought down five and a half Huns, made ace fighter pilot already, but better still, I've found the girl of my dreams. How could so much happen in so short a time?

If I die tomorrow, which is more than likely, it will be as a contented and happy man.

"I'd like it very much if you kissed me, Harry."

Greatly daring, heart thumping, "I thought you'd never ask!"

Chapter 21

The next five days were hectic ones, both for Rose and his squadron. There were more patrols than before, but no successful interceptions.

On the 26th, following the disastrous loss and damage to half (eleven merchant ships out of twenty-one) of the channel convoy CW8 on the 25th, with only two reaching their final destination, it was finally decided that channel convoys should only use the channel during the hours of darkness.

It would take some time though, to put decision into effect, and convoys were still at sea the following day. The weather was awful. Low cloud and heavy rain over much of Britain made flying extremely difficult.

Nevertheless, the Luftwaffe continued in attacks on shipping south of the Isle of Wight, and along the Channel coast, and, although Excalibur did no flying this day, some Hurricanes were sent out. The weather was responsible for more damaged aircraft than enemy action.

The loss of two Royal Navy destroyers on the same day was yet another bitter pill for the Admiralty. The country could ill afford to lose such valuable ships and sailors.

Saturday the 27th saw more attacks, as the weather partially cleared. There were further attacks on convoys still at sea, and concerted attacks on Dover harbour and the Royal Navy lost three more destroyers.

Losses were reaching untenable levels, after the events of the last weeks, and in addition to the losses endured at Dunkirk and in Norway. It was decided by those in Admiralty that something would have to be done.

Husbanding the remaining destroyers was vital, but it must be without appearing to surrender the Channel to the Luftwaffe.

For Foxton, there was an invasion 'scare'. A phone call came from London warning of an invasion fleet landing at Margate, and a flight of 97 squadron's Spitfires were immediately scrambled. There was complete chaos with half-dressed pilots of Excalibur arriving at the airfield in an exotic variety of cars and bicycles.

Sirens wailed and trucks brimming with soldiers raced importantly here and there amidst plenty of shouting and swearing.

The ground crews ran around desperately preparing all the aircraft for combat, and air defence searched the sky alertly for the first sign of approaching enemy aircraft. With his whole squadron available, Donald put up a rota of a Hurricane section for airfield protection.

Billy authoritatively confided in Rose of huge fires burning on the Channel, and hundreds of German dead were being washed ashore. Rose wondered about this, as Billy was still wearing his pyjamas beneath his flying kit, and had arrived at the airfield after everyone else. How could he know?

Meanwhile, everything was quiet and peaceful at Margate, and the Spitfires returned frustrated.

There was no invasion. No German dead. The only casualty was a soldier who accidentally shot himself in the leg as he fell off a truck.

Apparently it had been an exercise organised at Whitehall. An irate Granny swore to track down the faceless functionary who had phoned the warning, and shoot him on his next foray into London.

The air fighting was desultory until the 28th of July, when 'Sailor' Malan led his 74 squadron into a victorious drubbing of German forces, the Luftwaffe overall losing more than three times as many aircraft as the RAF.

Even the great German ace, Werner Moelders, was forced to an ignominious crash-landing, with terrible leg wounds that would keep him in hospital and out of the fighting for some time.

Many believed that it was Malan himself that was responsible for besting the great German ace.

This day was also significant in that it was the one when destroyers were withdrawn from the exposed confines of Dover harbour to the slightly safer harbour of Portsmouth.

The Navy were no longer safe in the waters they had so long claimed as their own.

After the RN losses of the previous days, it was amazing that the authorities had taken so long to act. Unfortunately, with the loss of destroyer protection, the task fell upon the RAF to provide additional defence.

An increased effort was to be required from RAF Fighter Command.

Excalibur however, did not manage to take part in any of the fighting that actually took place, although Sinclair and Billy did prosper, adding to the squadron score board, when they succeeded in cornering a Junkers 88 over Rochester, and shooting it down, with the loss of all aboard.

During this time, a bright spark at Group thought it would be a good idea to take the connection with King Arthur further. They put forward the suggestion that each pilot of Excalibur should have the name of one of King Arthur's knights on their Hurricane.

Donald himself, as 'King Arthur', was to have a gold crown painted onto his aircraft. It would be an excellent idea that could serve propaganda purposes. The newspapers would have a great story with the modern 'Knights of the round Table.' In the hour of Britain's Greatest Need, blah, blah, etc.

Donald thought the idea was appalling.

"Just imagine if I get shot down, Uncle," he confided to Skinner, "Group can't really appoint a new Arthur then, can they? And just think what a terrible thing it would be for the public to hear about! If the war carries on, it's quite likely that we're going to lose a lot of the 'knights' as well. You know what's what in wartime. No. I shan't approve the new paintings, or the whole diabolical scheme."

But Granny was vociferous in his protests. He loved the idea and did want artwork applied. But he had no interest in knightly emblems. It turned out that he was rather keen to have the picture of his current favourite female painted onto his kite, and she turned out to be the rather voluptuous Daily Mirror's Jane. Preferably nude and astride a charger (or, better still, astride something else...)

Donald had put his head in his hands. "Good grief! The saucy bloody sod. Tell him no. I have it on authority that Jane wasn't one of Arthur's knights."

Donald did not approve of Jane. And no scantily-clad girl would be adorning one of the planes of his squadron.

Air Vice Marshal Keith Park, AOC of 11 Group, as he regularly did with all his squadrons, flew in to see the young pilots of his two squadrons on the 29th. He jumped down from his Hurricane, still as sprightly as any of his young pilots.

He'd swept into the hangers to have a quick word with the

Flight-Sergeant, then onto the mess to see his boys. Rose had been standing nearby, talking with Granny, and the lean and hawkish Park spotted them and walked right up to them.

He'd nodded, stuck out his hand. "Hello, Granny. Nice to see you. Didn't recognise you there for a moment, thought you were the airman on latrine cleaning duties."

He'd frowned, looked Smith up and down, quirked an eyebrow. "I can see your sartorial skills haven't improved much. My God, man, what d'you wash your uniform with, engine oil? Oh, and well done on that bar to your DFM! Good man, very well deserved! Hear you're going to paint Jane on your 'plane." He shook his head slightly, eyes crinkling. "God help us! The service is turning into a circus." He turned those probing eyes to Rose. "And this is Rose, is it?"

Rose nodded, gaping and dumbfounded under the great man's gaze. The tall New Zealander had placed a finger lightly on Rose's chest, onto his AFC ribbon. "Well done. Heard all about it. Did very well under very trying conditions. Could do with a few more like you. Hear you've managed to knock down a few Huns since? I suppose this grubby rogue taught you a few of his tricks?"

Rose nodded again, dumbly. Park smiled warmly, his face creasing. "Good lad. Let the others have a few, though. Don't keep 'em all for yourself, there's a good chap. Nice to see a nice spotless tunic. Good example for Granny, though I fear he's a lost cause."

He'd nodded at Smith. "Try not to let this awful chap act as a model of service discipline for you, will you, Rose, alright?"

He had sat in the Mess and had a cup of tea with Wing Commander Heart, Donald and Squadron-Leader Cohen, CO of 97.

The other officers gathered at a respectable distance behind them. He preached the doctrine of attacking 'Head-on.'

It had certainly worked against the Stuka formation he had attacked with B-Flight, mused Rose.

"The bombers have got less forward armament and armour forward, so they're more vulnerable to a head-on attack. Also, they're flying in tight formation, so they've less room to manoeuvre. If you hit 'em head on, you'll likely break up the formation."

He'd looked round at the pilots sombrely, "But you must do as you see fit. It's easy for me to recommend a tactic, but it's up to you boys, when you're up there. You're the one's facing the bullets." The pilots thought over his words in silence. It was of course harder to accurately aim at an enemy coming at you head-on, and the danger of collision was uncomfortably high.

Then Park had made his way back to his refuelled Hurricane, stopping momentarily to have a quick word and a flirt with a gaggle of WAAFs coming off duty from the ops room.

As the sound of the Hurricane receded, Granny had said simply, "He's a fine man, that one. I'll tell you how we first met one day," and walked back into the mess. Rose wondered how Park had known him. But then, how had he known about Rose? It was the first time they'd met.

He'd have to question Smith at an opportune moment.

Anyway, Granny was right. AVM Park truly was a very fine man.

There were a number of air fights that day, and B-Flight took off, to intercept Heinkels that were stooging around off the Essex coast near Harwich. Sinclair was able to claim a probable, whereas Farrell received credit for one damaged.

The 30th of July was a day with low cloud and limiting weather. Fighter Command flew a large number of sorties, but there was no air combat on this day.

It was different on the 31st, although enemy activity was very light. The first fight of the day was actually one in which a RAAF

Short Sunderland four-engined flying boat chased off a Ju88 that was sniffing around the refitted merchant cruiser *SS Mooltan*.

Stukas bombed small convoys around midday, but managed to get away without RAF interception.

Later, in the mid-afternoon, Bf109 raiders were intercepted by 74 Squadron, and a dogfight developed over Dover and its environs.

Again a day of inactivity for Excalibur. But one appreciated greatly by the pilots.

Despite the continuous and busy programme of flying, the poor weather meant that the squadron managed to get some free time.

As was normal in Fighter Command at that time, usually the pilots received two days on duty and one day off. The days were a whirl of danger and flying during the day and wild mess parties or forays in the evenings.

Whilst not being stretched too hard, the pilots were flying far more sorties than were usual in a peacetime fighter squadron, and the tiredness was telling. So the day off was a valued time for the pilots.

They were also days of great satisfaction and pleasure for Rose.

His days off were ones spent with his friends, with the ground crews, or flight testing. The best part of his day off was sharing the preciously little free time that Molly had available.

He spent as much time as possible with her, enjoying moonlit walks through dispersals and companionable silences over tea. Yet they had not crossed the line into full physical intimacy as they were still, paradoxically perhaps, deeply in love whilst still desperately shy with one another.

For the moment, the kisses, hugs and caresses were enough. Rose was content, his tired mind soothed by the peace of her presence.

Nonetheless, on one occasion, he had been unable to resist running a hand momentarily over one smooth, slim calve, up her thigh and onto her rounded buttock, revelling in the exciting firmness of her flesh.

He remained the true gentleman, despite the raging ache in his loins.

She was a source of peace and happiness for him, and he valued the contentment he found with her more than anything else in his life.

More often than not, he would fall asleep in her embrace.

"It says a lot for my conversation," she would joke. But she would let him sleep, for the tiredness was already plain to see in his eyes.

He had written a long letter home about Molly to his family. He even learned the words to 'You've Done Something To My Heart,' and sang it tunelessly to her whenever he could until he decided to sing it to her in front of a truck load full of grinning erks.

Despite the dirge-like nature of his rendition, or perhaps because of it, they appeared to have greatly enjoyed it.

Molly was mortified beyond words. A little part of her was pleased, too. But it was a very little teeny-weeny part.

Understandably, she begged him to stop. "I love you, Harry, but you're no Al Bowlly."

He stopped. But only because she asked him to.

Granny was upset, because, being unable to sing to her, Rose now began to sing the song when he was with his friends.

Excalibur had flown many patrols that July.

The boys of the squadron would behave themselves in the presence of Molly, Dolly and the other WAAFs usually associating with the squadron, as the girls spent more time with the tired young men.

They were particularly bashful under the calm gaze of Rose's Flight Officer, although it did not prevent them from gathering around her whenever opportunity permitted. Not often enough for them, but far too often in Rose's opinion.

They were also frankly envious and fascinated by Rose's good fortune with Molly. She had seemed so cool and out of reach. How had Rose won her?

Out of bounds to them, yet along had sauntered this shy single-striper with his quiet ways and taken her from under their admiring gaze, and into his embrace. How on earth had the young devil managed to net such a prize?

"She only feels sorry for you, sweet boy, as you'll be dead soon," Ffellowes had considerately said, and offered him a cigar.

"Oh, well. At least I've still got my showgirls," Farrell had sighed.

"Damn lady-killer. You keep your eyes off my Dolly," Denis had shouted at him cheerfully.

"Good thing the Commandant of the WAAF ain't here," Billy had quipped, "'else Harry would be after her, an' all. I think he likes popsies with a few rings on their sleeve. Cheeky rascal."

Not only did he receive respect for his success against the enemy, but now he had notoriety as a lady-killer, too.

However, there was no one else but Flight Officer Molly Digby for him. In public, she maintained a professional distance, concerned about the possible erosion of her authority, especially with her girls.

Rose had also been out into London with Molly twice. The first time it was to dinner at the Savoy Grill, a favourite hang-out for RAF personnel, but it was not the preferred choice for Molly, and she'd decided they would eat elsewhere.

So, instead, Molly drove Rose in her smart little sports car ("Don't ask about the petrol ration!") to a Kashmiri restaurant that she knew of in London, for a spicy eastern meal.

Although it was packed with uniforms, a table was cleared immediately after Molly had a few quiet words in Hindi with the head

271

waiter, who seemed to know her. It was the first time Rose had eaten anything that resembled an authentic Indian curry, and the memory of it alone was sufficient to make his tongue tingle.

The whole of the journey back, feeling rather less of a man, he had found it difficult to talk, his mouth and sinuses feeling inflamed, his eyes red and still watering, despite the copious amounts of water he had drunk. He was grateful for the darkness. Molly did not seem to mind his quietness, but rather, she seemed amused by the effect of the meal on him.

He'd also learned that Molly's paternal grandmother had actually been an Indian princess, which explained her lustrous black hair, exotic beauty, and her apparent immunity to the effects of spicy food.

So, not only was she his senior officer, now he knew she also belonged (distantly) to aristocracy. He continued to wonder at his good fortune.

Despite the heat, and the tingling of his tongue, Rose had enjoyed the meal immensely, the food so unlike the milder 'curries' he was normally used to, although it had been necessary to dilute the spiciness with lashings of plain yogurt.

He had watched with envy (and not a little awe) as she had spooned the fiery food into her sweet mouth with no discomfort whatsoever, and manipulated the chapattis effortlessly with her fingers.

When he had tried to copy her, the thin pieces of unleavened bread had disintegrated into a soggy mess, leaving Rose with yellow, ghee-stained fingers and limp rags of bread.

By the end of the main course his mouth felt as if a tracer round had gone off and set fire to his tongue. He wasn't quite sure it was all still there.

The Brigadier at the next table, like Rose, was dripping with sweat and red faced, but he ate everything that was placed before him (which was quite a lot, and without recourse to yogurt) with a fortitude and pleasure that was impressive.

Rose felt a positive weakling in front of her, especially when the sirens had screamed their warning outside. Molly and all the others in the restaurant had not batted an eyelid. She did, however cock an eyebrow in amusement as he gradually slid lower and lower beneath the table.

As it happened, no bombs fell near them, but by the end of the evening, the beads of sweat on his brow did not result from the food alone.

The journey home had been just as frightening, as Molly had thrown the open top little car headlong down the darkened roads, chatting happily all the while. The one shaded headlight of the car offering no discernible illumination that he could see whatsoever, and the trip had been a terrifying headlong high speed dash into the darkness.

Rose was mildly surprised that he had not screamed once when they finally arrived back at the airfield. How she had managed avoiding an accident amazed him still.

And, incredibly, still in one piece, although he feared that he'd swallowed quite a number of insects on the journey back. He had prised his numb fingers from the dashboard and patted Genevieve thoughtfully and offered up a prayer of thanks. The skies above were not the only threat to life and limb.

Their second outing had been closer to home. Molly and Rose had both had an afternoon free, and so they managed to find time to watch 'The Lady Vanishes' in the small Gaumont cinema of the nearby market town of Damson-Le-Hope.

Much to his embarrassment and chagrin, he spent almost the entire duration of the film sleeping, dead to the world.

Molly had sat there with her hand in his, whilst the plot unfolded. The Lady and the whole film vanished as Rose slumbered unconcernedly, his strawberry ice forgotten and melting on the floor between them.

At least she had enjoyed the film. And better still, she had given him a photograph of herself looking very solemn and exquisite in the uniform of a Section Officer ("I was young and junior once, you know!").

Immediately he had asked for more.

"This one's for me, but I also need one for my room and one for my kite, and one for..." he had explained. Then another thought struck him. "Oh! Horatio Nelson used to carry a lock of Emma Hamilton's hair. Could I have a lock of hair, too, please, my sweetest flower?"

"Where on earth do you expect me to find a lock of Emma Hamilton's hair, you silly boy?" she'd scolded him mock-crossly.

Nonetheless, Molly duly supplied him with a lock of silken black hair ("I managed to cut this from the tail of that mangy old cow in the field over there"), tied with a bright pink ribbon, and one more photograph, in which her hair was shorter and in which she was dressed in a summery frock, smiling brightly into the camera.

"I was even younger then. Long time ago," then, pointedly, "About the same age as you are now."

He'd kissed her fondly, in reply. "Oh, Molly. You're such a withered old thing. But I do rather like those old bones." He'd laughed and jumped out of the way as she had tried to punch him.

The last six days were a quiet time for RAF Fighter Command overall, with minimal losses of Hurricanes and Spitfires.

So ended July 1940. In that time, Rose had become a seasoned fighter pilot and also found true love.

Very soon, the next phase of the battle would begin. One in which the squadron would play an even greater part.

Chapter 22

Thursday the 1st of August 1940 opened with fair weather, although at the beginning there was overcast and low cloud above the Channel, the Dover straits and the east coast. There were desultory raids on the Sussex coast, near some RAF airfields, and the goods yards at Norwich were hit.

Hitler, despairing of receiving a positive response to his 'Last Appeal To Reason' of July 19th, in which he had appealed to Britain to sue for peace, issued Directive number 17.

The war against Britain was to be intensified by both air and sea, with the end outcome expected to be that country's inability to continue the war, and resulting in her complete defeat.

Secretly, he wanted to start a front with Russia. Britain would be isolated, and with no hope.

Der Fuhrer had also decreed that the invasion forces would land on many points along the south coast, between Ramsgate and beyond the Isle of Wight.

The invasion would be codenamed Operation Sealion.

The landings should occur on the 15th of September, and the Kreigsmarine and Wehrmacht stepped up their preparations, as well as their arguing. The soldiers were keen on continuing onto their next battle, but the sailors worried about RN destroyers and light coastal forces cutting bloody swathes through their plodding fleet of barges.

The Luftwaffe fliers said nothing, but dreamed of orderly ranks of RN warships lined up to be sunk to order by air-attack.

The following two days were also ones with changeable weather over the channel, allowing attacks on northern cities, as well as attacks on a number of airfields in Essex.

One of these was against RAF Foxton.

The raiders attacked from low level, and there was little early warning.

Rose was walking to the fighter pen to check his beloved kite, and to chat with the ground crews.

Behind him, a Spitfire of 97 Squadron began its take-off run, and he turned to watch, never tiring of the glorious sight of a fighter taking off, all grace and strength and glinting edges.

The first that he knew was a strange faraway crackling in the distance. He cast a glance casually in that direction, saw a single-seater dip down and fly low over the grass at the far end of the field, and he shook his head to himself.

Silly sod, he thought. They must all be asleep in the watchtower. He looked back at the speeding Spitfire on the grass. Watch out, chum. One of your bods is about to buzz you.

Those Spit boys fly far too low. Someone's going to catch it. Don't they know one of their own is departing? Don't they care? Donald would have our hides if we did it…

Then he looked again, for the engine tone was wrong.

And he saw five more fighters emerge from behind the trees at the boundary, almost bounding over them like race horses at the Grand National.

Tiny lights flickered in their noses and along their wings, and strange lines of silvery wire seemed to reach out from them.

"What the…" his words trailed off as dreadful realisation hit him, like a machine gun bullet.

Sudden and awful.

They looked horribly familiar. He had seen something similar in his rear-view mirror.

The bloody things were Messerschmitt Bf109s!

And they were heading for him!

He stood transfixed in shock for one disbelieving instant.

How had they managed to get so close? There had been no warning whatsoever.

Where the hell were the air defence gunners?

All the questions suddenly disappeared as a petrol bowser exploded with an eye-searingly bright yellow-white flash, the crew around it enveloped by the fireball, followed by a bone trembling *THWUMPHH!*

A wave of sweltering hot air swept over and past him, and he became aware, nakedly aware, of his exposed position.

Tearing his eyes away from the sight of the oncoming enemy aircraft, he turned and ran for the nearest slit trench.

It was so far away!

His muscles pumped, legs pistoning and arms working, as if the force of his desperation may carry him faster. Each footfall jarred his spine as he ran.

He could almost feel the bullets and cannon shells tearing up the ground behind, and his world became a silent one, save for the pounding of his heart and the torn gasping of his breath.

At any moment he expected to feel the terrible lancing pain as the shells tore through him, or as an airscrew carved into his back to fling him high into the air. He did not know it, but he was screaming as he ran, bracing himself for the horrid impact.

Would he even know it when it happened? What must it be like to be torn apart?

But the seeming inevitable did not happen.

Instead he had a vague memory of throwing himself headfirst into the trench that was suddenly before him, dark and earthy, and oh so welcoming!

He fell in a heap onto the floor of the trench, and there was earth in his mouth. He spat out.

He was alone.

But he had managed to outrun the bullets, and Rose gasped with relief. Thank God. He was safe.

Hopefully. But what if they carried bombs?

Sounds suddenly crowded in on him, like a solid wall.

He tried to press his back further into the earth, cowering as the sound of British gunfire (at last air defence had opened fire!) chattered, the rising angry snarl of enemy engines and the shouting and screams (of warning or pain?) beat at him. In the distance, the climbing and falling of the siren wailed disconsolately.

God! How much safer it felt in the cockpit of a Hurricane, with a gun-button beneath one's thumb! Rose thought longingly of his revolver.

He could hear the whine, howl and thumping as bullets and cannon shells stitched the ground nearby, clawing deep furrows into the ground.

The sound rapidly grew louder and nearer, a shower of pebbles and clods of earth turning the trench into a churning thing of choking soil and sound, an airless world of terror.

An enemy fighter shot past overhead, a blurred shape flashing past (so low!), blotting out the light for one awful instant. So close, he feared it would crash into the trench.

Involuntarily, he ducked his head, covered his face with his hands.

He was buffeted by a whirlwind of sound and slipstream from the German fighter, air sucked away, unaware and unmindful to the dirt and grass that whirled around and covered and clothed him.

And then it was over. He opened his eyes, breathed in raggedly, trying to calm his racing heart.

And then something thumped into the trench beside him.

Rose recoiled in terror, thinking that it was a bomb before he realised that it was simply a fragment of shrapnel from the ack-ack.

It smouldered red hot, a jagged piece of twisted metal with razor edges six inches long, not a yard from his left foot.

He stared at it in horror, as it hissed evilly in its mound of disordered soil.

He began to move weakly away from the shrapnel, brushed away the loose earth, stones and grass that partially buried him. He spat out again, aimed at the shrapnel.

Thank Heavens he had not been hit by that! It would surely have killed him!

There was the sudden sound of running feet and two men threw themselves into the trench. One landed on top of him and knocked him flying, so that he landed, winded, on the floor of the trench. His cap skittered off and rolled down to the other end.

The man who had landed on him helped him back into a sitting position. Rose felt as if his body were made of jelly.

Bloody hell! What now?

"Sorry, sir. Din't see you." The eyes were wild and staring, a trail of saliva at one corner of his lips.

Rose looked at him. The man was almost crazy with terror, crouching down, his fingers clenched into white fists, clutching at the dark soil. He was like some wild animal pursued, unkempt and shaking, face flushed and wet from running.

Sweet God. Do I look like that too?

His mate was a Corporal armourer, with the sturdy solid build of a weight-lifter. Rose offered up a silent prayer of thanks. If the Corporal had landed on him, he'd have certainly broken a few bones, perhaps worse. What was his name? Quinn, Quirke, something like that.

The man who had landed on him was the opposite of the corporal, small and slight of frame.

Thank goodness!

"Sorry, Mr Rose." Although a big man, the corporal was soft spoken, and his voice was apologetic. Unlike his companion, he was calm. His nose was bleeding, the smudged red trail creeping down his chin, and spotting his tunic. "Didn't see you 'til it was too late. Are you alright, sir?"

There was real concern in his voice, but Rose was more interested in the sound of German aero engines as they rapidly receded.

Rose rubbed a sore hip, ran his tongue over dry lips. There was soil on his lips, and he spat again, but there was hardly any saliva. He wiped his mouth with his sleeve, which was no improvement.

The machine guns gradually stopped their chatter, trailing off one by one uncertainly. The Bofors guns had already stopped.

In the absence of their banging he could now make out the vengeful roar of Merlins.

The Readiness flight, trying to catch the hit and run raiders, but there was little chance of catching the faster 109s.

"Yes, quite alright, thanks." Rose sucked some air in, "Just had the wind knocked out of me. Not to worry."

He rubbed his hip, but knew that you didn't check who was where when Jerry was trying to part your bum cheeks with cannon-shells, you just ran like buggery for shelter. He almost giggled.

Pull yourself together, Harry. You're supposed to set an example. You're an officer. Bloody well act like one.

These two will be looking to you for guidance, reassurance. Wish that damned dirge-like siren would stop.

He took another deep breath. "No lasting damage, corporal, not to worry." His hip really ached. There would be a hell of a bruise there tomorrow.

He worked to lower his voice. Took another breath. And then another.

His heart was racing like a train.

OK, it's over. You hold the King's commission, for goodness sake! Get that hysterical note out of your bloody voice.

Try to be more like Granny.

No more sounds of enemy aircraft, just shouts, screams, the sound of racing vehicles, and that twice-damned siren. His nose filled with the bitter stench of gunsmoke and burning.

"Looks like Jerry's gone." He steeled himself, carefully stood up and peered over the parapet edge of the slit trench.

There was no sign of the enemy planes, the Bf109s had disappeared as suddenly as they had first appeared.

A single, long strafing run and scarper eastwards for home at full speed.

"The bastards must be well on their way back to Hun land."

His companions got shakily to their feet and joined him.

Just then two (where's the third?) Spitfires took off, climbing above them, their blue smoke-streaked undersides seeming close enough to touch, and turning rapidly. They've no chance of catching Jerry, thought Rose.

Wish I was with them, though. Always worth a try, particularly if the ack-ack wallahs had winged one or more.

Already there were men running in all directions, to tend the injured and to put out the fires. Three separate plumes of dark smoke reached upwards from the airfield, dense and oily, like accusatory fingers questing into the clean blue sky.

The remains of the bowser, blackened and split open, was burned fiercely, casting a pall above them. Further away, the wreckage of a Spitfire was burning in the distance, its tail broken off and untouched by fire. He could hear the sound of the bullets in its guns popping as the fire reached into the ammunition trays, setting them off.

No signs of any German wreckage, though, curse them!

Rose thought back sadly to the sight of the Spitfire he had stopped to watch, as it began to take off just a minute or so ago.

Poor bastard. He'd had no chance at all.

One moment he'd been racing along the runway, indomitable and proud in his shining kite, the next he lay dead in the glowing hot remnants that were all that was left of his Spitfire.

The siren finally ebbed and groaned into silence. The enemy did not reappear.

One slashing destructive attack, over in a handful of seconds and then quickly back over the Channel, to Schnapps and safety and congratulations.

"Come on, Johnny, boy. Best nip back; otherwise the Chiefy will have our guts for garters."

The Corporal turned to Rose. "Sorry sir. Permission to return to duties, sir?" He looked closely at the young officer. His chin and neck were streaked with blood and dirt. "You sure you're alright, Mr Rose, sir?"

Rose nodded irritably. "Yes, yes. Don't worry. I'm perfectly OK."

He didn't feel it. Felt bloody awful in fact. He brushed forlornly at his uniform. He looked more like Granny, now.

"You two had better get back. Get the MO to have look at your nose, though. Alright?"

"Yessir." They scrambled out of the trench and ran towards a small truck parked nearby. It was completely unscathed. Hope my Hurricane escaped, he mused as he watched them pile in and drive away towards the big M2 hangar.

Rose rescued his cap from the corner of the trench, shook it clean, pushed it onto his head, and pulled himself out, looking back at the cluster of airfield buildings.

And suddenly he remembered Molly.

Merciful God!

Molly! He started to run. His hip ached jarringly, but he ignored it.

Oh God! Please let her be alright!

The fear hammered a fresh tattoo in his heart as he watched an ambulance clatter its way away from the headquarters building.

Please God, help me!

Please keep her safe for me!

There were fresh reddish brown scars in the brickwork of the buildings where Luftwaffe guns had ripped into them, and many of the windows, including those of the Watch Office, had been shattered to leave gaping holes that stared emptily across the aerodrome.

He ran to a clutch of excited pilots, the shards of glass crunching beneath the soles of his shoes. More than one of them had cuts from flying glass, which left red trails down their cheeks and hands.

They turned to stare at the gasping apparition with the dirt-streaked face.

"Bloody Hell, Flash!" It was Farrell. The pilots had decided Rose, now an 'Ace' pilot, and with a smart and beautiful girlfriend, would be known as 'Flash Harry', or Flash for short.

"What happened to you?" like Rose, he was shaking and pale.

"Fell into a trench," Rose said shortly. He pointed at the departed ambulance. "Have you seen Molly? Who's been hurt?"

Denis clapped him on the back. "Christ! Thank God you're OK, mate. Thought you were a goner!"

He turned to the others, "Saw old Flash running up the field racing with a Hun! Still beat him, but must have been close!" he laughed wildly. "Never seen anyone move so fast, looked like he had a fucking 109 right up his arse!" he explained, then thought for a moment. "I think there's a line to shoot there."

Rose gripped his sleeve fiercely with one shaking hand. By now he was frantic with worry.

"Please! Tell me! Have any of the girls been hurt?"

Farrell rolled his eyes. "You randy old stoat! We've just been hit by some bloody Boche bastards, and all you're worried about are girls!"

Denis saw the worry in his eyes, squeezed his shoulder gently. "No, don't worry, mate. It was a couple of the ground crew boys and poor old Grant," he said quietly, mentioning the name of one of 97's flight commanders. "He caught one in the guts as he was trying to get to his Spit." He shook his head. "There's not much hope for him, I'm afraid. It's a bad wound." He wiped his eyes angrily and looked at the burning Spitfire, "I dunno who that was."

Amazingly, tears glistened silver in his eyes. "He had no chance at all, poor sod."

But Rose wasn't listening any more. He could see an ordered line of girls standing together near one of the grass covered shelters.

And she was there with them, slim and neat in powder blue.

"Thank you, God." He breathed gratefully. She looked so calm and in control, as she talked to her girls, and he felt proud in her and in them. No hysteria there.

So, at last, you know now yourself what it feels like to be under fire, my love. I can see you weren't found wanting, you look so calm an efficient. You're every inch the girl I thought you to be.

He began to limp to her, and then thought better of it.

Wouldn't do her authority much good if he draped himself all over her. Not in front of her girls. She saw him and smiled slightly, shielding her hand from the girls with her, she gave him a thumbs up.

Thank God she was alright!

"Good Lord! Whatever happened to you, Flash?" Skinner appeared as if by magic, and peered at him in surprise. "Not your usual dapper self. Is that one of Granny's tunics?" he poked Rose's grimy sleeve doubtfully.

Rose sighed, brushed his uniform again.

"Hello, Uncle. No. I jumped into a slit trench with a 109 close behind. He didn't manage to get me with his guns, so he tried burying me with stones and grass. Almost got hit by a piece of ack-ack shell casing, as well. Then an armourer decided to land on me, dented me a bit. That's why I'm a bit dirty."

"Probably black and blue, as well I shouldn't wonder. Some of those armourers are big lads. Built like brick shit houses." Skinner murmured. "I think you ought to go and check your leg with the Doc." He waved his arms vaguely. "No bombs, though, thank goodness. Could have been worse."

Uncle must have seen me limping, thought Rose. "I will, Uncle. Just as soon as I've had a word with Flight Officer Digby."

"Glad to see you're alright, dear boy," Skinner went on, "although… I remember the first time the old Hun strafed my airfield. It's old hat to me y'know. It was back in 1917, and this flight of Albatros' thought they'd come over and take a pot shot at us." He laughed at the memory. Nerves of steel in this old boy. "Never ran so fast in all my life, I can tell you…"

Rose looked longingly at Molly, as Skinner happily burbled away. Wish I could hold you, he thought. The past few minutes had left him dazed and grateful to be alive. Ground war isn't at all to my liking.

Molly dismissed her girls, and began to walk towards them. Then she noticed the state of Rose's uniform, and her eyes widened.

"Harry! Oh my God! What happened to you?" She ran up to them, took his stained hands into hers. She fixed Skinner with a hard stare. "Hello, Uncle. What have you done to my Harry?"

My Harry. She had said it aloud before them. How wonderful it sounded. I shall never tire of hearing you say that, my love.

Skinner held up his hands and shrugged. "Not guilty. But he's not yours, Flight Officer, may I remind you, and that he belongs to the RAF. As do you. However, to answer your question, I'm innocent, M'Lud. Your naughty young man fell into a slit trench. Seems alright, though by the size of that smile on his silly face."

She looked anxiously at him. "Oh my God, Harry. Are you alright? Oh, Harry!" she looked as if she might burst into tears.

Diplomatically, Skinner sidled away.

Hm. Suppose I could play the wounded hero a little.

"Oh, it's really nothing, Molly." He said self-deprecatingly. "I was very worried about you. I was so scared." He reached into his pocket, pulled out the little pink bear. "Here. You must hold on to her. She'll continue to bring you luck, and keep you safe for me. Take her back, my darling. She'll protect you. I couldn't bear it if you were hurt."

"No, Harry! You must keep her. She's taken care of you, and that's all that matters to me! Please, keep her with you?" tears finally spilled onto her cheeks, and his heart ached.

"I was so worried! I was safe with my girls in the shelter, we'd just

286

been warned, but all I could think of was you out there and unprotected! I was scared you might try to take off in the middle of it all."

He wiped her tears away, leaving dark streaks of dirt from his fingers on her cheeks.

"Please don't cry, Molly. I can't bear to see you cry. Look, OK, I'll keep her. What matters is that we're both alive, thank God."

Both still alive! *Thank you, God!*

Rose pushed Genevieve back into his pocket, groped around for his handkerchief, and wiped the stains from her face.

"It won't do for your girls to see you cry. Where's my tough little Flight Officer?"

Her nose was pink, her lashes matted with tears, cheeks smeared, and she was painfully, heart-achingly beautiful. She smiled, becoming still more beautiful.

"Thank God. Thank God you're alright. That's all I ask for." She looked up at the sky. "That's all I ask for. Keep him safe for me. Please."

Finally, not caring that he was covered with powdery dirt, or that everyone must be able to see them, he took her in his still trembling arms, and hugged her tightly to him, his lips hungrily finding hers. Bugger the regulations!

They embraced for a long moment, each grateful that the other had survived, whilst around them Foxton recovered from the enemy attack.

It had been the first Luftwaffe incursion against the airfield, and it would not be the last.

Chapter 23

Rose took off soon after dawn, deciding his Hurricane needed an air-test. The clouds to the east were painted like streamers of red and gold on blue, as the sun began its slow upward traverse of the heavens.

His Hurricane bumped along the grass, tucking in his wheels the moment he left the ground, and climbed at full throttle, his nose pointing skywards at a sharp angle.

Let 'em look at that, he thought with exhilaration as his Merlin roared.

As he passed a thousand feet he levelled off and circled the grey, shadowed airfield anxiously, checking for low-flying aircraft.

A section of 97's Spitfires had already taken off, when the first flush of dawn had lightened the eastern horizon. It was improbable, but the Luftwaffe may try for a dawn attack.

However, there were only the three Spits high above, no other aircraft, and no sign of the enemy.

With a last look at the watch office (might she be there, or would she be asleep?), and another quick glance at her photograph, carefully taped beside the altimeter, he pulled back on the stick, pointing his aircraft at the heart of a particularly thick mountain of cloud. The retreating darkness still cast a cloak of semi-darkness below him.

The 1030 hp of the Merlin thundered through the air, propelling the 31 foot long fighter higher and higher. Rose's eyes flicked from the instruments to the sky around, enjoying the freedom of the space that surrounded him, whilst not allowing his guard to drop for one second.

He had become used to the beautiful but unfaithful sky, knew that the empty loveliness hid mortal danger. But he loved it still (even if he did not trust it).

With so much cloud about, a squadron of Messerschmitts or even those newer He113's could easily be hiding up here, waiting to pounce on some unsuspecting pilot. Granny said that he'd never seen one and he didn't believe they really existed, but Wally and Billy had recounted a duel in which they'd fought together against two He113s, so they must exist, after all.

The morning was calm, little up or downdrafts, so little turbulence that the Hurricane seemed to cut effortlessly along.

He hit the base of the cloud, still climbing. Before him appeared the coastline, the water beyond shimmering a burnished silvery-gold in the post-sunrise light.

Much of the countryside below was covered with drifting wraith-like early morning mist, partially obscuring the fields. Here and there, the sun would catch the surface of a body of water, and it too shone silvery-gold against the drabness of the land.

He could just make out the faint shapes of the thin needles that were the distant pylons of the East Coast Chain Home station at Barhamwood, the two pale sets of masts pointing like skeletal fingers into the lightening sky.

The powerful sound of the Merlin was soothing, and he began to hum tunelessly. He shifted his shoulders in the narrow cockpit, settling his parachute straps into a more comfortable arrangement, squirming so that his buttocks sat more comfortably on his parachute.

The sun glinted, promising a painful glare, and he kept glancing towards it carefully.

What was it they used to say?

Beware The Hun In The Sun.

Unconsciously he stroked the red gun button on his control column with his thumb. The sun was still fairly low, so the likelihood of attack from that quarter was relatively low.

Best to be careful, though.

Granny had sniffed at him from behind his morning paper, and warned him not to 'Bugger about where the Huns could take a pot. No need to go over the North Sea looking for trouble.' He'd turned the page and broke wind. "Stay near, you tart."

Denis grinned at Rose. "Sounds like someone loves you, Flash."

Granny had blown a raspberry through the newspaper.

Rose smiled fondly beneath his face mask.

The old devil had sounded almost as if he cared. Who'd have thought?

He stole a quick look at Molly's picture. It was wonderful to have people who really cared.

As he continued to climb, he glanced at his oxygen connection, ensured that it was on and connected properly, checked flow. Granny had told him enough times about being careful with his oxygen.

Wouldn't do to pass out from hypoxia and splatter oneself against the pretty landscape.

He felt strangely invulnerable with Genevieve tucked carefully in his pocket and Molly smiling serenely at him from the instrument panel.

They were his good luck charms, and whilst he had them, he felt the Germans could not shoot him down. He took her photo with him every time he flew, now, as well as Genevieve of course, and he could not imagine going into action without either of them.

They were his shield against misfortune, but his heart still thumped for a moment when he caught sight of the shadow of his aircraft momentarily outlined against a cloud, as he weaved from one to another.

Thank goodness for the glycol pump that kept his windscreen from icing up.

At least up to about twelve thousand feet, or so, Chiefy said.

His wingtips scythed through the cloud, leaving spiralling vortices swirling loosely behind. He turned between the clouds, winding a twisted path between them, as if the openness between them were a road within a canyon. Exhilarated, he banked around, flinging himself and his fighter at the mounds of cloud, like a modern day Don Quixote tilting wildly at windmills, gasping with the excitement and the forces.

He felt a mad urge to spray the cloud with his machine guns, as if they were titanic foes, and he laughed at himself and his foolishness.

The spinning airscrew a few feet in front of him sliced pitilessly into the flanks of the cloud.

The sun had begun to burn off the early morning mist, so that the shadowed land below slowly became more visible, the vivid colours of the countryside were not yet brightly lit, and the landscape was still grey below. The world had not quite fully awoken.

Soon enough they would form a vibrant collage of greens and yellows and brown below.

But he did not look down, for the grey land was far beneath, and he and his Hurricane were all alone in this world, a world of brilliant blue and fleecy white.

Heaving his rugged aircraft around, he enjoyed the freedom, the tranquillity of his surroundings that brought in him an easing from the normal everyday tensions of his life.

For ten minutes he zipped from cloud to cloud, like a child playing tag on a summer's day. It felt wonderful to play, to actually just fly and be released from the strains that were part and parcel of his daily existence. He could clear his mind, and indulge himself.

Tiring of his game at last, but still revelling in the crisp freshness of the morning, he yanked his stick back, and the Hurricane responded like a thoroughbred, soaring gratefully upwards into the clear air again. The two of them were creatures of the air, the strings that bound them to the earth cut, so that they could fly endlessly, reaching up, ever up.

At twelve thousand feet, the last cloud tops and feather-tail wisps fell behind, so that all that filled his straining vision and his windscreen was a sunshine-filled blue.

The sky stretched vast before him, miles and miles of a deep azure bowl, nothing able to contain and hold him.

The fighter was like a champion racehorse, a living instrument straining against him, eager to throw herself forward, the power of her humming through his blood, the trembling of her exciting him and invigorating.

At 20,000 feet, he eased further back on the stick and looped the Hurricane so that the clouds he had left behind below were now above, then before him again. He rolled her so that she was pointing almost straight down again, and he held the stick tight as she rocketed sharply downwards, towards the stiff white ragged curtain of broken cloud, faster and faster. He was all alone, but he could see the light glinting off the surfaces of his wings, and he knew that he would be visible from afar, a plummeting shining sliver of metal, glowing bright, high in the air, falling, falling.

The sun was warm against his face and caught the metal and wood of his control panel, making them glow warmly, the instruments shining.

He fell quickly back to earth, down, down, as if to ram the ground.

He hit the cloud again, and pulled back, rolled and turned (easy there-mind the wings, don't want to lose them!), like a diver smashing through the surface of the sea. The horizon gyrated and whirled, this way and that, the world around one of movement and changing position, of light and shadow.

A sudden glint caught his eye, and he looked again. A momentary flash of light reflecting off glass. Instantly alert to danger, he steadied the fighter.

Yes, again. There.

Something on the surface of the sea?

A tiny cruciform shape crawling across the surface.

Worry prickled through him.

He turned towards it, checked the sky above, no bandits above, no trap. Perhaps it was an aircraft, flying low, really low. Without being aware of it, his body had tensed in the confines of the cockpit as the warrior effortlessly slipped back into the seat.

Why was it so low? Trying to avoid being seen? He felt suddenly cold, and his dry throat tickled uncomfortably. He was all alone up here.

Where it had been a delight a mere few seconds ago, now it was an uncomfortable position to be in. There may be more of them.

Quickly, he spoke to the duty controller at sector control, advised them of the situation.

Whatever it was, it was too close, dangerously close. And he was the nearest. He felt the coldness of fear nibbling at his periphery.

What's wrong with me?

The peace of a few moments ago forgotten as harsh reality loomed. The interception was his to do.

Gun sight on, guns to 'fire.'

It was difficult to see the other aircraft, for aircraft it was that he'd seen. The speed at which it was moving meant it could be nothing else.

A single aircraft skimming the waves at close to zero feet.

And it was heading for Britain.

Might it be a reconnaissance Dornier? No, they flew far higher, often far above the normal ceiling of intercepting fighters.

The painful shimmering of the sea making him squint, but still he could not see what it was, so he curved around, turning widely out above the icy sea, so that the sun was behind him. The aircraft before him turned from a glittering shape to a dark one.

No sign of any escort.

He drew closer, his finger poised, ready to pump lead into the other machine as he strove to identify it.

It was painted black on its underside, and as he eased himself nearer, he could now see that it had the peculiar yet familiar tadpole-like shape that was typical of the Handley-Page Hampdens that served with RAF Bomber Command.

One of ours. Not an enemy aircraft, after all. Thank goodness!

The twin-engined medium bomber had a narrow fuselage, that pinched in about half way along the aircraft, to form a thin fragile element, to which was attached a twin tail-fin arrangement.

There was a rear-gunner, and Rose took care to stay out of range. They might mistake him for a Jerry fighter.

How must they have felt? The coast of their homeland before them in the early light, a long dark night over enemy territory behind them.

They must have been relaxed, until they saw the fighter approaching from astern, their relief at seeing the English coastline dispelled by the fear at the sudden appearance of the unknown aircraft.

To have survived hours over hostile airspace, then to get home and see a fighter approaching must have been a terrible shock for the bomber aircrew.

Rose waggled his wings, waved apologetically at the faraway gunner in the open cockpit (must be frozen stiff, poor sod!), who waved back enthusiastically (must be bloody glad I'm not a Hun!).

He reported the nature and identity of the contact to sector control, and edged closer, moving forward so that he drew level with it.

He could see the battle damage and the stain of war on the skin of its fuselage and wings. Ack-ack bursts had streaked it grey-black, so that the dark green and brown of the camouflage was almost obscured.

There was also a sprinkling of ragged tears in the port rudder, the largest of which was over a foot in diameter.

The battered Hampden looked dirty and tired against the crisp water. It was a thing of the night, and somehow appeared uncomfortable and out of place in the daylight.

Rose looked past the shining arcs of the propeller to the high cockpit. He could see the pilot within, but the cockpit was in shadow, only the shape of the man visible.

There was a strange pride in him for his compatriots as he looked at the Hampden. The battered machine and its weary men had emerged from a hostile darkness, where all around them had been only the enemy and danger.

They had fought their way through a fiery gauntlet, and returned to a homeland washed clean and bright by the early morning sun. Brave men venturing alone deep into enemy territory to strike a blow against the enemy.

How glad and comforted they must feel each time their wheels touched the ground of home.

He took up a protective position above and behind. He had decided he would escort them, at least part of the way, home. He was their welcoming committee, and now he would be their escort. It was the least they deserved.

In the bomber the pilot wiped his face. He eased the bomber into a gentle climb as they passed over the coast.

He was the same age as the young man in the Hurricane flying alongside, but he had been flying bombers for three months, and had sixteen operations to his credit already. He was already a veteran of Bomber Command's war, and whilst his colleagues of Fighter Command were tasked with the defence of Britain, his remit was to attack the enemy in their own territory, in their own backyard, alone.

In the wee small hours of the night he and others had bombed one of the coastal facilities where the German invasion forces were gathering their assets.

There were shattered barges with dead soldiers inside them this morning because of his and his colleague's actions. Enemy soldiers that would never storm a British beach or port.

We'll keep them at bay, he thought, with a grim satisfaction, but there was no longer gladness in his heart, just the all-encompassing tiredness.

He patted the side of the cockpit. You brought us back safe and sound again, old girl. They called you a 'flying panhandle,' but there's nothing better than you.

You and little Harriet. The little panda bear, with one missing button eye, swung from a stanchion beside him. One eye was missing because he had 'tortured' the stuffed toy when he was eight. Harriet, however, did not seem to hold a grudge, for she had brought him back again and again.

There was a tap on his shoulder. It was his observer. "Almost home, thank the Lord. There's a little tea left in the flask, skipper. Would you like it?"

The pilot grimaced. "No thanks, John. Bit strong for me, and it's probably pretty well stewed solid now. You lads have it. Could do with a fag though."

The observer laughed and disappeared back into the tight dark space behind him.

The pilot glanced back at the Hurricane holding station on them. Nice to have an escort for a change. The yell from the gunner as the fighter had curved in from behind still rang in his ears.

Thank goodness it had been a 'friendly.' He was exhausted and did not feel that he would have been able to evade an attack after such a night. All he wanted was to have a bath, tuck into some eggs, and then straight to bed.

He sighed, scratched his neck. Fat chance there would be of that. The Intelligence Officer would be waiting with sharpened pencils to debrief them.

He yawned hugely. Lots of lovely cloud around today.

The bomber's enemy and friend.

He fumbled in his fur lined flying jacket for the picture of the girl.

She was a WAAF Flight Officer, stationed at a fighter airfield, worse luck. Wish you were based with me, old girl, he thought. I could keep an eye on you then, at least.

Maybe the fighter came from her field?

He looked back across at the Hurricane. I wonder if she knows you, my friend. Perhaps you could tell me how she is.

He smiled to himself.

Silly sod. What funny things to be thinking about at this time of the morning.

At last, he managed to free the photograph from his pocket.

The teeth of the zipper cut into its edges, adding to the worn appearance.

There was a scrawl in black ink on the back of the picture. An inscription that read, 'Dearest Edward, don't I look grand in this uniform! Flight Officer no less! You'll have to salute me, next time! Have to dash, so take care of yourself. Love always, Molly.'

The girl in the picture was smiling, a calm smile. Her eyes were dark, the long black hair he knew so well tucked demurely beneath her service cap, and the two rings of a Flight Officer proud on her sleeve.

"That's one more op in the bag, Moll!"

He had begun to feel that he may see out the end of his tour after all. Please God.

He pushed the photograph back into his pocket. He could not know that an identical photo, but without the scrawled message, was taped to Rose's instrument panel in the Hurricane that flew alongside.

It had seemed an age since he had last seen her, although it could not be more than two days since she had driven down to see him in her little sports car, and she had telephoned him the evening her field had been attacked by Bf109s.

He hoped that she was OK. He massaged his back with one hand. These long flights were hell on the old back.

The damned flight had seemed to last forever. They should be at the airfield in just a few more minutes.

"Chummy's off, Skip. Time to wave ta-ta."

The Hurricane on his port side waggled its wings, then tipped over and dived away.

He watched it as it grew small with distance, shrunk to a dot, then disappeared altogether.

A chance encounter, and a blessed one for the bomber pilot.

Whoever you are, thank you for the welcome home. God bless.

Chapter 24

The aroma of ripe fruit, foliage and wet earth was heavy in the air. The light rain that had fallen earlier that afternoon had brought a feeling of freshness, as if the world had just been crafted anew. Delicious and clean and pure, the scents and hues all around heightened by this sense of cleanliness.

Rose took a sip from his pint glass, and sighed, pleased that his world was so lovely and peaceful. As with all such rare opportunities, he took great pleasure in enjoying the simple delights of nature. They were a welcome and wonderful contrast with the sounds and smells of high-performance fighter aircraft and fighter airfields during wartime.

How strange it was that he had never been able to truly appreciate the true beauty of the countryside before. In the last few weeks it was a land for which he had spilled enemy blood and killed, and now he saw it as he had never done before.

The imminence of death makes one enjoy life and living so much more, allows one to experience its essences all the better.

The lull in the fighting of the last few days had given them all time to recover, to rest. Perhaps the Germans had decided not to invade after all.

But, of course, he knew better. It was a forlorn hope.

Molly laughed, the low, throaty sound like music to his ears. "Lovely moustache, Harry."

He smiled back self-consciously, and she leaned across the wooden table between them to wipe his upper lip with her napkin. He raised his glass of milk to her in thanks, watching her warm eyes as she critically assessed her cleansing efforts.

"Thank you, kind lady."

She tried to curtsy, but she was sitting down across from him, and it didn't come out right.

They were sitting in the garden of the Horse and Groom, in the shadow of a clump of trees that led onto part of the adjoining orchard.

Between them were the remains of a light lunch of bread, cold cuts of chicken, cheese and pickles that Jack had rustled up for them. Jack had also given them his 'special' chunky Piccalilli, although the strength of it made Rose suspect it may contain the stuff that flame-throwers used.

Molly seemed to enjoy it though. He'd decided that she must have a steel-lined stomach, and the appetite of an ox.

She traced swirling patterns in water on the table top, and watched him surreptitiously. With the lull in fighting, the pilots had been able to get some rest.

It had not been unusual for them to be flying three or more sorties a day.

The dreadful pallor of his face had gone, and the dark shadows under his eyes were beginning to fade. He still looked tired, lined and gaunt, and there was something in his gaze that made her want to take him into her arms and hold him tightly forever.

But then, she felt like that all of the time.

"Let's go down to London again, Harry."

He watched the way the beat in her slim neck pulsed. She was not in uniform this time, deciding instead to wear a simple dark blue dress that accentuated her figure beautifully, her narrow waist, and had also given him a tantalising glimpse of long, shapely legs.

He was still quite shy of staring at her, but whenever they were together, he had found that he could not help himself. "Yes. I'd like that."

Aware of his admiring gaze, she tossed back her hair and flicked water at him.

"Didn't mother tell you it was rude to stare?"

She was pleased but also a little embarrassed at his single-minded attention.

His eyes remained locked on her. "She said it was OK if the girl in question was staggeringly beautiful."

She snorted in amusement. "Flattery…"

He held up one hand. "I know, I know. It'll get me nowhere. It doesn't matter. I'm not saying it for some reward here on earth. I'm merely speaking as I find. You are just so very, very exceptional it entrances me."

And she was. With the sun behind her, her black hair was lit a glowing reddish-brown.

On the road, a despatch rider bellowed noisily past on his motor bike, a hateful and smelly reminder of that other world from which they had escaped, even though it were only for an hour or so.

Their eyes followed his passage south, until he disappeared where the road curved behind the trees bordering it, the sound and smoke a fading memory of him.

She raised one slender arm, to tuck a tress of hair neatly behind an ear. Her lashes were long and dark, and there was something in her eyes that spoke of hot winds and spice, an exciting and exotic mysticism harking back to her Indian heritage.

301

"I do so love you, sweet Molly. I wish I had the words to tell you how much."

She placed her hand on his, squeezed gently. "I know, my darling. You know I feel exactly the same. I love you with all that I am."

He took another sip of his milk. "Molly, why don't you come home with me, next time I go back? I'd love you to meet Mummy." The sound of the motor bike had faded, as the despatch rider hurried on to whichever destination he was heading for.

"She'd love to meet you. I've told her all about you."

"Oh dear. So she knows I'm a cradle-robbing old hag, then?" she grinned evilly, "Did you tell her that I'm about the same age as her?"

"Honestly, Molly!" His expression was severe.

"I'm sorry." She didn't appear sorry in the slightest. "What did you say?"

"I said that you'd love to see her, and that we'd come as soon as we could."

She groaned and looked away. "Oh, Lord! She'll be horrified when she sees me!"

"No she won't. She'll adore you." His stern expression softened. "Just as I do. I told her you're an absolute smasher!"

"I can't go, Harry," she said beseechingly, "She'll think me too old. Can't we just enjoy each other's company for the time being?"

"I want her to see you. And my family. They have to see the girl I've chosen."

"Your family too! Oh no!"

"Oh yes! Honest, Molly, they'll love you." He raised his eyebrows slightly. "You're exceedingly lovable, you know. A little bit like me."

"Hm, quite. Why must we get so serious, Harry? Let's enjoy ourselves, make the most of each day. Forget about the future, let's just enjoy now."

"Of course you must meet them!" He sounded scandalized, "They have to see my girl."

"Girl! Crone more like!" sitting before him, her head tilted so that her hair fell in a delicious cascade, she looked exquisite and delicate and, oh, so gorgeous. Crone could never be used to describe her, never in a thousand years.

Rose cleared his throat. "If we mean to take our esteem and regard for one another further, I feel that we must make some kind of formal arrangement, an understanding of sorts." he said, rather pompously.

She stared at him, suppressing the urge to shriek with laughter at his formality. "My God! What on earth are you chattering about, Harry?"

He could feel his neck and cheeks darkening. He groped around in his pocket, gripped the box hidden there fiercely. She was looking at him in some bemusement.

He slipped off his seat clumsily, dropped the box, fumbled for it, and went down on one knee before her.

He was conscious of a dull roaring in his ears, and the chalk dryness of his mouth, but all he could see was the surprise in her eyes, the perfect O of her mouth. Thank the Lord there was no one else here!

"My darling sweet Molly. I think you are the loveliest thing in my life and the thought of you makes each day of my existence a pleasure. I love you with every fragment of my being," go on, throw in a bit of science, "And it feels, um, as if each one of my atoms is inextricably linked with each one of yours, an unbreakable bond holds me to you, and attracts me to you. I've written a poem for you."

He cleared his throat again, placed one hand on his heart, struck what he hoped was a heroic pose (difficult to do whilst kneeling on one knee), and recited theatrically:

"Bewitched, I remain enthralled by you.

303

Helpless and enslaved, I seek not freedom from you, I seek
no release.
For when the thin white line of dawn splits the sky from land,
And when the sun's glare shines hot green through the canopy of
leaves above,
To the moment that day becomes fast receding, to the faint
refractive glimmers of flamboyant purple and red and pink,
And through the night when the milky skein of thin cloud over
moon lights the empty loneliness,
I can think only of you, endlessly of you, always you. Whether
awake or in my sleep, it's always you.
I love you, I adore you."

His heart was clattering along, and he had to gasp for breath.

"What I mean to say is that I love you, and I need you, and I would be honoured if you would become my wife. My own very sweet Molly, will you marry me?"

Oh, you old silver-tongued smoothie! He was quite pleased with his performance, despite the fact that he was trembling. Now for the next bit…

He opened the box and held it out to her. "Please?" Granny had taken him to London secretly, and Rose had bought his Molly an engagement ring.

He was aware that someone was watching from a shadowed window.

She took the box from him. "Oh, Harry!" she looked at the ring wistfully, "This is really beautiful!" then she shook her head. "But I can't accept it, my darling."

She closed the box with a sigh, and held it out to him.

He ignored her outstretched hand. "Why not? You do love me, don't you?"

"You know I do, of course I do. But, one day, you'll meet a girl who will be right for you. I wish it were me, but I'm not right for you. A wife is the last thing you need right now. Particularly one very much older than you. You're too young to get married right now." She stroked his cheek tenderly. "So, let's forget this nonsense, alright?"

"But I need you." His voice sounded petulant to his own ears.

"And you have me. I'm yours. Completely. Yours in every way." She dropped her eyes, folded her fingers between his. "In every way that you want. For as long as you want. Do you understand?"

His throat felt dry. He understood. But it was not enough. He wanted it all. "But I love you," he muttered feebly, standing up.

"I know, Harry, you silly sausage. I love you and I need you, too." She smiled self-consciously, "You are the loveliest man I've ever met, and I need you." Molly blushed. "I want you, too. In every way. Very much."

She tossed her hair anxiously, "For goodness sake! The girls are always going on about how dense men can be! Do I have to spell it out? I want you. In that way. *You know.* There. I've said it. Aren't I a dreadful person? It'll make your poor mother's hair go grey to know that her little boy is in cahoots with a shameless creature like me!"

"Ah." He was at a loss as to what he should say. His head was spinning madly…did she mean what he thought she meant?

Cripes!

She licked her lips nervously, and closed her eyes, her features downcast. "Oh dear. I think I've shocked you."

"No. Erm, no, not at all." His neck felt constricted, and his voice came out girlishly high pitched. He cleared his throat, and he felt his eyes might pop. Bloody silk scarf was too tight.

"I want to show you how much you mean to me. I want to offer you my commitment, for life." However long it might be. "You are everything in my life that matters."

"Harry, my darling love, the last thing you need right now is to worry yourself about a wife. You must put yourself first. Getting married will only complicate things for you. I'm not going anywhere, you know."

"But you said you love me. If you do, you must marry me. How can you love me but not marry me?" He felt tears burning hot behind his eyes, and he sat down again.

"That's why I want you to put yourself first, because I love you. Very much." She sighed. "Don't you see? You will be going back up there. I don't want you to think about anything else but taking care of yourself. I need you to concentrate on yourself while you're up there. I will do anything for you. Give you everything I have, everything you could want, but not that. I can't marry you. Not yet. Because I love you."

"You say you'll do anything for me. Prove it to me, then. Marry me."

She shook her head in exasperation. "Harry, you are so awful! We've been through this already! Are you listening to anything I'm saying?"

The corners of his mouth turned down. "Yes," he said sulkily.

"Enough, then, of this marriage talk. I'm flattered and proud that you asked me, so pleased that I cannot say. Your poem was the most beautiful I've ever heard, but this isn't the right time. You know that."

She sighed deeply, "You're very serious about this, aren't you?"

He nodded solemnly. "I've never asked anyone before. It's not something one does every day, y'know. It took me a lot of courage to ask you. The least you can do to honour my courage would be to say yes."

"You wonderful, strange, sweet boy." She kissed him lightly on the lips, once, twice, three times, touched his chin lightly with a forefinger. "Alright. As it means so much to you, ask me again in six months. If you're still interested then in this old girl, you can ask me again, and I promise I'll consider it then."

"Wear it for me until then? Please Molly? Please?" He looked so hurt, she relented.

"Good grief. It's like pulling teeth with you, isn't it?" Almost regretfully, she put the little box into her respirator case.

He glowered at her. Like so many of the WAAFs at Foxton, she used her respirator case as a handbag, whilst the respirator itself was languishing in a drawer in her quarters. How many times had he remonstrated with her about not carrying the damned thing?

"I'll keep it with me, Harry, but I shan't wear it. Not yet. Agreed?"
He grunted.

"And yes, in the meantime, I'll meet your family." His eyes lit up. "Don't get your hopes up. They'll probably hate me. You'll thank me afterwards for not agreeing to marry you."

"They'll love you, not because I do, but because you are just so very wonderful. You will say yes, one day. You'll see." The faintest of smiles, "You can't resist me."

She shook her head again. "Did I tell you that you were awful?"
He nodded.

"I did?"
Another nod.

"Good. Because you are. You're bloody awful." She smiled again fondly. "You are such a fool. A crazy, sweet, wonderful fool, and I love you. Very, very much."

"And I love you in return, because you are absolutely, sublimely, bloody marvellous."

"Yes, I seem to have heard that before." She stood, smoothed her dress, and held out her hand to him. "Walk with me?"

"Gladly." He didn't feel very glad at that moment. Instead he felt empty inside, where his heart ought to be just a vast gaping well of disappointment and sadness. What a bind! Once he had wanted so desperately to be an ace pilot, but all he now craved was the girl beside him. What else could possibly matter?

"I love being here with you," she smiled warmly and his heart skipped in its warmth, "I wish it could always be like this."

I don't, he thought, I want it to be like this *and* you with my ring on your beautiful finger.

They walked slowly along the tree line, quiet for a moment, each deep in thought. Once, he bent and plucked a wild flower and gave it to Molly. She arranged the white and yellow bloom in her hair.

"Do I look like a South Sea princess?"

"You were a princess before I met you, and now you are my princess." He looked again. "My! You do rather look like a delectable piece of Tahitian totty." He thought carefully. Was Tahiti in the South Sea? He couldn't remember. Never mind, it sounded right. Certainly suits my Molly. Beautiful tan, dark hair, laughing eyes and delicious smile.

"That's kind of you. I think. Although I don't think I'm too partial to being called a piece of totty. Makes me sound like a bit of confection."

"Tasty piece, fabulous to look at and awfully sweet."

"Don't waste your breath. It'll not get you anywhere, Pilot Officer."

There was a faraway growl of Merlins, but although they searched the sky, they could not see the fighters.

They continued in companionable silence, skirting the long line of trees that flanked the road, with their pale trunks and rich verdant lushness. To one side of them was the orchard, on the other the flatness of the surrounding countryside, with its abundant greens. The earth was twisted into dark brown ruts where the farmer had driven over the land in a tractor, and the opulent odour of fresh wet loam hung in the air, like a heady promise of a warm, rich and fertile future.

She had put her arm through his, and now clasped his hand tightly as if to hold on to him.

The freshness of her was far more delightful than the fragrance of the surrounding summer landscape, and when she tossed her hair, it swirled like a glorious cloud around her face momentarily.

They stepped carefully past the clods of earth and grass, staying on the surface of the road, where it was firm and safe. The first time they had taken a walk; Rose had stepped into a trail of mud, and had almost lost a shoe in the sticky thickness, much to Molly's amusement.

They walked carefully, for in some places the road was uneven, and the rutted furrows left by the tractor were filled with water and mud.

Once a lorry full of squaddies lumbered past, and Rose part-hated, part-enjoyed the admiring whistles from the khaki mass when they caught sight.

A cheerful voice called out, "All right for some!"

Another voice, "Officers always get the nice ones!"

He watched them disappear ruefully. "They liked you." He commented dryly, "the bastards."

"Well, you could always get yourself a girl with no hair, no teeth and a glass eye, I suppose. She'd probably get fewer wolf whistles."

"Much as the thought of it is attractive, and one I'd normally consider, I think I'll keep you. You don't have a glass eye, but I suppose you're passable enough."

She laughed, and tossed back her hair again, punched him lightly on the arm. "If it had been a truck full of WAAFs, I'd have had to put up with their admiration of my chap."

He smiled at her compliment.

Apart from the army truck, there was no movement around them, just peaceful countryside basking in the warmth and sunlight. The earlier rainbow that had painted an arch across the sky had long faded away. There was no hurry, no stress, and it felt wonderful to be alive and not feel the tension, or the need for haste.

In the distance, a herd of sheep dotted the green of a field like crystals of sugar on baize. Rose thought he could just hear the distant call of the shepherd as he worked with his dog.

They came to a low stone wall in an advanced state of disrepair. He spread out his handkerchief for her to sit on, and they sat down together, still arm in arm.

She put her head on his shoulder, and he turned his face to press his cheek against her gleaming hair. Her fragrance filled his nostrils.

The wall felt cold and knobbly against his buttocks, and he shifted slightly at the discomfort.

"Are you comfortable, Harry?"

"Whenever I'm with you, of course I am." He shifted again, and then sighed contentedly. "I feel totally at peace." The stones still dug him cruelly in the backside, but he ignored them. What did they matter when a girl like this was beside him?

He could feel the warmth of her body through her dress, the smoothness of her arm, the curve of her against him. What was I before I knew her? How could a man enjoy life if he did not have the love of a woman in it?

The slight breeze that had played skittishly with her dress earlier had waned away to stillness.

Sitting there in the still landscape, the calm making Rose feel as if he were caught in a still-life picture, as if the two of them were a couple, deeply, gloriously in love, caught for an instant in an empty, colourful world (not taking the shepherd, his dog or the sheep into account, of course).

After a while, she spoke again, her head still on his shoulder, her body tucked in against him.

"I meant what I said, Harry." Her voice was quiet, little more than a whisper, "Every word of it."

"I know. Don't worry, I shan't shoot myself, or anything like that. I'll wait, because I know you'll marry me one day. I am irresistible."

"No, that's not what I meant, my conceited darling."

"Oh?" Intrigued.

"What I said." Her voice again dropped to a whisper. "You know. Don't expect me to say it again."

"Um, what was it you said, then?"

She elbowed him painfully in the side, with a surprisingly bony elbow. "Sometimes I wonder if you're being purposefully dense."

"Eh?"

She sighed, vexed, looked away. "I said that I was yours in every way. In every way that a man could want a woman. Oh Heavens! You know. Do I need to draw a picture for you?"

"Oh. *Ahem!* Of course not, sweet girl," he muttered hastily. He suddenly remembered the picture of Vivien Leigh in his room. Oh Lord! I'll have to chuck it away before Molly sees it!

"Well?"

"What?"

"Do you want me, too?"

"Of course I want you! My God, how could I not? I want you more than anything I've ever wanted in my whole life. I've wanted many things in my life, but never anything as much as I've wanted you. I'd not have asked your hand in marriage if I didn't!"

Rose realized he was gabbling, and squeezed her hand gently. "I want to be with you in every way. I want you so very badly." He licked his lips, "So very badly that I can't sleep sometimes. All I can think about is you."

She lifted her head and looked straight into his eyes. He was surprised that he hadn't noticed before, but her deep brown eyes were flecked with gold.

"You can have me anytime you want. I was careful before, because I want what is right for us, but I love you so much, Harry. I thought things were complicated, but the way I feel for you has made me realise that it is just so very simple after all."

There was silence for a moment, and he willed her to speak again. "Harry. I want to be loved by you. I don't think there's anything I'd like more. I want you. I want to hold you with my hands and lips and body. And I want to feel your hands on my body."

Her cheeks had coloured slightly, but she did not look away. "I'm not a loose woman, or anything like that, I hope you realise that? I've never said this to a man before, you know."

She blushed darker, "It's just that you are such a terrific boy, and I love you. I want to love you in every way. I'm not that sort of girl, but I do know that I love you, very, very much. And I'd like to love you in that way, too."

She smiled then, despite her embarrassment; spoke lightly, "Perhaps I haven't made myself clear. Did I mention that I really, really, want you?"

He was embarrassed as well, stunned, but also enormously thrilled. He had wanted her for so long, but had been so scared. He had feared so much that she may reject his inexperienced advances, but now he knew that she, too, wanted him. And she wanted him in every way! Dreams come true.

Except…

"Molly. There is just one thing."

Anxiously, "What is it, my love?"

"Well," He took a deep, apprehensive breath. "I've never, um, I don't quite know how to put it, but, you see, um, well, oh hang it all! The thing is, Molly, I've, er, well, I've never been with a woman. Never. Ever."

The moment he'd uttered the words he could have bit his tongue. He groaned inwardly.

Why did say that? She didn't have to know that!

There, she'll think me less of a man now. He found it difficult to return her gaze. How can I make it special with no experience? I want to be all the man she could ever want, but she'll not want a useless boy sharing her bed.

Her voice was hushed, "Never?"

"Never, ever. I'm sorry."

Still looking at him, she smiled slightly, although her eyes were still serious. "That's alright. Actually, I'm a little bit glad. It means that we're both in the same boat. She cupped his face, and kissed him tenderly.

"You mean…?"

"Yes. I'm not as worldly as I may seem. I've never actually been physically intimate with anyone, either. I'd never found anyone before that I wanted in that way." Her smile widened, ever so slightly, and there was a mischievous twinkle in her eyes.

"Until now. And I'm willing to learn with you. Very willing indeed."

She took his hand gently, and placed it palm-first onto her left breast. He was so surprised that he almost fell off the wall.

"I want to learn about love with you. I want to share my body with you, Harry. I so want to feel your hands on me. We could learn so much together." He could feel her heart beating like a caged bird beneath his trembling palm, the tempo matching his own racing pulse.

It didn't matter!

It was as if a weight had been lifted from his shoulders. She didn't mind that he had no experience, and she still wanted him! He felt so light-headed and dry-mouthed, with one hand around her waist, the other cupping the fullness of her breast, her nipple erect and pushing hard against his palm.

"Are you sure, my darling?"

"I don't think I've been so sure about anything in my life. I'd never met anyone quite like you before, someone to whom I wanted to give myself to completely, except, of course," she smiled sweetly at him, "now I have. That's why I thought we could go into London," she continued. "One of my friends has a flat in Mayfair, and I thought that we could be together there. Spend a weekend there together, just you and I."

She looked down, red-cheeked, her neck still flushed.

"There. I've thoroughly embarrassed myself now, and you too." Her cheeks were colouring again, changing now from creamy warmth to a bright pink.

He felt as if he had a potato lodged sideways in his throat, and cleared his throat shakily.

Dear God!

"Molly. I love you." He pulled her back to him, enfolded her in his arms. "Yes. I would like that. Very much. I want you, all of you, so much! Mayfair it is." He licked his lips, tried to speak nonchalantly. "When shall we go?"

God! She must surely feel his heart clattering noisily in his chest.

"I'm off next weekend. Can you get away then?"

"Yes, I think I can do that." Stay calm. Of course I will, even if I have to kill someone to get a weekend pass!

She pressed herself against him. "It can be sooner, if you'd like?" Molly looked back, and he followed her gaze to the coolness of the shadowed orchard.

For a moment Rose pictured her lying naked on a soft bed of fruit blossom, eyes bright and expectant, and almost succumbed to temptation.

He licked his dry lips. "No. I can wait. I want to wait until next weekend. I want to treasure each second with you. One or two hours with you is not enough. I want to look at you, not for a little while, but for a long time. I want to hold you and not let go, I want to sleep with you. I want to listen to you as you sleep. I want to taste you with my eyes and mouth and skin and mind. I want it to be so special."

The stones were damned uncomfortable, and still damp. His bottom felt permanently dented, and he shifted again. A small stone, flat and smooth eased out, and he rubbed it with his fingers.

"Does this mean you will marry me after all?" he asked, hopefully.

She tilted her face up to catch the sunlight, and laughed huskily. "Oh no! You never give up, do you?"

"I won't stop asking until you say yes. I'm not going to let you get away from me. Ever. I love you, and I need you."

"Let's see what Mummy has to say when she sees me, alright? Better not make any plans, my crazy, cheeky boy."

He pressed his lips against her slim neck, breathed in her scent. Her breath played against the nape of his neck, and he squeezed her firm breast gently.

Wow.

"She'll love you, I know she will. How can she not?"

"We'll see. But make it soon, OK? I can't wait too long. I want you so very much, I wake up and my body absolutely aches for you." She looked up again. "Do you think I'm terribly forward? You're a little shocked, aren't you?" her eyes were anxious, "Do you think I'm a bit brazen?"

He stroked her cheek lovingly. So smooth.

"No. Not at all. I was a bit surprised, and terribly shy, but not shocked, not at all." There was so much adrenaline flowing that he

315

stuttered as he spoke, and he could feel the tremor of emotion in his limbs, threatening to change into uncontrollable shaking. His penis had stiffened, and it now felt huge and he shifted his position so she would not notice.

"I don't think you could ever do anything that could make me think badly of you. You are the most marvellous person I've ever met. I just can't find adequate words to describe what I feel for you, and what I think of you. I don't know how to tell you how much you mean to me. You are the perfect woman."

He thought for a moment, chose his words with care.

"I don't think you're forward at all. In fact I think you're quite sensible. You said what you said just now, because you appreciate how valuable each second is for both of us." Goodness! How stilted I sound, he thought. "We should enjoy each and every day together. I know now that if you and I live to be a hundred, I'll still not have had enough time with you. Now that I've found you, I want you. All of you. All the time. Every second of my life without you is a second wasted. So I will have everything that you give me. I want to share all life's experiences with you. And I'm grateful that you had the sense to say what you said. I was a fool, and was too shy too even think to speak it. "

He shook his head. "No. you aren't forward, sweetheart. You're showing me how much you think of me, you had the courage to say what I was too scared to. You aren't forward, but rather, you are a hell of a sight braver than I."

Her eyes were shining. "You think so?"

"I do. You've shown me just how much I mean to you. And I am so glad. You offer me such a precious thing, it makes me realise how highly you think of me. I can't tell you how proud you made me, or how pleased I feel by the fact that you've chosen me." He took a long ragged breath. "Because I need you too, in every way. Forever."

He moved even closer, and whispered softly in her ear, "But I still want you to marry me. Soon."

She laughed again, her peals of laughter rolling across the landscape. The mood of seriousness now dispelled.

"That's why I love you, Harry. So single-minded and committed. Be careful what you wish for, you sweet man. I may have to marry you after all."

"Please God. Yes, please. I want you. Forever. How can anyone else match you?"

She laughed again. "Gosh, I can't believe that I said all those things to you. I can't believe what we've just been talking about. We're terribly shameless, aren't we?"

It was strange that he felt so comfortable talking about things only hours before he would never have imagined discussing with her. He marvelled that he had been able to talk so freely about such things. But that's how it was with her. He was just so comfortable when he was with Molly. He could talk about anything with her. Despite their mutual shyness, of course.

"Yes, outrageous! I think it's terrific!"

She smiled. "Isn't it?"

They sat peacefully for a few more minutes, each comfortable in the love of the other. Finally, the wall became unbearable. Despite the delight of the woman beside him, his buttocks had gone numb, and his spine had begun to ache.

Why is it that the bloody wall doesn't hurt her bottom? He wondered.

I'm going to have to personally check why. A detailed and careful examination.

317

In Mayfair. Oh yes, please! Can't wait!

Finally, regretfully, unwilling to release her, but scared that if he didn't move soon, he wouldn't be able to, Rose stood up. His legs and back protested, and buttocks began to throb painfully.

I'm never going to sit on one of those blessed walls again. Look very pretty and scenic in pictures, but they're bloody hell on the arse. Bet I've got a wet seat to my trousers to boot.

They walked back towards the Inn, hand in hand. They were comfortable in their new understanding, and the increased, deeper feeling of intimacy that there now was between them.

They had the fluid intimacy of lovers whilst still innocents, unversed in the physical expression of the mechanics of their mutual love, now sharing a deep and fulfilling understanding with one another.

Chapter 25

The cloud formed strange shifting patterns of light and dark on the land, as the squadron climbed swiftly through the turbulent air, like the disorganised patterns drawn by a small child on paper.

They climbed fast and hard, and it was a bumpy ride, difficult to stay in formation, even one as open and spread out as this. Each of them fought hard to keep their formation together, even though it was a little ragged.

But soon the clouds had been left behind, and the air became less turbulent.

From their height, the ground, where still visible in isolated patches, became a grey flat parchment, with vaguely discernible features. Except for where the sun penetrated, and the flat grey land became a patchwork of shifting bright splashes, though with as little feature, little else.

There was no chatter, just the calm tones of the controller, and Donald's cool, crisp responses.

"Hullo, Kettle Red leader, Sapper control calling. Are you receiving me?"

"Hullo, Sapper control, Kettle Red leader calling, receiving you loud and clear."

"Hullo, Kettle Red leader, vector one-zero-zero. Fifty-plus bandits, approaching Dover. Angels twelve. Buster."

Fifty-plus! Good Lord above! A thrill of fear and anticipation coursed down his spine, and his stomach turned over. *You'd think we'd be used to the odds by now.*

No sign of trepidation in Donald's voice, though. "Hallo, Sapper control. Kettle Red leader calling. Vectoring to one-zero-zero. Fifty-plus at twelve. All received and understood. Listening."

Rose turned his eyes from their interminable search of the surrounding skies to look at Granny's Hurricane. *Bet Granny has a few choice phrases.*

As if reading his thoughts, Granny looked back to shrug and shake his head dolefully at Rose.

In the midst of his friends, he began to feel more at ease. The thought of imminent contact with the enemy less worrying than he had felt earlier. The churning in his belly subsided slightly.

They settled at fourteen thousand, and the cloud beneath them began to break up, the land below uncovered. But he did not see it, for now he searched for signs of the enemy. When he looked down, he did not see the land beneath for which he fought, but instead he searched for the tell-tale movement against the backcloth.

He continued the search above and below and to the sides and behind automatically, for the enemy could appear on the tail of the careless within seconds, as if by magic.

The pace of battle now was one of continuous, monotonous flying, trying to keep formation with your fellows, so that the mind became anaesthetized, and the mind began to wander. At any moment, the boredom could be interspersed with sudden, shocking combat, so that the dullness of the mind was terrified back into stark clarity.

That is, of course, if the battle had not already been lost in that first instant when it had been joined. In the fighting of the last month, many a fine fighter pilot had gone to his death without even seeing his executioner. Such were the vagaries of fighting and the twinned importance of luck and skill in the clouds.

Despite the tension, the mind began to slip, and the effort to concentrate left a man feeling as weak as a kitten, even after only an hour's worth of patrol.

And all of the time, there was the vague apparition of fear, which gnawed silently and perfidiously at the soul from the shadows.

So, as Granny had drilled into him, and as his war had reinforced the lesson, Rose continued his unrelenting search. Nonetheless, the cold, tiredness and lack of sleep were an enemy that ceaselessly circled at the periphery.

He adjusted the oxygen mask carefully, strained to concentrate and maintain his alertness.

Where were the bastards? There should be bombers and a higher fighter escort, heading straight for their targets, their airfields in France behind them.

He stifled a yawn, when suddenly he saw them.

So did the others, as the sound of excited voices called out over the R/T, until Donald silenced them firmly. The bombers were an unbroken group, a terrible dark war host that seemed to endlessly stretch back.

Still some distance away, and higher, a second, smaller formation of dots hovered.

Fighters!

Rose's neck had gone cold, and he felt the bitterness of the acid of his stomach, erosive and stinging. With a steady finger, he switched the safety on the stick to 'off.'

Donald waggled his wings. "OK, Excalibur, head on attack on the formation. Red and Yellow section first, then Green and Blue. Open up, line abreast. We may get only one shot before the escort get stuck in, so make it count. Tally-Ho!"

The Hurricanes were two thousand feet above and in front of the bombers, and Donald pushed them into a gentle dive that took them down into the face of the enemy formation.

The six Hurricanes of the first wave were still in position when they pulled up. Donald had calculated well, and they were suddenly within range, the pencil-thin Dorniers so close that he fancied he could see the bomb aimer in the nose of the one he had selected on the right of the formation staring back at him in horror.

Already a web of tracer weaved towards them, hunch down, steady.

He pressed the button, and the aircraft vibrated from the recoil of his Brownings, as did the image of the enemy aircraft he was targeting.

And then he had skipped over it, the blurred, vague memory of hits and smoke, smeared, spinning pieces of metal.

But he could not look back and see what damage there was, for there were plenty more of them before him. It seemed like hundreds.

Stretching back apparently unendingly into the distance.

His stinging eyes were already searching for the next one.

Rattle of hits against the fuselage, but it's OK, because she continues to fly.

Another appeared before him, and he pressed down the gun-button again.

There were so many! The Hurricane shook again, and he put in a two second burst that seemed to last forever, until the Dornier, blurred in his windscreen, smoking and massive, whipped past.

He shot through the trail of stinking grey-white smoke, and was turning and diving to starboard, so that they searched for the open air on the flank of the formation.

Had they turned to port, he and his Hurricane would have stormed into the centre of that looming formation, into the massed concentrated gunfire at its core.

Rose gasped. He had thought a collision impossible to avoid, yet they had passed one another with space to spare.

He stared behind. He could not tell what had happened to either of the twin tailed machines he had attacked, for the formation, once so solid looking and impenetrable, had opened up into a ragged and open formation.

Three machines were streaming smoke, and a fourth was falling slowly, burning fiercely (mine or someone else's?), whilst a fifth spun downwards out of control.

Parachutes opened, and men, once safe and invulnerable, were entering into captivity that might last for years. But then, they were the lucky ones.

Beneath the formation, a lone Hurricane was firing into the belly of a Dornier, whilst on the far side another was turning back into the attack.

A bomber exploded suddenly, whilst another fell away, a white thin ribbon marking its path like the glistening bitter trail traced by a slug.

Already some bombers had turned back. A whole group of three, still in formation, turned tail and fled back the way they had come, diving away as they sought salvation over the glassy waters.

Leave them. More than enough still on the original heading.

The sea shone silver, too far below to see the waves, like a stippled metal tray.

Glance left, right, above and behind.

Another RAF fighter behind, pulling up. How come there were fewer bombers? Where did they disappear to in so little time?

Another glance backwards.

There were suddenly more machines. Machines with square edged wings and yellow spinners. Bf109s!

The breathless fear hit him then, like a bucket of ice water flung over him, full in the face. But already his arms and legs were moving, manoeuvring his kite to counter the threat, to face them.

"Cripes!" The word was torn from his lips. He keyed the R/T. "Break! Break! 109's attacking from above!"

The shining arc of their airscrews was like the gauzy flicker of a wasp's wings, strangely adding to their malevolence. They were coming down in formations of four aircraft, line abreast it seemed.

And still he was turning. Harder now, gasping in exertion and fear.

More of them were diving down, difficult to count, dear God, so many, and then he was head on with the first group, and he barrel rolled, no time to aim, pressing the gun-button reflexively in the same moment, the swathe of gunfire reaching out at them in a spreading, outward spiralling cone.

If any of his bullets hit them, the damage didn't show, although they split apart into two pairs.

The 109's were firing too, but their own fire did not connect, the deadly sleet racing past him.

They did not manage any hits on his machine, whether because of his unexpected roll, or the sudden head-on attack, or perhaps because of both.

And then he was past them, some the 109's trying to follow, whilst the majority of them continued to the torn bomber formation. He aimed himself at a nearby cloud. With a little luck, they would be unable to catch him in there.

There were others coming. Two more 109s dropped down dangerously close behind him.

Bloody hell! They would catch him before he found the sanctuary of cloud.

I've had it!

Nothing but black-crossed machines. No chance to run.

Turn tight again, hard, pull back hard. Tracer and cannon shells creeping after him, trying to nail him down as he turned again.

Any cloud nearby? No. Side-slip, turn.

A German fighter soared past, so close that he saw the pair of wide open blue eyes staring back into his. A grey leather flying helmet, and then he was pulling the other way.

Another flashed before him, no chance of a shot.

He saw a Hurricane with two Bf109s on its tail, and then another two. Turn, you fool! Turn!

I'm going to die today.

The first pair fired and tracer converged on the fleeing RAF fighter, so that big pieces of wing and fuselage flew off. Fire blossomed its evil flower, and smoke poured back, thick and black and final.

It began to fall, but still they continued to fire into it tearing it apart methodically. No parachute.

"Leave him!" Rose shrieked. A Bf109 was close, closing behind. Twist the Hurri, and bank.

The last he saw of the other Hurricane was the sight of it as it disintegrated like wet paper suddenly ripped raggedly apart.

Still no parachute. Now there wouldn't be one. Just the ugly smear of thick black smoke against the dirty-white canvas of cloud.

Whose was it? Oh.

Goodbye, Desoux.

He felt the thump of hits against his machine, one, two, three, four, five and then he was turning again. Hits crashed into the armour behind him.

Tighten the turn, muscles aching and heart racing. There was no chance at flying in a given direction, for he would be chopped down without mercy. Sanctuary so far out of reach.

Vomit threatened to surface, and he swallowed convulsively.

The world outside was a turning, twisting, tumbling landscape, filled with tracer and silver grey machines. He knew he was not alone, for he could hear the others calling, but he felt as if he were the only Hurricane in the sky, the only target.

He could not aim and fire any longer, all his attention focussed on surviving. He cursed and the next few minutes were ones with desperate weaving and turning, until he felt as if he had been doing this for an eternity, arms and legs shaking with the effort, vision constricted, lungs burning. Eyes straining against the next slashing pass.

By some incredible good fortune, none of the occasional pattering hits on his aircraft proved mortal, and she continued to turn cleanly, the engine continued its reassuring growl.

And all the while, the Dorniers were getting away.

Seconds turned into minutes, endless minutes, and a straining eternity of struggling. How much more can we take? The Hurricane and he were straining against the forces, the Merlin screaming, and the odour of blood was heavy in his nose.

Stick right, kick rudder. Too much! Counter it. More. Yes, better.

The forces on him made his face feel swollen, tried to rip him free of his harness.

His hands felt like claws, cold with fear.

And then suddenly, he was in cloud.

One minute there was just the danger, the bright blue bowl filled with sharks, the next he was in cloud, heavy and grey white, and, oh so beautiful! Survival had appeared unexpectedly, and by chance.

It held him like a babe in arms, softly, and protective. A sanctuary of flocculent wool.

After the last few minutes (which had seemed like hours), he was feeling confused and spent. In the melee, he had lost all sense of direction and now he levelled out the aircraft, saw that he was at ten thousand feet, on a heading of one-eight-zero degrees. Due south.

The enemy had been heading roughly two-nine-zero.

The cloud held him comfortingly, but he knew that at any moment he may pop back out into the open. The Dorniers would be long gone, by now, so he would try and stay in cloud for at least a few minutes. Perhaps he might catch a straggler or a cripple?

He was fearful of the Bf109s (so many!), survival had been in little part due to luck, but there were still too many rounds in his ammo trays to run home now. Too many bombers that would still be on a heading for whatever target they were attacking. They were likely gone...

Damn it!

He pulled back the stick and zoomed back up at full throttle. He popped back out into the clear air five hundred feet higher up.

The sky was empty. He swivelled his head quickly all around, eyes straining, but there was no sign of any other aircraft.

Neither RAF nor Luftwaffe. Of the swarming Bf109s there was no sign.

There were just a few faraway streaks and contrails on the clouded horizon.

He checked his watch. He could not have been in cloud for more than a minute or so, and they had all gone.

So many Messerschmitt fighters, so very many, now none at all.

The R/T still buzzed with the sound of combat, and he gathered that the battle had moved north-west of his position.

He turned on a heading for where he estimated the enemy bombers would be, and pushed the stick forwards. There may be more beneath.

The cloud base was at nine and a half thousand feet, and he levelled out the Hurricane at eight thousand.

A fire was burning in a field below, dirty orange, whether from a crashed aircraft or from a building hit by jettisoned bombs he could not tell.

The minutes dragged by, and he began to think the fight was finished for him.

And then he saw the pencil-thin line in the distance.

The closer he flew, the more apparent the situation. Two 109s were worrying a smoking Hurricane like a rabid dog would snap at a sheep isolated from the flock.

It was twisting, but the 109s had it boxed in. suddenly it had pirouetted magically and was heading back the way it had come.

Rose pushed the kite into a screaming dive, keyed the microphone. "I say, is this a private party, or can anyone join in?" his nerves sang like railway tracks as a train approaches, but he held his course steady.

It was two-on-two now, but the other Hurricane was in a bad way.

"We must stop meeting like this, sir. People will talk!" It was Carpenter, breathing hard.

"It's only because you're so pretty. Can I have a go?"

"Be my guest, sir. My bloody guns have jammed, so these two gents thought they'd have a go."

But the enemy were already diving away, out of the fight, back to France. They had been late but finally victorious in their defence of the Dorniers, and with fuel depleted dangerously, there was no time for battle further, and they now left the battered Hurricanes alone.

Against all the odds, they had survived.

But Desoux had not been their only loss this day.

Barsby had been coned by return fire, and his damaged Hurricane had been easy meat for the Bf109s. Carpenter, from afar, had seen it all. There had been no parachute.

Rose was drenched with sweat, and he turned for home, Carpenter on his wing. At least the other Hurricane wasn't smoking now, but they needed to get back to Foxton at soon as possible. The fight, for them at least, was over.

Their Hurricanes both bore the ravages of the battle, and they had not achieved any appreciable results, but the enemy formation had been broken, and they had survived. Luck had been with Carpenter, too, this day.

They had survived. And in the end, it was enough.

Chapter 26

It was dark outside when the orderly clumped his way into the crew hut. The stove in the middle of the room was black and cold and Rose shivered as a gust of cold air blew through the open door into the hut, and pulled the thin blanket higher to cover his face.

The orderly placed his hand on Rose's shoulder and shook it gently.

"Four thirty, sir. Rise and shine."

"OK. Thanks," Rose slurred. He had been awake for at least fifteen minutes; the sounds outside as aircraft were readied, dragging him from a bottomless slumber.

He felt as if he'd been mummified.

"Tea's on its way, sir."

"Right."

His mouth and eyes were sticky and he wiped his face tiredly with one hand, bristles scratching against his palm.

The orderly made his way around the hut, shaking the occupants of the other camp beds in the hut. There were mumbled responses from the pilots.

Outside there was the sound of a Merlin as it coughed and spluttered. The ground crews would be preparing the aircraft for the approaching dawn and the new day.

He sat up, watched blankly as a drop of water wended its way down the fogged pane of glass, adding to the clear trails already there.

How hateful dawn readiness is, he thought, and yawned widely. He was loath to leave the cosy warmth of his little huddle of blanket.

"What a bind," muttered a dark shape from across the room. Granny. He broke wind explosively and coughed.

The others moaned, and the orderly, grinning, retreated hastily for the door.

"Phew!" Carpenter swung his legs out of the cot, "Best brush your teeth, Granny. Just got a whiff of your breath and it's flipping chronic!" Despite the cheery words the NCO pilot sounded exhausted.

"Whose side are you on, you smelly beggar?" Denis pulled on his trousers. "Where's my bloody gas mask?"

"It's not me, you swine, it's the bloody drains," complained Granny.

Rose ran his tongue over his furred teeth, swallowed dryly. His neck was stiff and his shoulders ached abominably.

I need a cup of tea.

The rest was automatic. Climb out of warm but uncomfortable bed, eyes closed, muscles creaking and tired. Pull on outer clothes, fabric and wool, unpleasantly stiff and cold against his skin. Mae West over the whole ensemble. Then the scarf, tied carefully around his neck. He fancied he could still smell Molly's scent on it.

The thought of the girl raised his spirits, dispelling some of the cranky gloom of his fellows and the melancholic mood of the pre-dawn darkness.

He patted his flying jacket pocket, made sure he had the little bear and the photograph safely tucked away.

Walk outside, inhale deeply of the chill, moist air, full of the rich fragrance of countryside, the sweetness of it hanging like honey. He shivered miserably.

Nevertheless it was a refreshing experience, after the noxious odour inside of the hut, despite being mixed with the multiple and varied smell of airfields and aircraft. He stretched arthritically; almost fell over as Granny pushed against him playfully.

Then on to his Hurricane, where it was sitting quietly in a small gathering of the sleek Hawker fighters, ahead of him, in the darkness. He quietly squelched his way over the damp grass to it.

There was the 'clang!' of tool on metal, and a 'plumber' cursing softly.

A quick chat and a joke with the ground crew, who had already been awake for hours readying his kite for dawn readiness, and then he checked his parachute.

As expected, it was waiting patiently on one tail plane, ready to be thrown on at a moment's notice.

He patted it (Hope I don't need you today, dear friend), then jumped (Careful! Don't slip!) onto the port wing root.

Canopy closed against the moisture still heavy in the air, proud line of four full and three half swastikas on the side of the cockpit denoting his confirmed and shared score of victories. He looked at the line, trying to remember the Rose who'd first arrived at Foxton, innocent, inexperienced, and very, very anxious.

He had played with the idea of painting Molly's name on the side of his aircraft, but had superstitiously decided against the idea.

Brace feet and push back the canopy, check the cockpit. Gloves and helmet ready, oxygen and R/T leads already connected. He lifted the helmet, checked the reflector sight carefully, and replaced the flying helmet again.

Careful glance at the instrument panel.

Petrol tank full.

Tail trim wheel neutral.

Airscrew pitch, set.

Directional gyro, set.

Then the glass of the canopy. Yes, it had been beautifully polished, each speck of dirt carefully removed, and then carefully rubbed dry.

In the air, a dirty speck could be mistaken for an enemy aircraft in the heat of battle, adding confusion where there would be no shortage of same.

Good. The boys had everything set up perfectly.

As per usual. Thanks, lads.

Doubtless one of them would pass a cloth over the Perspex again.

Then, as was his custom, he sat on the leading edge of the wing, offering his 'plumbers' a cigarette from the packet of Players he kept on him solely for them, and they chatted again for a few minutes.

Then it was back with Granny and the others to the Readiness hut.

The trees at the edge of the airfield and the hangars were still indistinct, dark shapes looming, and the sky was still deepest royal blue, although he thought he could already detect a faint line of grey on the horizon. The sound of rustling of leaves reached him faintly, as a whisper of wind twitched the trees playfully.

Rose shivered again, pulled up the collar of his jacket, wishing he could have a wash and brush his teeth.

With a bit of luck, someone should have lit the stove in the readiness hut. There'd be some chance of a bit of warmth, perhaps.

He rubbed his cold hands vigorously together, brought them to his mouth and blew warm air on to them.

Granny spat on the grass, coughed, blew his nose and spat again.

"Got a stinking headache, Flash." He had drunk liberally the night before. As usual. Granny searched his pockets, "Think I should have a fag."

Rose shook his head. "Be the death of you, chum."

Granny grinned grimly. Waved a tattered cigarette. "Not these, old son. I think my old mate Adolf will oblige in that department."

They stepped into the hut, nodded to the tubby orderly (Dobbs?) manning the telephone, and pulled a pair of chairs close to the lit stove.

Squadron-Leader Donald was already there, sleeping peacefully in the armchair behind the orderly. He would be leading the readiness flight today, Denis taking Yellow section, with Granny and Rose as his number two and three, respectively.

They dozed for half an hour, as the little stove valiantly crackled the cold away.

Rose opened his eyes as the sound of a car pulling up came to them from outside the readiness hut, and a few seconds later an airman came in carrying the container with their breakfasts.

Probably congealed, thought Rose. Never mind. What I need is a nice hot cup of char. Sweet and hot. The hotter the better. Despite the pleasant warmth of the hut, he still felt the cold deep in his bones.

The airman began laying out the mugs and thermos. There was something lumpy, grey and oily and unappetising on a plate, as well as some thick slices of bread.

Taking a mug gratefully, Rose brought it to his lips, and took a mouthful of the hot sweet brew. It burnt his tongue, but the warmth took off the deep chill he had been feeling, and he took another sip.

"Here, Flash, get this into you." Granny passed him a slice of bread thickly smeared with bright yellow butter.

"Thanks, Granny."

Rose slumped back into his chair, and let the warmth from the stove play over him. He took another sip. The tea was hardly the nicest he'd had, it was already quite stewed, but at least it was hot, and that was exactly what he wanted. He took a bite.

Behind him the telephone suddenly jangled hideously, the

half-expected discordance startling him, so that the tea slopped hotly onto his leg, and his breakfast went flying. He cursed as the fluid burnt his leg, whilst all around the others stared at the orderly, frozen into still-life as he spoke on the phone.

The orderly jumped up and shouted shrilly, *"SCRAMBLE! A-FLIGHT SCRAMBLE!"*

Rose could feel the strange, sinking sickness already, as he ran for the door, spitting out his bite of bread.

How he despised that blasted bloody awful telephone! Bloody, bloody, fucking, bastard thing.

Behind him, his slice of bread had landed butter-side down, on the muddy floor, following the rules of physics that customarily govern all flying pieces of buttered bread.

As usual, it was Granny who saw them first.

"Bandits, nine o'clock low. Heading two-seven-zero."

"Tally-Ho!"

They were Messerschmitts, not the Bf109s, but the bigger, twin-engined 110s, the much vaunted 'Destroyers' Rose had first fought.

Rose picked them out against the landscape, a shoal of ten or more, sweeping low, from right to left, over the marshy ground of northern Kent.

The dark shark-like shapes were doubtless one of those hit-and-run flights sent out to attack targets of opportunity wherever they presented themselves.

The low lying sun, crawling on the horizon in this strange world of retreating darkness, caught their surfaces brightly, picking them out perfectly for A 'Flight against the darker land below. The RAF fighters, however, had the darkness behind them, so it was much harder for the Germans to see them.

Six of us to ten of them, he mused. He searched for higher formations of fighters, but there was no sign. Check behind, left, right, above, below. Check the 110s, then around and behind again.

Smoke poured suddenly from Donald's' exhausts as he took them into a shallow dive at full boost, lining up for an attack astern on the port quarter of the 110s.

They must surely see them at any moment, and Rose hunched forward in his cockpit, willing his Hurricane faster.

The enemy aircraft grew larger agonisingly slowly, yet luckily they seemed not to have noticed the diving Hurricanes, coming out of what remained of the darkness.

And then objects suddenly fell away from them (bombs?), and the enemy formation split apart. They'd spotted the Hurricanes.

Two pairs of 110s on either flank pulled upwards out of the formation, whilst the centre of the formation remained steadfastly on course.

"Red Leader to Yellow section, we'll take the four to port, you take the ones to starboard. Keep an eye on those up ahead. They may circle back and take us from behind."

Denis replied crisply, "Yellow Leader to Red Leader, message received and understood."

The 110s were still climbing and turning, straining upwards, desperately trying to bring their cannon to bear. These ones weren't going to try and make a circle, like the wagons in the westerns. They were going to fight it out.

Evenly, Denis called, "Yellow Leader to Yellow section. Spread out. Pick a target."

The range was great, but Denis fired a long-range burst that brought a shower of hits and a puff of smoke from one of the enemy. It fell back out of the formation, rolled over and dropped away rapidly. Good shot!

A moment later it caromed into the ground, in a blistering gout of bright flame that lit up the grey land below them.

Rose applied right rudder, allowed his Hurricane to drift a little to starboard. Glance behind.

Almost there, light pressure on the button, tracer climbing, too far to hurt him.

And then the machine on the extreme starboard position of the enemy formation was lined up just right, and Rose pressed the button on his spade grip.

Once again there was the familiar blurring, and flashes sparkled convulsively on the port wing of the machine, shredding metal and tearing the engine into shattered, burning metal. Still trying to turn, neither the pilot nor his gunner was able to bring their guns to bear yet.

Suddenly there was another ahead, arrowing in hard towards him.

He cringed back as the approaching 110's nose lit up. Orange blobs floated up towards him, slowly, almost as if they were hardly moving, then suddenly they grew to the size of oranges, seemed as if they would hit him head on, crumpling him up.

But there was no crash of exploding cannon shells, no bone-wrenching pain, and the enemy fire passing harmlessly above.

Lucky!

Then they had raced past each other, the Me110 a grey flash zipping beneath his port wing, and his Hurricane juddered in the turbulent air, and his target had disappeared.

Rose waited for the order to tighten up the formation, or to separate and find another enemy, perhaps pursue that last one.

Suddenly, Donald's voice, cutting through the HF incisively, "Yellow section! Bandits closing behind! Get out of the way!"

The central part of the original formation had turned back, and the two 110s were lining up behind Yellow section, although Donald had called out before they had managed to get within effective range, the enemy almost but not quite having trapped Yellow section in a loose closing pincer.

Except the two remaining machines of the original four (did I get one?) of the savaged starboard formation had decided to call it a day. They were pointing out to the sanctuary of the open sea, and running away now, fleeing hard at full throttle. No time to pursue them. They'd had enough, and were out of the fight.

"Break, Yellow section!"

Kick rudder, push on the stick, full boost again, pull up hard.

Rose felt (heard?) a bang as something thumped heavily into the fuselage behind him. His Hurricane jerked, settled back normally. Pray that the 'something' that hit her hasn't done any major damage.

Please God.

Grey smoking lines streaked past, not ten feet from the cockpit.

"Break! Break!"

Now whipping around in a sharp, screaming turn, the forces gripping him and pummelling him, the greyness threatening to enfold him in its caress.

Nothing in the mirror, look up, directly through the canopy, and there they are, two thin birds of prey following Denis down.

"Yellow Leader! Two bandits on your tail!"

The sight of smoke streaming back suddenly from Denis' fighter, and then he rolls sharply, drops away.

Check behind, all around, nothing in the rear-view mirror.

All clear behind.

They might be able to get away if he didn't get after them immediately.

Flash of light, burgeoning, expanding glaringly.

God! Was that Dingo Denis?

"Got you!" a high pitched scream of triumph.

Granny, crowing victoriously over the HF, and one of the two that had been trailing Denis was no longer there, just a tumbling, flaming torch that smashed into the ground below, scattering fragments of metal everywhere.

The remaining 110 was climbing, now desperately turning for the sea.

Try and cut him off.

Where are the others? Red section had disappeared completely.

The Messerschmitt 110 was below and before him, passing from left to right, the landscape below a barely noticed blur. Concentrate on it, he instructed himself.

But don't forget to watch your tail.

Open the throttle wide. Don't let him get away. Watch out for the gunner.

No sign of Denis' Hurricane. Was he gone or had he managed to get away? How had they managed to get so close to hit him? He must be even more tired than I am.

The 110 was travelling flat out, each second taking the hateful enemy intruder closer to safety.

Bank steeply to starboard, follow him down, cork-screw to port and check the turn when wings level.

Nothing behind, the distance ahead decreasing rapidly.

The Luftwaffe flyer was on the horns of a dilemma, should he head for the sea, and offer a straight-flying target? Or should he turn and jink, evade the British bullets and lose his advantage of speed gained, and thus allow more hunters to close with him?

He chose the straight and level option, try and flee, hope that speed was enough for salvation.

Adjust the aim to allow for his speed, press down the button, and eight guns roar, the sound sweet music to his ears as he drops it down onto the enemy machine.

The enemy gunner swings round his gun, a string of tracer reaches back like some evil silk from a spider's spinneret, trying to ensnare him within it. Stomach turns to a solid ball of ice as the line of tracer arches closer.

Concentrate on him.

Centre the dot. Half a ring. Press.

He had judged perfectly, for his first, tentative burst splattered viciously against the port engine, ripping the Daimler-Benz DB601 engine into fiery ruin. Flame gouted back like acidic vomit, searing and unforgiving.

Then he had to pull hard to port in a climbing turn, the smoke belching from the burning engine hiding him from the rear gunner, and preventing accurate return fire.

The 110 was slower now, losing height, so there was no need for emergency boost to keep up with it. He curved around tightly into his second pass. The Me110 was slowing now; smoke billowing in irregular gouts, like a message in Morse code, telling a sorry tale of destruction and death.

He closed, so close that the wingtips of the enemy fighter were intersecting with the reflector sight's edges. Smoke obscured so much and he prayed for good fortune.

The enemy was ruined. There was no way that the 110 would survive a trip across to France, but still he pressed the button, and once more his guns poured fire into the luckless German fighter.

His bullets splashed across it, from nose to tail, scraps and shreds of metal flying from it, the hits sparkling a bright pattern of destruction and death.

Kick rudder left and right to spray the German fighter with

death. Tiny shattered pieces of metal spattered the Hurricane harmlessly.

The stench of cordite, mixed in with hot metal and smoke, was suffocating, and Rose's empty stomach churned.

And then there was just the pneumatic hiss as his guns finally fell silent. He had used up all of his ammunition.

Yet the Messerschmitt still flew on. The fire had turned into a wan streamer of long flame, but it had lost its earlier violence.

Oh, it was losing height all the time alright, but still it continued to fly, straight and true.

Rose was filled with the urge to destroy, to kill this trespasser against his land. But his bite was toothless, his fighter now an empty threat.

Once, twice he pressed the gun button hopefully, but he knew it was a futile action.

The enemy was done, his battle lost, but the fire still burned in Rose's belly. He wanted to send it, for to him his foe was an it, evil and nameless, flaming into the ground.

The rear machine gun lolled, like a marionette with its strings cut, and now he could see that the long glasshouse canopy had been shredded into a charnel house and splattered red by his bullets.

Aboard the enemy heavy fighter, all life had been extinguished by his guns.

Slowly, instincts screaming, like a feral cat creeping into a backyard, he eased into formation, moving nearer. Watch that gunner, he might turn in a split second and hammer the Hurricane with his machine gun.

Except that there was no longer any danger, because the gunner had no head. All that remained was a body, hanging forward in its straps, still clutching the MG15 machine gun.

He felt like giggling, and stifled it with a gloved fist.

With no head, the gunner could no longer sight on him, and so was no longer a threat to him, as he had been just minutes earlier.

The giggles still bubbled upwards. What the hell was wrong with him?

Bullet holes had scarred the entire length of the Me110, scouring away the paintwork with the life from the occupants of the big aircraft. There was little glass in the canopy now, and what there was, was painted a horrible patchy fluid red of lost dreams and terrible harm.

And the foulest thing was that he was glad.

The coast was close now, but the heavy fighter would never reach it.

It slipped lower and lower now, faltering, as if it were battling on, even though it no longer had the energy to continue the struggle, like a punch-drunk boxer hanging from the ropes, refusing to admit defeat.

The blur of trees and hedges and marshy ground below drew nearer, and Rose pulled into a gentle climb, his eyes never leaving the 110.

And then there was no more height, and the Messerschmitt skidded into the ground, smearing itself messily across the landscape it had come to destroy. A destroyer no longer.

The dead men were immolated in the bright flare of the explosions that rent the fragmented wreckage, a Valhalla of sorts, for fighting, flying men.

The sea swept towards him, and he curved around in a gentle, climbing, arc, to level off at a thousand feet.

The flight was forming up, and there were two plumes of smoke that marked the lost machines of brave men.

Granny tucked himself in comfortably beside him. He had his hood pushed back, and had a pattern of bullet holes stitched across his fuselage roundel.

"I saw yours, Flash. And the one you damaged. That makes you an ace, confirmed. Did you see mine go down?" he laughed, "that makes sixteen, confirmed."

"Yeah, Granny." He was still breathless, "Bloody good shooting. I saw you get the one who shot up Dingo. Did he get out of it OK?" Anxiety fluttered inside him, "Is he OK? Where is he?"

"He had to take to his umbrella, but he got out OK." As if reading his mind, he added, "Don't worry, Flash, he'll be fine. I kept an eye on him until he landed. He landed near a road, and there was a car coming, and he'll probably cadge a lift. Probably be back at home before us, I shouldn't wonder."

"Hope so."

"I know so. I bet he'll end up in a rich widow's house or something."

Rose's heart rate began to reduce in tempo, although the adrenaline was still jolting through his system

"Let's go home, Granny. I've had enough. And my guns are empty."

"Me too. I need some ammo, but I could really do with is a nice cuppa and a fag."

Three thousand feet higher up, to the west they could see another two Hurricanes.

Donald sounded reassuringly cheerful. "Come on you pair of reprobates, form up."

"Received and understood, Red Leader. We got one each. Dingo got one too. They got him but he got out OK."

"Good show, lads. That'll teach the buggers to try to sneak in and pinch our bums in the night."

Carpenter was missing, and had last been seen chasing a 110 south. Donald had also got one for sure, and damaged another with the new boy, Sergeant Jenkins. That meant four shot down for sure, perhaps one or more probable, out of ten bandits, for the loss of one Hurricane. It had been a good interception, and the German dawn attack had been foiled.

Not a bad little score for the morning, and it had been nice to be attacking rather than defending, although Rose still wondered why the Germans hadn't adopted one of their usual defensive circle formations.

With the immediacy of danger temporarily gone, although the brightening sky could still hide dangers, the energy seemed to drain out through the soles of his feet in an instant, leaving Rose feeling suddenly tired and shaky.

I need some sleep, some peace. Place a hand over the pocket, feel her picture there. Beside his heart. I do so need you, Molly, my love. Just a few days now.

Oh God, when will they stop coming over?

Rose cast an eye wearily at the columns of smoke, now behind them. He had killed at least two men this day, gained his fifth confirmed individual victory, and yet the morning was still young.

Had those men watched the sun rising as they had speeded on to their target? Had they wondered if it would be their last sun-rise?

They must have felt so strong, flying side by side in those big powerful fighters.

They would not know that they had only minutes of life left to them, before he had tossed them into death with a pitiless hail of bullets, and sent them into that cold, cruel darkness.

Without thinking, he patted his pocket, eyes automatically searching for a hidden enemy, reassured by the bear's bump.

But I'm alive.

I'm still here to see the sunrise.

Thank you, God. You've given me the gift of one more glorious dawn over my country.

Still alive.

Chapter 27

The 8th day of August, 1940, was a day of unsettled and wet weather interspersed with intervals of brightness. There was cloud over the Channel, but not enough to put off the bombers.

Another convoy, it had been decided, would have to be pushed through. Presented with such a tantalising target, the Luftwaffe were not shy in taking up the challenge.

It would have an effective balloon barrage, and fighter support.

The morning saw a number of raids.

The main attacks were by a formation of Ju 87 dive bombers and Bf109 fighters. It was met by Hurricanes and Spitfires.

A second, similar raid, just after midday, and consisting of the same enemy aircraft types, was met by RAF fighters again.

Both times Excalibur were unable to intercept, leaving them seething and frustrated. It was always galling to see the enemy, yet not be able to engage.

Raids in the afternoon, where there was less cloud, were enough to cause the convoy to scatter, and thus offer easier targets to the enemy bombers, resulting in losses.

A third main raid, the biggest of the day so far, was detected in the late afternoon. This one consisted of over a hundred bandits.

The convoy, split up after the previous attacks, was vulnerable, the defensive balloon barrage no longer as protective a shield as before.

This time, Excalibur Squadron was there. Fighter Command had ensured a presence throughout the day, and they were ready for attacks as they developed.

Because of the continuity of a convoy fighter escort, the squadron had been able to get into that extraordinarily unusual situation, an advantageous position and height at just the right time.

A-Flight had been cruising at twenty-five thousand feet, the Hurricanes wallowing uncomfortably in the thin air, when they caught sight of the first elements of the big raid. Immediately, Donald ordered the six Hurricanes of B-Flight, eight thousand feet lower down, into the attack.

Already the high escort of enemy fighters, flying at eighteen thousand feet, were visible as a cloud of midges. B-Flight should be able to inflict some damage before the German fighters came down.

The Junkers were about to begin their attacking run when the Hurricanes of B-Flight screamed down out of the sky and lanced painfully into their flank, like a pack of wolves slamming into a herd of sheep.

Except, of course, these sheep were armed with an aft-firing 7.9mm MG15 mounted in the cockpit. From his position above, Rose watched his friends smash into the dive-bombers, like a battle-axe smashing into the armoured breast plate of an enemy, rending the neat ordered lines asunder.

Tracer formed a fine, delicate criss-crossing cage that caught one Hurricane and set its engine aflame, and it fell away. In response, though, the score was heavily in B-Flight's favour. They were taking a toll of the enemy machines.

Two Stukas were already falling, and another two were dropping

346

out of their neat, ordered ranks, wobbling and smoking. A third ballooned outwards in a catastrophic explosion.

Parachutes were blossoming, including one that was white. The pilot of the damaged Hurricane had managed to escape his crippled mount. The Hurricane tumbling crazily down, shedding fragments.

Poor Farrell. Bad luck. At least he'd got out.

Perhaps he had been successful this time before he'd had to hop out.

And then the covering 109s of the high escort were diving, trying to intercept the Hurricanes of B-Flight, and allow the Stukas a breathing space in which to rally and escape or continue the attack.

It was the German fighter's turn to be 'bounced.' They had not even seen the second flight of RAF fighters above. And as far as Rose could see there was no second bunch of Bf109s above the first.

Denis, quiet, crisp. "Red Leader to A-Flight, time for us to join the party! Tally-Ho!"

One by one, the Hurricanes of A-Flight leaned over into a dive and made for the plummeting Bf109s.

They were two arrowheads of three, glittering shapes where the sun caught their canopies, falling like thunderbolts from a clear blue ceiling.

Rose glanced down, as the twisting aeroplanes below grew larger and larger in his sights. This time, however, he was primarily concentrating on the sky behind, and in also in keeping formation with Denis. He would stay strictly on his section leader's wing, taking a backseat role of watch and cover and protect.

The formation of German fighters was below them, the enemy at an angle of dive shallower than that of their pursuers.

There were three formations of enemy fighters, each containing four Bf109s. Fairly evenly matched, then, but still his heart thumped anxiously inside him.

"Red Leader to Yellow Leader, you take the starboard four. We'll have a bash at the others."

"Received and understood, Red Leader, last one in's a rotten egg." cackled Granny. God, how does he stay so cool?

The two sections separated, and Yellow section closed until they were three hundred yards above and behind the four 109s when Denis opened fire, grey trails streaming back from his wings.

They had caught the enemy completely unawares, or so it seemed. Was there already another formation of fighters descending on them? But there was still nothing above them.

Denis' aim was excellent, and his bullets splashed across the 109 second from left.

Immediately, the enemy machine came apart, exploding into a blazing ball that corkscrewed out of the formation, its pilot already dead.

At that instant, Rose opened fire on his target.

Pieces flew off the right wingtip of the Bf109 that Rose had targeted, and then it abruptly rolled away, white smoke pouring from its exhausts.

He let it go.

The fighter formation was split up. But there were no congratulations or calls of triumph, just a terse, "Tighten up, Yellow section."

Stay in formation.

Concentrate on the machine next to you, but don't let down your guard. Snap off a quick burst if the odd chance permits.

Then they were racing through a gaggle of Junker 87s. The gull-winged dive-bombers scattering from the tight formation of three Hurricanes that came as if from nowhere like a bolt from the blue into their midst. His ears buzzed, the Bf109s forgotten.

For an instant, a Stuka was in his sights, and he pressed hard on

348

the gun-button, a one second burst that flayed uselessly at the open air, missing the dive-bomber and its terrified, staring crew completely.

He cursed obscenely.

Denis was pulling out, and Rose dragged at the control column, muscles straining, vision greying, and the Hurricane shuddered as it tried to recover from the screaming dive.

He ought to have throttled back, would not be able to stop.

They were going down too fast, and, unable to recover fast enough to intercept, sweeping past the Stukas, which were only so many blurred streaks that disappeared behind them as if standing still.

They finally managed to level out a few hundred feet further down. Immediately Denis had cranked over in a turn towards a Stuka that had been surprised by the nightmare of their sudden appearance, and seeing the unwelcome attention it had received, tipped over into a dive to escape.

Rose worked to hold position with Denis, already sliding and slipping after the dive bomber.

Throttling back so as not to overshoot, Denis locked his sights onto the Stuka, ignored the return fire and shredded it with a two second burst, destroying the dive-bomber with contemptuous ease.

Small pieces all that were left, to fall like errant leaves twisting to the ground in autumn.

"Any more?"

"Come on, Dingo!" Granny sounded thoroughly browned off with his supporting position, he was accustomed to leading and was itching to hunt his own. Rose glanced quickly into his rear-view mirror again, and saw the danger.

"Two bandits, He113's, five o'clock high, descending!"

Can't climb or dive. Have me on a plate if I try that. Best to turn and face them.

349

"Yellow break! Break, chaps!"

Kick right foot on the rudder bar, pull back and to the right on the control-column, and the Hurricane is suddenly twisting hard around, banking upwards to face the enemy. His vision greyed again as the tremendous forces pushed the blood from his head.

When the mists cleared sufficiently from his vision, he sighted carefully on the turning shape, pressed the gun-button.

He had misjudged deflection in his haste, and his two second burst arced uselessly away behind and beneath the enemy aircraft.

Rose could see now that it wasn't a He113 as he had initially thought, but another Bf109 with its squared-off wingtips and big airscrew.

The engine cowling and airscrew of the other machine twinkled with bright light, and orange blobs were racing towards him, slowly at first, swelling and expanding, and then they were whizzing past to one side as he eased rudder and side-slipped away from them.

A second later, the Messerschmitt had shot past, and the Hurricane wallowed in the turbulent air of its passage.

Fight for control, keep her under control, come on, my love.

There was just a hubbub of shouts in his earphones, and a confusion of aircraft all around him.

Wheel round, stick back, left rudder. Blacked out momentarily again.

Granny meanwhile had whipped around too, and his aim was better than Rose's. His first burst sawed into the first Bf109's Daimler Benz engine, he rolled, and his second burst caught the other 109 on the wingtip.

The first machine's propeller windmilled before it tipped drunkenly downwards, the pilot already pulling back his canopy.

The second Bf109, faced by the two Hurricanes and seeing his colleagues plight, decided he'd had enough, and dived away, plunging out of trouble. A parachute blossomed as the doomed Bf109 fell away.

Denis, meanwhile, had disappeared, and then Granny too, had gone, as he half-rolled and dived after the second 109. "Come on Flash, we can share this one."

Another Stuka passed below Rose from left to right, heading for the convoy. Already two ships were burning, and another was sinking, low-down at the bows, its speed dropping off sharply.

He dived down, and a thread of tracer swept up to meet him, above, tracked downwards, *thud-thud-thud!* Sound of a cricket bat on sandbag. Something *spanged!* against the side of the cockpit, one panel crazing and frightening him badly, and then the stream of fire had washed past below.

Bullets had torn into the port wing, and now a long thin section of fabric tore back like a long streamer, and flapped frantically like some long strange banner, the vibration from it pulling at him, but at least the bullets had missed anything vital.

The ribbon lengthened as the slipstream pulled at it, but it would not tear off, dragged at him instead as he held her steady.

But at least he'd survived the bead of tracer. They'd missed his wing petrol tank, God be praised!

My turn, he thought savagely, and his thumb jammed down on the gun-button.

The Stuka was banking to port, sun catching its cockpit cover harshly, when the bullets from his guns crashed in a concerted storm against the fuselage and starboard wing of the enemy aircraft. Metal flew back, and the enemy machine shivered under the assault.

The enemy gunner was firing again, and Rose's Hurricane shuddered against the new hits, the big Merlin caught, just for an instant, and so did Rose's heart, and then it was purring again, and the enemy pilot had dragged his aircraft around tight, a piece of one of the dive-brakes whirled off, and the Stuka, trailing more pieces, suddenly tipped over and tumbled down.

Was he hit badly, or was it a loss of control? Or perhaps a controlled spinning tumble? But there was no time to follow him and find out. He'd hurt the Stuka, and that was enough.

The Hurricane was vibrating disturbingly, and fighters were somewhere behind him, hunting him.

And then there was only a hail-like rattle of bullets or shrapnel against the armour plating behind him, more thuds against the fuselage.

The aircraft shook and juddered even more under the violent onslaught. For a terror-filled instant he thought he was lost, but then his reflexes took over.

Automatically, he banged hard on the rudder, and the trembling Hurricane swerved wildly to starboard, dropped a wing tip and pulled back hard into a steep bank.

My God! Survived it!

Even as he was turning, two more Messerschmitts sped past him, guns still winking, so close that he saw a face looking directly at him, brown-helmeted head and a pale blur of a face, features indistinct, and then the contact was swiftly broken.

The Stuka had disappeared, grateful for a chance to escape by the sudden reprieve.

Watch out for a second pair. Search this strange whirling confusion, yes, two more, falling down at him. There're too many!

Calm, calm. Reduce the turn, pull out a little.

Vibrations worsening, not from the wing-fabric though, finally ripped off by the sharp turn. Vibrations must be from some of the damage done by the machine gun bullets.

Pray to God she stays together. Please, my darling, don't let me down.

Please, please, please... *come on...*

Mumbling the mantra quietly, desperately, unaware he was doing so.

Still too far, but the Bf109s suddenly break off, dive away.

What the...?

There! A Spitfire, curving around behind them, light sparkled from her leading edges, and smoke ripped back from the second Bf109 of the pair.

Off to his left, a burning Hurricane whirled past, cockpit empty and harness flapping, it's rudder and tail plane ripped apart, angry orange fire rippling back from the exhaust stubs, the propeller stopped and broken.

He tried to pick out whose it was, but it had disappeared below before he could pick out the code-letter. At least the pilot had managed to get out. We've lost two at least, then, but not me, thank the Lord. Not so far...

And then there were no more aircraft nearby, just the shouts over the R/T, and a few planes turning and fighting, far off. A trail etched harsh against a cloud showed the death-dive of yet another aircraft, but with no sign of its identity, or of the victor of the fight, whilst below, three mushrooms, only one of them white, had blossomed, like peculiar airborne mushrooms. But at least that was one RAF pilot saved.

In the moments of sudden quiet, he tested the controls, glancing nervously into his mirror and all around him. The torn hole in the fabric of the wing had left a few of the members of the wing exposed, scratched bright by the impact of bullets.

She responded well, no apparent damage to the vital systems, but there was still that damn strange vibration. The motion made his hair stand on end and his nerves tingle with anxiety.

Sod it. What could be causing it? The engine sounded fine and the propeller arc shone smoothly before him.

There was still ammunition in his guns, but he no longer felt certain that his aircraft was prepared for further combat. Better, perhaps, to break off, and make for base. At least he'd damaged two, and maybe a third. No definite kills today, though.

His body was shivering as if in sympathy with the fighter, and he was ashamed, but it wasn't worth the risk to get back into that maelstrom.

There may be something seriously damaged, if the vibration was anything to go by. He'd been hit many times, and it was a miracle if nothing vital had been damaged. It was bloody miracle he was still flying!

Better, by far, surely, to live to fight another day?

Yes.

He felt a coward, but decided that it was unlikely that he could add significantly to the fight, particularly as it had drifted off to the east.

He pushed down the nose slightly, pointing it at the nearby coast, took a heading that would get him back to Foxton.

The vibration unsettled him, and he was keen to get home, eyes anxiously flicking at his mirror.

Chapter 28

The first sign of more trouble was a sharp staccato series of bangs, the Hurricane shuddering more violently in sympathy, the control stick shaking in his trembling hands, then a large gout of thick black oil vomited back to splatter like dark, sticky treacle against the windscreen, obscuring the checkerboard of fields below.

Rose cursed and made to slide back the canopy hood.

And then the engine abruptly cut out.

The shimmering disc of his propeller disappeared, as the whirling blades slowed, windmilling, and finally came to a stop.

Thankfully, there was no sign of fire.

Just the sound of wind whistling on surfaces and ragged, torn and damaged areas, and the peculiar tink-tink-tink as the Merlin cooled, and a slight, strange grinding.

Fucking Hell! He licked dry lips, wiped his goggles automatically.

Hold her steady, drop the nose a little, before speed drops off too much. Turn off the engine, trim the kite's tabs gently for a long glide.

Five thousand feet, and can't see a bloody thing.

Anxiously he searched the sky around, for he was a sitting duck, easy meat to a marauding enemy kite.

Push back the hood, lock it open, and lean forward into the sudden cold blast of air.

Can't reach.

Don't panic. Loosen straps, try again, and try to wipe away the oil.

Hold her steady. He looked down and the slipstream tore the hanky from his fingers, as he tried to mop ineffectually at the stain. A thick droplet whipped back and splattered stickily against one of the eyepieces of his goggles.

He recoiled. Ouch!

But not in hurt, just shocked by the impact of the viscous glob of oil.

Careful. Keep wings level, watch your airspeed.

That's no bloody good. There was still a thick skim of oil across the windscreen, and he was peering through smeared goggles.

Time to ask himself the question he would have preferred to avoid.

What should he do, stay with her or bale out?

She might be OK, might be able to make a good landing. Don't much fancy hitting the silk. Rather a long way down and it feels much safer to be surrounded by a rigid protective skeleton.

They'd been a victorious team together, torn out the enemy's throat together more than once.

And, after all, she'd taken care of him so far...

But was there fire hiding inside the engine, was the integrity of the airframe compromised?

Sod it. He'd earned an AFC bringing back a damaged aeroplane in the past, he could do it again.

Anyway, the kite may spin out of control if I try to step out of the cockpit, thought Rose. And if I leave her, she may land on a school or something...

Stay with her, then.

"Slipper Yellow Three to Turnip," Turnip was sector control, "My

356

engine's conked out, so I can't get back home. Am going to pancake, um, about ten miles north of Pevensey Bill."

But there was only silence in reply. He tried again, but with no joy.

The airframe shook in the turbulent air, and he wrestled with the controls.

Keep your airspeed up, keep the nose down, but not too far, maintain airspeed of at least 120 mph. Compensate for drag on the aircraft. Keep the glide angle shallow as you can.

Make sure she doesn't get too tail-heavy, or else airspeed may bleed off, and off you stall.

He tried to still his trembling fingers.

Oh God, help me!

Watch your wings, keep 'em level, watch out for wobble, don't let her go into a spin either, or else you're done for.

Got to look for a good landing site. Poke your head into the whistling slipstream, look ahead for a suitable site.

Shouldn't be much of a problem; find a field, preferably without any of those anti-invasion traps.

Sure. No problem at all.

Oh, please help me!

Take another breath, got to stay calm.

A moment's lack of concentration, you lose control, and suddenly, it's all over and you're dead. Not desirable when you've got an intimate rendezvous planned with the best looking WAAF in Britain.

Rose smiled at the delightful memory of her nipple, firm and erect beneath his palm, the suppleness of her breast and her gasp as he gently grasped it, the desire hot in her eyes, then he shook his head and looked at the instruments.

The needle on the altimeter was winding down terrifyingly quickly.

Sky still mercifully clear and free of enemy aircraft, the blue empty all around.

Ah. There we are. A long flat rectangular shape that was a freshly turned field, lovely and brown, but the loose earth would not be able to support the three ton Hurricane, it would dig in on contact, likely ground-looping, and the chance of coming to a sticky end would be far higher in such a field.

A sticky end! He grinned to himself tightly, but without humour, eyes grim and continuing the search for salvation.

But at least he could still smile. And the thought gave him courage.

Then he caught sight of a lovely evenly rectangular field of long grass further ahead, and it was clear, or at least appeared so from this height.

Turn, to starboard, turn gently; slide over with a judicious use of rudder. It was large field, bordered by hedgerow, but to him, as he approached at what seemed to his anxious eyes as too high a speed, it appeared about as large as a postage stamp.

Careful, careful! Don't let your airspeed drop! Don't stall her now!

Blimey! That ground was coming up jolly quick.

Easy, easy now. Tighten straps.

He patted the spade grip of the control column gingerly. Come on, my love, come on, keep on flying, just for a little longer.

Oh God, save me. Please!

He stole a glance into the rear-view mirror again. Don't let a raider or fighter pop into sight as I come down. I'm a sitting duck, here, just waiting to be plucked.

With the engine off, he stood no chance whatsoever against enemy fighters. In fact a Stuka would have had little difficulty in knocking him down.

He watched the ground rushing up towards him, throat bone-dry and ticklish, and his eyes smarting painfully. Altitude seemed to be running out too quickly.

He glanced down at the little windows beside his feet.

Oh shit! The wheels! They were still up!

With the engine out of action, the hydraulics and the engine-driven compressor were out of action.

He would have to do it by hand. Feverish burst of activity as he selected 'undercarriage down,' then wrestled with the hand-pump lever on his right, interspersed with anxious glances out of the cockpit at the fast approaching ground. Heart thundering as wings wobbled terrifyingly.

Thank heavens there would not be cause to use the red-painted foot-pedal.

A thump as they came down.

There, down and locked.

Careful, compensate for the increase in drag.

Now, don't forget to pump down the flaps. Move selector to outboard position.

Keep wings level! Careful!

You're not going to make it! A sick feeling in the pit of his stomach.

Shut up. I'll make it. I've got a date with Molly in Mayfair, so I'm bloody well going to make it.

His clothes were stuck to him, his body wet with strain.

I'll make it, of course I will. Done alright so far, haven't I?

Cows scattering slowly, like big white sluggish blobs, at this great dark silent bird swooping low. Everything else a green blur, as he concentrated on the field ahead.

Five hundred feet.

Approach speed 110 mph.

Mouth dry, the horrid coppery taste of fear on his tongue. Swallowing so very painful.

Not much further to go. Hedgerow reaching terrifyingly up for him.

At one hundred feet he pulled back, flaring out into a shallow angle of approach, the speed well above stall speed as he raised the nose.

Tongue poking out with effort and concentration.

Again, the whisper: you're not going to make it!

Shut up! He banished the thought from his mind.

I will! *I must!*

As he passed low over the hedgerow, his speed was down to 90 mph, and he eased the stick back further, as the field came up to meet him. He glided down, and he tucked himself forward, head down near the Sorbo crash cushion, and then the main wheels hit, the Hurricane bouncing a few feet back into the air again, before jarring hard against the ground again. He was pitched forward, but his straps held him firmly.

Thank the Lord he had remembered to tighten them!

Bit of a heavy arrival, but the undercarriage had not collapsed. His forehead hurt from where he had caught it.

The tail wheel settled onto the ground, as he eased further back, did not slam into any hidden obstacle, and he was down proper, jouncing hectically along the uneven field, everything outside just a speeding blur.

Down! Thank the Lord!

The wheels bumped across the rough, uneven ground, shaking him and jarring his teeth against each other. He clamped shut his mouth grimly and fought to keep her steady.

But he was safely down.

Safe and sound, and still blessedly alive.

As he rolled and jolted along, at last daring to breathe, a worrying thought hit him. The ground was uneven. What if the long grass hid a sharp dip? He would have no warning before piling into it.

But, at last, after an anxious eternity measured in seconds, the Hurricane rumbled to a stop at the far end of the field, without (thank goodness) encountering any hidden traps.

There was just the continued sound of metal cooling, tinkling from the engine, the distant whirr of insects, and the high hawthorn hedge rising before him, partially obscured by the raised nose and unmoving propeller blade. No fire.

He slumped in the cockpit in a daze for a long, grateful moment.

Oh God, oh God.

A quivering, painfully deep breath.

Still alive. Drained and sweating and faint with fear, but still here.

Squeeze the little bear in his pocket.

We survived again.

God only knows how. There are such things as miracles, after all.

Dear, sweet, kind God, Thank You.

Incredibly, unbelievably, still alive.

How long he sat there, trembling and faint, he could not recollect, but finally, with unsteady hands, he unstrapped himself from his aeroplane, disconnected his leads, and raised himself out of the cockpit.

His descent onto the wing walkway was little more than a controlled, stumbling fall, and he had to sit down on the wing-root trailing edge quietly, limbs trembling, gazing unseeingly at the long, straight trail of crushed, flattened grass that his Hurricane had left behind it.

He removed his flying gloves and took out the NAAFI chocolate he had placed in his pocket earlier, and, with a little difficulty, he unwrapped it. What he really wanted right now was a Mars bar, but this would have to do.

The bar, soft and warm from his pocket, trembled stickily against his incisors as his hand shook, but then at last, he managed to bite off a piece and was sucking the rich, dark sweetness, the rush of saliva finally moistening his dried mouth and throat.

But his poor, beloved Hurricane was a mess. Joyce and Baker would be cross.

The lower part of the rudder and some of the anti-spin fairing, the strake, had been shot away, leaving a tattered hole in the framework arrangement, and lopping off the tail navigation light from the rudder tab. Luckily there had been no damage done to the tail wheel.

A 20mm cannon shell had torn into the rear fuselage on the port side, removing part of the skin with her P code-letter, the ragged edges of the horribly large hole exposing the bare ribs of the wooden dorsal formers.

The upper longeron was still whole, although shrapnel had scoured glittering silvery scratches on its surface, and splintered a number of the formers. Thank goodness none of the compromised elements had broken.

It was only by a miracle that the exploding shell had not sheared any of the tail control cables, or hit the flare launch tube. He felt sick, but doggedly pushed the chocolate into his mouth again.

On the wing, the torn fabric had pulled away a hole that exposed the wing stringers and aluminium alloy wing ribs, but, luckily, damage to the wing sections was mercifully light. If fortune had not been on his side, the wing or fuselage may have folded during some of the harsh manoeuvring.

It was a sobering thought. It had been close, very close.

She was also liberally peppered in the wings and rear fuselage with lesser damage through bullet holes, but this seemed like nothing when compared with the great rents torn into her.

It was incredible that she had handled so splendidly despite the extensive damage done to her, and that she had managed such a rough landing. If he'd known the extent of the damage he may have taken to his parachute after all!

It was a testament to the amazing strength of Sydney Camm's design that she had been able to take the punishment she'd endured and carry on flying through it all.

He reached up and stroked the plywood skin panel behind the cockpit gently with one gauntleted hand, played with the bullet hole there with one finger.

"You brought me back," he whispered, feeling both serious yet daft at the same time, "You brought me back safe. I owe you my life," and he did. "Thank you my precious. Thank you."

But it was obvious she would need some fairly extensive repairs before she was fit to take up again into combat. She may have brought him back safe, but she had suffered badly in the process of doing so.

Truly, she had saved his life. He patted his pocket gratefully. As had his lucky mascot.

He slipped carefully off the wing, threw down his parachute and lay down in the long, fragrant grass, closing his eyes, unwilling to further see the wounds inflicted upon his poor Hurricane.

Perhaps, if he lay here for a minute, the trembling would stop.

Finally, as he lay in the shadow of the port wing, his head pillowed on his parachute pack, and munching the last soft lumps of chocolate, the tiredness claimed him, and he drifted off into a blessedly peaceful, dreamless sleep, free of fire, smoke trails and Messerschmitts.

The sun was a little lower on the horizon, the shadows longer, when he finally awoke.

"Hullo! You there! Do you need a hand, there, young man?"

Rose opened his eyes to see a stout country-squire type standing some distance away. He sat up.

"Ah, er, good afternoon, sir. I'm sorry if I'm trespassing, but I had to land, because my poor old kite just couldn't carry on."

The other nodded slightly. "Yes, I do see. You're RAF?" he made no move to come closer.

Rose, surprised by the strange question, turned to stare at the Hurricane. Yes, the roundel was definitely visible. It was only her code-letter that had been shot away.

"Yes, of course I am, sir, Pilot Officer Rose, Royal Air Force, Fighter Command."

Who the hell do you think I am, a member of Haile Sellasie's air force? Silly old codger!

"Nowadays, you can't be too careful, y'know, old boy. You could be one of those Huns dressed up. Can't be too careful, Fifth Column and all that sort of thing, of course." He thrashed at the grass with his walking stick.

Rose felt like laughing, the few minutes of rest had been a godsend to him, and he felt refreshed, the effects of the high fight and the unpowered landing a tough memory. "Yes, I know, it's the war."

He felt ridiculous standing here talking politely with this country squire, when he should be trying to contact the squadron, tell Molly he was OK, find out how the boys had done.

The other looked at him for a moment, and then nodded sagely. "Quite. Would you care for some tea? You could call your chaps on my telephone."

"Thanks, I'd be most grateful."

"Splendid. You can't possibly be a Hun, then. Buggers don't drink tea, what? Come along." He stared at Rose closely. "You look awfully pale, my boy, are you quite alright? Not hurt, are you?"

364

"No, thank you. I'm fine. Just a little tired, is all."

The other turned away, looked back. "Well, come on, then, dear boy."

Rose looked doubtfully at his aircraft. "I shouldn't really leave her here…" After what they had just been through together, it felt wrong to leave her here alone in the meadow. She had protected him and brought him safe from the fight.

Besides, she was government property, and it was improper procedure to leave government property unattended and unguarded.

"Oh, my dear boy, don't worry about that, nobody ever comes here. Your aeroplane will be safe here. We'll call some of my chaps." He glanced at him keenly, "I'm the local commander of the LDV, you see. We'll call 'em when we get back to the house. I'm sure they'd be more than happy to supply an armed guard until we can contact the local army barracks. Sound alright to you?"

Rose nodded, "That sounds a very reasonable arrangement, sir. By the way, sir, as I mentioned, my name's Rose, Harry Rose."

The man cleared his throat noisily. "Good gracious, how terribly remiss of me. You must forgive me, forgetting my manners. Inexcusable, absolutely inexcusable. Bloody war, of course. The name's Fitzwilliam," he waved the gnarled walking-stick again, "pleased to meet you." He stared at the Hurricane with frank curiosity, and appreciation.

"What a lovely thing. Must be wonderful up there in the clouds in it."

Rose turned to look back at his aeroplane fondly. "Yes."

The Hurricane was not an 'it.' She was a she.

But Fitzwilliam was right, she was a lovely thing.

A wonderful, fantastical and lovely thing that had brought him back down to earth safe and sound.

He felt a traitor leaving her here in the empty field, but he was conscious of Fitzwilliam's gaze on him, watchful, and wondering at this quiet, stained and strained young man who had descended from the sky in this beautiful fighter.

He patted the bulge in his tunic pocket unconsciously, squinted upwards. "Yes. You're right. There's nothing that compares with it." He thought back to the flashing aeroplanes up in the bright blue sky, twisting and turning, sometimes tumbling out of control.

It wasn't always wonderful up there in the clouds.

But she was, and she had brought him back down safely. He reached out and touched her side for a moment.

Thank you.

Fitzwilliam saw the touch, and smiled at him, nodded as if satisfied about something.

"Come along then, young man. Perhaps we can talk a little about it before I get my chauffeur to give you a lift back to where you need to go. I was on the Somme, you know. Lost the best part of a battalion in less than a day. Lucky to be here, really. Bloody awful. I know it isn't all soft light and music."

Probably thinks I've got the 'twitch' or something, maybe that I'm off my rocker, thought Rose.

He could pretend to be civilized again for a few short hours, amongst those who could not know what it was like, before they sent someone to pick him up, or he was dropped off by Fitzwilliam's chauffeur.

And, most importantly, he was still alive.

Tired and stained, perhaps, but very much alive.

Chapter 29

August the 12th had started as a lovely clear day, with scattered patches of fine mist lightly cloaking the airfield at Foxton.

Excalibur squadron had had a rough day on the 11th. They had been scrambled four times, three times unsuccessfully, and had been able to intercept the enemy only once, on the third occasion.

They had been sent to support the convoy 'Booty' off Harwich, but had been unable to close with the attacking Dorniers before they had in turn been intercepted by the escorting Me110 Zerstorers.

The German fighters had fought valiantly, but there had still been losses for the bombers they had been escorting.

A replacement in B-Flight, young Sergeant Ryan, was shot down and killed, in the ensuing combat, but Billy had avenged him.

Rose, flying in a replacement fighter, and the rest of A-Flight had had an inconclusive but frenetic fight in the gathering cloud, and were unable to make any claims at all.

Carpenter had received a bullet in the arm, but had been able to force-land his aircraft safely. He would not be flying for at least a week or maybe more.

He'd smiled at Rose, "Can't say I'm sorry. Could do with a break!"

Rose had pretended not to notice the teary eyes of the tough and dependable NCO.

Another raid had come soon after that, but the weather quickly made fighting dangerously difficult, and Excalibur were recalled, the pilots grateful for the unexpected respite.

There had been no party that evening, just clumps of tired pilots sitting together, talking. Molly was able to see Rose for an hour, but they had said little, just comfortable to be with each other, holding hands and secure in each other's love, and glad they had seen out the day. Already the walk and the conversation that they had shared seemed so long ago.

The mist was almost clear when the first attacks began. First of all there was a fighter sweep by Me109s, and a flight of the now rather battered 97 Squadron brought them to battle, without loss to either side.

Then there came a serious development. A brilliant Luftwaffe officer, Hauptman Walter Rubensdorffer led his unit on an assault on a number of RDF CH stations in the south-east of England, including the nearby station at Barhamwood. The stations were left damaged, although not permanently, by the very nature of their structure, although with many dead and wounded. Many of these casualties were the heroic and unfaltering WAAFs who played such an important part in operating the complex equipment.

A-Flight were scrambled, but yet again, were unable to intercept the raiders, who made good their escape, disappearing gratefully into the poor visibility over the morning sea.

A shaken and pale Denis had taken them low to survey the damage done to 'their' CH station. A number of the girls on duty there were regular visitors to the Mess, and the personnel were old friends to Foxton.

Angry tears and a sour bitterness welled in Rose as he saw the piles of rubble that had once been the buildings of the station. There were still men and women searching the piles of wreckage, but they must have little hope. The damage was too severe.

Only the barracks of the guarding troops appeared untouched, the rest of the Nissan huts and brick buildings having been levelled.

Of the Receiving Hut itself, the heart of the CH station, there was no sign, just a deep, still smoking crater.

The two groups of skeletal transmitter and receiver towers, however, also showed amazingly little damage, only one of the four in one of the two sets being crumpled into what now resembled a confused and twisted pile of matchsticks by the storm of bombs.

He was grateful for the height, as it hid from them some of the true awfulness of the attack, the battered corpses and torn uniforms that were their own.

The return to Foxton had been silent, as they mourned those they had lost, and hoped for those who might yet be saved. Behind them, the pillars of smoke rose into the air accusingly, and each man felt again the guilt and pain that comes when someone close is hurt, and nothing can be done to help, or help is too late.

But, despite feeling ashamed, Rose still found some comfort in the fact that the attacking Me110s had not continued their attack against Foxton, which was dangerously close by to Barhamwood. 'His' beautiful WAAF was still safe.

Granny, face terrifyingly cold and stiff, as if carved from marble, had echoed his thoughts, whilst the Hurricanes were quickly refuelled. "If they'd continued on track for a few minutes, Flash, old son, they'd have caught us with our pants down. They can't have realised how close we were, the fuckers."

He had been quieter since Carpenter had been wounded, his

ebullience replaced by some of the hardness he had displayed when Rose had first arrived. Rose was worried, and a little scared by the change in his friend.

Smith had been fighting continuously longer than most, and the strain must surely be affecting even him. Then he remembered that one of the girls that Granny had been fond of (Sally?) was an operator at Barhamwood.

Not a girlfriend (or was she? There were so many!), but a dear friend certainly. He looked back again at his section leader and friend.

Granny had pulled out a Churchman cigarette, looked at it reflectively, looked up at the bowser refuelling his aircraft, and put it carefully in his pocket.

Poor Granny. No chance of leaving Foxton, or of even a telephone call.

How does one ask such a thing?

Again, it was as if Granny's thoughts followed his own. "Too many people have died to mourn for one person, Flash." His eyes glittered, "But we have to make sure the bastard's pay. I'll not forget." His voice had become a cracked whisper. "We have to make 'em pay in full, right?"

Rose patted his shoulder awkwardly. "We will, Granny. We will." And then, "I'm truly, truly sorry."

Oh, how hollow were the words, how little they helped.

He was surprised by how much Granny had come to mean to him.

He closed his eyes in tiredness, and didn't notice Granny looking back at him, and could not have known his thoughts.

Granny could not dispel the sight of the devastated CH station from his mind.

Oh God. Why must so many good people die? When will it end?

He knew of course that Sally must be dead, for it had been her shift in the Receiving Hut. Like so many other good friends past, but he could not show his sorrow. The lads needed his strength. His eyes glared at the sky above, but his thoughts were with the petite brown-haired girl who would meet him at the old *Ship's Bell*.

Sweet Sally, heart of gold, confident smile, eager body and small, delicate hands that could work miracles, both in and out of bed. RIP, sweetheart. I'll not forget you. Ever.

Merciful God, at least take care of this boy, and Molly. Even if you take me, let him see this through. He deserves a good and long life. He's a good lad, not an old devil like me. I've lived to the full; he has yet to do so.

Give my boy and his girl happiness.

They deserve it.

A big raid at lunchtime hit civilian and military targets in Portsmouth and severely damaged the CH station at Ventnor.

The enemy suffered heavily in return, losing many aircraft and crews, as well as the experienced Oberst commanding the bomber Geschwader.

Then, later, that very afternoon, British fighter airfields came under attack. Manston, Lympne and Hawkinge were attacked in turn.

Once more A-Flight was scrambled, Donald was leading, Dingo his number two, this time to intercept the raiders attacking Manston. It was the second raid of the day on the airfield, and Donald managed to catch one of the fleeing groups of Dorniers just as they crossed the coast, heading east-north-east.

The hard-pressed covering Messerschmitts were embroiled elsewhere with other Hurricanes and Spitfires, and the four twin-engined bombers were on their own. When they caught sight of the fighters, they closed the formation, tightening it to try and maximise the efficiency of defensive cover provided by their formation and rear facing machine guns.

Seeing this, Donald raced ahead of the bombers with Red section, whilst Yellow kept station behind, throttled back so they stayed out of range.

Both Donald and Granny, the latter leading Yellow section, each had a replacement pilot flying in the number three position.

Rose craned his head this way and that, watching for enemy fighters carefully, his fingertips tingling with nervous tension.

The nearness of the sea, two thousand feet below them, didn't help. He hated flying over water, remembering the fear he had for it and the sight of the Me110 pilot floating all alone in his little dinghy. Besides, as poor Renfrew had once put it, 'I'd hate to swallow seawater, 'cause fishes pee, fart and screw in it.'

I bet Molly's a bloody good swimmer as well, he mused, she seems so adept and confident about everything. She's just such an amazing girl.

Then he thought back to the car-rides. Involuntarily he shuddered. Perhaps not that good at driving, though.

Then he rebuked himself mentally. She hasn't pranged the car once yet, so she must be good, particularly at the speeds she does. Memories of the drive back from the Horse and Groom made him shudder. He could have sworn that she had been going at about the same speed as his Hurricane.

Then the sweet memory of her hair streaming elegantly back in the airstream, and the sound of her voice as she had sung 'The Nearness of You' to him, made him smile despite the grimness of his mood.

And even though the hateful yet graceful shapes of the Dorniers were so close.

My God, Molly, how much I love you, he thought. It still amazed him that she had chosen him over all others.

And then the three Hurricanes of Red section appeared out of the haze before them, and bore down on the four bombers, spitting lead in a continuous, long stream.

The head-on attack had the desired effect. A long streamer of eye-searing white flame appeared from the leading machine, and the formation split apart.

The damaged bomber fell away, leaving the one on the left of the formation to rear up and turn away to port, whilst the two on the right hand side lurched downwards and to starboard, holding formation with one another.

"OK, Yellow Leader, take the two together. We'll finish off the loner."

Granny keyed his microphone. "Received and understood, Red Leader."

Granny led them in a graceful curve, suddenly broken as smoke streamed thickly from Yellow Three, the new Polish NCO, Sergeant Cynk, as he pushed past Granny and Rose in emergency boost.

"Bloody Hell!" bellowed an astonished Granny. "Yellow Three from Yellow Leader, where the hell do you think you're off too? Get back into position, you silly bastard!"

"So sorry, my Sir. But there are two German samolot. You give me one, you take other. Yes?" the Polish sergeant's voice was apologetic, as he twisted after one of the Dorniers, making no move at all to re-join.

"Well blow me down with a feather! Yellow Leader to Yellow two; take care of that other one, Flash. I better keep an eye on that silly Polish bugger. God help us!"

Granny rolled after the fast diminishing pair of aircraft, leaving

Rose and the other Dornier alone. The one damaged in the head-on attack had disappeared.

Rose glanced all around again, and then pushed forward the stick, dipping the nose of his Hurricane, and he dropped in behind the Dornier in a shallow dive.

On the R/T he could hear Red section as they fought with the remaining Dornier, as well as Granny alternately swearing, pleading then ordering Cynk to get back into formation.

Each time Cynk would acknowledge, his voice loud and high-pitched with excitement, but regretfully ignoring Granny's orders, instead continuing with his attacks.

And then the rear gunner was shooting at him. Flecks of bright yellow sprayed towards him, tearing through the air towards him, but nowhere near enough to cause him any worry yet.

He pressed the rudder bar, one way then the other, so that he slipped from side to side, and the range had finally closed to two hundred yards, and he placed the dot of the reflector sight in front of the cockpit of the enemy machine, and pressed the gun-button.

The Hurricane shuddered with the vibration, but he played with the rudder again so that his long burst clattered from one wingtip of the enemy machine to the other and back again. A flash lit up the port engine, there was a ribbon of fire, and then it went out.

He was shouting now, defying the bullets that seemed to reach out. The sight of the tiny figures clambering over the rubble at Barhamwood was still fresh in his mind.

He hunched his shoulders tautly, waiting for the impact.

The blurred image of the Dornier grew larger and larger, until it came to completely fill the gun-sight, spilling over on either side, and he jerked back, felt his stomach drop away as he leapt over the struggling bomber, holed and battered.

His mouth gaped wide as he pulled back with all his strength, and the guns fell silent as he released the button.

Then he felt the hammer blows as bullets smacked into the underside of his Hurricane.

Thump-thump-thump-thump-thump!

God! Still lucky! His hands ached but he tightened his grip even more on the control column.

He raced on, kept going for a mile or so. The Merlin was still roaring, reassuring and sweet, and the control surfaces were unaffected. There were a pattern of bullet holes where the enemy gunner had hit him, but he had not managed to cause any serious damage.

Rose rolled into a turn to port, climbed up two hundred feet.

The Dornier was coming towards him, still flying, damned thing!

No fighters around, push back into a shallow dive, ease back the stick a little, rudder to port, squeeze down and allow for the Hun to fly into his swathe of bullets, release for a moment, and press the trigger again. Keep adjusting stick and rudder, allow for deflection, keep firing, keep firing, and spray him with lead.

Ooh, too close!

Pull back! Stick hard back, hard back into his stomach. Vomit bitter at the back of his throat.

More thumps, *thud-thud-thud!* And he flinched, as bullets buried themselves somewhere behind him, into the body of the aircraft, one banging into the armour plate directly behind him.

One caught his canopy, starring it, and another smacked into the mirror. One moment the rear-view mirror was there, the next it had gone, as if it were never there.

He twisted his aching neck, strained to look behind.

The blasted thing was still flying!

"What more do I have to do?" he whispered.

Battered and struggling, peppered into a colander, yet the bloody thing just wouldn't go down!

Full throttle, wheel around into a hard, tight turn to starboard. Grimace at the forces; resist the greyness at the edges.

And level out.

Right, you bastard. I'm going to shove this right up your bloody arse! Keep an eye out for the escorts, wherever the hell they were.

Back down again, continue down, past the Dornier's level, down five hundred feet. And then pull again on the control column, not too far, watch the airspeed, come up from underneath and behind. Watch out for the lower gunner...

Except there is no lower gunner, just a torn, ripped hole in the underside of the fuselage. He hadn't even noticed the damage in either of his previous attacks.

Either he had done that, or, more likely, the gunners at Manston were responsible. Whichever, it was his lucky day.

The enemy bomber was jinking, port, starboard, then port again, but Rose easily corrected.

Sight carefully, closer, bit more, and then press the button!

Hits sparkling on the enemy bomber, thin line of smoke from the starboard engine, but no flame.

The sun was bright on his neck, but he did not look for enemy fighters that might be hiding in its light. Instead, all his attention was focussed on trying to shoot down this accursed intruder. Had there been enemy fighters nearby, he'd never have noticed them.

But once more, Lady Luck smiled down on him, and there was no trap, and no enemy fighters appeared.

"Burn, you bloody bastard! Burn!" He'd hit both engines, but they continued to run and it didn't burn! Aim for the cockpit, kill the sods!

How much more did he have to do? Any decent bloody Hun would have fallen out of the sky by now.

"Why don't you burn?"

And then a new-born flame reared back to lick hungrily against the engine housing. The flame became bigger as it began to burn in earnest, and the Luftwaffe pilot hurriedly feathered the engine, the glittering arc of the propeller breaking up as it slowed then stopped.

The enemy pilot must have realised the danger to him, for he lowered his wheels, in the universally accepted sign of surrender, and began to turn his aircraft ponderously around, gesturing hopefully at Rose through a shattered panel.

There was no chance that he might make friendly territory now, but still he could make landfall on the nearest land, which was, for him, unfortunately still England.

Or he could ditch and hope that the German Air-Sea rescue services would reach them before the British, or the elements, could get to them.

Obviously he had decided that his best interests lay in making for land. His aircraft was so damaged that it would probably not be able to survive a ditching in the sea; trying to land it would be easier on land particularly as the undercarriage was still functional.

They flew back, victor and vanquished. Rose taking care to keep far back, well out of range of the machine guns. The fires of hatred that he had felt earlier had now been extinguished, leaving behind it only a cold anger.

Twice the pilot almost loss control of the aircraft, but each time he expertly managed to slip it back into level flight. The engine was still smoking, but the fire had gone out, and Rose could imagine the desperation of the pilot, then the relief came, sharp, like cold water to a thirsty man, as the east coast once more slipped into sight through the haze.

The masts of a nearby CH station were in sight as the Dornier pilot prepared for landing.

There was a long, flat stretch, strangely enough, quite close to the station. Even more strangely, there were none of the obstacles placed as a precaution against invasion.

Probably thanking his lucky stars, mused Rose grimly. Bloody aircraft's like a colander, got two battered engines, one stopped and on useless, yet he still manages to survive. I'm not the only lucky one, after all.

The Dornier began to turn, and a few of the station personnel, rather than taking cover, bravely gathered to watch the unexpected sight of their enemy land. Perhaps the sight of Rose's Hurricane emboldened them.

But the Dornier did not have enough power, and as his speed bled off in the turn, what power remained bled off too. With the loss of power, so too was there a loss of control, and without warning, the big German bomber began to slide down.

As the bomber slid, then spun downwards, its weakened port wing broke off outboard of the engine, and sliced into the ground a few hundred yards from the CH station perimeter fence.

Like the huddled watchers on the ground, Rose was stunned by the sudden switch from deliverance to destruction as the 52 foot long Dornier smashed into the ground a quarter of a mile from the station, with an impact *Crump!* that he felt, even circling above at an altitude of a thousand feet.

The wreckage flared wickedly bright in an expanding, shocking fireball, and a dense cloud of smoke billowed upwards from it.

But there was no pity in his heart for the immolated enemy aircrew.

Instead Rose felt a strange mixture of cold satisfaction and regret.

Satisfaction that he had made someone pay part of the debt created that morning at Barhamwood, and regret that he would not be able to show off his 'captured' bomber.

The German may have been an outstanding pilot, but in Rose's eyes, he had also been a Nazi, and he felt no sadness at the death of the Luftwaffe aircrew.

Not so lucky after all.

The memory of Farrell, machine-gunned beneath his parachute, was still in his mind.

How fickle luck is, he decided. I thought that bugger was the luckiest German flying today. He survived all my attacks, and then he comes to grief not a million miles from the aerodrome he bombed, and within walking distance of a CH station.

To Rose it smacked of poetic justice, and a curious, inappropriate gladness swept over him.

Feeling cheerful, he roared over the CH station, executing a crisp victory roll as he did so. He felt slightly guilty at disobeying Donald's order against such reckless aerobatics, and realised the danger that his Hurricane's airframe may have been seriously damaged by the enemy gunfire, but he had to do it.

It felt right.

It also felt very, very good.

And luckily for him, the damage done by the enemy guns was not enough to prevent him from successfully completing the manoeuvre. Nothing fell off, and he didn't join the Dornier below on the ground, burning.

He breathed a sigh of relief as he rolled level again, for it had been an incredibly stupid thing to do.

Goodness only knows what the station onlookers thought as they saw him celebrate the sudden and shocking demise of the Dornier. They were lucky the Dornier hadn't landed on their heads, in one last blow before dying.

Without ammo, Rose would have been about as helpful as a chocolate teapot to them.

Nevertheless, Rose handled the controls gingerly after that, and he breathed more easily as he made his way back to Foxton, leaving the seven towers dwarfed by the rising pillar of dark, dirty smoke behind them. He patted Genevieve again, safely tucked into his pocket, smiled happily at the photograph of Molly.

Still alive, my sweetheart.

In the absence of its squadrons, Foxton, too, had been hit by a raid.

Whilst A-Flight had engaging the four Dorniers, a small staffel of six Junkers 88 bombers had raced in and unloaded their bombs in a single pass from east to west over the field.

The staffel of Bf109s that were acting as escort also made a single cannon-firing pass, and then the whole formation raced away at top speed for France.

A squadron of Spitfires, curiously enough, themselves from battered Manston, caught them out over the sea, and sent one of the bombers flaming into the sea.

Rose saw the smoke of Foxton from a distance, and pushed the throttle 'through the gate,' despite his low fuel state.

The airfield was cratered, although it was still possible to land. One of the hangers was a burnt out shell, whilst another had lost its roof. The equipment store had been demolished, and the ops block, armoury and sergeants mess had all received varying amounts damage. In one of the fighter pens, an aircraft burned silently, and smoke drifted over the airfield, like a malevolent cloud.

Although it looked terrible, Foxton had come off lightly in comparison to the other fighter fields. But Rose could think only of Molly, and an icy chill of fear settled over his heart.

"Excalibur Yellow Two to Felix, request permission to pancake." His voice cracked. Even from here he could smell the airfield burning.

"Felix to Yellow Two, permission granted." From below, two green flares came arcing up.

Instead of circling, he pointed his nose towards dispersal's, and with trembling hands, lowered his undercarriage and flaps, reducing the throttle to skim rapidly down onto the grass, bounced once, twice (what a terrible landing!), and braked as soon as he got to the dispersal area. Two Hurricanes were already there. Granny and Cynk's.

Good. They're back.

Baker and Joyce were waiting for him, faces pale but with welcoming smiles. Thank heavens they're alright, at least!

Baker saw the bullet holes and pursed his lips tightly, shook his head slightly.

Joyce was clambering onto the wing when Rose hastily un-strapped himself, pushed back the hood, and tried to get out of the cockpit. He was stopped and pulled back by the still-connected leads of the oxygen and the R/T.

Angrily, he disconnected them hastily and pulled off the flying helmet, left it perched on the control-column.

"Any luck, sir?" Joyce asked at him. His cheeks and face were black.

"What happened, Joyce?"

"Jerry called while you gentlemen were away, sir. Some damage and some of the lads in the hanger copped it when the bastards came over."

"Oh no! How many have we lost?"

"Don't know for sure, yet, sir, but over twenty. I think."

"Oh God! They hit you all while we were chasing around somewhere else. Bloody Hell!" the air was hot and dusty, the smell of burning thick in the air. Somewhere, rounds of ammunition were popping. "I'm sorry, lads."

Baker came up, sucking his hollow tooth. "Best thing, sir. They'd 'ave caught the squadron on the ground, 'coz there weren't no warning." His voice was gentle, "They'd only 'ave shot up the old girl if she'd been 'ere, and there'd 'ave been no chance to take-off."

He nodded his head sagely, "Better you was up there already when they come callin'. Anyway, it's good to see you back safe and sound, sir. Glad to see you've been busy too. 'Ope you gave the bastards a touch of their own medicine?" he asked hopefully, his eyebrows raised.

Rose looked around desperately. He had to find Molly. "Oh, yes. Got a Dornier. Crashed and burned near Manston! She was running sweet as a nut, as usual. Thanks, boys. Look, I have to go…'"

They beamed with pleasure at his news of the victory and the compliment for them.

Joyce raised a finger. "Oh, Mr Rose? Flight Officer Digby called dispersal's a quarter of an hour ago. Asked if you'd 'phone her at the signals office when you got back?"

"She called a quarter of an hour ago? Was she, er, OK?"

Joyce nodded firmly, "Yes, sir. Right as rain."

She was alright! Thank God!

Joyce's face crinkled again. "In fact, she said that if you hadn't got one, we was to re-arm you and send you straight back up!"

He could feel the relief coursing roughly through his limbs, and he laughed. "OK, Joyce. I'll come back and see how the repairs are coming along later on. Probably have to go up again. But, thanks again." He patted the fuselage. There were a line of holes horizontally stitched through the roundel. "She was wonderful up there!"

"Well done, sir. But I'd not 'phone from dispersal's yet, though. Best wait a minute or two. I think Mr Smith's in there, um, talking to that foreign fella."

"I'll bet he is!" Poor Cynk! He'd know better after Granny gave him a bottle.

He felt like singing joyfully.

Molly was alright! Thank you, God!

She's still alive!

And so am I.

Thank you.

He gathered her into his arms and held her tightly to him.

Molly's face was dirt-streaked, and her lovely eyes were watering from the smoke. "Oh, Harry! You might have called to tell me you were on your way! I could have slapped on a little war-paint! I must look a state!"

"You look bloody marvellous!" He kissed her forcefully, "Thank goodness you're alright! I was so worried!" At first, he thought she was trembling, then he realised it was him.

"Why Harry, you're so sweet when you're worried!" She was touched by his concern, and surprised at his trembling.

"No, I mean it. I saw the damage, Joyce said some people were killed, and I was terrified."

"Now you understand how it feels when someone you love goes in harm's way."

"Yes, I suppose so." He looked doubtful.

"Why do you think it might be different for us on the ground?"

"Well, because you're a girl, and war should not be for you."

"Why do you think I'm wearing this uniform, stupid? I'm as RAF as you too, y'know. Why shouldn't I serve, take the risks we've come to expect of you and others like you?" she sniffed, "I'm glad to share the danger with the man I love."

"War is not for women," he said pompously.

"What rubbish. Tell that to the Germans who're bombing the cities."

"I want to protect you."

"How do you think it must feel to be hiding in a shelter when you're up there fighting?"

"I don't know what to say, it just seems wrong to me. I want to protect you, not have you near danger." He scratched his head. "But you're a girl, and it's not right."

"I'm glad you've noticed! But what's it got to do with anything?"

He was stumped. "Anyway, it's not right." He repeated.

"Yes, I know. You said so."

"Will you promise to be careful for me?"

"Only if you promise to come back to me every time you take off."

He kissed her lightly. "Absolutely."

"OK, then. That's agreed. Now give me another lovely big hug. Oooh…yes, that's it. You've made me feel so much better. Hey! Oof! Be careful, otherwise I'll have to go and see the MO for cracked ribs! I'll have to get bombed more often! You're extra nice when you're concerned."

She smiled prettily, "and I think that you're going to bruise my leg if you continue to press that thing of yours against me. You'll get your chance soon enough, naughty boy, not long to wait."

He grinned sheepishly and adjusted his hips. "Was there any danger?"

"We just managed to get to the shelter. Two of my girls fell down the steps in their rush to get inside. They were lucky, though, they'll be fine."

Rose was triumphant. "There, what did I say? You see? It's too dangerous."

"Be a love and be quiet and hug me. Mm…that's lovely. As usual, you're talking a lot of nonsense. I think we should be quiet now. I think I'd like it if you kissed me, so I think you'd best do so, Pilot Officer."

"Yes, please, Ma'am."

Chapter 30

Thursday, August the 15th was a fine day over much of Britain.

It was the day when Feldmarschal Herman Goering decided to throw his Norwegian and Danish-based air fleet, Luftflot 5, into the battle.

Attacks would be carried out all along the southern and eastern coast of the United Kingdom, from Scotland down to the south. These attacks would mean that 11, 12 and 13 Group would all now be involved in intercepting and engaging major raids.

Close to midday, 60 Stuka bombers with a heavy fighter escort attacked Lympne, Hawkinge and Manston. Even though they inflicted extensive damage, they suffered a very bloody nose at the hands of 54 and 501 squadrons.

An hour or so later, the aircraft of Luftflot 5 came streaming in from the east, their targets being airfields of the north. They too, inflicted much damage, though not on their target airfields, with Luftwaffe losses being serious, whilst the RAF fighters engaging them suffered no losses at all.

Luftflot 5 would not attack Britain again by day. They had been taught a harsh lesson by Fighter Command, one they'd find hard to forget.

Messerschmitt 110 and 109 fighters came in low over the waves in the early afternoon, and strafed a number of airfields, causing many casualties, particularly at Manston amongst the vital, irreplaceable groundcrews.

10 and 11 Group were now to receive an increased workload, as a large number of south-eastern coastal towns were attacked.

RAF airfields were to receive further attention too.

Rose and the rest of A-Flight were at immediate readiness when it began.

The tannoy suddenly screeched metallically, "Scramble A-Flight!"

Rose's heart lurched painfully as the fitter fired the starter cartridge to start the Merlin engine in a sudden rush, it coughed out a cloud of blue smoke, and began to bellow throatily, the roar blending with the other Hurricanes to either side, music to his ears.

Signal chocks away, check the ground crews are safe, push throttle wide open, bugger which direction wind is in, just get off the ground, lickety-split.

Quick as you can, each second precious.

Quick check of the knobs as you bump along, switch on the R/T.

Watch out for the others, no time for the niceties of a pre-war check list. But then, how many times had he checked everything already in the long crawling minutes as he had sat waiting for this sudden rushed moment?

Hands trembling with fear and excitement, as the ground rushed past in a blur, and then fell away below.

Up, up, into that beautiful pale blue sky, sun streaking through the canopy onto him, but no time to enjoy it, concentrate on Dingo as the flight climbs up.

"Turnip to Carrot Leader, vector one-twenty, Buster."

Reflector sight on, wheels up.

"Carrot Leader to Turnip. Received. Vector one-twenty, buster. What angels?"

Switch on R/T, twist the catch to 'fire.'

"Turnip to Carrot Leader. Angels one."

Angels one! One thousand feet?

Low-level raid indeed! Almost bloody ground-level!

Even over the R/T, Denis sounded just as surprised, "Carrot Leader to Turnip, please confirm, Angels one?"

"Turnip to Carrot Leader, confirmed. Vector one-twenty, angels one." The tone of the controller's voice seemed to imply 'of course,' as if he did not care to be questioned.

"Christ! Jerries! 11 o'clock low!"

Rose squinted ahead, but at first he could not make out the camou-flaged shapes against the darker ground and trees.

Where the hell are they?

Then he saw them, ten pencil-thin straight shapes, broad wings, sliding silently over the landscape, a couple of hundred feet below them, and the sun suddenly catching their glazed noses, canopies and propeller discs. They were still some distance away, but the distance between them was rapidly decreasing.

They were Dornier 17s, and they were on a course straight for the station A-Flight had just left.

The most important question was, had they come alone, or were there any fighters up there, hidden high above them?

Rose glanced up and around, but the sky above was clear. He followed the others down as the flight curved into a head-on attack.

Might they be able to attack without any rude interruptions?

"Tally-ho, lads. Break the bastards up! Only one chance! Make it count!" Denis' voice was high-pitched.

The closing speed was phenomenal, and Rose had only a few seconds in which to allow for deflection, push down the nose, and press the gun-button.

Smoke trails twisted their way towards the Dornier on the port side of the formation. The enemy bomber rushed past like a dirty grey streak, but not before he thought he had seen some puffs of smoke where his bullets might have hit.

Pull the fighter back in a tight loop, barrel roll right way up and level at the high point of the loop, push forward the stick to dive back the way he had come. Black spots dancing before the eyes as he fought against the forces that pummelled him, and strove frantically to pick up the enemy bombers against the ground below.

For a moment all he could see was another Dornier skidding away to starboard, breaking up and trailing a thick cloud of smoke, and losing height.

Then as he looked again, he saw that the enemy formation had split, but there were at least four, no, five bombers still on a bearing for Foxton, already visible before them as a sprawling bright rectangle of green.

Full boost, playing catch up. If he lost the game, his friends on the ground would pay the forfeit. He banged his thigh with his throttle hand as he willed his Hurricane on.

Come on!

Tracer streaked silently up towards him from one bomber, floating slowly up to rush past above the glass of his canopy. Side-slip, take avoiding action, don't lose 'em.

No time for fear.

An unusual feeling of confidence and harmony as the wings of the Dornier slipped into place between the range bars of his reflector sight.

The enemy gunner was good, *thump-thump-thump* as the enemy

guns punched hot lead into his fighter. She faltered, but kept right on flying.

He replied with a one second burst, but he had not judged deflection carefully in his haste, and the torrent of bullets passed beneath the twin tailed machine to fall harmlessly away below.

He squinted, murmuring to himself, but he was conscious that the station was close. He jabbed on the button again, Molly's nearness driving caution from his mind.

The clean, sharp lines of the bomber blurred as the vibration from the guns rattled along the structure of the Hawker fighter.

Enemy gunner still firing, fortuitously not close this time, whilst the De Wilde bullets sparkle as his gunfire splatters against the port wing of the bomber, ripping the engine cowling away, and the enemy pilot started to turn, port, jink to starboard, then reversed back onto course.

Check behind.

Still no enemy fighters.

Details of the enemy aircraft were imprinted on his mind even as he jockeyed into position.

Not grey as he had thought, but a deep bottle-green paint scheme above and pale blue beneath, yellow stripe just before the tailplane.

Rose's Hurricane bucked as he passed through the German aeroplane's slipstream, and he fought to control her.

The trees below seemed to reach up for him.

Oh shit! Ground's too close, get clear!

Rose rolled to port, stick back and into a steep turn, wings feeling as if they were perpendicular with the ground, but not before he saw the Dornier turning ponderously to starboard, an evil clutch of bombs falling slowly from its belly like some horrid offspring, to explode harmlessly well short of the target, violent fountains of soil erupting on the airfield's perimeter, ripping apart the fence and empty ground.

Check all around, no enemy fighters yet!

Unbelievable! Where were they?

Surely the Germans had not come without an escort?

Oh well, don't look a gift horse and all that.

Rose pulled back into the attack, his Hurricane sweeping smoothly around to continue his pursuit of the Dornier. None of its fellows were visible anymore.

The bomber no longer carried any bombs, but the German pilot persisted in continuing his attack run, still a danger to those on the ground, as he still had machine guns on board, which were firing at targets below.

Quick look, still no other fighters or bombers visible, follow him down at zero feet.

Snapshots of all around. Before them, made tiny by distance, a khaki ambulance speeding helter-skelter beside the squadron hanger, rushing like a tiny scurrying beetle.

An airman in blue, legs pumping as he races on a bicycle towards the watch office, flurries of dust where strafing German bullets reach for him, unsuccessfully trying to pluck him from the saddle.

Sky now pocking with puffs of dirty brown smoke with fiery red cores as the ground defences opened up on the bombers.

To one side, near the buried, protected fuel tanks, ugly geysers of earth and grass shot upwards, as another raider planted his load, causing no damage except for tearing a line of ugly craters across the smooth grass. Visible now as he struggled for height, bracketed by ack-ack.

Smoke curled from a fighter pen to starboard, fire licking an upturned elliptical wing. At least one fighter had been caught by this low level raid, then. Please let the pilot have been saved…

'His' enemy bomber close in front now, fire carefully, and try not to hit anything on the ground.

Aim carefully, for your family is down there.

Short, sharp bursts, one-two-three, and flame curls back in reward.

Thump! Something unpleasant bangs into a leading edge. Has the gunner found the range again, or is that a piece of Dornier? Might it even be Ack-Ack?

"Shit-shit-shit," he mutters to himself, unaware he is chanting the words, like some incantation, to himself.

The Dornier loses even more height, slipping towards the hangers. Beneath, its shadow races to meet up with it, like an eager friend rushing forward with a warm embrace.

Puffs of smoke shoot up beside the fighter pens at the western end of the field as the other enemy opens fire with all of his machine guns.

A vivid orange flower, near the MT pool, opens its ugly petals as a bomb from another of the raiders slams into a QL fuel tanker.

And then a liquid stream of painfully bright tracer sped up from one of the gun pits, stitching holes along the starboard wing of the Dornier, and the little flame Rose had started spread to form a white sheet of boiling fire, that seemed to spread almost instantly across the entire length of the enemy bomber.

The tracer from that unknown anti-aircraft gunner had hit a fuel tank.

Ack-ack continues to burst all around it, but the enemy is doomed, with no hope of survival.

They are far too low to hope for escape by parachute now.

A hot blob of flame, it suddenly exploded, fragments of fuselage and wing cartwheeling across the ground, like shattered fragments of a broken toy.

One of the engines, prop still turning, flew through the air, crashing into another fighter pen, this one mercifully empty.

His Hurricane passed through the roiling black smoke cloud, tiny pieces of smashed aeroplane clattering against the Hurricane, but there was no serious damage to his fighter.

One down! It didn't matter that he could not claim it. That had been good shooting by the unknown gunner. He deserved to keep that one.

His admiration was cut short as one of the Bofors gunners turned his fire onto the Hurricane.

Malevolent bursts of dirty grey-brown smoke began to sprout all around him, and then that trail of fiery tracer curved around onto his bearing.

"Crikey!"

Rose stared at the flame filled hearts of the anti-aircraft fire and waggled his wings desperately, trying to show his roundels.

"Don't shoot, I'm British!" he shouted, but it was useless. They couldn't hear him.

He felt the tremor as shrapnel punched into the fabric of his fighter, the 40mm Bofors rounds exploding closer and closer, buffeting him by their blast.

Something thumped hard against the armour plate at his back.

Good Lord!

All around, more guns were tracking him, seeing only the enemy and still firing, and desperately he pushed her down, well down so that it seemed to him that he could no longer be flying any higher than about ten feet, his 11-foot propeller skimming just above the earth, and slightly turned the Hurricane to port, passing between the trees at the south-eastern part of the main airfield complex, and out over the other-rank's married quarters.

"Shit-shit-shit!" he held onto the spade-grip with both hands, keeping her steady, as the ground-effect made his Hurricane bounce as if he were riding a raft on a river.

Rose had a vague impression of neat little houses, transfixed by the vision of street-lights, then green tracery of tree tops, whipping past terrifyingly close, the topmost branches level or even above him.

Within seconds, he was through the other side and safe, pull back the stick and turn to port, away from the main complex of the aerodrome, back into the sanctuary of the sky.

Best stay low 'til he was a safe distance from the 'drome, though!

Bloody hell! Still alive! My God!

Thank God the gunners were better against the Dornier than they had been against him.

It probably helped that it had been larger, slower and damaged.

For a moment back there, he had thought himself a goner. It was hard to believe that he had been under fire from his own side, could have been killed by them, even harder to believe that he had survived the experience more or less in one piece.

He sucked air into seemingly-shrunken, starved lungs, turned in his seat to look behind.

All the other Dorniers had disappeared by now, the sky around him completely clear, leaving behind the wreckage of two of their number flaming on the ground.

Could it truly have been less than a minute since they had curved into the attack?

He circled the airfield in a wide orbit, still taking care to stay well clear of the Ack-Ack, as he listened to the sound of Dingo and Granny as they pursued another of the enemy bombers, eyes straining as he looked for more dark green shapes sliding in low over the trees.

There may yet be more of the enemy, a second wave, perhaps.

Damn it all, he must have been cracked to fly over the field in the midst of an attack. What were the gunners supposed to do? Stop shooting?

Idiot!

Of Sampson and the new Polish NCO pilot, Sergeant-Pilot Cynk, there was no sign.

He continued to circle protectively for ten minutes, until a jubilant Denis and Granny returned, all that remained of their victim tiny shards of metal scattered around a smoking hole fifteen miles to the east.

They maintained a combat patrol for a further ten minutes, before a green flare came arcing up, and they were told to 'pancake.'

Gratefully, they landed and taxied towards dispersal, before aligning their aircraft into a rough T-shape arrangement, noses pointing inwards, then switched off and jumped gratefully down from their cockpits.

Rose felt as if he had been connected to an electricity mains point. His body was trembling both with excitement and nervous reaction to the experience of combat and of being fired upon by the airfield defences.

Despite that, however, he felt pleased with himself. True, he had not managed to score a victory, but he had helped in the destruction of one, and more important, he had prevented the bomb-load hitting its intended target.

Best of all, Molly had waved at him from the ground as he was landing.

He hadn't worn his flying boots, and inside his shiny black shoes, his feet and socks were soaked with sweat. He walked forward tiredly to the laughing Denis and Granny. It seemed they had, in addition to destroying one, they had badly damaged another.

Whilst they talked, a small, triple-hosed fuel bowser was brought up and pushed in between the Hurricanes. Whilst the hoses were being deployed from their long, stamen-like, metal movable tubes, anxious groundcrew rushed up and busied themselves over the aircraft.

It was extraordinary how they all suddenly appeared from nowhere and swarmed over the fighters like an army of worker ants.

One erk moved quickly from machine to machine, unscrewing the fuel cap on the port wing, just outboard of the fuselage. Once the refuelling had been done, he would then check the oil tank.

Armourers scurried forwards with a flat-bed trolley loaded with belts of .303 ammunition, the fitters checked over the aircraft, and radio technicians cursorily examined each of the TR 9D radio transmitter/receivers.

Granny lit a Players cigarette and offered it to Rose. "Here, Flash take a drag on this. It looks like you could do with it."

Rose smiled and shook his head, "Thanks, Granny, but I'm OK."

Granny nodded towards Rose's machine. The fuselage had been rent by a number of pieces of shrapnel. "Looks like you had a warm reception from Jerry, chum."

"Bloody hell, I'll say! I was chasing that Dornier," he waved at the mass of still-smoking wreckage near the watch office, "And the flippin' Ack-ack started having a go at me!" he could still see the dirty puffs of smoke sprouting around him, and he shuddered.

Denis clapped him on the shoulder, "Well thank heavens they didn't get you, mate, otherwise that would have been an end to what is going to be a long and distinguished career!"

Rose grinned, delighted at the compliment.

Granny stared over his shoulder. "Uh-oh, here come the ladies."

Skinner was driving towards them, and Rose was surprised to see the slight figure of Molly with him.

Her face was flushed, and her eyes shone with pleasure and excitement, and she gave him a quick peck on the cheek, careful not to catch

396

him with the brim of her helmet, and conscious of the groundcrew gathered around the Hurricanes, even though no-one seemed to be looking at them.

"Thank God you're alright, Harry! I saw you come after that Dornier and bring it down! It was the most wonderful thing I've ever seen in my life!"

Rose coloured, half-pleased, half-embarrassed by her words, and aware as Denis and Granny exchanged amused glances with each other.

He coughed self-consciously, his voice gruff. "Ahem. Well, to be honest, I think it was the gunners who got him really, Molly."

She looked absolutely breath-taking, and he felt like taking her into his arms and squeezing her tightly to him. Two bright spots of pink burned on her cheeks.

"Only after you'd damaged him. You'd have got him anyway, you had him dead to rights. I couldn't believe they were shooting at you. I thought they were going to get you, too! When you disappeared behind the trees, I thought they'd shot you down!"

Skinner laughed and clapped Rose on the shoulder. "I found Molly at a gun-emplacement having a go at the gunners. What she didn't say about the army's abilities in aeroplane identification! Little fire-cracker, I can tell you! Poor buggers didn't look like they knew what had hit 'em. I think the Corporal in charge was crying when I managed to bring her away! I've already remonstrated with her about being out of the shelter during a raid! Anyway, I'm glad you came out of that little lot safe and sound, Flash. We thought you were a goner! You're a crazy bugger, and no mistake!"

Then he turned to Denis, his face serious,. "Well done on the Dornier, Dingo. I'm afraid that A-Flight will have to get back onto immediate readiness once you're re-armed and re-fuelled. Looks like there may be a lot more business for you very soon. Some of the other fields have taken a pasting, far as I can make out. Manston got it bad, I believe. No chance of a hot meal either, I'm afraid, but I'll get them to send over some bully beef sandwiches and tea as soon as."

He put a hand to Molly's elbow. "Come on, young lady. Time we left these chaps to get on with it. You need to get back to your girls, and you really must stay with them in the shelter this time!"

He looked doubtfully back up at the sky. "We may get some, um, more company quite soon."

Suddenly there was the throb of an engine and a sleek shape skimmed low over the airfield. A Bofors gun began to bang away, but stopped almost as soon as it had begun.

"Silly b-," Skinner bit back his words, one eye on Molly, as Cynk took up his Hurricane into a vertical climb. He sighed and shook his head. "Ah well. He seems pretty pleased with himself. Must be good news."

Rose touched her hand for a brief instant, before she was shepherded away. Despite the presence of the others, he had understood her unspoken message, had felt her love and her concern.

"Still no sign of old Speedy." Granny had voiced their unspoken concern.

Denis stared at the Polish NCO's Hurricane as Cynk landed and taxied towards them. "Yes, but he might have landed elsewhere." His voice was harsh. "You'll have to excuse me, boys, but I think I shall have to have a word with our dashing young sergeant."

Granny shook out another Players cigarette, and made as if to light it.

Denis shook his head.

"Aw, fer Christ's sake, Granny, put it away can't you? If you light that, you're likely to send us all up into the wild blue yonder, without our kites." Dingo waved at the fuel bowser, and the faint but just visible green haze of 100 octane fuel vapour that hung low over the Hurricanes. Wait for the gas to disperse, at least, can't you?"

Granny made a face to Denis' retreating back, shook a fist. "Just because I let you share my Dornier! Get your own next time!" He pushed the cigarette back into the packet disconsolately. "I'm parched. Where's the bleedin' tea?"

Chapter 31

There were twenty Heinkel 111 bombers, flying stolidly three miles ahead and to port, four thousand feet further down. Unfortunately, they were not alone.

Weaving on either side of the formation were a number of Me110's, describing circles as they strove to keep in formation with their charges, whilst further up, tiny dots at the same height as Excalibur showed the trailing Bf109s.

There were not that many of them, though.

Rose squinted, counted the 109s.

There were only six apparent to him. He counted again, but came up with the same number. They must already have met with RAF fighters, for indeed, an almost-invisible trail of smoke was being drawn along by one of the Heinkels, and as it drew closer, the formation looked less ordered with less of the usual Teutonic meticulous precision.

Only six. Still enough, really, if the hammering in his ribcage meant anything.

Donald's voice, deceptively soft over the crackling R/T.

"Red Leader to B-Flight, you go for the Heinkels, we'll take the 110's. Watch out for the the 109's. Tally-Ho!"

Rose glanced quickly over the instrument panel as the five

Hurricanes of B-Flight nosed downwards, pointing themselves like manned spears at the plump, evil shapes of the enemy bombers.

The Me110s continued to weave circles in the sky, almost as if they were playing tag with one another.

Surely, they must have seen us, wondered Rose.

B-Flight swung into line-astern, and then the 109s above pounced.

"Red leader to A-Flight, Tally-Ho, chaps!"

Sunlight catches the canopy of one of the falling 109s, so that it gleams like a falling star. What a sight this could be were it not for the evil in the enemy's heart.

Somebody in B-Flight (Fellowes?) calls excitedly as his bullets rip into the fuel-tanks of a Heinkel, and a violent, searing-white explosion wipes the bomber from the sky.

Rose concentrates on the diving Bf109 before him, as it steadily expands.

Tracer leaps up from the tangled mass of bombers now, reaching indiscriminately at the fighters, regardless of the markings on their wings.

At last, the Me110s become aware of the danger, but instead of trying to block the diving Hurricanes of A-Flight, they huddle into a defensive circle, one on either side the now disorganised bombers.

No time to wonder at the craven behaviour of the big twin-engined fighters, for the Bf109 was in front of him.

It turned after a Hurricane that was harrying a Heinkel, seemingly unaware of the presence of Rose so close behind.

Rose pressed the firing button, and suddenly bullet-strikes puff starkly against the side of the Messerschmitt.

Quick glance into the mirror…

Fuck! More 109s screaming down! Where the hell did they come from?

Key the R/T. "Break! Break! Yellow Two to A-Flight, Bandits above and behind!"

No time to follow his 109, and he slammed the Hurricane into a viciously steep turn.

All around, Hurricanes are taking avoiding action, and the Bf109s overshoot, splitting into two formations of two, continue their dive before straightening out.

A single Hurricane dances inside the spinning circle of Me110s, as if it were at some crazy ride at the fair, where the only prize can be survival.

The second pair of Bf109s climb in a wide turn in front, and Rose lined up on them, adjusted the stick minutely, pressed once again on the firing button, and once more the airframe vibrates in sympathy with the thundering of its Brownings.

Bullets splatter in a wide swathe across the trailing 109, and white smoke gouts from beneath the engine cowling. A large chunk of aileron flashed past, and Rose carefully lined up for another burst, when suddenly tracer flashed past in front of him, angry and burning.

Shit! Someone behind!

No time to think or wonder, as reflexes take over.

Stick back hard into the stomach, harder, grimace as the forces pummel him.

Black spots dance before his eyes.

He must have overshot, follow him down. Anger burned like acid in his mind, and the redness overtook him.

Aileron turn, down. Forget the others, have to get him.

Bastard!

Far below, two aircraft, the 109s that had a go at him?

Disappointment. Just a pair of Spitfires (Where did they come from?) pursuing a 110, already burning brightly like the torch at the '36 Berlin Olympics, falling, falling, dying.

So where did he go?

Search the landscape below him, the sky above, but apart from the Spits and their prey, there is only a single pair of Heinkels, made tiny with distance, high-tailing it eastwards into the distance. Damn! No chance of catching them and the 109 seemed to have disappeared altogether.

Pull carefully out, ease back on the stick, muscles straining.

The Hurricane pulls out, whilst high above, far above, tiny shapes continue to whirl about.

Three palls of smoke on the land below, another Spitfire turning far ahead.

Still alive, thank goodness, though with little to show except for perhaps a couple of damaged.

The Spit settles onto a course towards him. Shit! Better make sure he doesn't think I'm a Jerry!

Begin a gentle turn, show your roundels, but be careful. Bugger may need spectacles.

Wait. That profile…doesn't seem like a Spitfire after all…

Behind the goggles, his eyes widened.

Uh-oh.

That's no Spitfire…it's a bloody Messerschmitt!

His heart was beating fit to burst, but he kicked rudder and he hauled back on the control-column again, so that the Hurricane twisted around to point directly at the approaching enemy fighter again.

Hide behind the reassuring bulk of the engine, not close enough yet, but he fired his guns anyway. Perhaps the sight of the oncoming tracer would put the enemy pilot off his aim. Side-slip and jiggle.

Fiery balls of tracer zip past overhead, seeming to be just inches from the perspex of his canopy, and he screwed shut his eyes, jaw

403

clenched, hands tight on the paddle-grip, holding her firmly on this flight into likely oblivion.

A second of heart-wrenching terror and then the Messerschmitt has passed above him in a great buffeting rush of sound and air, apparently as undamaged as he.

He banked around into a tight turn, fighting through the disturbed air of the 109's slipstream.

The Messerschmitt was speeding away now, not even bothering to re-engage Rose.

Rose straightened out and ripped after the other at full throttle.

Not so fast, matey! Glance in the mirror.

The enemy pilot ahead was heading south in a dive, and the advantage meant that he was steadily pulling away from Rose's game but slower Hurricane.

Bloody hell! This bastard was going to get away as well! In the last few minutes that his part in the fight had lasted, he had taken shots at three Bf109s, but hadn't managed to properly wing even one.

The anger was still burning at him, and a scowl settled on his features as he resolved to pursue this last chance for a victory.

The enemy fighter was lower now, almost skimming the meadows and fields, its shadow leaping up and down frantically beneath it. Low over a field, sheep panicked into flight by the sudden appearance of this monster from the sky. Nothing behind.

The range was too long, but he caressed the gun-button nonetheless. It was a gamble, but there was the outside chance of a lucky hit with a well-placed shot.

Carefully sighting, he pressed the gun-button for a short one-second burst. Don't waste it. Lord only knew how many rounds he had left in his ammunition trays.

Uselessly, the bullets flayed the freshly-ground earth of a

newly-turned field, then he snatched back his thumb, for a farmhouse, barn and outbuildings loomed suddenly out at them, bursting up at them out of the landscape, like a picture in a children's pop-up book.

Mouth dry, he pulled up the nose. That barn looked awfully big. Thank God that he had decided only on a one-second burst, that he had already stopped firing, otherwise he could have easily peppered the farm and possibly its inhabitants.

That would have been a terrible thing, a terrible thing that would have made his life impossible.

But, almost as awful, was the realisation that had been his last chance, and the thought left a harsh sour taste in his mouth and a seething frustration in his heart.

He was certain that the Messerschmitt would be too far ahead once he pushed down back into the chase, and the fight, such as it was, would be over.

And, of course, that is exactly what would have happened, if it were not for one thing.

The farmer, entertaining a mistaken belief that the embers of his fire would fall back onto his roof from the chimney, had lengthened and reinforced his smokestack to quite an impressive dimension, so that when anything once-hot did float down, it would have lost any ability to cause him damage by alighting on the roof.

This belief would be the factor that changed everything unexpectedly for the Luftwaffe pilot, and turned the entire situation drastically around into Rose's favour.

With one eye on his pursuer, the other on his fuel, and knowing that to gain height may result in his losing some of the preciously gained advantage over the Hurricane, meant that the German pilot was ill-prepared for sudden avoiding action.

He adjusted slightly, but it was not enough.

At a speed in excess of 300 miles per hour, the Messerschmitt's starboard wingtip sliced into the farmer's pride and joy, leaving behind part of the wing as shattered pieces of curled metal fragments amongst broken brickwork on the farmhouse roof and courtyard.

The terrible impact twisted the aileron and made the 109 swing to starboard, and suddenly the German pilot was fighting to control his machine, pulling back hard and correcting for the fleeting contact, as it threatened to smash itself into the ground so close beneath it.

The wounded Messerschmitt soared upwards and slowed, fighting for height, straight into Rose's sights.

Stunned but thanking his lucky stars, Rose closed in quickly behind it and placing the red centre dot of the sight before the swerving enemy fighter, and jammed his thumb hard down onto the button.

Incendiary and AP rounds ripped into the enemy aircraft, and the next instant, Rose's fire had ignited the fuel in the Bf109's fuel tanks, blowing the trim little fighter into a thousand flaming pieces.

The farmer poked his head out of a window and shook his fist at the triumphant, soaring RAF fighter, climbing in a graceful curve high above the pillar of smoke that marked the death of his opponent.

"Look what you done to my lovely chimney, you Brylcreem bleeder!"

And he'd bloody wet himself!

Bloody flyboys!

Chapter 32

They had been sitting in their cockpits for half an hour now, strapped in and on immediate readiness, and Rose was hot and weary and half asleep.

The irritation at having to wait in the heat had faded to a grumbling annoyance. For about the hundredth time, he swatted at the bluebottle that seemed to be extremely keen to land on his sweating face.

He wiped his cheeks, and thought longingly of another grapefruit squash, even though Baker had brought him out an icy cold bottle less than fifteen minutes earlier. There wasn't even a breeze to give them some relief. They'd have to switch off the engines soon as well before they overheated.

How much longer would they have to wait before Sector Control allowed them to take off? If there were some enemy kites around, they'd have cleared off long ago, surely. Laughing all over their silly fat faces at the absence of the RAF.

Rose looked around, saw that Denis was deep in his own thoughts, while good old Granny was snoozing with a newspaper, his beloved Daily Mirror, shading him from the burning sun.

Without warning, at the eastern end of the airfield, a column of roiling orange fire suddenly leapt skywards, almost knocking down the water tower, and reducing the trees around it to firewood.

The sound of the explosion came next, a flat, sharp report with a deeper, rolling undercurrent that was like a heavy wooden door slamming shut, or the crack of thunder. The ground seemed to vibrate beneath him, the shock travelling up the undercarriage of the Hurricane.

For a second he thought a petrol bowser may have blown up through some idiot piece of carelessness, for there was no sound of aircraft, no sign of an enemy at all.

Almost immediately there was a second eruption, and then a third. The crash of the explosions was belatedly joined by the slow, mournful wail of the sirens around the station.

Desperately he waved for the chocks to be pulled away. Thank God his propeller was already turning. Baker came running, "They're dropping bombs, sir! Watch out! Take off!"

Rose nodded and pointed, "Get under shelter!" he shouted.

Immediately he revved his Merlin, and with the chocks pulled away, he eased off the brakes so that his Hurricane slowly started to roll forward. God, so slow! Pull forward the hood, close out the din. Watch out for the others…

Dear God! Caught with our bloody pants down! He looked up to see layered rows of silver shapes glittering in the sun as they crawled across the blue backdrop, the elliptical wings of Heinkels. They droned slowly overhead, passing almost leisurely from east to west, as if they were on a restful stroll through the park.

Anger flared hot in him.

So much for the bloody lookouts! Bastards on the tower must be half-asleep as well! How had the Germans managed to get so close without someone seeing them?

And where were the blasted AA defences?

Molly! Rose looked back at the administration building. Molly was there!

He felt a mad urge to leap from his machine and go to her, but he knew he could not. His place was up there, as was his duty.

They had to be stopped.

Run Molly, hide!

Moving, bumping along faster, faster.

Please, God, give me the strength I need!

Take care of my beloved, my sweet Molly! He grasped the little bear without thinking.

Belatedly, "Excalibur squadron scramble, scramble!" about bloody time!

Already, like Rose, Donald was moving, jouncing along the grass as he desperately tried to get into the air. Except, he was flying towards the columns of fire that were erupting like cancerous growths along the recently filled-in ground. Beneath him, the ground heaved in sympathy.

Come on. *Come on.*

Damn the take-off drill! No time for that now. He had to get up there *now*. He'd checked everything a dozen times already, anyway, during that interminable wait of before.

Something in the region between the equipment store and the station chapel exploded searing white, adding to the cacophony of the bombs falling and exploding, Bofors and machine guns clattering now, shouts of running men, and Merlin engines roaring angrily at emergency power.

Quick, oh fuck, *quick.*

Another bomb exploded inside the already ravaged hangar, further shattering the wrecked walls. He cowered as a flying clod of earth bounced off the engine cowling.

Smoke was already climbing into the sky from a dozen different sources, drifting heavily along. Perhaps it would help to make it harder to bomb, he thought hopefully, although it was likely they would already have dropped all their ordnance already. But there may be a second wave…

Oh, Molly! Run! Run, as fast as you can! Get under shelter.

Already Donald was in the air, his undercarriage legs folding beneath him, and then he was gone, plunging into the thickness of the wall of clinging smoke.

Where was Granny?

Denis was in front of him, Cynk beside him, as they raced at break-neck speed across the grass, towards the advancing columns of fire and smoke.

Run, Molly! You have to live! *Run!*

Rose blanched as a Hurricane suddenly received a direct hit, the racing sleek fighter instantly crumpling into a shattered flaming ball of debris that continued along, caroming in the same direction for fifty yards, shedding fabric and metal in its wake.

Several unknown somethings *cracked!* against his canopy, followed by the clatter of stones and earth, and he flinched back again involuntarily.

The burning Hurricane came to rest at last, just a mass of blazing ruin. Oh God! Whose was it?

He looked ahead, tearing his eyes from the conflagration that contained his squadron mate, and gasped, as Denis' Hurricane, clawing for the sky, was tipped over by the blast from another exploding bomb, sliding out of the air to careen messily across the grass, ripping up great clods of turf, its wheels collapsed, the propeller shattered, falling apart like a toy thrown by a spoilt child.

And at that moment the terror squeezed his heart harder.

Oh God, don't let me die like this, not here, not on the ground. Give me a chance, please! Let me get up there.

Up to that point, they had still been together, and he had always been so confident in the company of the others, flying alongside his fellows.

But now, someone was blown up and must surely be dead, Denis lay wounded, maybe dead in the battered remnants of his own Hurricane.

And where was Granny?

Then Cynk had disappeared into the huge thick bank of smoke that roiled fitfully towards them, like a malevolent cloud, and Rose was alone, blasts buffeting him mercilessly.

Please, God, let me get up there; not here, let me die up there, not uselessly on the ground, but clawing and ripping and screaming defiance in their faces, curse their craven hearts..

Molly, run, my love, hide!

Behind him more bombs burst like malevolent flowers amidst the airfield buildings, levelling the signal section and part of the sick quarters, killing and further wounding the survivors of the previous day's attack.

He was alone, the black wall of smoke speeding towards him, like a monstrous evil that would swallow him into a world of twilight.

Granny, where the hell are you?

"Red Leader to Excalibur squadron, no chance of forming up boys. Get altitude, and get stuck in. Tally-Ho! They're killing our people, don't leave a single one!" Donald's hoarse voice steadied him, pushed back the fear that threatened to swallow him in its grey maw.

The Hurricane was bouncing and bumping interminably, shaken by the blast, the Merlin screaming like a banshee, the surroundings a blur of blue and green and brown, and before him the hungry amoebic darkness. He could sense the evil within it.

85 mph! Un-stick speed! Pull back, jolt as the kite clears the ground.

Flying, flying smoothly now, oh, what a darling you are!

Reflector sight on, adjust for 150 yards, get in close and kill 'em! Twist from 'safe' to 'fire,' the action steadying him further, although the icy fear still ate at his innards.

Another series of incessant explosions, *crump-Crump-CRUMP!*

Each of the geysering eruptions was closer, disturbed racing air jostling and swinging and threatening the Hurricane.

Oh my God, save me, *please*...

Threatening to upset his fragile inner courage and stability.

Ease back, back, don't let your speed bleed off, evil blackness blotting out everything before him...

And then he had plunged into the shadowy world where there was nothing but his Hurricane, as if there were a limitless abyss and not ground but fifty feet below.

He was engulfed and swallowed by this emptiness, and momentarily disorientated, he forced himself to look down at the instruments, his cockpit suddenly shadowed and dull in this world of no light.

And just as suddenly, two seconds after entering the stinking and bitter darkness, he tore through the other side, trails of smoke wisping back in oversized spiralling vortices from his wingtips, the Beech trees of the north-eastern boundary passing just below his wings, the airfield behind him and hidden by the drifting black gulf.

He thought despairingly, guiltily, of Molly, half-grateful for that obscuring curtain, which hid the savage wounding of his home.

One last glance back, then he swallowed and blinked away the tears, concentrated on the fast diminishing Hurricane (Cynk's?) clawing for height ahead of him. There was no sign of Donald.

But he had survived that inferno.

He himself still lived, Praise God! Yet behind him the people that he had lived with, his family, were dying.

A moment ago he could not believe that he might survive, and now his heart was still beating as fast as the revolutions of the Merlin, or so it felt. The cloying sweat that bathed him was cold and grasping.

God had listened to his prayers, and given him the chance he had asked for, unlike those others who had not managed to take-off.

Where was everybody else, for goodness sake?

He was climbing too slowly, he'd never catch the bombers at this speed. What was wrong? Perhaps he had been damaged in that crazy take-off. Anxiously, he scanned the panel, and then he saw his omission.

Idiot! He saw that the undercarriage light was still on! The damned things were acting like a speed brake, slowing him down.

For heaven's sake! You're behaving like a bloody novice! Tuck your bloody wheels up!

Hand from throttle to undercarriage lever, then back again.

Another, slight, jolt as the wheels retract into their wells.

The altimeter was reading five hundred feet, when he noticed three dots, low down, almost invisible against the darkness of the ground, heading at high speed in towards Foxton from the north-west.

Jerries!

Fucking hell! A low-level strike to follow up the high level one!

He was trembling, swallowed again, his throat like cardboard. His head was throbbing, and the buzzing deafening in his ears. But the fear had disappeared, instead the anger in his heart had begun to burn brighter, the flames flaring white-hot, and threatening to consume his reason.

They were twin-engined jobs.

Junkers 88s?

No, thin shapes, twin tails, no glazed nose - Me110s. Bloody 110's *again*.

413

They seemed to tear across, at an angle towards him, the combined speed bringing them rapidly together at a point of intersection.

They were below, but they had to have seen him, for they turned slightly to head towards him.

With their nose-mounted cannon and machine guns, they were formidable opponents in a head-on attack.

If he had not spent a moment retracting the undercarriage, he would not have seen them, and they would have sped past beneath him (if, that is, one of them had not taken a hopeful shot at his fighter as he climbed above them against the bombers), to hit poor, battered Foxton again, from an unexpected direction.

But it no longer seemed to matter. He was a dead man flying. He had not died down there (Thank you, God!), and now he would sell his life for German blood. He would see some of them die before the light faded from his eyes, go to his end with their blood beneath his fingernails.

What was it the Ghurkhas shrieked into battle? '*Ayo Ghurkali!!*'

Molly would understand.

Behind him, Foxton burned, and he knew that only he lay between his people and the German bullets, as the survivors of Excalibur raced madly, desperately to close with the departing bomber formation.

No Bf109s, Thank God!

Yet.

Oh, Granny, I need you here.

And then they were in range, for their noses suddenly flared bright, and orange blobs of fire lifted from them, floated on twisting tails of smoke, and then dancing progressively faster, madly at him.

Bang on the rudder bar, right, left, right, hurl the aircraft from side to side, jinking wildly. Press the button, the vibration of the guns and the bitter reek of cordite comforting. Keep on sliding around; lay down a curtain of lead, through which they *must* fly!

"Ayo Gurkhali, you fucking, motherless bastards!" if only I could bury a kukri right up to its hilt into your damnable chests!

Then something thumped into his Hurricane, and he momentarily lost control. At first, he thought he had collided with one of the 110s, before he realised that instead, one of them had hit him with their fire.

Falling, stomach lurching with fear, there, easy my darling, easy, got you, level out, easy there…

He was so low, so low that he thought he would plough into the swaying sea of green below him at any moment. The aircraft faltered again, and then she was clawing her way back up.

He tested the controls carefully, craning his head around to check if one of the enemies was coming after him.

Gentle, turn to port.

One of the Me110s had pointed its nose up, and was climbing, hoping perhaps to whip around and dive on this impertinent Englander. Except that it passed directly over the airfield, high and in plain view of the gunners.

Smudges of grey-brown puffed all around it, as the anti-aircraft gunners caught sight of it and turned their guns on it, and then, realising its mistake, it was desperately diving back down again.

Too late. Too late now, you fucking, bloody swine.

Instantly, a 40mm shell had ripped into one wing, igniting the fuel there, and turning the fighter into a plummeting, smoking torch.

Indirectly, he had made his contribution to the Messerschmitt crew's deaths, and his heart sang joyously at the knowledge. The crew of that one were surely dead!

Thanks be! Die, you murdering bastards!

Another of the 110's was turning distantly, almost end-on to him. Perhaps the fate of its compatriot had dissuaded it from attacking Foxton. The wounded lion still had teeth.

Of the third Me110, there was no sign, just a straight, thick line of black smoke that led straight down into the pall of dust and smoke shrouding the airfield.

Had he got that one?

At least he had disrupted the low-level attack. Rose grinned fiercely, so hard that the muscles of his face ached.

He looked back upwards to where the enemy bombers had been, but they were now just a distant glinting group of dots almost invisible in the glaring blue.

They were too high, too far away, and he would never catch them now. But they had not escaped, for there was one which tilted, then fell away, twisting down into a splash of flame on to the countryside below.

"Got him." Donald's voice, faraway, subdued. A distant curving plume of smoke where another of the enemy had died.

But the massed bomber formation lumbered on its way, like an elephant ignoring insectile pin-pricks.

The anger bit deeply at his guts again, taking off some of the acidic dread that surrounded him. He had wanted so to smash into the bombers, rip them apart with his guns, ram them if need be, for they had destroyed his home, and killed those he thought of as family. He could feel the screams building in his throat.

He would make them pay for those murdered, stolen lives dearly.

Where are you, Granny? Where the hell is everybody?

Damn you all!

Stick back and push right rudder, bank around. The remaining 110 was still there, turning towards him, closing the range with him.

Surely he too, must feel the anger now. One of his friends shot down by the airfield defences, another badly damaged at least by this lone defiant Hurricane.

They would flash towards each other like Knights at a joust.

Rose smiled coldly.

Perfect.

We can die together.

Tracer sailed towards him, flecks of glowing fire that streaked by him like a stream of angry wasps, each with a fatal sting.

Crush the gun-button with finger, a long burst that scythed at the heavy fighter. A burst that sprayed anger, defiance and hate.

The two fighters approached each other at a closing speed of almost six hundred miles an hour, each firing streams of death.

The first one to break away from the head-long rush would receive fully the punishment being meted out by the other.

Except it no longer mattered to Rose that he might be dead in the next few seconds. His mind seethed for vengeance, and survival was no longer a factor. All that mattered was that he spilled enemy blood today. That he killed as many as possible.

And if he died doing it, so be it. He had been given this chance, to repay the Luftwaffe for what horror they had sown, and he was grateful.

Thank you, God, for my life and your other mercies, and for the love of my Molly, and for the friendship of my friends. And, of course, for this last chance to hurt the foe. I could have died down there, and it would have been a terrible thing, but I'll gladly die up here.

The thoughts raced through his mind, hazy and half-formed, his eyes fixed on the onrushing fighter, time slowing, the fear and the anger replaced by a calm peace. An acceptance of his fate, and more than a tinge of sadness for the lost happiness he had hoped, and longed for, with the beautiful dark-haired girl that he adored.

Behind the mask he smiled as the Messerschmitt swelled in his sights, how would it feel to die?

Would there be any pain? Or just a flash and then instant darkness?

He did not care, and looked from the windscreen to the photograph on the panel.

I'm sorry, Molly. I love you…

He did not see the Me110 twist to one side, the pale belly exposed to him, nor see the bullets that ripped from his guns into one of the two Daimler-Benz engines, flaying it into ruin in an instant, before it had passed him, scant inches from him. He was aware of the shadow that he thought was the onset of the darkness, but was in reality the fuselage of the Me110 just missing him.

He cursed, having fully committed himself to ramming the enemy.

The Hurricane shot through the smoke streaming from the 110's engine, and the odour of smoke, oil and burning metal roused him out of the strange suicidal reverie that he had fallen into, whilst the aircraft wallowed and faltered in the slipstream of the Luftwaffe fighter.

Automatically he took control, glanced quickly around for other enemy fighters as his trained reflexes took over again.

It was then that he realised that he was still alive, and that the 110 had disappeared. Just the vague smeared splash of a droplet of oil on his windscreen, and streamers of fabric flailing in the slipstream. He hadn't even felt the impacts. The oil left a smear that quickly vanished.

Mine? Or his?

All this in the blink of an eye.

Dear Heaven! What had come over him? He shuddered, his skin cold by the thoughts in his mind. He had been ready to die, to fall from this world a few seconds ago.

Dear God! I must be going crazy! It won't do to die. You're on borrowed time, he rebuked himself, so use it well. One Jerry isn't enough. You need to kill more of them. As many as possible.

For the ones who no longer could.

Press the rudder bar again, roll to the left.

Where has that Me110 gone?

Look all around you, check behind and beneath. Nothing near him.

A tiny dot receding, low-down on the horizon, leaving a faint smear behind. It hadn't even turned to continue the fight, but was high-tailing it out of Dodge.

He shook his head, unable to believe that they had both survived that insane, head-long dash, when seconds before death had seemed the only possible ending.

It was a miracle.

He rolled after the 110. The game was not yet over, for either of them. There was just a heavy feeling in his heart, as if his insides had been turned to cold tar, the white fire cooled. The hatred in his heart had hardened to a solid, hard little evil ball that dripped venom and pain inside him.

But he could not let the 110 go. The debt had to be paid, by those who shared in that collective guilt, and that debt was a terribly large one.

This Me110 would be one, small part of that repayment. There could be no mercy. Not now.

He concentrated on the German aircraft.

You have to die.

Push into emergency boost, catch him. He had the edge on speed, and normally, he would have out-distanced Rose, but he was obviously damaged, otherwise he would have climbed and disappeared into the suddenly hazy sky.

Faraway, he could see a single aircraft spiralling down, catching the light dully as it fell.

The smoke from his home was a great wide pillar of blackness, the base of which contained a faint reddish haze and innumerable, scattered pinpoints of flame.

He could hear the sounds of the distant dogfight over the R/T, the faint voices of other squadrons calling out as they joined in the fight against the hated raiders.

The fight had entered the high broken cumulus, and Rose knew that any more victories would be so much harder to achieve.

And then Donald was calling, his ammunition gone, returning to his battered home, and Ffellowes shouting out as a Heinkel blew up beneath his guns. Rose had not even seen Ffellowes escape the destruction, but that coldness hard inside him gloated at the thought of yet another Hun kite torn from the sky and the survival of another of his friends. But they were more than that, they were his brothers.

There was no sign of any other Me110s or Bf109s. Not even one of the elusive He113s. Can't be many of those about, he'd yet to see one.

And where the fuck was Granny?

Those three Zerstorers must have decided to strafe the airfield on their own, following up the terrible attack just as the men and women thought it safe to emerge from the shelters to fight the fires, to rescue the wounded.

Except they hadn't gambled on the possibility that one of the fighters that rose out of the destruction might catch sight of them as they sped in at extreme low-level.

He had split them up, and ruined their attack.

And of the three, perhaps only this one remained.

The airfield defences had nailed one, he or they might have been responsible for the second, and now he must catch this last one. Finish them all.

The enemy *was* damaged, for the distance had lessened, the details of the Me110 clearer. It had not managed to use its advantage in speed and climb rate to escape into the sparse cloud.

Rose wondered how much ammunition was still in his ammo pans. He had already fired two longish bursts. Would there be enough to finish the 110? He would have to fire carefully, conserve, and use it well.

They must not escape.

Close the throttle, he was close now, could see the pale oval that was the gunner's face staring back at him, eyes wide, except he did not fire back at Rose, the MG15 7.9mm was pointing upwards, barrel moving, and then it spat tracer up at the empty sky.

Your aim's rotten, you Nazi shit, thought Rose.

And then a huge dark shape dropped down in front of him, grey trails already streaming back from its wings, filling his windscreen, so close that he thought he would crash into it. He flinched and exclaimed in fear. What the -?

Rose dropped the nose slightly and wrenched the aircraft in a long skid to port, his aim put off by the near collision, heart hammering, instantly losing height.

"Fucking hell!" Torn from his very soul by the suddenness of its appearance so close before him. His heart had almost stopped in terror. He hadn't been watching his tail as he slavered for blood, and it could have been his undoing.

But, thankfully, the shape before him was another Hurricane, and it had almost collided with him. A second later and it would have flown through Rose's fusillade, and he would have likely shot it down.

He couldn't decide whether to be grateful that he hadn't been bounced by an enemy fighter, or be annoyed by the blatant theft of his 'kill.'

He decided it was better to be infuriated.

"You mad bastard!" He raved vehemently. And then he caught sight of the code-letter on the other RAF plane.

Cynk!

Bloody Cynk! That greedy Polish so-and-so…

He keyed his microphone. "Cynk, you bloody bastard! What the hell do you think you're doing?" He choked in anger. He felt a mad urge to open fire on the Hurricane, quashed it hurriedly.

"So sorry, my sir. Please to watch above. His friends come, maybe?"

Well! Of all the bald faced cheek! Amazed, Rose allowed his Hurricane to drift back in a covering position, to allow the Polish pilot to continue the attack, automatically checking for enemy fighters.

Obviously the mad bugger had not taken Granny's 'bottle' to heart!

"You cheeky big fucker…"

He watched from a quarter of a mile behind as the Polish pilot poured one, then a second long burst into the Messerschmitt, ignoring the return fire. He didn't aim for the wings or engines, just for the fuselage. For the men sheltering inside.

The Me110 started to slip drunkenly to one side in a wide, flat turn, Cynk close behind. He had silenced the gunner, and there was no more exchange of fire.

"You try now." Cynk's voice was timid, not quite apologetic. "I think nothing in gun."

The silly sod had run dry.

What a way to fight a war!

Rose shook his head again. "Alright. Get out of the bloody way, will you?"

"Please. I get out of bloody way, my sir. You come now."

They were down to four hundred feet, and the Me110 continued in its wide turn. Rose looked at it doubtfully.

"It's going to crash; he's got very little control. Be a waste of ammunition."

"No, no! He boom on it the base. Please, you try."

The Messerschmitt *was* heading back in the general direction of Foxton.

Maybe Cynk was right. Perhaps he would try and make a last attempt at shooting up something, or crashing into something at Foxton....

Well, he wasn't trying to land, thought Rose doubtfully, and he's probably has got stacks of ammo. That's good enough for me.

Might as well use up the last of the ammo, no point taking it home.

His heart flinched.

Home. What there was left of it.

Rose curved in from starboard, setting himself up neatly. It was so easy. The enemy pilot wasn't even trying to evade, just staring ahead. He was a sitting duck. The MG15 machine gun wobbled, but it was only from the dead (wounded?) gunner sliding down in his seat as the machine tilted back into level flight.

It *was* heading for the airfield.

Rose sighted carefully for a no deflection shot from directly astern of the enemy machine, placed the dot over the port engine, jammed his thumb down on the gun-button.

His Hurricane juddered as the guns clattered, but only enough for a two second burst of bullets and tracer before the roar ceased, and there was just the pneumatic hissing for company, which announced that he too had used his last rounds.

423

But it was enough.

A tiny flame licked at the starboard engine cowling, and then there was a small explosion, the flame spread, and the wing began to blaze all along its length in earnest. Thick blackness billowed back at him and he pulled up hurriedly. No need for smooth, showy climbs.

There was no doubt now, for it was finished, and he was glad. His bullets had been the final nails in the coffin of the German crew.

The Me110 wobbled, then spun viciously to starboard, losing height, and smashed nose-first into the ground, scattering fragments and disappearing in a glowing, sun-bright orange fireball.

But already it was behind him, the sight he dreaded more than anything before him instead.

Cynk was whooping happily on the HF, but Rose felt no joy, the nightmare ahead transfixing him.

That thick horrid pillar of smoke from Foxton, fed from dozens of fires, stained the sky before them, the sight fetching hopeless despair dully into his mind.

It had been hit hard. Dreadfully hard. There would be many, many casualties from damage like that. It was a great pall of black and dark grey smoke, and a strange diffuse red-brown-white flattish cloud that hung over the field. A hideous canopy over what had been his home.

Please God, let Molly have survived. You brought me safely from perdition on the ground to victory and life in the air. Please, please, let it be so with my beloved.

He found he was muttering his prayer out aloud. Anguish had settled over him like a heavy mantle. One part of him wanted to ram the throttle through the gate; the other wanted him to stay away, to hold back the bad news.

"You not worry, my friend. She not killed, too pretty."

Rose could not smile across at the Pole, his features so stiff, that cold ball hardening once more inside of him, awful despair, as the revolutions of his propeller drew them ever nearer.

The airfield was closer now, and the rolling smoke could not hide the dreadful hurt inflicted on the station.

It lay before them like some terrible child's playroom, stuff thrown haphazardly and without care this way and that, like unwanted playthings.

There seemed to be fires burning fiercely everywhere he looked, and so many of the buildings had been reduced to rubble that he found it difficult for a moment to orientate himself, for the hangers appeared to have disappeared altogether, and the region of the water tower was pitted so that that part of the field resembled the moon. It was a scarred, barren plain.

Rose's heart sank. Dear, sweet God. The bombs had ripped the station to shreds.

RAF Foxton wasn't damaged, it was *destroyed*.

Obliterated.

How could this happen? He could feel the heated stinging behind his eyes, and his mouth was dust, so dry that his tongue felt like a dry potato that threatened to choke him, and he couldn't speak.

A single smudge of smoke erupted fifty yards in front, before the trigger-happy gunner realised the two fighters overhead were 'friendlies.'

Cynk pulled back his hood and shook his fist at the gunners.

Rose noticed none of this, his spirit immersed in sorrow; instead he was looking for a clear landing place, for the field was strewn with burning, burned out or damaged aircraft and vehicles.

The pall of dust, soot and smoke that pricked at his nostrils covering the airfield like a hazy, choking shroud.

There were two Hurricanes parked up beside the covered fuel

dump, men working feverishly around them, and he side-slipped down, then whipped round dangerously, almost on one wingtip.

He could smell the stink of devastation and death from inside of the cockpit and he thought his heart would surely break apart.

Chapter 33

Rose unstrapped himself from the Sutton harness, all fingers and thumbs, and hastily pulled off his flying helmet with shaking hands, letting it slip to the floor of the cockpit, even as his Hurricane was still rolling to a stop.

With a single effortless motion, he pushed back his stained hood, tumbled down from the cockpit and stepped out into a dark world of confusion and sound, his mouth sour with dread.

The odour of smoke, cordite, burning metal and wood was mixed horribly with that of freshly turned earth and masonry dust, filling his nostrils until he coughed and gagged, wiped his rapidly-tearing eyes, momentarily overwhelmed by the foul atmosphere.

At the eastern end of the field, the skeletal remnants of one of the hangers collapsed, like a tired house of cards, the fall of wood and steel dull and final, crashing to earth amidst a storm of whirling dancing cinders and sparks, flying high and wide.

Joyce came running up to him from a bank of smoke, "Oh, Thank God! Thank God you're alright, Mr Rose!" he was wild-eyed, smoke stained and had lost his cap.

Rose thought for a moment that the man would hug him, and tried to force a smile to his face. He couldn't. "Can't get rid of me that easily, my old son. Where's Baker?"

The reply came out as a dried croak.

"I thought you was done for, sir. Baker is helping with the bowsers. He sent me to look after you. He was shoutin' like a fuckin' nutter! When you took off through the smoke...we thought...we thought..." He gulped convulsively, his Adam's apple bobbing up and down, and there were tears in his eyes.

He held Rose's sleeve gingerly, "We all thought you was a goner... oh Thank God you're alright!" he coughed and spat, wiped his mouth with a dirty hand, "Thank God!"

Rose placed his gloved hand over Joyce's, and looked around him. Where would she be? Please God she had managed to get down into one of the shelters. What the hell was the shelter number for signals section?

Oh God. His mind had gone completely blank.

Joyce's hand was trembling convulsively (or was it his own?).

Rose pointed back at his Hurricane. "Look, will you take care of her for me? Get an armourer too. Top her up and reload. I got a few licks back. There may be more of the bastards along shortly." He looked up as he passed his gauntlets and silk gloves to Joyce, but the sky, what he could see of it, was empty of enemy aircraft.

Instead the airfield was in a false twilight imposed by the smoke and dust canopy overhead and the thickly swirling fluffs of soot. He was in a nightmare world of abject chaos and disorder and horror.

Thank goodness most of 97 squadron had already scrambled. At least they escaped this bloody awful shambles.

"Yessir. Any luck?"

But Rose was already running towards the shattered heart of operations, collapsed and broken, half-hidden beneath the brooding pall of brick-dust and smoke. His chest felt as if there was a great weight resting upon it, as if it were in a vice, and he fought to suck air into himself, and it seemed to his shocked mind as if he were wading through thick syrup as he raced as fast as he could to the ruins.

God help us if Jerry comes back.

But we're finished, even if he doesn't.

There's nothing left to bomb.

He had been, still was, so concerned for Molly that he had not even noticed the holes and torn fabric, signs of the bullets and the fragments of exploding bombs in the smoke-stained dirty skin of his aircraft.

Joyce had noticed, and he pursed his lips thoughtfully as he trotted to the Hurricane. We'll need more patches there.

He caressed the aircraft. Poor old girl, what have them bastards done to you? Tears coursed down his stained face.

Behind him, Cynk's Hurricane bumped down, rolling over the grass and coming to a stop.

A party of men ran past Rose, but his legs felt stiff with fear, and it still felt as if he were stumbling through treacle. All around there was clamour, but the roaring in his ears dimmed the shouts and sounds of activity.

The operations block seemed miles away, and it seemed as if the journey to it took an interminable eternity, and he wondered if he might really be in some kind of terrible nightmare, always running, getting no nearer, and he would suddenly awaken from this horror to an unscathed Foxton.

Outside the fire section building, he was surprised to see Skinner sitting on the grass minus his jacket and shoes, a bloody cloth wrapped around his head, a trickle of blood disappearing beneath his rumpled collar.

Incongruously, there was a wrecked fire tender lying on its side five feet from him, on the edge of a bomb crater. The two cylindrical red tanks had been ruptured by shrapnel, and water dribbled like blood from its side. There was no sign of the crew, just a suspicious trail of red leading away from it.

Rose bent down beside Skinner. "Uncle? Are you alright? Have you seen Molly?"

Skinner looked at him blankly, muscles slack and eyes glassy. "Pardon, old chap?"

Rose swallowed painfully. "Are you OK, Uncle?" He was looking very pale and very strange.

"Is that you, Carruthers, old man? Is the old Brisfit ready?"

What? Who the hell was Carruthers?

Oh no. Rose shook his head. "I'm not Carruthers, Uncle. It's me. Pilot Officer Harry Rose. Flash."

"Rose? Rose? Don't know you, old man. Never heard of you. Don't want you. Where the devil's Carruthers?"

He tried to stand, tottered unsteadily, and fell back down onto his backside. He grimaced and lay back on the grass and closed his eyes.

"Oh dear. Think I'm a bit tipsy. Perhaps I shouldn't fly today. Never mind. I'll just lay down here for a while. Would you mind telling Carruthers for me?"

"Uncle, have you seen Molly, or Granny?"

Skinner opened his eyes and looked at him doubtfully. "Granny? Why are you asking about Granny, old chap?" he stared at the fire tender, but not really seeing it. "No good asking about Granny. She isn't here. She's tucked up safe and sound in Blighty. This isn't Cheltenham, you know."

He closed his eyes again, cupped his hands in front of his mouth, and shouted, "Carruthers, come here! You can't go up there without me! Come here, now, you rotten scallywag! You need me to protect you from that silver nosed bastard." He groaned and closed his eyes.

An airman ran up to him, "Leave him be, Mr Rose, sir. Someone will be along in a tick to take care of him. Could you come and give us a hand, please?" The man looked exhausted, "A bomb hit shelter number four. We're trying to get the people out. Please help."

Everything seemed to press in on him. Bomb shelter number four?

Oh dear God, no.

Dear God. Please, no.

Oh God.

No, no, no.

Shelter number four was the one to which the WAAF signal section were normally assigned, he remembered now.

Rose grabbed the other's arm forcefully, "Did you say shelter four?"

Skinner opened his eyes, looked from Rose to the airman, "I say, old bean, have you seen Lieutenant Carruthers?"

The airman ignored him, his eyes pleading. "Please, sir, we need help digging out the bodies." He began to cry quietly.

Without another word, Rose was running, looking only to where shelter four had once been, but where there was now just a smoking mound of hateful fresh earth, filled with men digging, and passing back debris along a daisy chain made of men in dirty uniforms.

A flying leap and Rose landed on the earth, a stone sending a jarring shock lanced painfully up his right leg. Immediately he started scrabbling crazily at the earth, and a splinter of wood dug into his little finger, but he did not even notice, his chest heaving, and droplets of blood from his fingers spotting the fresh earth.

The sergeant in charge glared at him. "Stop that! There may be an air pocket down there. You might make it collapse. Leave it to us." His face, large and red like the others around him glistened with sweat, his voice ragged with anger and despair.

Rose stopped and sat back on his knees, eyes staring. "Quick! Help me, please! There are people down there!"

The big NCO looked at him for a moment, and the anger in his eyes dulled slightly.

"Slow and sure, sir. Just you step back over there, alright?" the sergeant spoke patiently, as if speaking to a stupid child. "Leave it to us." He pointed again with a thick finger. "Please. Just. Step, Back." His voice held the ring of authority. "Now."

Rose began to obey, when suddenly he caught sight of a tarpaulin spread out to one side, laid out roughly over a number of somethings.

Oh dear God.

He stared, not wanting to believe. The shapes covered by the tarpaulin were bodies. A pilot was standing there, his head bowed.

As if in prayer.

He could feel the wrenching hopelessness rising up within him, like a wild bird that threatened to escape through his throat.

He felt he would go mad.

No. Please don't. No.

His feet were solid lumps of lead that required all his concentration to move and he staggered to the row of shapes.

There were about twenty of them there, their feet and ankles uncovered. A few of them wore RAF shoes, one Army-issue boots.

But the rest of those feet were in stockings.

The majority of the shapes were girls.

They were WAAFs.

The Signals section.

A void gaped hugely within him, dark and empty and bottomless.

He was not even aware of it, but he was keening.

A low, barely audible, soft moan of pain that stretched up from the deepest parts of him, without solace or hope, just an upwelling of pain from his very soul.

The other pilot had noticed Rose's approach, and he looked up. It was Denis. He had a nasty gash on one cheek, a black eye, and his right trouser leg was torn.

His face was wet and stained and forlorn.

"Flash?" He sounded so terribly tired and wretched. "She's not there, mate."

Rose ignored him. He could not keep his eyes from those feet, small, delicate, some with painted nails, none with shoes. Where had their shoes gone? The inconsequential thought flashed through his mind.

"She's not there, mate. Honest. I've already checked. Neither is Dolly. They've taken her to the hospital. She'll be safe there." He looked up emptily at the canopy of cloud and smoke and dust. "Those bastards will be back."

But there was one pair of ankles in ripped stockings that seemed somehow familiar.

Right at the end of the line.

"I don't believe you." The darkness was gathering around his soul, pressing against him. He thought his chest might cave in, the emptiness within him cold and harsh, like a vacuum.

He walked to the shape on the end, bent to pull back the sheet, and Denis laid a hand on his shoulder. "Look, I've checked already, for Christ's sake, Flash, leave it alone, can't you?"

His arms felt like weak twigs, but Rose twitched back the sheet, terrified, but desperate to know, and his mouth was filled with the greyness of ash. Around him the smoke and flames were nothing, as if they were no longer there.

He was in a silent, empty world.

His eyes moved over the girl's face.

A lovely girl to be sure, but, it wasn't Molly.

Her hair was fair, and the loose wavy tresses moved gently, not from some cool breeze, but with the draught from the burning buildings nearby that tugged at them. There was a smear of dried blood at her blue lips, and her skin was deathly white beneath the smear of dirt, otherwise she might have been asleep.

It was Janet, once bright and young and sweet, and now she was very dead.

Her eyes were almost, but not quite, closed, the blue irises faintly visible behind the slits, and he half-expected those long lashes to part and for her to sit up, laughing at them. Those once daring and bright eyes now dulled in death.

How could this be?

She would never laugh again. There could be no more happiness for her.

And there would be no more laughter in this grim field of smoke and blood and death. Only tears, endless, deluging rivers of them.

"Oh, Janet, no." The harsh grief cut into him with shocking pain.

It was as if his heart was punctured, and the energy drained from him.

He fell to his knees, and the tears came, sheets of tears. His body wracked by sobs, and he bent forward with the rending pain of it. The tears ran down his cheeks, cutting runnels through the stain and grime, and soaking his collar and tunic.

Nearby, some ammunition popped ridiculously, like party crackers, but it meant nothing to him in his world of private torment.

There was a strange, quizzical expression on her face, as if she could not quite understand what she was doing there, as if she were confused and a little scared. The expressions twisting her pretty face into a confused almost-frown now frozen in death, and twisting his insides in sympathy and painful self-loathing.

"Dingo? You're sure?" His tears fell unchecked onto her stiff dead face, and he felt like reaching out to her, comforting her. The last seconds of her life before she had gone into that dark valley were ones of confusion and pain and fear.

Oh, Janet. I failed you.

I failed all of you.

"She's not here, mate. Honestly. I'd not lie to you. Not about something like that."

A faint glimmer of hope flared in the darkness of his aching heart, but it was extinguished almost immediately, could not survive with the evidence of this cold, dead girl before him.

She'd not have left her girls alone, if she could help it.

Once so full of laughter and life, now totally devoid and empty, like the discarded doll of some petulant child. It was impossible to think of this corpse as the Janet who laughed and smiled so engagingly, smiled at him once, too, her eyes dancing with interest and mischief and promise.

Why? Why these girls?

There was a large red wound in the middle of her chest, covered with a piece of torn tunic through which the blood soaked, like some dirty stain.

It was as if something had pierced her to stab out the life from her body. It must have been instantaneous, or almost so, otherwise there would only have been the pain on her face, not that questioning look. But it did not comfort him.

Tenderly he brushed the hair from her bloodied mouth.

"Oh Janet, I'm so sorry."

How can this be war? What kind of monsters were they?

435

"What a bloody shambles. We let them down, mate." Denis' voice was a whisper. He looked like he may drop with exhaustion and grief at any moment. "We failed."

Rose's voice broke. "I know, Dingo. God help me, I know."

Gently, he covered her up again. I'm sorry. I never really knew you, Janet, and now I never shall, although Molly always spoke kindly of you. She liked you, was so fond of you.

It's so unfair. So very unfair.

Rest in peace. God bless you and give you peace.

"Where is she, then? Tell me." he could not keep his eyes from the covered girl.

"I don't know, mate. I haven't seen her at all." Denis' eyes were far away, another time, another place, a road in Belgium, choked with civilian dead. He had seen the effect of German bombs and strafing before. The nightmare he had dreaded for so long had finally become reality. The same sights, yet the dead this time were British. This time they were his family.

Rose glanced back towards the work-party. "Oh, God, Dingo. She might still be down there." His chin began to tremble.

"Leave them be, Flash. They'll tell us if they find anyone. Keep it together, mate."

"Flash! Where the fuck have you been?"

Granny appeared from out of the smoke, grabbed Rose, and pulled him up by his collar. "Flash, for Christ's sake! I've been looking all over this mess for you! Thought you'd copped it up there!"

"Oh, Granny! I've lost her! I think Molly's dead!" Rose started weeping again, his body shaking again, not caring that they were watching him. A blob of mucus stretched and fell slowly from his nose onto the ground.

Granny shook him roughly, "No, you haven't, you silly bastard! She's alive!"

Had he misheard? "Alive? What…?"

"She's hurt." He saw the pain on Rose's face and continued hastily, "No, not too badly. She won't die, Thank God." Granny looked grimly at the line of bodies. "But she's been wounded, and they've taken her to the station sick quarters. What's left of it, at least. But you needn't worry. Arrangements have been made for Molly and some of the others to go to the hospital in the town."

He grabbed both Rose's shoulders, and shook him again, roughly, "But she's alive, d'you hear me? She's alive and she'll be alright!"

Rose wiped his nose with a sleeve. "Granny? Take me to her?"

"Bloody hell, Flash! Why d'you think I'm here? For a kiss and a cuddle and a fag? I've been looking for you for fucking ages! She wants you! Gawd only knows why! My company isn't good enough for her! I daren't go back without you! She'll have had my balls for a pendant if I don't go back with you, so move your worthless arse."

Granny nodded to Denis. "Dingo, it's good to see you're still with us, chum." He squinted at Denis. "Eye looks nasty, impressive shiner. Best get it looked at." He rubbed his chin, dread in his eyes, "Dolly…?"

Denis wiped his reddened eyes. "She'll be OK, mate. She's been taken to the hospital. Cuts from splinters. Don't worry about me, I'll be OK. Now get this young sod to his girl!"

They stumbled from the debris of Shelter Four, picking their way past the barracks and parade ground, and between the photo and radio section buildings, the narrow alley half blocked with rubble.

Behind them, Denis squatted down and shook his head. "What a bloody shambles." He whispered again. He reached out to rest his hand on a girl's covered form.

"I'll pay them back, sweetheart, I promise. On my life, I swear it."

437

Rose was amazed at how much damage had been inflicted in so short a time. Here and there, scattered amidst the wreckage and smoke sat or lay the wounded, awaiting medical attention.

Occasionally, they would also pass a covered corpse, although the shape beneath the covers sometimes seemed to be too small for a human being. The bombs had obviously had a devastating effect on the bodies of some of the dead.

Shoes and caps were scattered around as if forgotten by their owners. A pair of spectacles without lenses, a pair of gloves, cigarettes strewn about.

Shattered glass and broken bricks and other fragments crunched beneath their feet like crystalline sugar.

And everywhere, that awful metallic, coppery stench.

As they hurried to Molly, Granny explained what had happened whilst Rose had been breaking up the attack by the Me110s.

As the bombing began, Molly had taken her girls down to the shelter after the first warning that a raid might be imminent, and then she had been called away to the headquarters building for some necessary duty or other.

Then, short moments later, the bombs had fallen, and the shelter had been hit in her absence. Granny had seen the bombs hit, and knowing how risky take-off was, had leapt out of his kite hoping to help. The girls were special to all of them.

Whilst the squadron had been fighting and Rose had faced the Me110s in his own arena, Granny had helped to drag the broken bodies one by one from the earth. And then the headquarters building, in turn, had been hit.

Molly had saved lives, it seemed. She had gone into the burning building, and had guided out the wounded, supporting and encouraging. She had personally saved three men, including the Wing

Commander, although he was severely injured, before another bomb had fallen. And this time, her luck had run out. She had been caught by the shrapnel.

But she's alive, he reminded himself. That's all that really matters. She's still warm and alive, not lying out there cold and blue and torn beneath some anonymous sheet of tarpaulin, like those poor girls. With her spirit, and my love, one day she'll be strong again. She's alive!

Chapter 34

The desk had been removed from the Chief Medical Officer's office, and dumped unceremoniously upside down outside. Thus cleared, three stretchers had been placed in the office.

The sick ward was already filled, the cloying stench of blood and antiseptic mixing with the ever present smoke and dust. The over-fill of the injured had been laid out on the grass outside, between the sick quarters and the MT pool. The eastern wall of the building had been knocked down, and he could see some of the vehicles, dented and damaged and under debris and rubble.

Beneath their feet, glass and vials and powder and tablets crunched and popped.

The concussion from the bomb blasts had knocked down the neatly arranged mirrored medicine closets, strewing the contents across the floor in a multi-coloured jumble. Blood and soot had dirtied the once gleaming white walls, and dirty, bloodied dressings lay in a pile in one corner.

Doubtless Griffen must have been apoplectic.

It was a far cry from the scrubbed and polished sick quarters in which he had lain so very recently. She had visited him, that time. This time, the positions were reversed. Please God she had escaped as lightly as he had.

Granny stopped and turned to him. His voice was quiet, "She's in there, mate. She isn't feeling too good, she's been given a shot of something. I've had a word with the doc. She's going to be alright. Remember that. You've got to be strong for her, OK?" Then he stepped aside to allow Rose in, patted his shoulder. "I'll be outside, chum. Shout if you need me."

Rose nodded his thanks, not trusting his voice, the dread squeezing his heart like a vice again.

Molly was on a stretcher pushed up against the filing cabinet that housed the medical records.

She was laying facedown, her slim form covered with a grimy sheet spotted with blood. Her tunic rested by her side.

Her lustrous black hair, now speckled with dust, was spread out around her head. Her exposed, smooth shoulders were scratched and pale, the skin milky white. The word URGENT had been scrawled across them in watery blue ink.

Beside her, there was another WAAF, a corporal according to her accompanying tunic, but the girl's eyes were closed, her face untroubled and mouth slack, relaxed in the drug-induced oblivion of unconsciousness.

Rose squatted down beside Molly, and reached out, thought better of it, withdrew his hand.

"Molly. I'm here, my sweet love." His voice fractured, and he sucked in his lips, closed his eyes, as the tears spilled from his eyes. His sinuses and nose were heavy with mucus, so that his voice was thick, as if he had a head cold.

"Harry?" her voice was weak, almost inaudible, the very merest of whispers. "Oh, my Harry, is that you? You're alive? Thank God…"

Even lying there, semi-conscious, injured cruelly, all she could think of was his safety.

441

"Molly, my darling, what have they done to you, my sweet girl?" his hands were shaking uncontrollably, and he could not keep the keen of pain from his voice. He bit his lip to still the sob that threatened to escape.

Control yourself, you stupid, bloody fool.

She turned to face him, and he was shocked by the waxy sheen of sweat on her pale (Dear God, so very pale!) face. Her eyes were half-closed, her soft lips devoid of their usual brightness, bruised where she'd bitten them. The swollen dark purple-blue bruise breaking the paleness of her complexion, angry and livid, on the side of her pinched face. The sight of her made him feel as if he had been kicked in the stomach, and he felt the strength drain from his muscles.

He felt he would surely faint when a low moan escaped her lips. But she was still alive.

Thank you, Dear God, still alive.

Her voice was so low, slow with pain and morphine. "What's this? Is my brave RAF hero crying? Better stop, you'll scare the kiddies and the animals..."

"I thought I'd lost you."

She swallowed dryly and closed her eyes, "I'm not dead, y'know. Still here..."

Thank God! "How do you feel?" he tried to make his voice sound light, but he could not keep the worry from it. What a stupid question to ask! She's laying there before me with her back torn open, and I'm asking her how she's feeling like some fatuous moron!

"Like the sky fell on me... I feel so tired, Harry." Her voice was slurred. "My mouth's so dry, but they won't give me a drink..." Above her head was a scrawled note, bearing the legend, *'Nil by mouth.'*

"I must look dreadful. Don't look at me." She turned her face away, but not before a tear glistened slowly down her nose.

"Oh, Molly, you're the loveliest thing in my life. I think you're beautiful." Carefully, he bent forward and kissed her hair. She was still fragrant, despite the stench of smoke, blood and open wounds, and the awful experience she had suffered.

Where was the bloody MO? "Molly. I love you. I want you. Have you decided to marry me yet, or must I wait more?"

Rose listened for the sound of unsynchronised aero-engines. The sooner Molly was sent to a hospital, the better, as far as he was concerned.

Lying there, she and the other casualties were terribly vulnerable if the Luftwaffe returned, and frantic apprehension gnawed at him.

"Harry...I love you, too. Always will. Will you hold my hand, please?"

She must have been given something strong, he thought, for she seemed to fade in and out of consciousness. He was content to squat beside her, holding her cold hand, trying to warm it with his. He smoothed back the hair from her forehead, moist with sweat. His knees ached, but he dared not move.

Then she was awake again. "Harry...is that you?"

"I'm still here, my love."

"Thank God...I thought I'd been dreaming."

"No, still here, large as life and twice as ugly."

"I think you're dashing...wish I could give you a kiss...we'll have to cancel our weekend in Mayfair..." Another tear coursed down her cheek.

"Tell me about my girls, Harry?"

He was silent, what could he tell her? The truth? That they're all dead?

"Um, I don't know, Molly. Granny brought me straight here. I'm sure they'll be alright, love."

443

"Tell me, please. I saw the shelter hit, Harry. I know what happened. I should have stayed with them. They all trusted me. Tell me."

Still he was silent. What could he possibly say? Helpless, Rose looked round. Where's that flippin' MO?

"Oh, Harry…they killed my girls…" Tears began to flow in earnest now; she sobbed bitterly, shoulders shaking, her soft fingers tightening around his.

"They shouldn't have died alone. I should have been with them… they were my girls, Harry. My responsibility. What right have I to live instead of them? Why them and not me? They were so young and good…"

"Nobody should have died, my sweetheart. I couldn't bear it if you were gone. I couldn't go on. Thank God you were spared. I couldn't bear it if you had gone."

"Why…?" A despairing whisper, full of hurt and liquid pain.

"I wish I could take it away, my love. I want to take all the hurt from you."

But still she asked, "My poor dear girls. Why…?"

He could not answer her; the words stillborn on his tongue, the pain in her voice cutting sharply at him like the cold sharp scalpels on the steel tray outside. How could he answer her, when he could not explain it to himself? How could he comfort her, when the sights he had seen, and the injuries to his sweet Molly left him with incomprehension that his home, his world, familiar and friendly, was forever gone?

How does one explain what is impossible to comprehend?

He could only kneel beside her, her hand like ice in his, his eyes staring in apprehension at the raised area where the covering sheet was being kept away from her lower back by a support frame. Momentarily, she had sunk back into unconsciousness.

What had they done to her? What awful hurts lay beneath that sheet?

The cold anger was forged afresh, in those minutes. The young pilot, kneeling beside the battered body of his beloved, felt the bitter stinging hatred burgeoning, tempered and hardened by those bitter tears, by her poor battered form and by the endless sea of pain.

He tried to soothe her, murmuring meaningless nothings, but in the end, it was the tiredness, despair, and her injuries, that had sent her sliding back into unconsciousness, the pain fading, but the wetness of her cheeks and on the fabric of her pillow a remembrance for the departed.

A stained button on her tunic hung loosely from torn thread, the sheen gone, and he ripped it off, pocketed it. It would be his battle talisman.

It would serve to remind him, wherever he was.

He would pay them back a hundredfold for what had been wreaked here today. A thousand fold. He would become like Cynk, living only to kill.

He would kill them at each and every opportunity. Such monsters could not deserve mercy.

They had hurt her, the one thing that mattered most to him in this world. They had gouged his heart, and he would not bear the pain alone. He would hurt them the same way. They had no sense of what was fair, and deserved no fairness in return.

Where was the justness of dropping bombs on girls, or machine-gunning a man beneath his parachute?

There was no honour in it. The swines had no honour.

His shirt was drenched, and he picked it away from his back, struggling with the Mae West he still wore.

She had asked what right she had to live when others did not. He had no answers, but he knew that she had been chosen to live. It had not been her time, not yet. Thank goodness.

He leaned his head against the filing cabinet, and the tears streaked through dirt, and oil, and smoke stains. He cried for what might have been, and for what his world had now become.

For the enormous pains, and for the horrendous hurts, both physical and mental, inflicted upon her.

But most of all, he cried because she had lived through that day of fire, death and damnation, when so many had not.

Whatever else happened, she had lived.

There could be nothing more important than that.

Nothing.

For while they both lived, their dreams still held substance.

He was not aware of how long he had been there, except that he had drowsed beside her, and then he was suddenly alert.

There was a muffled cough, and another tap on the door. Two orderlies stood uncomfortably there, faces tight, a stretcher between them.

Perhaps they were embarrassed to see one of their pilots, one of the nation's darlings he thought bitterly, kneeling there with a snotty nose and tears on his cheeks.

The smaller of the two orderlies smiled uncertainly, colourless eyes blinking hugely behind thick lenses in the subdued yellow light.

"Begging your pardon, sir, but we're from the hospital. We've come for two RAF ladies. Flight Officer Digby, and, er," he consulted a clip-board, "Ah, Miss Simons. Is that the young ladies there?"

"Yes, this is Flight Officer Digby. I don't know if this one of is Simons, sorry. It's a bit cramped in here. Wait a minute, I'll come out. Give you a spot of room to work in."

"Harry, is that you?"

"I'm here, my sweet. Don't worry, it's alright, my love, these chaps have come to take you to the hospital. They'll take care of you. You'll be comfortable there."

He gently lowered Molly's hand, hating to let go of it, and climbed unsteadily to his feet, thigh and calf muscles straining painfully.

The orderly with spectacles deftly squeezed past him, and laid down the stretcher beside her.

In no time at all, they had transferred her gently to the stretcher, and out into the waiting service ambulance, with its great red crosses.

Rose hopped up into the ambulance while the orderlies went to fetch Miss Simons (whoever she was).

The interior, once so light when he had been admitted so recently, was now dark, and the walls seemed to absorb the low pitched words as she raised her head to him.

He leaned forward to listen carefully, but it was difficult with the wheezy breathing of the drugged airman already there.

Her hair hung forward like a curtain, hiding her face from him. "Oh, Harry, I don't want to leave. I don't want to leave you." In her half-closed drugged eyes, there was at last a trace of fear. "Take care of yourself, please don't die..."

The last time she had left those who meant something to her, they had died. She had lost her girls, and now she feared terribly for him.

Rose nodded soberly. "I don't have any plans to, my sweetheart."

He remembered the madness in his mind as he had raced towards the Me110 so recently, banished the thought to a distant place, "Don't you worry about me, my darling heart. I'll be OK, you'll see."

He patted his pocket. "Genevieve will take care of me. She'll see me right. You just concentrate on getting better, agreed?" *I should have given her back to you, they could never have hurt you then.*

"Be careful?"

447

He stroked her feverish, moist brow. "I'll be jolly careful, I promise." He smiled carefully, "I've found you now. I shan't ever let you go. I intend to live so I can be with you, so you better live for me."

The orderlies had returned, and the little man with the spectacles had heard her, and he leaned forward, "Don't need to worry about him, miss, he's a big lad. I'm sure he can look after himself." He grinned apologetically to Rose.

Granny was standing outside the ambulance; "I'll take care of the little sod for you, Molly. You take care of yourself, and leave me to look after him. Fair enough?"

"If you don't…" she whispered.

Rose put a finger to her lips. "Enough talking. You rest now. I'll come and see you as soon as I can, but you must know that I love you dearly, and will do forever."

He bent forward and kissed her lightly, his lips just brushing hers, but already she was slipping back into the protective state of unconsciousness as her body fought the injuries she had suffered.

It was the hardest thing he could do, to step down from the ambulance. He did not want to let her out of his sight, but to hold her close, never let her go.

Together, Granny and Rose stood in the unnatural twilight, and watched the ambulance slowly make its way to the main gate, until it had disappeared from sight through the gloom.

Granny patted his shoulder kindly. "She'll be fine, Flash. They'll look after her. Come on, let's go and scrounge a nice cuppa. I think the planes will have been refuelled and re-armed by now."

His hand gripped Rose's shoulder firmly, shook him slightly. "We have to be ready if there are any more attacks."

"Yes. I'll catch you up in a moment, Granny, just have to go and check something, OK?"

He picked his way past the wounded back to the Chief MO's office, to discover that the remaining WAAF had also disappeared, and had been replaced with some badly wounded soldiers from the airfield defence unit, plasma bottles snaking from their arms.

Those still conscious watched him silently, with pain-filled faces, and he felt like a trespasser.

Molly's tunic had been carefully folded and placed in the corner. I'll keep it safe for her. When I go and visit her, he thought, I'll take it to her.

Rose picked up her tunic and hugged it tightly, wiped his face with her sleeve. It was then that he saw the great star-shaped tear in the back of it, a good three inches across. The torn fabric edges were caked stiffly with dried, black-looking blood.

Dear God. He held it up to the light. The wound must be terrible. Yet she had lain there quietly. Despite the Morphine, she must have felt such agonising pain.

He felt an urgent desire to go straight to the hospital, to be with her as he should, but he knew that his duty lay here, with his squadron. He had to trust them with her, even if his heart pleaded with him to go to her. He had to defend those who were left behind.

He gathered it up and put it over his arm.

There was a photograph poking up out of her side pocket.

Curious, he pulled it out. There was no one watching, but he felt guilty nonetheless. It was like going through her bag, an invasion of her privacy.

The photograph showed a young man, smart and correct in RAF uniform. Like Rose, he wore the single, thin rank braid of a Pilot Officer, and the silken cream wings of a pilot. He could not have been more than nineteen or twenty years of age.

The face stared up at him, blandly indifferent to his confusion.

What did this mean? Why was it in her pocket? Who was he?

Beneath the photo, a message had been written in a neat copperplate style:

Dearest Molly,
Thinking of you, old girl. Keep your head down!
Love, Teddy.

Teddy? Who in the name of holy heaven was this Teddy?

The photo stared back at him enigmatically, not offering any answers, just a mystery.

He could not understand it. What was a picture of a young pilot, not unlike himself, doing in her pocket? Might she have had it in safe-keeping for one of her girls? Or perhaps it had been placed in her pocket by mistake?

No. The message was addressed to her. Dearest Molly. It could not be for someone else.

He meant a lot to her, for she carried it everywhere with her, as Rose carried hers wherever he went.

Sweet God. What did it mean? His battered mind was thrown in shocked turmoil. He'd been through monstrous waves of pain already, and now this came out of nowhere to further shred his already frayed heart!

When she held him to her, when she kissed him passionately, was this other in her thoughts? When he touched her cheek or her breast, did she wish it was this other, this damned Teddy?

Had all she had said to him been a lie? All the protestations of love a sham? Was this blasted Teddy her true love?

He felt dead inside, his chest cavity as cold and cavernously hollow as a burnt-out grate, as if she had cut out his heart and lungs.

450

Did she say the same words of promise to this other, too? All the intimacy, was it the same for this man? Did she, God help us, feel the same for him?

Was he her lover? Had he enjoyed her in that way? The very thought of her with this 'Teddy' was almost too much to bear. Surely, it could not be so?

The thought of another man's hands holding and caressing her was abominable.

Oh, bloody hell! You are my perfection, and mean everything to me. Why can't I be the same for you?

Oh, God. So much pain, why must there be more?

What have I done, that I am tortured so?

It was as if his innards had turned to powdered ash, dust blown away by hot, scalding wind, leaving him scoured of all happiness and empty.

Thinking of you.

Like cold steel stabbing wickedly into his heart. Another man, thinking of my Molly.

Except she's not mine alone. She's shares her affections with another man.

And sudden revelation. So, *that's* why she won't marry me! She wants the other more than she wants me!

Who are you, bastard?

How could she do this to him? It was as if she had no feeling for him. She must have been laughing at the pair of them, each of them thinking she was theirs alone.

But that was not the Molly he knew. Not the girl he loved. It could not be as he feared; she was too good to have done this, surely?

Why? Why?

Oh Molly! What does it mean?

451

His mind was a swirl of jumbled, confused questions. It was the shattering of his world, shattered into a hundred million tiny pieces. The loss of innocence that he had thought the fury of war had already taken from him these last few cruel weeks.

He had never thought that betrayal could be so harsh. It left a taste more bitter than anything he had ever known, just wave after wave of unbearable incredible pain.

A hurt so brutally intense, like the excruciating agony he felt when he had seen her laying there, hurt and weak, when he had known that he had let her down.

Let them all down.

He felt a sudden desperate yearning to be amongst his own kind. The world he understood. There was no excruciating pain like this with the boys, just friendship and companionship. The risks were straightforward enough. There was nothing hidden, no falsehoods.

He looked up at the darkened sky, but instead of the smoke and soot and dust, he saw only the cruel dejection of loss and loneliness. He had thought her dead mere moments earlier, and the joy of her incredible salvation had been so bright, to be tempered then by this monstrous disclosure.

She was not even his, after all.

Never, ever, had he felt so very alone.

Rose pushed the photo back into the tunic pocket, his hand unsteady.

He hugged the torn and dusty tunic tightly to him, as if it were she, tried to find her lingering scent, but this time, like her, it was gone. All that he could smell from it was smoke and ash and her blood. The smell of broken dreams mixed with the shock of cruel reality.

It was as if she truly was lost to him, after all.

God, why did he have to see this day?

Far better to have rammed the 110, after all. The pain would have been only for an instant, and he would never have discovered this betrayal. Would not have had to feel this awful hurt that was like nothing he had ever experienced before.

Better to have died ignorant than to have experienced this. The pain felt as if it would cut him into two, as if it would kill him.

A despairing sigh, like a silent cry of unbearable sadness escaped his lips, and he closed his eyes as he mourned all he had lost this terrible day.

As if it would block out everything. But, it could not.

His life could not be the same ever again.

But despite everything, he loved her still. He would always love her, even though he knew that she could never possibly reciprocate his feelings.

He cursed himself for being such a fool.

He would not share her with anyone. If she would not be his alone, he would not be hers.

He would forget her.

Teddy could have her. She must care more for him anyway.

Fucking Teddy, the bloody bastard. I'm going to keep your picture, you dog, and if I ever meet you, I'm going to knock you out.

And, anyway, he was not truly alone, no matter how much he felt it was so.

For he still had Excalibur squadron, and his friends.

Those, at least, that had survived this terrible, terrible day.

And of course, there was still the fight up there, amongst the clouds. He would put his heart completely into his business. He had been trained for it, and he was a veteran now.

The Germans had brought to him this shocking day. In this afternoon of fire and blood and broken dreams, they had brought to an end all the hopes and aspirations that he had formed over the last few weeks.

They were responsible for taking her from him, they were responsible for shattering the dream he had been stupid enough to believe in.

He must repay them in kind. Return the favour they had done him.

There was so much pain, so very much, that there was more than enough for everyone to share.

And he would make sure that they shared it.

And at least she was alive. She may not love him, her heart may not belong to him, but she was alive.

And in the end, that was all that really mattered. Because he would always love her, no matter what.

Chapter 35

The devastation done to RAF Station Foxton that day, the 16th of August, had been severe.

By some incredible fluke, no bombs had fallen on the married quarters, and there was not a single injury amongst the civilian dependants.

Miracles still happened.

The same however, could not be said for the rest of the station.

The enemy bombers had planted a plentiful amount of explosive on the vital heart of the station, wrecking the guard barracks, the armoury, photo, parachute and radio sections, one of the squadron hangers, and both the repair and maintenance hangers.

Extensive damage had also been done to the watch, signals and meteorological offices, MT pool, and to the vital ops room and station headquarters.

Fortunately, however, the fuel dumps, and the ordnance depots had largely escaped damage. The loss of life, already dreadful, would have been even heavier.

The Wing Commander had been seriously injured on the ground, the gallant old fellow had been trying to get to his Gladiator, and now it was expected that he would not survive his wounds.

So much lost.

Despite the despair, individual acts of heroism shone through. By ground crews, members of the Army guard, and not least by the WAAFs of Foxton.

Nerves had broken at other stations, too. At Manston, on the 12th, hundreds of the station personnel had hidden for days in the catacomb-like caves running beneath the airfield.

Aircrews were forced to perform a lot of the vital tasks done by men now cowering in the underground natural shelters. The women of the WAAF silenced their critics forever with their epic courage in those dark August days.

To all intents and purposes, the Germans had removed the airfield from Fighter Command's list as an effective base of operations and fighter aerodrome for the two squadrons based there. It would be months before the damage done could be put right, and weeks before it could be used again as a fighter airfield.

With the damage done at Foxton, the two squadrons were, at least for the short term, homeless.

There would be no more operations from Foxton for the foreseeable future.

The Spitfires of 97 had escaped destruction (even though their ground crews had suffered), and although Excalibur squadron had suffered, it was still an effective fighting unit. It had lost six Hurricanes on the ground, with three pilots killed and two injured, although the acting MO had promised they would both be flying again within the week.

Billy, one leg in traction and an arm in plaster, had vowed from his hospital bed to be back in the air within a couple of days.

Rose had been shocked by the transformation overnight in his CO.

The normally unflappable Donald had developed a tic in his left eye, and was gaunt with grief at the loss of his pilots, the ground crews and the station personnel. It was something Rose could understand completely, though, for the face that stared back at him in the early light that morning from the mirror showed the same pale drawn features with the haunted eyes and down-turned lips.

Fighter Command, in their wisdom and need, sent 97 to Duxford, part of 12 Group, whilst Excalibur squadron was to be re-deployed to the small satellite airfield at Keeleigh.

It had been a civilian field, a Flying club in the 30's, and the facilities were woefully inadequate, but it was a functional site from which to fly and fight.

Corporal Fricker threw together a few items for each pilot, placed a grouchy Hermann into his cage, and drove to Keeleigh to begin the preparations and to set up amenities and accommodations for the pilots before they arrived.

Excalibur circled Foxton once in salute and farewell, the airfield a sorry sight now that it was no longer shrouded by smoke, even though not all the fires were out.

Donald led the surviving six Hurricanes of his squadron to the new field, whilst the remaining three pilots were sent off to collect new Hurricanes from Brooklands.

The ground crews, air defence and the essential support elements, with a dented but thankfully recovered Skinner, would come by road, once the necessary vehicles and spares could be scraped together.

With a bit of luck, there would be replacements sent to them soon. Until then, they had to make the best with what they had.

RAF Keeleigh matched the grim mood of the six pilots as they came into land. It was a large flat grass aerodrome, with a clutch of wooden buildings, something that looked like a concrete type pillbox (that was in actual fact a rudimentary watch office), a single large wooden hanger that suspiciously resembled a barn, and a windsock.

Beside the wooden 'barn,' a timber and canvas Bessonneau-type hanger had also been erected.

The first element of the support personnel had already arrived, and after the comforts of Foxton, it felt like being banished to Siberia.

Foxton had been home to them for so long, it was hard to accept this unfinished and bare place as their new one.

At the far end of the field, a crop of drab olive-green tents had sprung up, neatly laid out in four rows. It was like one of those black and white Times photographs of the '30s showing an army encampment on the North-West Frontier.

These would be their new accommodations, a far cry indeed from their previous lodgings. Amongst them were a single ambulance, a fire-tender, and some 15cwt trucks. No sign of any of the AEC refuelling bowsers, not yet.

After landing, they left their aircraft bunched together at the southern end of the field, near the hangers, partially hidden by hastily applied camouflage nets. It would be some time before the main body of 'erks' would arrive to tend to the fighters.

A small truck, with No1 Works Area (Field) written on the side, collected them and took them to the field kitchen and the new 'mess,' a long canvas tent that smelt of damp and mildew.

A trestle table had been set up inside, with a pair of tea-urns and plates of bread and jam were awaiting them. But there was little appetite in them, and they slumped down into the chairs in grim silence, lost in their own thoughts and memories.

After a while, he could stand it no longer, and Rose stood up again. He wanted to get back up there.

"Sir, when do we go on patrol?"

"We're going to have to wait for the supply train to catch up with us, Flash. I know we're rearmed, but we haven't the fuel for a proper patrol."

"Will you give me permission for a test-flight, then, sir?" he looked out through the tent flaps at the distant Hurricanes. "The tank's almost full, and as you said there's a full load of ammo."

Donald looked at him shrewdly. "You'll get another chance for a crack at the enemy soon enough, my lad." He closed his eyes, and sighed. "Be patient. There's going to be a hell of a lot more fighting before the month is out. More than enough for everyone. Besides, who knows, sector control may get on the blower for us. God knows they need every fighter that's available."

He rubbed his eyes wearily, lowered his voice. "She'll be alright. The matron was an old friend of my wife's. Just a matter of time. Be patient, Flash."

"Yes, sir. Thank you." Rose replied dully, looking longingly at the clutch of Hurricanes.

"I heard about you breaking up the low-level attack by those 110s. They would have made things a lot worse. Between you and me and the table leg, I believe there's a Mention for you on the cards. You did well, Flash. I know it's hard to believe right now but it could have been even worse."

"Thank you, sir." Could have been worse? How that was possible was difficult to imagine. Even the thought that he might receive a Mention in Dispatches did nothing to cheer Rose. It meant nothing. Nothing seemed to mean anything anymore. All there was now in his life was sorrow.

Donald watched him compassionately. "You've nothing to reproach yourself about, Flash. You did extremely well in a damnable situation. There's nothing any of us could have done. We all wish we could have, of course, but we couldn't."

He ran a hand through his hair, "At least we hurt them back. I know it doesn't help, but there you are. We all lost a lot of people who meant a lot to us. And we managed to get some of the sods."

"Yes sir." The words held no comfort.

He felt dead and cold inside, and he walked out into the daylight, but the bright sunlight did not warm him, and there was nowhere to go. He was trapped alone with this deep well of sadness and depression.

He could not get the image of Molly's tear-stained face out of his mind, the pain in those large brown eyes, those warm, beautiful eyes that had sparkled mischief, but had become deep pools of pain.

With Granny, he had visited the little country hospital, late in the night, but she had been unconscious the whole time, following the general anaesthetic given her for the surgery.

The doctor had warned that it was possible that she might also lose her foot. It was so badly broken by fragments of bomb casing. And they still had to determine the damage done by the shrapnel that had pierced her back. He had assured Roe that she would walk again, that any damage to the spine was temporary.

The most important thing was that she was alive. And with so much death in so small a time, her survival was a wonderful miracle.

Oh, Molly. I loved you so very much. Why did you have to love another? Dear, kind God, why can't she be mine? She's all I could have ever wanted. And now, she's badly hurt, and I could not even say goodbye before we left.

The nearby odour of manure did nothing to cheer him.

There was a low cough beside him, and he turned to see Cynk standing beside him. He had been so caught up in his thoughts; he had not even heard the Polish sergeant approach.

"I walk too, yes? With you?" he smiled widely, revealing gold-capped canine teeth and orange nicotine-stained incisors. His concern was obvious. Rose tried not to stare.

"No," said Rose, shortly. "I'd prefer to be alone, Sergeant."

Cynk ignored him. "Not be sad. I tell you about Poland, yes?"

"Are you deaf? I said no." Rose started to walk away.

Cynk fell in with him. "Come on, Flash, stop being such a sulky little shit, talk to me."

For God's sake! "Sergeant, I want to be alone! I don't want to know about Poland. Leave me alone, that's an order!" then he realised Cynk had spoken to him in perfect, unaccented, English!

The other gazed at him blandly, with wide open grey eyes, eyebrows raised. "In Poland, young man, I was a Major. They outrank Pilot Officers, you know. Even a sergeant in the RAF, however, deserves a little respect."

Rose shook his head in wonder, held up his hands apologetically. "I'm sorry, er, Sir. I shouldn't have shouted at you like that. I apologise. But...um...?"

Cynk smiled gently, "What you've seen so far was an act. I am Polish but I grew up in England, went to boarding school in Hampshire and I read History at Oxford. However, for the present, I prefer to remain a stolid Nazi-hating Pole with little English. I'm only interested in killing Nazis."

Still stunned by the revelation, Rose nodded ruefully, "Yes. I had noticed. You're pretty single-minded."

"If the authorities knew that I spoke good English they'd give me a squadron of Polish airmen to train and command. How can I kill Jerry if I'm trying to herd together a flock of bloodthirsty young Poles whenever I'm in the air? I'm not interested in being a nursemaid."

Rose shrugged wearily. He didn't have the will to argue anymore and he was more than a little intrigued by this revelation. He sat

461

down on the grass. "Oh. Yes, alright then, er, Major. Sir. Tell me. About Poland?"

"Where shall I begin? Let's see…Well, I was born in Szczecinek. Nice place, huge forests, glittering streams. Lots of pretty girls. A little bit like Scotland, just much nicer. The most beautiful place in the world. My father was both a Cavalry officer and diplomat. Still is, as it happens."

He pulled out a cheroot, lit it with a silver cigarette lighter.

Puffing heavily he tossed the lighter to Rose. Engraved on it was an owl inside a triangle, and beneath written '113 Eskadra-1 Pulk Lotniczy.'

Rose handed it back. "113 Eskadra…113 squadron. Your squadron?"

Cynk took a long drag from the cheroot. The evil odour of it made Rose's eyes water. It was even more overpowering than the cologne that the Pole seemed to douse himself with. He tried not to choke and Cynk grinned at Rose's expression.

"Yes." He thumped his chest, and Rose winced. "We belonged to the Brygada Poscigowa. The air defence Brigade for Warsaw."

"And you were the squadron commander?"

Cynk thrust out his chin pugnaciously, nodded. "Absolutely. I shot down five Nazi planes in my PZL P11c. we knocked down a fair number of the bastards before the government capitulated." His eyes clouded, "We should have kept right on fighting."

"In a PZL p.11c?" Rose spoke with new-found respect, seeing Cynk in a new light. He had already downed five Nazi planes in an obsolete aircraft!

The P.11c was a light, gull-winged aircraft with an open cockpit and fixed undercarriage. Once a cutting-edge design, by 1940, it was outclassed by the aircraft in the Luftwaffe's stable of aircraft.

"Three Heinkels and a pair of Stukas. Then, on the third day a

Messerscmitt raid strafed my squadron, blew up my P11c on the ground." He spat a glistening glob onto the grass. *"Ghwovvno."*

He took another long drag, and then rolled back his left shirt sleeve, to expose a smooth patch of shiny pink skin. "Missed me, the devils." Getting down on one knee, he pulled up his left trouser leg. There was a pink, dimpled area, where a bullet or piece of shrapnel had obviously passed through the soft part of his calf. "See?"

He stood up again, jammed the cheroot back into his month. Rose tried hard not to cough, wiped his eyes.

"Next time we meet, I'll kill more of the bastards."

Rose held out his hand. "We'll kill them together, Major."

Cynk grinned widely, his metal crowns gleaming dully, and took Rose's hand. "I look forward to it."

Rose sighed, looked towards their Hurricanes. "I wish we could start now."

"Your beautiful lady, Molly, tell me, is she OK?"

The mention of Molly made his heart clench painfully inside his ribcage. *God help me, I do love you so much. Molly, how I wish you really were mine.*

"Yes, Thank you, sir. I believe everything will be alright. She was hurt badly, but they said she'll make it. It'll all be alright in the end."

How I wish that were truly so, thought Rose.

"God willing." Strangely, an expression of sadness flooded across Cynk's face. "I had a very beautiful lady, too, once. Her name was Helena."

Carefully, Rose placed his hand on Cynk's shoulder. "Tell me about her. If you'd like?"

"Yes. I'd like to, very much. She took my heart." He reached under his Mae West. "We met in Cracow. When she was at medical school. Young and very, very beautiful. We were married the year she graduated."

He sighed, a long wistful sigh, "The most beautiful thing I saw in my life. She took my heart."

He pulled out his wallet, a battered brown leather thing, with the emblem of the Polish Air Force on it, and took out a photograph.

Rose took it from him. It was well thumbed, a little faded, but it showed a girl in her mid-twenties, high cheekbones, dark eyes and wavy fair hair piled high, one raised eyebrow and a faint smile. Cool and elegant.

He handed it back. "She's very beautiful, major. A real beauty. You are a very lucky man."

Cynk smiled sadly, looked down at the picture. "I was. Once. Not anymore. She died." He slid it carefully, lovingly, back into his wallet.

Silently, Rose cursed himself. Idiot! Wasn't thinking. "I'm sorry. I am such a fool. Forgive me, please?"

Cynk sniffed, spat again. "They killed her when they bombed Warsaw. Fucking shits. I think they don't care what they bomb or who they kill, the bastards. She was caring for the first casualties in her hospital when they bombed Warsaw. Mother was helping her." A long, drawn out sigh, "Both gone, now. That's why I won't stop until they're all dead…" He sighed again, patted his pocket gently.

"She took my heart," he said it again, almost as if he were speaking to himself, deep sadness darkening his voice.

"I'm very sorry, Major. Truly sorry." Rose felt uncomfortable. What could he say that could help? Rose was the lucky one. His girl was not dead.

"We'll make them pay, won't we, old chap?"

"We will." Cynk looked around, "Don't tell them, Harry. Let me stay with you chaps. I need to avenge them. I can't do it if they give me a squadron to train. Please keep my secret. I need to fight, more than anything, that's what I need."

Rose was ashamed. Even though she may love someone else, at least Molly was still alive. It was he who was lucky. It may hurt that she did not care for him, but at least he had not had to witness or experience the pain of her death.

He had not had to suffer that, like poor Cynk. Nevertheless, the thought of what he had lost still hurt him. She was not dead, yet she was lost to him nonetheless.

But she was alive.

The thought of operating from Keeleigh had made Rose feel dismal, he had missed Foxton, but now the satellite airfield did not seem so bad. At least he was still at home, still in England, not kicked out, like this poor devil. Cynk truly was far from home. Flying from a foreign land, whilst his own country lay beneath the heel of a brutal conqueror.

Cynk had real reason to feel despair, yet he fought on regardless, determined to get revenge on those who had hurt him so cruelly. No wonder the man lived to kill. He had a lot of revenge to take. It was all the Germans had left him with.

Rose was grateful to the man.

Cynk had made him realise that things were not as awful as they could be. He thought of her sweet face, and the sadness washed over him again. It still hurt. But with men like Cynk with him, he would never be alone.

And those were the things that really mattered.

He grabbed the Polish Sergeant's sleeve, indicated the mess tent.

"Come on, Major, let's go and have a nice, hot cup of tea."

"Yes. I'd prefer something a bit stronger, but tea will do nicely. My mouth's as dry as a bear's arse."

There was some desultory conversation between the pilots, and now Corporal Fricker had appeared and was waiting beside the urn of steaming tea, from which he deftly poured two mugs, passed one to each of them.

Cynk patted Rose's back, and made his way over to Donald.

As Cynk sat down, Fricker leaned closer to Rose. "Saw the sergeant get down on one knee, sir. Thought he was asking you to wed him. Seems a funny sorta bloke."

"Actually, Fricker, he's had a rough time of it, but he's a good fellow. Might seem a bit peculiar, but his heart's in the right place." He sipped carefully from the steaming mug, eyes on the Pole.

Fricker looked doubtful. "If you say so, Mr Rose, sir." He looked at Cynk again. The other pilots were trying to convince him not to sing one of the terribly sad, dirge-like songs of his homeland.

He watched Rose wander off curiously.

Bit peculiar? Bloody strange, more like. Fricker sniffed. Still, Sergeant Cynk was an overseas gentleman. That explained everything. They were different.

Not his fault, really. He sniffed.

He was foreign, after all, couldn't help that, could he?

He stirred a mug of tea for himself, with extra sugar, just as he liked it. What was it Mr Rose had called the sergeant? Major? What was that all about?

Wait until he told the lads. They'd be gobsmacked!

He sipped his tea moodily, and burnt his tongue.

Bloody war.

Chapter 36

Rose sat down on the camp bed gingerly, and although it creaked slightly, it did not collapse as he had feared it would.

No tent for him. The fears he had of living in a tent had proven groundless. There would be no experience like that awful childhood trip to the Isle of Wight and that field of cows.

The first morning he had awoken on the island to the sight of a cow looking down on him through the flap of the tent, and he had run in terror, clutching dew-filled shoes in one hand, cold wet cow turds squelching beneath his bare feet.

Instead, the pilots would be sharing rooms with each other in the main clubhouse. Rose was to share his room with Cynk. No distinction between officers and other ranks here. The pilots all flew and fought together, and now they messed together.

Their room, once the flying club's stockroom, was whitewashed, with plain walls and a neat wooden floor. They were at the end of the corridor, so the washroom was just opposite.

Cynk was trying to clean the little square window, but the dirt was impossible to shift. Tiring of his cleaning efforts, Cynk popped it open. He turned to Rose with a grin. "See?"

Rose gave him a thumbs up. "Lovely. Nice fresh air."

Thank goodness the window could be opened. The mustiness of years of misuse could not compete with the powerful scent the Pole wore. And if he lit one of those blessed cheroots in here, Rose would definitely need to don his respirator.

Either that, or suffer death from asphyxiation.

He smiled to himself. He could still joke about it, despite the pain that gnawed at his very soul.

Life goes on.

The sparseness of their furnishings somehow firmed Rose's resolve. No more comfort. Now it was time to concentrate on fighting, and killing.

The Germans were fighting a single-minded war. No quarter for women or children. Bombs could so easily have fallen on the married accommodation at Foxton. It looked as if the rules had been thrown out of the window for the duration.

They were fighting for centuries of tradition and culture, for so much that had gone before. And for what was yet to come.

The sight of so much, the things that had become his new home and new family smashed into shattered ruin had been like a cleansing fire, scouring and burning him with its pain. But it was a fire that did not destroy, instead it made him stronger, had hardened his mettle even further, burned away softness.

He knew now that it was likely that his death would be soon, and it would not be an easy or peaceful one. He knew it, and accepted it.

Cynk turned towards him. "Harry, shall I sing us a song? A good song?"

Bloody hell. That's all I need. "Er, no. Thank you, Major."

"Ah! Don't worry, I'll pick you a nice one." Cynk bowed. "And forget the Major nonsense; I'm still a Sergeant officially. My name is Stanislaw."

Rose stood and held out his hand. "How do you do, Stanislaw. As you know, they call me Flash. May I call you Stan, if that's not too cheeky?"

"Please do." Instead of taking the proffered hand, he crushed Rose into a crushing bear hug, and kissed him wetly on both cheeks. It was rather like being attacked by an enormous, scented, hairy dog. "Might as well do it the proper way. How d'you do?"

Something heavy banged against the door, and it swung open.

Granny stood there, red and sweating. "Which one of you hounds has nicked my blinkin' bed?"

He noticed Rose and Cynk in their embrace, eyed them warily. "I'm not disturbing anything, am I?"

Rose backed away from Cynk hurriedly. "Granny, thank God you're here! Didn't hear you fly in!"

Granny sniffed. "Christ! Have you had a tart or something in here?" he looked under the nearest camp-bed. "Smells like a bordello in Paris I used to visit!" he lifted the coarse blanket, "Are you in there. Natalie?"

Cynk looked confused, "Tart?"

Granny stamped across the wooden boards and threw himself onto Rose's bed. Amazingly, it did not collapse.

He sighed contentedly. "Bloody hell! I've just traipsed about fifty miles with my parachute. The petrol wallahs at Brooklands hadn't filled up our new kites properly, so we had to make a landing in a flippin' field somewhere over there." Granny waved vaguely towards the open window.

"Terrible place. Cows shitting all over the place. Farmer's wife looked about eighty, ugly as bollocks." He took off his Mae West. "What a benighted dump this is! Flash, my old son, I'm pooped. Think I'll snatch forty winks. Would you tell me when the bowsers get here? Have to collect my Hurribag later."

469

"Certainly, Granny." He hesitated. "That's my bed, you know, Granny."

"RHIP, chum."

"RHIP?"

"Rank hath its' privileges. It just so happens that the powers that be have made me up into a Flying Officer, and the Old Man has just asked me to take over as acting A-Flight commander. Just until Dingo re-joins us, though. Means I'm an acting Flight-Lieutenant, as well, I suppose. So a little bowing and scraping wouldn't come amiss, doncha' know."

He broke wind and sighed. "Apparently, they've also decided to make old Nosferatu here a Pilot Officer." He glared at Cynk and then shook his head sadly.

"The poor old duffers at the Air Ministry have finally gone completely bananas. So, you should be honoured to give me the bed. If I'm feeling well-disposed to you, I may let you put the new stripes onto my shoulder straps, so behave yourself."

Rose turned to Cynk, "Stan, this calls for a celebration. Granny just loves old songs, perhaps you could sing one for him, when I'm gone?"

"Yes!" Cynk bowed again. "How you do, Mr Smith. Welcome!"

Granny stared at him as if he had just fallen from the sky.

"Lord help us. What have you done to the mad bugger?" he breathed.

"You and I are going to teach Stan some English, Granny." Rose winked at Cynk.

Granny rolled his eyes. "God Almighty!" He reached down, and felt around in the small bag he had brought, finally producing a dark-green shot-glass bottle. "Nicked this from the admin office at Brooklands. Thought we could drink to the new place. I don't suppose you drink, then, do you?" the last question was addressed to Cynk.

Cynk nodded eagerly. "Yes, yes! Give me!"

"Thank goodness for small mercies," Granny glared at Rose, "At least I shan't have to spend my hours sharing a room with a weedy youth who can only sup milk."

The effort hurt, but Rose forced a grin onto his face, and he stuck up two fingers at Granny.

With a struggle, Smith sat up. "We'll drink to the Stationmaster, too. I heard that he died this morning. Poor old sod. Grand old chap he was."

He threw the bottle to Cynk, who caught it deftly, removed the cork and took a mouthful of the clear fluid in one smooth unbroken action.

Rose put his head in his hands, groaned to himself. If the contents in the bottle were what he thought it was, they were in for a lot of trouble and serious earache.

He thought longingly of his revolver. How does one prevent an inebriated Pole from singing songs of his homeland?

Chapter 37

It had been another fruitless day of patrols and missed opportunities, and to cap it all, miscalculation by a replacement controller had placed A-Flight into a position where they had ended up in a long stern-chase of a very fleet group of Junkers 88 bombers.

Just as they had been about to move into a favourable position, they had been bounced by a small tight formation of Bf109s, and the new pilot officer, Bracknell, had been shot down into the sea.

There had been no parachute.

Just one swift firing pass, swooping down on the little group of RAF fighters, and then the Germans had continued on to dive away, not even staying to tough it out, leaving behind them four surviving Hurricanes in disarray, and yet another dead RAF flyer.

Another young man dead, with nothing to show for it, nothing to redress the balance for that death.

Rose stared at the dented tin plate before him, the lump of corned beef before him sat sullenly in a cold and greasy gravy, surrounded by an entourage of hard peas and sliced tinned potatoes.

In the dim yellow light of the storm lanterns, it seemed defiant. Go on, it seemed to say, try and eat me. I promise you I shan't stay down. Once I get down there, I'll be coming straight back up.

He put down his fork, and looked up. In this battle of wills, the corned beef would win.

Even just looking at it made his stomach roil, filling his mouth with bitterness. It would not take much to make him vomit, even though there was so little in his stomach anyway.

I must have some more of those liver salts, he resolved, but even their efficacy seemed to have lessened against the liquid fire that burned at his innards.

Opposite him, Granny was stabbing at his meal unenthusiastically, fatigued.

Each time he poked his piece of corned beef, his fork would make a thin *screak* against the metal plate, like nails scraping offensively against a blackboard. Another spatter of gravy joined its contemporaries on Granny's tunic. Even he had lost his usual meal-time gusto. He would normally greet any food with enthusiasm, but this meal time was more of a battle, as their tiredness threatened to render them powerless against the tough meat served up by the Field kitchen.

Screak, screak.

Ffellowes opened one eye. "Must you make so much noise, old man? I'm trying to sleep."

"God!" blustered Granny gloomily, "this bloody thing must be older and tougher than me. I bet old Stuffy got the army to disinter their Boer war supplies." Rose tried to grin, but it seemed too much effort. Granny didn't even look up.

Screak, screak, went his fork, but the lump on his plate just slid around the plate in its puddle of gravy. The damned corned beef was hard.

Screak, screak, the sound ear-piercing in the quiet meal tent. Skinner, in his adopted capacity as mess waiter, flinched at the sound. No-one had the inclination or the strength to talk.

Denis was asleep before his plate, snoring gently, head bent as if in prayer, the plateful of bully beef untouched. His tie hung down in the gravy.

Granny caught Uncle's strained and baleful eye, and grinned infuriatingly at him. Rose shook his head wearily, as Granny resumed his assault on the meal. "I'm away to bed, Granny. I'm bushed."

"Okay chum. Do you want that?" he eyed Rose's hunk of corned beef.

"Have it if you want it, but don't come crying to me if you break a tooth."

"Ah!" Granny tipped the contents of Rose's plate into his. Just for a moment, there was a flash of his old enthusiasm.

"Good heavens, Granny," murmured Ffellowes disbelievingly. "You must have a tummy like a tin trunk!" His own plate was untouched.

Granny burped loudly. "It may be old. But it's still good for you, old boy. So eat up." He finally managed to separate a chunk from the mass, popped it into his mouth, and began to chew it gingerly.

Ffellowes spoke mildly, "When I was very small, my dear old Pa took me to the zoo, and I saw a great big dirty hairy cow-thing from the Highlands of Nepal having its lunch." He stared pointedly at Granny, "Wonder what made me think of that?"

Granny ignored the jibe, and smacked his lips. "You mustn't scoff. You don't know how lucky you are. When I was stationed on the Northwest Frontier back in '37, we used to have this bully beef roast thingy with spices and stuff. Bloody tasty but it'd sear the lining from your mouth and guaranteed to give you the screaming squits for days afterwards."

"Good grief," Rose laboriously got to his feet, arms and legs creaking. "If there's anything worse than listening to Stan sing, it's having to listen to Granny gibber on about the way it used to be in the good old days. I'm off. See you later, chaps. Night, night."

Granny watched his back retreating. "Poor wee lad. My stories are an education. He's the one who's missing out. Anyway, there we were every night, with boiled rice and that flippin' roast…"

Chapter 38

The early-morning haze had melted away under the harsh glare of the new sun, and the birds were singing in the far distance.

The mingled sounds of men, machinery and engines could mute their song, but could not dispel the simple joy they expressed.

Rose was slumped tiredly in one of the sagging deck chairs lined up inside the sad khaki affair that was the readiness tent. Beside him, the RNVR Yorkshireman, Sub-Lieutenant Haynes lay sleeping, his mouth ajar, a trickle of saliva gliding down his cheek. Were it not for the almost imperceptible rise and fall of his chest, he might well have been a corpse. His slack face was suddenly creased by a bad dream.

Poor bastard.

Straight off Swordfish and onto Hurris.

Hell of a transition. Poor bastard. We must be scraping the barrel.

Strangely, and fortunately, Rose's sleep was unmarred by nightmares.

When he slept, there was nothing. That is, of course when he could manage to sleep. How he wished he could sleep now, but it proved elusive. Despite his tiredness, he found it increasingly difficult to sleep.

It had been a week since the move from Foxton, but had felt like a month. Seven days of continuous flying, but always too late or too early to be part of the main action. There had been only one contact involving the squadron (such as it was). A short, confused and inconclusive tussle with a bunch of Bf109s east of Walton-on-Naze.

There had been no word from Molly, and he had been unable to trace her whereabouts. She had been sent to a specialist hospital for her surgery.

He still yearned for her, and her absence was like a festering tooth, lingering and aching and always there, in the background, whatever he was doing, wherever he was.

Rose's gaze was fixed on the tied back tent flap, still faintly wet with the moisture of a new day. Scant seconds earlier, he had watched with no little trepidation the shadow of some crawling beastie against the outside surface of the tent. It had obviously marked the passage of some creepy little thing out on a foraging expedition for its breakfast.

His level of apprehension had increased when the shadow had disappeared behind the folded back tent-flap. The thought that the spider or whatever it was may come into the tent was daunting to him. He supposed that it was childish that he should be scared of such a little creature, but he could not help himself.

He was as scared today of creepy-crawlies as he had been as a child.

And it had been a bloody large shadow on the tent-flap.

Normally, he would have got up and joined Granny and Cynk outside, but the flying of the last few days had left him feeling washed-out, and weak as a kitten.

Yet still sleep would not come.

So he sat there in the semi-darkness, idly watching the tent-flap, half-listening to Granny talking to the newly-commissioned Polish pilot, and wondering whether he should have taken out his pistol and taken a pot-shot at the beastie whilst it had still been visible, albeit as a shadow. But then again, with a bit of luck, perhaps it would be attracted by the moisture trail of Haynes' drool. Perhaps the sleeping pilot would do him a favour and swallow the little devil.

Somebody dropped a tool outside, and the clatter made his muscles tense and his stomach to spasm painfully. Haynes sat bolt-upright, eyes wide, like a marionette suddenly jerked into life.

Rose shook his head. "It's alright, Des. Just some silly sod outside."

Haynes licked his dried lips. "Blimey!" He reached for the cup of water by his feet, took a swallow of the tepid water. His hand shook and Rose looked away.

Six dented tin-cups had been tied together, and suspended with telephone wire outside the control-room. The sound of them being been bashed with a metal ladle to signal a scramble was a lot like the clatter he had just heard.

Rose sighed and looked at his watch (*oh Moll, how I need you*).

It was seven-thirty. Another half-hour, then they could go to half-hour readiness, and the tea would arrive. And breakfast.

His stomach contracted at the thought, and he swallowed away the burning acid that always seemed his constant daily companion, particularly at readiness. I must get something for my tummy, he thought for the umpteenth time.

A shadow blocked out the light and for an instant he thought the spider had come grabbing hideously for him. He almost called out.

But it was only Granny, his tin hat perched jauntily. He grinned amiably at Rose.

"You lazy hound!" There was forced jocularity in his voice. He had been trying to lessen the dark mood that had settled over Rose, although with little luck. "What are you doing in there? Get your bum out here, into the sunlight. Stan's threatening to sing a song to the boys. A mutiny is the last thing I need right now. Give us a hand? You talk to him and I'll knock the bugger out."

Rose waved a hand languidly. "Later, Granny. I'm just going to rest awhile. I'll be out in a few moments. OK?"

"Fair enough, chum." Granny stared at Haynes. "If you can bear to leave sleeping beauty, here."

Shaking his head sadly, Granny turned and left, but not before Rose saw a large black beetle-like thing perched on his shoulder.

Thanks, Granny. Hopefully, that's the creepy-crawly situation sorted out. Now all I need is another half-hour of peace and quiet.

But of course, it wasn't to be.

Exactly half an hour later, the four Hurricanes that formed the very much depleted A-Flight were climbing steeply above the glittering waters of the Thames estuary.

Granny had evolved a stepped up formation of two pairs, with Rose as the second element leader. Haynes was faithfully tucked close to his Hurricane.

Cynk saw them first, a solid mass of Heinkel 111 bombers at twelve thousand feet. There were about thirty of them, but to Rose they looked a hundred plus.

Their own small formation seemed to shrink further in size.

What the hell are we supposed to do against that?

But there were a few brown and green shapes already darting in amongst the large dark formation. Hurricanes from Rochford.

"OK, boys. The escort's busy elsewhere. Don't muck about, just get stuck in. Free-for-all. Yellow Two, stick with Yellow Leader, don't go swanning off."

Haynes. "Understood, Red Leader."

"Tally-Ho!"

That old familiar feeling again as he switched on the reflector sight and set the guns to 'fire.' That dryness of the mouth, innards contracting into a hard little ball, icy cold like the sweat that sprung from his pores.

They were still climbing, and Rose set the red aiming dot carefully in front of one of the bombers, one of the formation sub-leaders.

He fired, and the Colt-Brownings rattled their deadly tune for a two second burst.

That two second burst sent over two hundred and fifty rounds into a two feet diameter area two hundred feet in front of his nose.

The rounds raced ahead of his machine, a deadly cocktail of armour-piercing, ball and incendiary rounds, to strike fiercely against the port wing of the bomber, outboard of the engine.

Rose pressed rudder slightly, so that he could line up for a shot against another of the trailing aircraft. All the fear and sickness was forgotten, as he concentrated on fighting his aircraft, and staying alive.

Tracer zipped towards him from the machine guns in the glazed noses, but it was well off, no danger to him at all.

He fired again, his bullets (and Haynes's?) turning the cockpit of the second bomber into a shattered charnel house of blood and horror.

He did not even feel the hammering as bullets punched into the fuselage behind him.

The Heinkel reared upwards, exposing more of the pale blue underbelly, like a fish struggling at the end of a line, before stalling and falling off to one side. Its companions trying to keep away whilst maintaining position.

But Rose was already curving away, diving and turning for a beam attack on the rear of the formation.

"Yellow Leader to Yellow Two. Good shooting! We'll go back in again. Stick close."

No reply.

Rose craned around to stare at where Haynes had been just been seconds before.

His wingman was no longer there. He was all alone.

Shit! Where had Haynes got to? He must have been hit. Damn, damn, damn!

Cynk had already got one too, and was roaring gleefully over the R/T.

"Yellow Leader to Yellow Two, acknowledge." He grinned humourlessly behind the mask. Yellow Leader, if you please! That was a bloody laugh! He was the leader of a section that consisted of only one aircraft! Eyes swept across the sky, searching for Haynes, searching for enemy fighters.

He tried again. "Yellow Two, come in. Can you hear me? Acknowledge, please."

Still no reply.

No time to worry about Haynes. There were still no enemy fighters around; he should be able to get in at least one more good attack.

A bomber, slipping out of the formation, both engines on fire. Forget him. He won't get far; go for those who can still hit their target, whatever it is. No sign of the second bomber he had hit with Haynes. Had it gone down? Must have, they'd hit it hard. There was just so much confusion, it was impossible to tell.

Bugger it.

There were still enough undamaged bombers to chase. More than enough to go around.

You've done your bit, muttered that treacherous little voice. You've damaged two, probably downed one of them. It's enough. Live to fight another day. Go home, nobody could blame you.

And then there was no more time for thinking as he came up against the rear of the enemy formation.

481

A pair of Hurricanes were already harrying one of the bombers, which was in a very sorry state, and the enemy gunners did not seem aware of him as he curved in on a quarter-astern attack, coming in from slightly underneath.

You've done enough. But more of them need to die for Foxton.

The dive had given him extra speed, and he attacked the rearmost bomber of an echelon of three that formed the last vic on the port side of the formation.

The bomber ballooned in his sight as he raced towards it, and then he had jammed down his thumb again, smoke trails leaping from his machine-guns, flinging bullets ahead of the bomber in a converging course. He touched rudder again, and this time the bullets splattered against the bloated shape of the Heinkel's fuselage.

He was sweating, and he wiped his goggles irritably, licked dry lips.

He placed a long five-second burst into the enemy machine, closing the range from two hundred and fifty down to one hundred yards. He waited for return fire, but the gunner had disappeared, and there was none.

He looped upwards above the damaged Heinkel, tracer whipping around him from the enemy formation, twisted into a half-roll before diving down again for a second shorter burst.

Still, there was no return fire from 'his' bomber.

Instead, streams of tracer from three other enemy bombers converged on his machine.

There was a crash as a bullet smashed against one of the panels of his canopy, before careening off back into the blue. Then more rounds smashed into his machine.

It sounded and felt as if he had flown into a sleet storm, and he quickly banged down on the rudder, skidding her again, as more rounds punched through his starboard wing, dragging her out of the line of fire, almost careening into another lagging bomber. He fought with the controls, and he had an impression of a great dark shape looming suddenly, and the staring eyes in the tiny white pinched face of its terrified gunner, before it had disappeared beneath.

His heart was pounding madly, his temples throbbing from the effects of the sudden manoeuvre, but he felt like laughing madly at the horrified expression he had seen.

That poor gunner had thought his time had come when the Hurricane had swooped over him, like some harbinger of doom. The two aircraft must have missed each other by scant inches. He had not even thought to fire his machine gun at Rose.

Check the mirror; pull back on the stick, two Hurricanes diving down from above. Sweep around in a great parabola to approach the ragged formation of bombers.

Reinforcements.

That was more than enough. Time to go home. He had to survive so that he could kill again.

He looked again at the Hurricanes.

Big black crosses, edged in white, on the Hurricanes, because they weren't bloody Hurricanes after all, but Messerschmitts!

"Fuck!" He mumbled, and keyed the microphone, pulling around, "Excalibur Yellow Leader calling all aircraft. Bandits! Descending, high from the east. "

His kite was still flying smoothly, nothing untoward, so hopefully any damage done by the gunners wasn't critical.

Lucky, very lucky. Again.

But for how long?

He tightened his turn, eyes flicking from the enemy fighters to all around and back again, so that he could cut across and beneath their path of flight. They had not yet noticed him, and were continuing their downwards, to come up behind the RAF fighters worrying the bombers.

He closed quickly, held his breath, sighted on the second of the two Bf109s. Quick glance, lightning quick, in the mirror, one last sighting adjustment, check deflection, and press the button.

Brrrrrr! Brrrrrr! The eight machine-guns spat out the .303 rounds and punched viciously into the Messerschmitt. It was as if the enemy fighter had slammed into a brick wall. There were flashes along the length of the machine, a great gout of yellow-white flame vomited out, and the engine cowling and canopy disintegrated under the onslaught. It rolled over and entered a shallow inverted dive.

It continued along for a few seconds, before dropping steeply away below, a guttering firebrand leaving a thick black trail of hot oily smoke behind it. One wing folded back, broke off and spiralled slowly away from the fuselage.

Rose grinned, a terrible and strained grin of victory and blood lust and revenge, a drawn grin of sharp teeth and hunger.

That was one more.

Another of the bastards who would not sing the bloody 'Horst Wessel' ever again! Lots more left to kill, though.

The other Bf109 had immediately tipped over and dived away, white smoke streaming from its exhausts. Of the bombers, there was no sign. They had disappeared in that strange way that was so common in combat.

One moment the sky was filled with whirling aircraft, the next just an empty, pale blue bowl.

There was a sudden crash, a staccato bang, shocking explosions, all rolled into one, the sour stink of burning metal filled the cockpit, and the Hurricane lurched viciously, the stick wrenched momentarily from his shocked hands.

Apply coarse rudder and grab for the stick desperately. Try to get her back under control.

Damn it! He'd been bloody bounced!

No time to hang around, bang the stick hard into the right leg, and then yank it backward, hard back into his stomach. He was mildly surprised when it didn't break or come away in his hands.

The Hurricane rolled over and nosed down vertically (good girl!), screaming downwards, out of the stream of enemy cannon and machine-gun fire.

He cursed. Whilst he'd been watching the first pair, a second pair of fighters must have dived down on him. He had allowed himself to be duped like someone straight out of training.

Down, down, he plunged, slipstream whistling hollowly through the bullet holes in his machine. Streamers of fabric fluttered wildly, and one ripped away to disappear. He had been hit umpteen times by fire, the fuselage and wings riddled, but the Merlin was still singing sweetly, and apart from a slight vibration, she wasn't complaining at the rough treatment she had received.

Thank God, dear old Sydney Camm had designed such a solid, durable kite. The enemy could keep hitting her and she just kept on flying.

Bless you, Sydney, old chap. The Hurricane was a real marvel.

Then, suddenly he was in cloud, safe in the soft white embrace, and he pulled gently out of the near-vertical dive, The sudden roll, dive and pull-out had left him feeling light-headed and faint, and he blinked rapidly to clear his clouding vision.

He pulled her slowly into a series of gentle, weaving, irregular turns, just in case they had followed him down.

His body had turned into a block of ice, and his limbs were trembling uncontrollably.

That had been too close. He had come within a hair's breadth of becoming a victory symbol on the rudder of a Messerschmitt. Indeed, the way he had suddenly whirled away, the attacker may well think he had inflicted mortal damage on Rose.

Perhaps they had not decided to follow him down? His mouth was dry as dust, and he swallowed painfully.

Control column forward, pop out of the base of the cloud, lush green and brown quilt spread out below, the flatness marred by slight folds.

Rose dropped one wing, pulled into a gentle turn. Glance all around, squint into the mirror,

Nothing. No planes, no smoke, no flames. So peaceful, whilst up above men died or were maimed horribly.

Thank God. The enemy had stayed up there.

They hadn't followed him down, and he was blessedly alone.

Ahead and in the distance he noticed the familiar wedge of an airfield. At his angle of approach, its camouflage of painted hedges and fields was ineffective.

The needle on the engine temperature gauge was beginning to rise, even though the throatiness of his Merlin was as healthy as always.

Tiredness washed over him like a grey wave, and he decided to make use of the fortuitous appearance of the 'drome, and land.

As he drew closer, he could see the tiny shapes of two Wellingtons in black livery outside a hanger.

So. A Bomber Command Airfield. Thank goodness for that.

Bomber airfields had lovely long runways.

Wheels down, and with a reassuring thump, they locked into the 'down' position.

Next, he selected 'flaps down,' but this time, only one flap came down. Hastily, he selected 'flaps-up' again. He groaned inwardly. Without flaps, his approach speed was too high.

Smoke had begun to stream from the engine, and he could smell the burning metal odour again.

Shit! He switched off the engine, the propeller windmilling, and the smell and smoke cleared.

He could see now that he was going to overshoot, but to go around meant certain death. There was no choice but to get her down. God grant there weren't any trigger-happy gunners down there, or he was dead for sure.

Gentle adjustments to line up with one of those wonderfully long runways.

Side-slip, and again, lose height, God! Airspeed still too high! Push her down. A red flare arced up from the watch tower but he ignored it, all his concentration on the runway as it rose up towards him.

Easy, easy now…

There was a screech of rubber and he bounced back up into the air, once, twice, three times, before he finally thumped back down and stayed down with an aching creak of the undercarriage.

But, amazingly, it held, and he raced along the runway for what seemed like miles before the tail-wheel finally kissed concrete for good and the Hurricane was finally, properly, down.

With judicious use of the control surfaces, his nose filled with the odour of burning rubber, he finally brought her to a stop.

Still in one piece, by God!

Rose shook his head dazedly, eyelids heavy, energy suddenly drained from his body. So very tired.

That had been a flight and a half, and no mistake!

He closed his eyes, let out his breath in a long sigh, and leaned back his head tiredly onto the seat-rest.

A dodgy landing again with a knackered Merlin, the second time in one month, getting to be a habit. The relief coursed through him like cold water, and reaction set in.

He patted the spade-grip with a shaking hand. Next time, old girl, we'll go our separate ways. I'm going to try my 'chute out. Don't think my heart can take another unpowered landing.

But, we got down safely (thank you), and that's what matters.

Thank God.

Still Alive.

Should get out, in case the kite begins to burn...

He must have dozed for a moment, for the next thing he knew, an officer with rather a lot of rings on his sleeve, and scrambled egg on his cap, was standing on his wing and glaring down at him.

"Don't they teach you what a red flare means, young man?"

"I'm sorry, sir. My engine was finished, and I had to put her down quick. Your field was a godsend." He shook his head, his voice slow and cracked, "I'm really very sorry."

The Group Captain looked at him; saw the waxy paleness of Rose's drawn face, the tremor in his hands, and his own face suddenly crinkled into a smile. "Never mind, lad." His eyes narrowed shrewdly, "You're safe, now. Well done. Are you hurt?"

"No, thank you. Sir, just a bit bushed."

A small crowd had gathered around the ragged Hurricane, and Rose noticed a couple of pretty WAAFs on bicycles watching curiously.

The sight of them made his heart contract painfully. Oh God, Molly. Where are you? Are you thinking about me or about...him?

The grizzled senior officer saw the glance at the girls, but not the pain, and his smile widened.

"Hm. You must be all right. Come along. I'll take you to the Mess." His eyes took in Rose's strained and lined features, the tired,

red eyes. "I daresay you could do with a mug of tea, or perhaps something a little bit stronger?"

Rose licked his sore lips. "A cuppa would be nice, sir. Nothing I'd like better."

"That's settled then. Come along, now. My chaps will look after your kite." He patted the impressive line of swastikas beneath the cockpit. "She's a veteran, too, I see."

Rose undid his straps, clambered painfully from the cockpit. The Group Captain sprightly hopped onto the ground and offered him a helping hand.

"Had a busy morning?" He raised his eyebrows mildly, "You can tell me about it over the tea, eh?"

Rose nodded. In the distance a thin column of dark smoke rose into the sky. "Got a Bf109, lost my wingman, winged a pair of Heinkels, too, I think."

The Group Captain clapped his hands. "Capital, my dear fellow!"

Chapter 39

After his forced-landing at the bomber airfield earlier, Rose had contacted the squadron, and Granny had flown down in the early afternoon, with the two-seat Magister, to pick him up from the bomber station.

Rose's battered Hurricane would be checked over later by a team from Brooklands before being returned by road on one of those huge RAF flatbed road transporters.

In the battle, A-Flight had downed two Heinkels, and two Messerschmitts (one of them Rose's) confirmed, with four Heinkels as probables, and another three damaged.

But the story was not one-sided, for the Luftwaffe had managed to get a few telling blows in, too.

Haynes had been shot down and killed in the fight that morning, and two other Hurricanes had returned with battle-damage, one to be declared a total loss.

With Rose's Hurricane temporarily out of action and still at the bomber field, Excalibur was left with an operational strength only four airworthy aircraft in total.

Donald had declared the squadron non-effective for a minimum of forty-eight hours, whilst new aeroplanes and replacements were sent for.

It was very likely now that they would be declared B-category on 11 Groups' inventory of operational squadrons.

Donald had seen the strain on their lined, prematurely aged faces, faces that mirrored his own, and decided to give them each a two-day pass.

A short respite was exactly what they needed. Each of the pilots was worth his weight in gold, but he knew they were dangerously tired, pushed beyond rational limits, and they desperately needed a break.

If they carried on like this, the squadron would cease to exist in very short order.

And so, the squadron had been granted a much-needed break by Group.

Cynk had decided to visit compatriot friends of his flying fighters from Hornchurch, whilst Granny decided it was time to take Rose out on the town. As he had explained, "I'm responsible for your social development, Flash, my old lad." He still wondered at Rose's change in behaviour.

He'd winked salaciously, and flapped his denture with his tongue.

It turned out that he'd arranged female company for them both, but as he'd explained, "Need to see you develop properly, now you seem to have lost interest in Molly. I dunno why, but at least I can take you out."

Rose, feeling self-righteous, had given him an old-fashioned look and said, "I couldn't possibly walk out with that sort of girl." And then, to himself, "I want a girl who's interested in me alone."

Granny had been outraged, "That sort of girl? What sort of girl, you worm? The type who does it for money? Tarts? Is that what you think? What do you think I am, bloody hard up? I don't pay for it, damn it!"

He'd shaken his head in indignation. "You bloody cheeky cove! Girls do it with me for love, you know!" the outrage had evaporated, and he'd smiled serenely. "They can't help themselves. They see me and their drawers fall down."

They had met up with Granny's current girlfriend of the moment, a slim blonde named Jane (just like the one in the paper - surprise!) in Piccadilly in the late afternoon.

Waiting with her was a friend, an attractive and quiet redhead called Anna. Her gentle eyes had lit up when she saw Rose, and she had not let go of his arm once.

It had been strangely comforting to have her beside him, and in his longing for Molly, Rose felt ashamed to be with another girl, although when he thought of Teddy, he didn't feel that bad.

Granny had explained that Jane and Anna were both nurses at St Thomas' hospital.

After a delightful cream tea on the embankment, they had seen a rather risqué show, and then Granny had treated them to an exquisite meal at Humphrey's.

Whilst there, emboldened by Anna's interest and her physical closeness, and still recovering from the events of the morning, he finally began to unwind.

During the meal at Humphreys, Rose had added half a glass of wine to the large brandy he had been given by the bomber boys. By the end of the meal he was feeling pleasantly relaxed.

So, lonely and heartbroken, he overcame his shyness, and welcomed Anna's interest, drinking in the attention she gave him, trying to fill the aching hole in his heart.

She had a habit of touching his hand lightly as she talked, and the gentle contact somehow seemed to ease the terrible emptiness of his being, as if the light pressure acted to draw off the dark shadow of pain.

But despite everything, his heart still cried out for Molly, and he wished he were with her, rather than this warm, sweet and pretty girl.

The evening had progressed gently, and he had grudgingly and hesitantly accepted her closeness and presence, although a part of him still felt ashamed at his response.

After the wine, the shyness and inhibitions he had felt when they had first met seemed to evaporate like the early-morning mists, leaving in its place a strange feeling of recklessness, mixed with an aching, despairing hunger for company.

How he wished to be held in those smooth and gentle arms once again. To forget that awful unforgiving world of endless, nauseous terror.

He wanted to forget everything.

The four of them had finally stumbled, arm-in-arm, back to Jane's basement flat at ten o'clock. A slowly cycling Air Raid Warden had almost hit Granny, and had disappeared into the darkness disgustedly mumbling about 'drunken fools.'

And now he was here, bleeding and befuddled after missing the last step of the staircase and falling against the dustbins, leaning awkwardly against the doorjamb of a basement flat in Soho, pleasantly tipsy and covered with vegetable peelings.

With a girl.

A lovely, attentive, and quiet girl, at that.

A girl that the boys would have described as 'very tasty.'

Just as they had once described Molly.

A fresh wave of pain and loneliness washed over him.

After much confusion and fumbling, the flat's front door was finally opened and they piled, laughing, like a rugger scrum into the small flat.

In the darkness, a clock ticked loudly, and then his foot had caught on something on the floor, and he fell down.

493

Granny promptly fell on top of him, squawking a cloud of alcoholic fumes into his face.

There was the fearful gap of his missing central incisors because he had left his denture out. As he had explained, "Best to keep 'em out. Lost the last one in the loo when I'd had a few, and anyway, if I haven't got 'em in, the beer goes down faster."

The impact of Granny's ten stone lanky frame made Rose grunt.

"Are you all right?" asked Anna from the blackness, then in outrage, "Oh no! Jane! How many times have I told you to pick your undies off the floor? What are these two going to think?"

Granny belched. "Don't mind me, girls, leave 'em on the floor! Best place for 'em! Save me peeling 'em off!" he cackled, picking up something lacy from the floor and examining it closely.

Rose looked up surreptitiously, from his position on the floor, as he tried peering up the girls' skirts. But it was tantalisingly too dark to catch sight of anything interesting.

Jane giggled. "You know me, Smithy! When you're here that's where they stay!"

Granny chortled, "Just the way I like it," bathing the gasping Rose with another noxious cloud of fumes. This must be what it was like to experience a mustard gas attack, he thought grimly as he turned his face away from Granny.

"Is the blackout curtain in place, Annie? Daren't switch on the light, yet. That old windbag upstairs might report us again."

"It's alright; I've tucked it in place, Jane."

There was a click, and the hall was dimly lit up, the naked bulb casting a dingy yellow light over them, like dishwater over a grimy plate.

Something tiny gazed in surprise at Rose not three inches from his nose, before skittering rapidly away into one of the dark recesses where the pool of grubby light did not venture.

As Granny and Rose shakily got to their feet, the girls stepped into the tiny kitchenette.

The clink of cups, splashing water into the little sink.

"Cup of tea?" asked Jane.

"Make yourself comfortable, Flash." Anna was all consideration, "I'll get some warm water and a cloth. We'll need to bathe your cut hand, and for goodness sake, get your tunic off. I'll give it a wipe. I daresay we should be able to clean you up a bit." He sensed the smile in her voice, "Have you right as rain in a tick! You sure you're OK? I fell down the steps once and sprained my ankle. Hurt something chronic, I can tell you!"

Granny dug Rose in the ribs, "Cor! She's keen," he whispered, before picking up a wrinkled and laddered pair of stockings that were hanging from the dented radiator beside him.

"Don't worry about the tea, Cinders," he shrieked gleefully, "I've got something here that you've got to try on! It ain't made of crystal glass, but if it fits, princess, I've got something else that'll fit you, too!"

They sat together, so close that their knees touched. The contact was simultaneously disconcerting and delightful to Rose.

Granny and Jane had disappeared into her room, and he was uncomfortably aware of their subdued mumbling interspersed with peals of laughter.

Soon, all conversation ceased, and something began to creak rhythmically in the room. Uncomfortably, he looked around the little front room, unable to meet Anna's eyes.

He was very embarrassed by the knowledge of what was happening next door, and that they were shamelessly carrying on so close to them.

It was made worse by the quiet presence of the girl, and the occasional coy glance she gave him.

Her head was bent down, as she gently washed the cut on his hand. Her red hair, shorter than Molly's and cut into a bob, fell forward and hid her face from him. The cigarette she had lit glowed softly in the cracked saucer beside her.

"She sounds really nice. I can understand why she means so much to you."

He realised that he had been talking about Molly all evening, and apologised.

"I'm sorry, Anna. I've not been good company, you must have found the evening deathly boring. I've just been prattling on like an idiot. What a horrendous bore I am!"

She looked up, her grey eyes meeting his, pupils huge in the dimness, and despite his discomfort, he found himself returning her gaze boldly.

"Don't be sorry, Flash. I think it's wonderful that you love someone so much. Shows you're not a selfish so and so," not like so many others, she thought.

She smiled, carefully, looked back down. "I'm sorry about her being hurt, but I bet you'll see her again, soon, when she's better. I'm sure of it. You're really nice, she'll not let you go, you know."

You don't know the half of it, he thought glumly.

Anna pulled deeply on the cigarette before replacing it back on the saucer.

"She's a lucky girl. You really love her a lot. I think it's wonderful to care for someone so much." Smoke escaped from the corner of her lips as she slowly released it.

She rummaged in the biscuit tin that passed for a 'first aid box', then placed a clean white gauze dressing on the cut, expertly winding a strap of bandage around it, and fixed it with a safety pin. "There we are, good as new."

She took his hand, "You just need a rest, maybe a little sleep, and you'll be ready for everything again."

Daringly, he kissed her hand, and released it.

But she did not let go of his hand.

"Thank you, Anna. You're an angel." The warm smell of her filled his nostrils and he suddenly felt a wave of giddiness mixed with nervousness wash over him. He looked down, uncomfortably conscious of the erection in his trousers.

The creaking from next door reached a crescendo, something thumped the wall, and his cheeks burned as Jane cried out.

Bloody hell!

He could not meet the girl's eyes.

"You're very welcome. It's what I do." She noticed his discomfort and laid a hand on his cheek.

Jane cried out again. Good grief.

"Look at me?" he looked back at her, to meet her gaze, her warm, eyes direct and serious. "I think you're lovely, Flash."

He looked at her in befuddlement. Beneath the dressing, his cut was stinging, and the light-headedness and confusion he still felt threatened to overwhelm him, "Um, thanks…"

She touched his lips with the back of her hand, looked deep into his eyes, and he could see her longing, feel the hunger coming from her, like the hot glow from the radiator, it seemed to sink deep into him, and he could feel himself responding. His skin started to tingle, and his eyes prickle.

"Will you hold me, please?" she asked.

His throat was dry and the blood was pounding in his temples.

Uncomfortably, he put an arm around her.

She could feel his beating heart, could sense his mounting excitement, but also his shyness.

"I don't want any promises from you, Flash, I like you and I just want to be with you tonight, and that's all. I think we both need to be with somebody tonight."

Suddenly, she was nestling hard against him, and automatically he put both his arms around her.

She was trembling (or was it him?) from emotion or need, he could not say which, and her soft breasts and nipples were pressing uncompromisingly against his chest.

The slender body pushing against him brought a treacherous electric tingle to his groin, and he could feel his manhood swell further, knew that she must feel it, and he knew he should let go of her, but he could not.

The world seemed to spin, and his throat was raw, his face burning as if with a fever.

She pressed herself harder against him, and he bent down, to lay his cheek against her shining hair.

Then she looked up and suddenly her lips were on his, and he was kissing her deeply, her moist tongue working hungrily in his mouth, her soft lips pressed firmly against his.

Her hips pushing insistently up against his, and she swung one leg smoothly over him so that her pubis pressed hard against his.

Strangely, he felt no sense of betrayal or guilt. Had Molly done anything less to him?

For a week, he had only seen death and pain, had seen the girl he loved so very desperately been hurt, been hurt so cruelly himself, had seen old friends disappear in the blink of an eye, to be replaced by other youngsters, who disappeared at an even faster frequency.

His life had shrunk to a cold and vicious world of sleeplessness and pain and fear. It was a world deeply lacking in softness and warmth and love.

And now, his starved body rebelled against his mind's commands, and all resistance drained tiredly from him.

She pulled away from him; dress rucked up to her waist, smooth slim thighs and white knickers, her cheeks pink, eyes shining brightly, hair awry. She made no effort to cover herself.

"Flash, I want you to love me. It's been so long." She was gasping with emotion now, breath hot and fragrant against his cheek, "Please love me? I need it so very much…"

He could only nod dumbly, his world filled by her warm grey eyes and moist pink lips, the fragrance of linen and perfume.

She gently took his hand, taking care with his dressing, and led him to her room on the far side of the flat. He couldn't take his eyes off her exposed buttocks.

Behind them Granny laughed at something Jane murmured.

Rose followed Anna through a doorway in the hall and into her darkened room. A single ring heater cast a warm orange light against the furniture in a small but neat and ordered bedroom. There was a framed photograph of a soldier on the dresser, but it didn't seem to matter anymore. To either of them.

She pushed him gently onto the bed and as it creaked slightly beneath him, she lifted the dress deftly over her head, and dropped it to the floor before climbing on to straddle him. She leaned forward to kiss him, and his hands moved as if independent of his control to slide down her hips to slip beneath the waistband of her knickers and onto her smooth rounded buttocks.

Her tongue pushed greedily against his lips, her pelvis pushing hard against his, her pubis pressing against his genitals pleasurably.

Anna's questing mouth opened his, and clamped against it greedily, her tongue flicking against his, wet and hungry.

The blood was pounding in his temples as his fingers kneaded her buttocks hungrily, and then she was pulling the clothes from him until he lay there naked and faintly disbelieving in this girl's bed, as she teasingly removed her underclothes slowly before him, her eyes on him and a gentle smile on her lips...

His eyes wondered at the sight of her slender body, pale and limned by the light from the heater, small breasts topped with hard erect nipples, flat stomach, and smooth slim thighs framing the wispy triangular tuft of reddish-brown hair. In the poor light, her skin had the sheen of smooth burnished copper, her hair glowing bronze.

And then she was straddling him once more, but now there was no barrier between them, and she firmly grasped his rigid penis with one gentle hand to guide it into her.

She was already wet, oh, so wet and he slid smoothly into the warm tight moistness of her with little difficulty as she pushed herself down onto him with a low moan of pleasure.

Involuntarily, Rose gasped in wonder, and then was lost in her as their bodies began to move rhythmically together.

Rose stared fondly at the snoring figure of Granny, sprawling comfortably on the back seat of the early morning bus as it slowly trundled along the lanes that led to their new field. Dawn was already colouring the sky beyond the smudged windows.

He felt completely shattered, but for the first time in many days, the pain that had become so much a part of him had dulled into a deadened ache, the sharp edge blunted.

The warm euphoria of the incredible experiences he had discovered with Anna still held him in their afterglow, and he fancied he could still feel the heat and tightness of her upon his manhood. He had not managed to wash after that last time, and the dried stickiness of his crotch was another, very pleasant, reminder of her.

It had still been dark when they had roused to catch the early morning post train from King's Cross. He still ached all over, even in places he had never even felt before.

The two girls had stood on their doorstep in nightgowns tightly drawn around them, bidding them farewell with tears and kisses, and Anna had hugged him tightly, whispering in his ear, "If you'd like to see me again, call me? I'd love it. Very much. You've given me the strength to carry on."

And then she had smiled, eyes bright with unspilled tears, and said again, "Your Molly's a really lucky girl. If she's got any sense, and I'm sure she has, she'll be back for you soon. If you were mine, I'd not let you go."

She'd sniffed and wiped her eyes, "Take care of yourself, Flash; don't let the bastards get you." Another smile, sadder now, "Don't forget the address, now. It'd be nice to see you again. Even if you just need a friend. And something a lot more if you'd like…"

One last tender kiss, unlike the hungry, all-consuming ones of scant minutes before, when he had lain on top of her that last time, still deep within her, her crossed ankles locking him into position.

This kiss instead delicate, gentle, "You are really special, you know. Take care, sweetheart. God bless."

And then they were in the cab, heading for the station, the slim girl with red-gold hair a dear and wonderful memory. The best thing after a horrendous week of agony and strain.

It had been surprising at how close they had become in just a few hours of meeting one another.

He smiled fondly to himself, remembering the series of desperate bouts of lovemaking interspersed with short naps that had made the wee night hours flash by.

After the first time, sated and spent, they had lain beside one another, two people who had found comfort and some peace from the realities of their lives in the intimacy of one another.

They had caressed, kissed, made love, and spoken of their lives, and Rose had found her a sympathetic and attentive listener as he told her of his fears and the pain he suffered.

He loosened his tie, re-arranged the lapels of his tunic. He fancied that he could still smell her fragrance on his freshly washed clothes, a mixture of the lightness of her perfume, blending smoothly with the heady musk of her own scent. The memory of her vulva lingered pleasantly on his lips, and he remembered with pleasure the taste and softness of it.

Rose was worn out, and he settled back, putting his feet up on the seat facing him, and lowering the cap visor over his eyes.

She had told him of her life as a nurse, of the dreadful injuries that she had to treat on the inhabitants of the City and East London every day during and after the raids. A tale of suffering that had made him thank his lucky stars that at least he could fight back and not just have to sit and take it like Anna and Jane had to.

She had made him appreciate that although it may not immediately seem so, he had much to be grateful for.

Anna was a wonderful and sweet person, a healer of sorts, and he was grateful for all that she had given to him and all that she had shared with him.

It had done something for him. He was not sure what, yet, but the cold, cutting, bleak despair that was a constant companion to him since that last attack on Foxton, was somehow gone, leaving him suddenly feeling lighter.

He still felt Molly's absence, but the keenness and depth of it on his heart and mind had been blunted by the experience he had shared with Anna.

The time he had spent with the young nurse, and the special bond that had formed between them, was something that would always be important to him, something that he would never forget.

He owed her a great debt in the way she had changed him, and for the healing her words and caresses had miraculously performed, and he knew now that he had come to love her too, but differently.

Granny was right, nurses could soothe the cruellest hurt, and the two nights with Anna had given him the thing he had most needed. She had blunted the edge. But she was not Molly.

He still loved Molly, and missed her so very, very much; but now at least he could live with the pain.

From across the aisle, Granny opened one eye to peer at his friend. Rose was snoring softly, and his shoulders rocked gently with the movement of the bus.

Granny smiled affectionately, for he had noticed the difference in Rose, and knew his young friend was no longer the same despairing and angry young man he had been the previous day.

Anna, bless her soft and caring heart, had done all that he had hoped for. She had been exactly the medicine Rose had needed.

His friend was back. He just had to make sure he kept him alive, so that one day he could re-unite the young lovers once more.

God willing, of course.

He sighed, and tipped his cap over his eyes once more.

Bloody war.

Chapter 40

Rose collapsed into the armchair they had 'liberated' from the nearby alehouse with a sigh.

"Hello, Flash. How was your trip to London?" Startled, but too tired to jump, Rose opened his eyes and looked around the poorly-lit room.

A match flared and Stan lit a cigar, the shadows cast by the sudden bright light giving him a demonic sneer.

"Crikey! You startled me, Stan," In his weariness. He had not even been aware of the other's presence. "I'm glad you got back OK. I heard that you'd borrowed a kite at Hornchurch and scrambled with them?"

"Sorry, Flash," appearing anything but, Cynk puffed foul-smelling smoke at him, his eyes glinting hard.

Rose could sense something not right, and he leaned forward, his back muscles creaking painfully. He really must go for a hot bath.

"Something's wrong, Stan. What is it? Are you all right? You're not hurt?"

"Oh, Flash. I'm tired of it. Of all of it. The whole stinking mess. I want to see my home again. I miss it."

"Crumbs, chum. Never heard you like this before. What's up?" Rose sighed again. "We're all worn out, I think. I'm so tired that I don't think I'll be able to get out of this chair."

"We keep killing them, but they keep coming, the bastards."

"Yes. I know, Stan, but we'll beat them in the end. You see if I'm not right." Who're you trying to kid? The squadron was still reeling from the continuous loss of pilots that were its lifeblood.

Apart from Rose and Granny, the only pilots still on the squadron from the early July days were Dingo and Donald. With the loss of Haynes two days ago, the squadron was only ten pilots strong, four of those new and without any combat experience whatsoever. How much longer could they survive?

"I just want to see my home, go fishing in our lake." Rose had never seen the big Pole like this and he was anxious to soothe him.

"This is your home, too, Stan. We're one big happy family."

"Dear, good Flash. I'm not so sure. I flew with some of my chums at Hornchurch, as you know; they found me a kite. We intercepted thirty Dorniers over Dungeness, and I got two of them, but I got hit in the engine, and so I had to take to my parachute."

He puffed ferociously on the cigar, "I was lucky, got picked up by the army so I was back at the 'drome for lunch."

"Thank Goodness," said Rose warmly.

Cynk continued as if Rose hadn't spoken.

"One of my friends had been shot down too, but he didn't make it. Oh, he managed to get out OK, but he landed in a field. Poor bastard couldn't speak much English." Cynk looked at Rose with glistening eyes, "Do you want to know what happened?"

Rose nodded, dreading what might come next, scared to speak.

"He came down safely on a farm. The farm workers couldn't understand a word of what he said, the thick fuckers, thought he was German spy in RAF uniform, so they stoned him and strung him up. He'd just shot down a Dornier defending Britain, and they battered him then strung him up from the nearest tree."

"No, Stan, no, surely…"

Cynk puffed moodily on his cigar, the red tip glowing furiously.

"Oh yes. I saw him there with my own eyes. We'd gone to pick him up. They'd even stolen his things as mementoes. If the police weren't there I think I'd have killed some Englishmen. What do you think of that? Executed by the people you've saved. What a laugh, eh?" His voice wavered and he pursed his lips.

"Dear God, Stan, I'm so sorry…"

"Don't be. That bastard Hitler started all of this, in the end it's his fault. They're the ones occupying Poland right now, so they're the ones who should have to pay. The Doc wanted me to take some pills and take some time off, but where can I go? Can't go home, can I? All I want to do is kill Huns. So I told him to go fuck himself and if he grounded me I'd chop that lousy excuse for a head from his silly shoulders, and spit the pills down his neck. He didn't say anything after that. Seemed a bit shocked, actually."

Rose thought of the young doctor assigned to the squadron, a medical student just six months earlier. "Yes, I can see that that might have made him reconsider his advice, Stan."

Rose felt like weeping at the infinite sadness in Cynk's voice. "Can I buy you a beer, Stan?"

"No, thank you, Flash. I just want to have a bit of time on my own. When this is all over, those of us still around will properly remember the ones who don't make it." He coughed a sob, pinched the bridge of his nose. "Flash, if I'm not one of the lucky ones, will you take my things?"

Oh Lord. What use did he have for a dozen pint size bottles of eau de cologne (although it seemed to work miracles when it came to attracting the opposite sex), or all those boxes of malodorous cheroots or cigars?

Cynk extinguished his cigar and smiled sadly at Rose. "Don't worry Flash, I'll be fine. Just give me a bit of time, eh? And If I don't make it, will you go and see my Dad? He's on Sikorsky's staff. Tell him that I love him, and that I'm sorry I didn't say it often enough."

"Of course, my dear chap." Rose got up stiffly and made his way out, stopping briefly for a moment to put his hand awkwardly on Cynk's shoulder.

The big Pole patted it silently.

Rose squeezed his shoulder, and left, leaving his friend in the shadowed darkness, with his memories and the spirits of the dead for company.

Chapter 41

"Scramble, SQUADRON SCRAMBLE!"

"Beachy Head, 18,000; thirty plus bandits approaching from south-east."

Startled into wakefulness, neck stiff, eyes feeling sticky and gritty, so very tired. Fighting to climb out of the deckchair liberated from Southend beach.

The reports of starter cartridges, Bang! Bang! Bang! Clouds of acrid blue smoke billowing outwards.

Bell clanging and haring across the grass, chipped porcelain mug lying on its side, forgotten, the sweet tea already soaking into the discarded book. What page? Couldn't even remember what he'd been reading.

Pilots fanning out as they headed for their Hurricanes, parachute arranged and ready on the tail, pull it on, crawl onto the wing and heaved into the cockpit.

"Thanks, lads…"

Engine turning nicely, backdraught blowing the cap from his head.

Forget it, they'll recover it for him. Pick it up when you get back. If you get back.

Straps tight and snug, pulling the helmet on, shrug into the gloves, rapid check of the controls, tanks full, trim neutral, gyro set; oxygen and R/T attached.

Mouth dry and heart thudding, tug the Mae West down. Turn to check canopy runners, sight of a tubby armourer puffing after his cap across the windswept grass. Must collect it later.

Check position, chocks back. Squirm into a comfortable position, eyes flicking around the cockpit.

Get the aeroplane into position and then racing across the grass, the green blur speeding fast and then falling away as the Hurricane bites into the air, pull the lever and clunk of undercarriage, switch on the R/T and the kites pull together more closely.

Passing through 10,000 feet already, seven shabby Hurricanes, climbing hard, Merlin's screaming and metal gleaming bright as it caught the sun, hauling themselves to altitude.

Rose cleared his throat, one eye on Denis and the other on the sky around them. Would they get to the bandits before they'd bombed, would they get to them at all?

The constant attacks had pushed the detection and communications network almost to breaking, covered in brick dust and lines broken, they continued to provide the vital information to vector the defenders into position, albeit with some delay.

"Spanner Leader, hullo, Spanner Leader. Steer one-six-five, Angels 18 and above. Buster!"

Trails of smoke belched from the exhaust ports. Seven Hurricanes, turning gently.

"Spanner Leader, received and understood." Couldn't see them yet, "Spanner Red and Green sections, bandits above, eleven o'clock, straight through them, pick your targets, fellas."

God, Denis had good eyes, a small cloud of Heinkels, sunlight bright as it danced on curved Perspex bubbles. No fighter escorts?

No sign of enemy fighters at all, just these fat bumbling bombers, could it be that they were alone?

Rose sucked in a deep breath, oxygen sweet in his lungs, gun-button to 'fire', reflector sight check, bright enough - yes.

The Hurricanes were still climbing as the two-tiered German formation loomed and he was firing, tracer flickering back at him from the nose gunners of the bombers. He couldn't see where his bullets went, but he closed his eyes for a second as the Heinkel he had chosen became huge in his sights, its brothers smeared blurs on either side. When there was no collision he opened his eyes, and let out his breath, before him the sky was empty.

A clatter of hits pebble-like against his port wing reminded him that the rear gunners of the Heinkels were on the ball and dangerous, and he pushed the nose down, full throttle, trying to evade the threads of bullets that were reaching back for him. Where had the others gone?

Another Hurricane, Granny, twisting and turning as he evaded the return fire from the bombers, but a thin stream of white vapour showed that he'd not run the gauntlet unscathed.

"Spanner Red Leader," Granny, trailing out of the fight, "Engine caught a packet, it's playing a bit rough, heading for home, best of luck lads…"

He was at his weakest, and Rose longed to escort him home but he knew that the bombers were his priority. Granny would have to look after himself for the time being.

"He's done for, Jerry bastard…" Denis's voice, laconic, steady amongst the frenzied chatter in his headphones.

Hard turn to starboard, get back into the action, head swivelling and eyes staring in all directions.

Then he saw the second wave of bombers, around twenty of them, except…they weren't bombers at all, but the absent escorts, twin-engined Me110s, caught napping or just late at the rendezvous and unable to deflect the initial stabbing attack by the Hurricanes, but now storming in hungry for vengeance.

"Spanner Green Leader, bandits, 110s, coming in twelve o'clock…"

Forget about the bombers, got to try and break up the 110s to give the other Hurricanes a few more seconds against the Heinkels. Rose lined up on the leading rotte of twin-engine enemy fighters.

A smaller cloud of shapes appeared behind the Me110s, Dear God, more of them?

And then the flare of an exploding German motor, thick smoke tracing a line, twisting raggedly to port.

Not enemy fighters but another Hurricane outfit, a flight of six machines that bounced the approaching German escorts, turning them from a neat formation into a startled mass of aircraft turning and diving, another of their number already falling, and the blot of its demise curving downwards like a smudged black question mark against the lighter sky.

Rose forgot about the Me110s, turned back after the bombers.

A Heinkel was out of formation, and he closed on it from behind, slowly approaching the enemy bomber from dead astern.

Just as he was about to give the Heinkel an experimental squirt, there was a loud Bang! And the Hurricane staggered sickeningly. Rose struggled to regain control as his attacker, a Me110, passed low. Almost directly over his head. He cringed, but there was no crash of impact.

Where're the others, he wondered as he dragged the Hurricane into a skidding, wallowing turn, just as a second Me110 slid past, a dark shape too fast for even a snapshot, and he kept turning, glad to have survived any return fire from the second twin-tailed machine.

Time to get out of it…

* * *

511

"Harry, you silly bloody clot, what in the name of all that that's holy were you doing up there?" Granny was incandescent with rage, "you almost rammed that fucking Heinkel up there! You may want to the easy way out of this, but we can't afford to lose the kite!"

He looked searchingly at Rose. "Are you OK, matey? What the hell were you thinking?"

Rose stared tight-lipped at Granny for a moment, then sighed, this was his dearest friend, and Granny had become closer than a brother. He owed him an explanation for the way he'd behaved.

"Does it really matter, whether I live or die, Granny? I mean, what difference do I make, anyway? I thought there was something to live for when I was with Molly, but…"

"You silly sod! How do you think she'll feel if you get killed? What happened between the two of you? You were crazy for her, but as soon as she gets hurt, you change completely!" he shook his head in mystification, "What happened? You never stopped talking about her before, now you don't even mention her name. She doesn't deserve to be treated like that!"

Rose reached for his pocket, "Oh, you think so? Well what do you think of this?" he pulled out the photograph and brandished it at Smith.

Granny took it from him and looked at it. "Well? What about it, you silly tart?"

"Are you stupid, Granny, look at it!" A single tear dribbled down his cheek. "There was somebody else! I thought she loved me, but she had this other blighter in her life."

Granny smacked him hard in the chest with the picture, and Rose almost fell.

He was stunned at the intense fury on his friend's face.

"Oh my God, you stupid little shit…" Granny clenched his hands and turned away. "For fuck's sake. Why did you keep this to yourself? You should have spoken to me! That's a picture of Molly's kid brother! Pilot Officer Edward Digby, flies medium bombers!"

"Oh…" suddenly Rose felt very small and incredibly, unbelievably stupid.

Then it dawned on him, there was no one else after all! Her feelings for him had been genuine! Everything that had passed between them before that terrible raid on Foxton had been real, after all! All his suspicions, all his anger, all the grief, all misplaced.

Shocked by the revelation, with legs turned to jelly, he could not stand, and he sat down, hard, on the grass.

"Oh Granny, I thought she felt nothing for me." and then, "What if she finds out about Anna?" he stared at the picture, "Oh my God. Oh my God!"

"She'll never find out, Flash, and you mustn't tell her, OK? Why should she find out? It's up to you now to make her happy. You have to find her and look after her. But to do that, you're going to have to survive this. Don't throw yourself away like some suicidal idiot. You needed Anna, and I reckon she needed you. It was a nice time you both enjoyed. After everything, you needed a spot of fun, and I think that poor girl needed it too. Forget about it. It was just a bit of fun. You love Molly don't you? Despite what you thought?"

"Of course I do, Granny. She means everything to me. Everything."

"Well then, least said, soonest mended, eh? When we get a spot of leave again, we'll find her, OK?" He winked at Rose, "Unless you fancy another trip down to London with me? I know Anna would love to see you again." he leered lewdly.

Cynk walked up to them, his face stained and a cheroot hanging from his mouth. Granny glared at him and coughed pointedly.

The Pole smiled beatifically at them both and blew smoke in

Granny's face. "Got another today, Flash. Blew it up, killed 'em all. How did you do? Any luck?"

It hadn't taken Granny long to realise that Cynk wasn't the simple Pole that he professed to be, and he'd promised to keep silent so that they could continue to fly together. They'd discussed the notion that Cynk might be a Nazi spy using a Polish identity as subterfuge, but the Pole's clear delight at killing large numbers of enemy aircrew was genuine. He could not be a Nazi spy. Not in a month of Sundays.

Cynk noticed the photo in Rose's hand.

"Pretty boy, Flash. Not your usual type, though. I thought you liked girls?" he looked around, spat out a lump of tobacco, narrowly missing Granny's flying boots.

"I need some tea and an iced bun. Where's the NAAFI wagon? Is the cheeky little blonde one with the tits on today?"

Chapter 42

The letter from Molly came the very next day.

My darling Harry,

I pray with all my heart that you are safe and well.

I miss you.

I am much better now. I can sit up comfortably and I went for a little walk this morning. The foot doesn't hurt as much as it used to.

The doctors say that I'm healing quite nicely. They gave me the piece of the shrapnel that got me, and I've kept it. What is it they say about keeping your enemies close?

The rumourmongers are saying that I'm to receive the George Cross, although what for, I can't think. I still can't remember much of that dreadful day. But I do remember you crying, and it broke my heart to see it.

My sweetest, I have to tell you something very important. You are a beautiful man, and one day, with God's sweet mercy, you will be a father, and what a wonderful father you'll be!

However, the little shiny piece of metal here beside me on

the desk hurt me quite badly, and the surgeon believes that the
damage done means that it is quite likely that I will never be
a mother. I can never be the mother of your children, though I
would give the world to be.

And so, you must forget me, my darling love, as I shall try
to forget you.

You will always be in my heart and in my prayers. May
God always keep you safe. Keep Genevieve close always,
promise me?

Bless you, my precious, wonderful man. I'll always love you.
Goodbye.
Molly xxx

Oh Molly, I'll never forget you, he vowed, clutching the piece of paper in his hand as he watched, through tearful eyes, Granny and Cynk tussling on the ground for a newspaper, scattered shreds of paper around them.

I'll find you, my sweetest beloved girl. No matter where you go, I'll find you.

Forget you? How can I?

Without you, I am nothing, I am incomplete. Nothing can replace you, and I'll not rest in this life until I find you.

And when I do, I'll never let you go again.

Ever.

Chapter 43 – Prologue Reprise

Death was close... he could feel it.

Quartering the vivid sky, exactly as Granny had taught him to, an endless eternity of just a few months ago, rapidly yet carefully, Rose searched.

Eyes strained, squinting against the light.

His eyes flicking from one quarter to another, not lingering for even a full second; it was not long before he caught sight of the little group of tiny dark specks in the brightness, tracking across the nose of his aircraft.

He glanced quickly to the Hurricane flying alongside, piloted by young Sergeant Morton, tucked close into his port quarter.

"Sparrow Red leader to Sparrow Red Two, bandits at ten o'clock, we'll give 'em a nasty nip on the arse."

God! He sounded so confident, as if he really knew what he was doing!

"Give the tail end Charlie one quick burst, then tuck in tight, keep 'em peeled and no heroics, over," he licked dry lips.

Say it.

"If I buy it, lad, keep turning, get low and get the hell out of it, they'll not have fuel to play with, OK? No heroics."

"Sparrow Red Two to Sparrow Red Leader, received and understood, out." Calm, thoughtful with a quiet voice.

A smooth round eager face, bright brown eyes, looked about ten. Good lad. But if it all went tits up, he might be dead within minutes.

It won't happen. Not while I'm alive, he thought grimly.

"Sparrow Red Leader to Baseplate, four bandits in sight, am attacking, over."

The cool voice of the young WAAF, miles away, "Baseplate to Sparrow Red Leader, understood. Good luck and good hunting." What does she look like, he wondered, and what is she thinking?

Two against four, rotten odds. The same bloody story all through the summer. Always outnumbered, the poor bastards.

He turned gently to starboard, staying below the height of the enemy aircraft, and taking care to keep the channel behind him, to (hopefully) merge into the sunlit and glittering expanse of water behind.

Any glint of light on Perspex or other surfaces would (hopefully) be missed, mistaken for the golden light dancing and shimmering on the wave tops.

The gentle turn guided the nose of his Hurricane into an approach from below and into a five o'clock position on a loosely arranged quartet of faster light-grey, sleek Bf109s.

Luckily (?) the enemy fighters were flying at a leisurely pace, otherwise Rose and Morton would never have managed to close the range.

Four, or were there more, waiting to spring a trap?

He was sweating, nerves crawling as he waited for the enemy to react at any moment, but incredibly, there was no response to their approach.

Don't muff this up, he thought to himself.

Rose had already set his guns to 'fire', and his thumb rested lightly on the button.

With young Morton keeping a keen look out around them, Rose was able to concentrate carefully on the rapid approach, although he continued to glance in his rearview mirror and check the clear blue around them, whilst selecting the number three aircraft in the enemy formation as his target.

He licked dry lips once more, "Sparrow Red Leader to Red Two, second pair, I'll Take the number three. You take number four, but keep 'em peeled. This could be a trap."

The Rotte of four enemy aircraft bobbed lightly above and before them, thin, almost invisible, trails of grey exhaust streaming behind, gleaming blunt noses pointed purposefully for France, looking forward to a glass of wine and a cigar, the arrogant bastards.

Again, check the airspace all around, eyes straining in the aching brightness, he swallowed painfully, wishing for a cup of tea and searching for those enemy silhouettes that would be part of the trap that spelt instant death, despite Morton's continued vigilance as his wingman.

All clear, no signs of a trap.

In this high cerulean arena the hunter and the hunted regularly exchanged roles.

The buggers must be asleep, confident in their self-perceived aerial superiority.

The two Hurricanes were now behind and below the fast moving Bf109s.

The curving line of approach had brought them together perfectly, despite the higher speed of the Messerschmitt's.

Incredibly, they hadn't been sighted during the approach, and now the range was close enough to fire worth a damn.

Better make it count, just going to get the one free shot.

A last glance at the pale undersides and dark dappled flanks of the bandits, quick check on deflection, press the trigger – fingers crossed!

As soon as he saw the casings cascading back from Rose's Hurricane, Morton opened fire on his target.

Rose's aim was good, and 'his' Bf109 flew straight through his burst, but, his only reward was a panel of metal detaching lazily from one wing and a single puff of smoke. The enemy aircraft he was targeting serenely sailed through the tight spray of rounds, outwardly unscathed.

Damn it all!

His heart was hammering inside him so painfully that he thought he would have a heart attack. He lined up again, brow furrowed in concentration, eyes flicking behind and above, finger mashing down savagely for another short burst.

Morton, however, had better fortune, and his bullets splashed the underside of the German fighter and chewed the tail plane of the fourth enemy machine into ruin.

As pieces of the tail were ripped away, the smoking Bf109 wobbled unsteadily and then began to skid sideways out of formation, dropping away, beginning to flat spin, cartwheeling out of control.

You jammy bastard!

Incredibly, Morton had scored, one down confirmed, three to go.

At last thick smoke poured from their exhausts, the leading pair of Bf109s increased speed to climb rapidly away.

Morton gave them a hopeful burst but without result as the range widened. Thankfully, his success did not entice him into breaking formation to chase the enemy fighters. Faithfully, his Hurricane remained tucked in close to Rose.

Bollocks, thought Rose savagely, edgily lining up on the third Messerschmitt again. It hadn't altered course (the bastard must be asleep!), and he squeezed the trigger again.

This time the enemy machine began to smoke and the Bf109 began to roll, to dive and turn away, but, the young Leutnant from Bremen was unlucky and inexperienced, and he turned his aircraft straight into the path of Rose's guns.

Puffs of smoke and glittering flashes splattered along the stricken German fighter.

Rose's bursts splattered messily across the side of the German fighter, tearing ruin into the enemy machine as it passed before him.

The Bf109 shuddered beneath this third onslaught, first the propeller blades and then the Big Daimler-Benz engine ripping free of the fuselage, a big chunk of metal whirling dangerously away, the side of the fighter seeming to collapse beneath the onslaught.

A ribbon of flame, instantly thickening, surged from the ruined fuel tanks to engulf the fuselage, which dropped straight downwards, but the pilot was already dead, killed instantly in that devastating third burst from Rose's machine-guns, schoolboy dreams of glory turned to blaze and devastation.

A thick black plume of smoke behind marked the vertical fall of his victory, whilst Morton's, 'kill' augured into a freshly ploughed field far below.

But there was no time for looking at the tumbling, disintegrating enemy.

Already Rose was searching for the other pair of Bf109s – Damn it! Where the hell were the bastards? One minute they were there, and then just so much empty sky, stained by the pyres of their two victims.

Unconsciously, he touched the little pink bear in his tunic pocket. They'd been lucky, he knew, incredibly lucky, but now there would be the reckoning.

"Sparrow Red Leader to Sparrow Red Two, I can't see the leading pair of Jerries, d'you see the blighters, over?" he craned his neck around to check behind.

"Sparrow Red Two to Sparrow Red Leader, sorry, I lost sight of them, sir." Morton said with some embarrassment.

Probably watching his first victory go down, Rose thought crossly. But then, it was hard to blame him.

It was so hard to stay focussed after that first kill, the urge to watch the vanquished fall so very strong, but it was those few seconds of inattention that killed. He would have to give the boy an ear bashing once they'd got back safe and sound.

If they got back safe and sound.

He desperately searched the sky for any sign of the German fighters, gently rocking his fighter from side to side, his heart thumping painfully in his chest, throat like dust.

"Sparrow Red Leader to Sparrow Red Two, OK, keep looking out for those bandits, and bloody well done on your Jerry, over."

"Sparrow Red Two to Sparrow Red Leader, Received, thanks sir, bet they're not all as easy as that!"

"Sparrow Red Leader to Sparrow Red Two, dead right chum! Keep your peepers open, over."

Morton had opened the distance between them, but remained close.

Rose was sweating copiously beneath his oxygen mask, and he desperately wanted to scratch his cheek, "Sparrow Red Leader to Base Plate, scratch two Jerries, D'you have any more trade for us, over?"

"Well done, Sparrow Red Leader. Please stand by." Voice still calm, but she sounded pleased. Had she lost someone, did the fires for revenge burn in her heart?

Nothing to see, just empty sky, Where are the buggers?

Dear God, please let them be high tailing it for the French coast...

"BREAK! BREAK!" Morton's desperate scream of warning was like a sharp knife slicing through his innards and he instinctively hauled his Hurricane into a straining starboard turn, tight, tighter, muscles straining and his face set in a grimace, vision greying.

They'd almost been killed because he'd allowed them to get bounced!

'THUMP-UMP-UMP!'

Three strikes crashing close together, merging into almost one bowel-weakening sound, and he fought to control the machine momentarily as three shells smashed through the machine guns in his Hurricane's port wing, punching through the other side, thankfully without immediate apparent catastrophic structural damage to the wing.

At least it didn't fall off as he continued his hard turn outwards.

And then the tracer was whipping away below him as he out turned the plummeting pair of Bf109s. The wing might fall off. But if he didn't get out of the way, he was done for anyway.

Morton's Hurricane had broken away to port and now he too was turning tightly, Perspex flashing, as the shark-like enemy fighters zoomed through the airspace the Hurricanes had occupied scant seconds before, battering him by the closeness of their passage.

His heart was hammering and his muscles ached, vision greying.

Thank God for young Morton.

The Bf109s had dropped away, but were climbing up and away again, fast as lightning, already turning to line up for another slashing pass.

Where the fuck was Morton? He searched desperately, ease back, turn to port. Neck twisting painfully.

Oh. Closing rapidly from port.

The Germans would love to split them apart, but Morton was closing the distance again, was reforming with him.

"Sparrow Red Leader to Sparrow Red Two, fire when you see the whites of their eyes."

"Sparrow Red Two to Sparrow Red Leader," the boy was panting hard, and his voice was strained, "yes, sir!"

The enemy were two dark dots now, racing from below towards them nose-to-nose, tracer and cannon fire already reaching out towards them, smoke trails twirling upwards.

Rose cowered behind the deceptively comforting protection of his Merlin engine.

He pressed the gun button again and his guns roared a final time, and the Hurricane shuddered around him.

A Bf109 loomed huge before him for a heart stopping instant, a dark streaking blur, was that smoke…?

And then there was a neck-wrenching blow, and suddenly the Hurricane staggered nauseatingly in mid-air, and was flung over and was falling. The stick flopped uselessly in his gloved hands.

Time slowed, through the top of his canopy he saw with shocked eyes his propeller, tips bent sideways, and lazily turning end over end, curve slowly away and disappear out of his field of vision.

The fight was over.

Time to go.

Rose reached against for the quick release lever for the canopy, fighting the forces that gripped him. With an effort he grasped the lever, and pulled hard.

It didn't shift as he heaved on it.

He tried again, but no luck.

Fuck.

There was another bang and a juddering as his falling Hurricane was raked again. The instrumental panel shattered, and vibration in the tumbling ruin of his Hurricane worsened.

He was about to bang the canopy with his elbows when something smacked his leg to one side, knee cap cracking painfully against the side of the cockpit.

There was a dull 'whump', and suddenly flames, painfully bright, were licking around the edges of the cockpit. He could smell his aircraft burning, and he desperately reached again to dislodge his canopy. He was gasping now, unable to speak, eyes wide behind his goggles, muscles straining against the sides of the canopy, but still it wouldn't shift on its runners.

The world outside began to spin as the weakened wing broke in half, ground and sky exchanging places with a sickening rapidity, the sun flashing on-off-on-off in his eyes.

It was becoming increasingly harder to move his arms, and detritus from the floor of the cockpit whirled around him.

Got to get out of here...

He tried again to grab the sides of the cockpit, fighting the forces that held him in his seat, whilst around him ribbons and droplets of blood, dust, dirt and grass danced and looped and spun around him.

Shining a brilliant scarlet in the vortex, his life-blood flicking to splash against him and the inside of the cockpit, against the Perspex, and still he couldn't reach the canopy with his gloved hands.

Instead he reached for the bump in his flying jacket that was the little bear. All that was left to him.

The inside of the cockpit was like an oven now, and the rising heat was unbelievable, whilst flame continued to lick back from the ruined Merlin engine, darkening the Perspex above him.

I'm going to die, he realised. I'm going to die.

It's my turn today.

He closed his eyes, holding hard to the useless control stick.

525

The R/T was silent now, no Morton, no calm WAAF. Nobody, and Morton was on his own now, poor lad.

He was surprised that it didn't seem to matter anymore. No regrets, he'd lived by the sword, and now he would die that way. It had been good to love the girl, and at least death would take away the pain of her loss.

The spin pushed him hard against his seat.

At last, Lady Luck had turned her back on him.

He could feel the darkness gathering as his consciousness slipped away.

No chance to see Molly, no chance to tell her how much he loved her, no chance to tell her how much he missed her, no chance to say goodbye.

He thought of her, wondered if she would care when she heard of his death.

Of course she would.

He realised that he was crying, and opened his eyes.

Blood splattered across his goggles.

Suddenly, a white flash.

Piercing, shocking, silent, and the world finally turned black.

Epilogue

A light, cold rain was falling, but the RAF flyer was as stolid and unmoving as the gravestone before which he stood.

Eyes closed and head bowed, the bitter icy droplets speckled the exposed nape of his neck above his silk scarf like beads of crystal.

They had been standing there for some time now, and he could sense the restlessness of his companion, although she remained as silent and still as he.

The man who lay in the grave before them had been an important part of both their lives, but the airman with the stripes of an RAF Squadron Leader on his greatcoat knew her thoughts were elsewhere.

Still he stood, honouring the dead, but the tears would not come.

It was October now, and the German assaults had turned into a night bombing campaign, and the scrambles each day were becoming fewer.

The Battle was over.

With so much pain and death, tears should have soaked his cheeks, yet they would not come, just the uncaring rain that ran down his face, and the smell of wet grass and fresh turned earth filling his nostrils.

She sneezed beside him, and he knew it was over. Their time here was at an end, and it was time to go.

He reached out to the pale gravestone, touched it gently with his fingertips for a long moment. "Cheerio, mate. God bless."

He turned away, knew that she was following him as he strode through the tree lined path.

He stopped just once, at the gates, looked back once to whisper, "You'll never be apart again, together forever. Just as you wished."

Sadness, deep and black and forlorn.

Yet still no tears.

The gates creaked closed behind them, and then there was just the rain and the sighing of the wind and the silence of the stones beneath the leaden grey skies.

The girl placed the china teacup carefully beside him, yet still tea slopped into the saucer. She smiled brightly, but the bandages still covering his eyes prevented him from seeing it.

"There you are, milk and two sugars, just the way you like it. Would you like some biscuits with it, Harry?"

"Some custard creams, if you have them?" Anything but those bloody rock cakes.

She tapped one incisor with a fingernail. Still felt a touch tender. She knew better than to try another of *those* cakes.

"No custard creams, but we've got some crumbly digestives, more than a bit crumbled, though, I'm afraid, some coconut macaroons, rich tea biscuits, and, um, there're still some of Matron's rock cakes?" she sounded hopeful.

Not likely, love, not if I want to keep my teeth. "No, thanks, Iris. Just the tea will be fine."

"I tell you what. Let me check if there are any in Professor Owen's

528

tin, OK? Bet the old sweetie's got some hidden away. Be back in a jiffy." she brushed an invisible speck of lint from the foot of his bed and bustled out.

He shifted in the armchair set beside the open French doors, careful not to upset the cup and saucer. His feet rested on his slippers, and he wiggled his toes leisurely in the late afternoon sunlight.

The shrapnel wound in his left calf didn't sting any more, but it still ached dully.

He wished he could look out onto the gardens, but the eye specialist, Professor Owen had been firm. "No, Harry, the bandages are to stay on for at least another three to four days. We must ensure that your poor eyes have enough time to recover from the flash they were exposed to. Don't worry; I'm sure the war can wait. Be patient."

He heard the door swing open and he turned his head, "That was fast, any luck?

"You silly boy, I'm always lucky. Totty just falls at my feet, can't help it, just the way God made me. You're an ugly little bastard, so you'll not understand."

Rose stood, a huge smile on his face. "Granny, you old dog!" the teacup wobbled dangerously, but stayed in the saucer. Smith hugged him, a sudden welcome bouquet of tobacco, rain and machine oil in Rose's nostrils, and then stepped back.

He looked carefully at his young friend, noted the softening of the facial lines Rose had developed over the last few weeks, the bandages over his eyes. Rose would have been touched by the fatherly tenderness in Granny's eyes.

"It's Squadron Leader Old Dog, if you please, brat." Smith's smile matched Rose's.

"Dear God, you, a Squadron Leader? Granny Smith? Has the Air

Ministry gone bananas? Who'd you steal the stripes from? Is everyone else in Fighter Command dead?"

The smile dimmed slightly, "No, mate, even though old Jerry has had a damn good try." He unbuttoned his greatcoat and slumped on Rose's bed, smile brightening as he saw the picture of the girl propped against the little pink teddy bear on the bedside cabinet.

"It's acting rank actually," he explained, "Substantively I'm actually a Flight-Lieutenant. The powers that be, Gawd bless 'em, decided they needed someone with a spot of experience and devilish good looks to take over a Spitfire outfit in Wick. I'm taking Uncle, Fricker and Hermann up there with me. Fuck knows how I'm going to find Totty up there, though. It's in Scotland, or something, you know," he added helpfully.

"You're going to Scotland?" Rose's smile was gone now. "What about us? What about the Squadron?" he blushed, "What about me?"

Granny puffed out his cheeks. "They've withdrawn what's left to Acklington. Morton got another Bf109 before the squadron was pulled out. His fourth. He'll do well, given half a chance. Reminds me of a cheeky young bugger I met a few months back. I still can't believe that you got thrown out of your poor old Hurribag when she blew up, though. Talk about nine lives! Young Morton saw it all, reckons the Hun you hit went down, too, so you'll get a probable at least for it. They've made Dingo Denis CO, but it's a toss-up if they'll disband us altogether. There aren't many of us left. It's been a rough few weeks, and I'm sorry that I couldn't come any earlier, but there's been no chance of getting away."

He shook his head ruefully. "You need a rest, mate. We all do. Don't rush back. Let your eyes heal."

They would always be a part of Excalibur, even if the squadron ceased to exist. They could never forget their band of brothers.

"What about old Stan?"

"Somebody found out the smelly bugger could speak proper English, so he's been bumped up to a Polish mob at Church Fenton, Squadron Leader as well, poor bastard. Quickest promotion in the history of the RAF! Pilot Officer to Squadron Leader in a day! That'll teach him for smoking those bloody awful smokes. He said he'd come and visit you as soon as he could, so better warn the nurses to keep their knickers glued on!" he looked around.

"And talking of which, where are they all? I thought you'd be surrounded by sweet lovelies. But here you are, all alone. Good God, man, what kind of fighter pilot are you? More to the point, what kind of girls are they? They should have shagged the arse off you by now!" he sniffed, "Promise me you'll offer each of them a fuck? Even the ugly ones, OK? It's your civic duty to give 'em a damn good shag. In fact, I'm making it an order. Don't disappoint me!"

Rose grinned, "Good grief! I didn't realise that Squadron-Leaders had such a fine appreciation of official duties!"

Smith grunted and reached over and picked up a cake from the cabinet beside the bed, sniffed it, considered it, then took an experimental bite.

"Phwaauugh!" pieces of rock cake and saliva sprayed across the room.

"Good to see that you've remained as refined as always, Granny, at least the stripes haven't changed you," Rose said drily.

"Urgh! Oh my God!" Smith probed his mouth tentatively; "I think I've broken a tooth!" he took out his denture and looked at it. "What the bloody blue blazes was that? It tastes like something that came out of the back end of a goat and dried out in the sun! I thought that they were supposed to look after you! Is Stalin running the kitchens around here?"

531

"Ah, you found a bit of Matron's detestable rock cake. I think half the people in this hospital are still here because they ate something kindly matron brought in for us."

Smith grimaced, "I feel ill already. I might go see if there's a bed for me. Perhaps I can get an Angel of Mercy or two to minister to me," he scratched his crotch. "I definitely have something that needs to be taken care of."

Rose shook his head ruefully, "Bloody hell, Granny, even when you've been poisoned all you can think about is women!"

"A warm, friendly girl wearing a big smile and bugger all else bouncing on one's willy is all that makes life worth living, Flash my old mate." He thought for a moment, "That, Roast Beef, Yorkshire Pud and a good pint, of course."

"Well, I've got no beer, Granny, but you're welcome to a drop of tea."

Smith jumped up and brushed past Rose, "Cheers, my old son. You're a life saver." Smith swept up the cup and saucer and slurped Rose's tea noisily.

"Ah! That's better!" Smith burped loudly, and then broke wind, "Oops! Better out than in, as my dear old Ma always said. Thanks very much. Now it's my turn to give you something, Harry, so stick out your hand, old chum!"

Rose put out his hand, palm upwards. "What is it?" he asked suspiciously "not some old snot filled hanky, is it? I've still got the one you gave me last time. It's still stuck to the inside of my tunic."

Smith put a piece of fabric in his hand, "Almost, but no coconut. There you go. Don't say I never give you anything."

Rose rubbed the little piece of fabric between finger and thumb, "What is it?" he asked.

"What does it feel like, you twit?"

"Erm…" It felt silky-smooth and rectangular, but what was it? It seemed familiar, but he couldn't quite tell what it was.

Smith enlightened him, "You are a silly, ignorant sod, Harry Rose. It's a ribbon, a medal ribbon. I have the honour to inform you that you have been awarded the Distinguished Flying Cross for gallantry in the air. You earned it. Bloody well done, Harry!"

And then, a little self-consciously, "I got a DFC too, and Stan, though God only knows why, mad bugger. Dingo got a DSO to add to his half-stripe, Dolly's going to have to get one hell of a big stick to beat the crumpet off him."

Rose reached out to grip Smith's arm for a moment, sharing the emotion. "Good God."

The Distinguished Flying Cross?

He didn't know what to say.

He was now Pilot Officer Harry Rose DFC, AFC, RAF.

It sounded good.

Good? It sounded bloody marvellous!

Just a few short months ago he had been a scared young man being thrown around the back of a lorry on his way to his first operational posting, and now he was here, a veteran and victor of great air battles, a killer of his enemies, a survivor with a DFC to add to his AFC.

Smith cleared his throat, surprised to find that his cheeks were wet. "You're going to need time to recover, Harry. Don't rush back, chum. You've done more than enough. The bastards will post you wherever they want you, soon enough." He turned away to wipe his face even though Rose couldn't see his tears.

"So many have gone now. I was at Donald's funeral this morning. I think the Old Man never got over her death, but he's with her again, now. He'll be at peace. He was a good man. There's a posthumous

DSO for him. He more than earned it. Ten times over. I'd have given him a VC if I had anything to do with it. He did a good job with Excalibur. The best."

They were silent for a moment, remembering the dead and the wounded. At least Billy, Ffellowes and Carpenter had survived. It had been a cruel, harsh summer for Excalibur Squadron.

And then the old Granny was back. "Get the ribbon sewn on PDQ, matey, all the girls love a hero, and what with your DFC, AFC and the Mention, well, the knickers will be dropping wherever you go, even though you're such an ugly bugger. I've already put my ribbon up, and to be honest, I think my poor old todger will be glad for a totty-free time in Scotland. But don't tell anyone, I've got a reputation to keep, and I can't stand to see the girls cry."

"Granny, you're incorrigible, you know those Scottish girls are gorgeous!"

They chatted for a few minutes, and then Smith suddenly smacked his forehead.

"Cripes, I forgot! I had to give you the other thing."

For a moment he searched fruitlessly through his pockets, "For Gawd's sake, where is it?"

Rose chuckled to himself, same old Granny!

Granny tut-tutted, "I must have left it outside, Harry. Sorry, mate. Give me a moment to go and get it."

"Granny, honestly, you're hopeless!"

"You'll get nowhere in this air force if you don't know how to address a senior officer, you cheeky little bugger," and Smith swept haughtily out of the room.

Almost immediately the door swished open again, but the steps were lighter than Smith's. Iris must have returned with his biscuits, "Did you manage to find any, Iris?"

He put the precious DFC ribbon in his trouser pocket and held out his hand.

But instead of some biscuits, a slim, smooth hand slid into his.

A familiar fragrance that he'd feared he'd never smell again filled his nostrils and his heart hitched painfully for a second.

She was here! He gasped in thrilled disbelief and wonder.

The hand pulled him forwards into a ferociously tight bear hug and the air was almost squeezed out of him by the girl's powerful embrace.

Elizabeth Arden soap really washes away the day.

Soft lips brushed lightly across his, leaving a wonderful smear of lipstick and sweet wetness.

He gasped again. Rose's heart racing as he felt her pressed against him. Her hair was wet against his cheek, breasts delightfully pressing against his chest, her back firm and sweet beneath his fingers (don't press too hard, remember that awful wound, it must still be sore).

He kissed her back and could taste the salt of her tears on his lips.

Rose tried to speak, but his throat felt tight, and no words would come.

He could hardly breathe, a song of purest joy thrilling through him. He felt as if his feet weren't touching the floor, that he was floating in a cloud of bliss.

And then Molly spoke, her voice sweet, her breath fresh and delightful. All his dreams made real, the incredible miracle of his beloved in his arms.

The voice he had yearned to hear. The first words he'd heard her say for so long.

"So... who's Iris?"

Author's Note

I would like to thank my lovely wife, Zakia, for the love and support that made it possible for me to write this book, and my wonderful children Adam and Saphora for all the hugs, kisses and sticky sweets.

And to my wonderful little sister, Mursila, I thank you with all my heart for your invaluable guidance, advice and assistance. You made all the difference.

To So Few is a story of a young man's experiences at a dark period of time when the future of Britain looked extremely bleak.

A number of campaigns and battles during World War Two were key stepping stones in the long and difficult journey to the final victory in 1945, and the Battle of Britain was one of these.

To me, it is the most important of them.

Had the Luftwaffe been victorious, and had Britain fallen, with the resulting capitulation of all British and Commonwealth forces, Hitler could have invaded Russia in 1941 secure in the knowledge that his only front was to the east.

With the full might of his forces concentrated against it, might the USSR have also succumbed? Our world could have been very different from the one we know.

Some believe that the Royal Navy could have prevented the invasion, but I believe that had air superiority belonged to the Luftwaffe, it would have been a very different story.

As the evidence of history has repeatedly shown, determined air attack is cruelly effective against naval vessels.

The Royal Navy alone would not have been enough to save Britain from invasion (sorry, Jack).

But, of course, the Battle of Britain was only one of the many stepping stones to victory, and many more sacrifices would need to be made by so very many to achieve it.

The wartime generation was one filled with countless heroes and heroines, incredible people who paid for the freedom we enjoy today at great cost.

Nonetheless, my greatest champions will always be the extraordinary men and women who defended Britain in the desperate months of that long ago Summer in 1940.

This is my tribute to them.

To So Few.